D0816386

Burying Father Tim

Tom Robertson

authorHOUSE®

AuthorHouse™
1663 Liberty Drive, Suite 200
Bloomington, IN 47403
www.authorhouse.com
Phone: 1-800-839-8640

This book is a work of fiction. People, places, events, and situations are the product of the author's imagination. Any resemblance to actual persons, living or dead, or historical events, is purely coincidental.

First published by AuthorHouse 10/3/2008

ISBN: 978-1-4389-0985-1 (sc)
ISBN: 978-1-4389-0986-8 (hc)

Library of Congress Control Number: 2008908765

Printed in the United States of America
Bloomington, Indiana

This book is printed on acid-free paper.

For Sandy, who after laughing at my jokes for almost forty years when almost no one else did, saw something in this story that she wanted others to see…and refused to take no for an answer.
For Katie and Kelsey, who made an old baseball player love books, and who make every day Father's Day.
And for my dad, who I wish had lived to read this – I think he would have liked it.

Foreword

Burying Father Tim is, at its core, a story about the power of memories. Between the hilarious accounts of childhood escapades and the timelessly poignant theme of loss, it is no wonder that the narrator's voice oscillates from time to time. Perhaps consistency is unimportant, however. The struggle to reconcile our most glorious moments with our darkest is certainly a familiar one. At times, our experiences change our lives from summer to winter in an instant and then, just as we think that winter will never end, the first bud of spring pops its head through the snow. Perhaps the true beauty of this narrator lies in his ability to wait out the winter, knowing that the warmth of summer will return. His voice is one of simple humanity, of a man empowered by his joys and sorrows. As for me, the voice I hear reminds me of myself-warm and joyous in one moment and fearful the next. Those familiar shifts tell us to go ahead and rejoice while we can and take comfort in the pattern of our memories. The pattern suggests for us, as it does for our narrator, that regardless of the depth of the apparent winter, spring will indeed come again.

Katie Robertson
July 2008

Prologue

11:10 A.M.

THE SOUND OF TIRES SCREECHING on the pavement jolted my attention back to the present. A battered Buick had lurched to a stop only a few feet in front of my rented Lexus. I had allowed my mind to wander from the shingle-sided buildings and the heavily-barred windows of the neighborhood passing by outside. It was a blistering hot summer day. The heat rising from the pavement made images appear to move gently in a breeze that wasn't there. Traffic inched along between stoplights that seemed to take forever to change. Without even thinking about it, I had reached for the electric door locks several blocks back.

I felt completely out of place in a place that had been home until I left for college, a little more than thirty years ago. Once familiar street corners now looked as though I was seeing them for the first time. The old drugstore where we bought "penny candy" was now a pharmacy superstore, complete with a drive-through lane.

I drove past the barbershop where I used to sit on a board laid across the arms of the chair so that the barber could reach me without bending over. The windows and doorway were bricked up. The old red, white, and blue striped barber pole that hung from the outside wall was long gone. Only the rusted metal brackets from which it once hung remained.

The limestone bank where everyone in the neighborhood kept their life savings had been knocked down and replaced by a concrete parking garage. On the sidewalk was a kiosk with a cash station machine.

Lining both sides of every cross street were rows of bungalow homes, standing shoulder to shoulder, one after the other, with only the patterns in the wrought iron porch railings to distinguish one from the next. Every so often, a weathered canvas awning jutted out from one of the bungalows, its monogrammed letter corresponding to the last name of an owner several re-sales ago.

Up ahead on the right was St. Basil's Church. Magnificent from a distance with its stone walls and twin steeples, each home to a bell tower, on closer inspection, it was showing its age and then some. Built to last forever by immigrants for whom the church was their foothold in a new country, St. Basil's was from another time.

I went to grade school at St. Basil's. The Sisters of the Sacred Heart, in their long white habits, with veils flowing down from the stiff white cardboard that left creases in their foreheads, were from another time as well. I was an altar boy here, when the Mass was said in Latin and no one ate meat on Fridays. To my friends, I was Mike, but to the nuns and priests of St. Basil's, I was Michael.

Now, inching my way through traffic, I watched the old neighborhood slip past. I was looking at the road, but my mind had gone back in time. I nearly slammed into the Buick when the unmistakable sound of tires on pavement suddenly brought me back. With my turn signal on, I returned my attention to the two steeples, and to the task at hand.

It had been years since my folks had moved away from the old neighborhood, and even longer since I had left. What brought me back today was a need to close a loop in my life. A need for closure. A need to say goodbye to an old friend. I came home to bury Father Tim.

Chapter 1

I MET FATHER TIM THE year that my brother got sick. It was hot that summer. Hotter than usual. We didn't have air conditioning, but if we had, my mom wouldn't have used it. Henry was sick and she was constantly worried that he would catch a draft and end up in the hospital again. There was an old metal fan in the front window that made a pinging noise as the blade turned. The fan was pointed out of the window, blowing the air from the house out into the yard, because it was warmer in the house than it was outside.

What I remember most about the summer that Henry got sick was the way the smells changed. Instead of the smell of hot dogs cooking on the charcoal grill outside, or the scent of cinnamon on an apple pie baking in the oven, the house now smelled like medicine. Strong, metallic smells from the medicines and the distinctive odors of detergent and bleach from the bedding that my mom changed twice a day. I have long forgotten the colors, but the smells never left me – medicine, and bleach, and leather.

Dr. Heintz carried a scuffed and battered black leather bag. He came by the house most afternoons on his way home. Doctors still came to the house back then. My mom didn't have a car, and Dr. Heintz knew that it was very hard for her to bring Henry to his office, so he came to them. He told my mom that it helped him to see Henry in his own bed, but she knew better. There was tape wrapped around the handle of the little black bag, where the leather had worn away. He'd been visiting sick kids in their own beds for a very long time.

The summer that Henry got sick, my parents grew old. The laughter that had been contagious, the corny jokes that my father used to tell at the dinner table turned to whispers and furtive glances. Henry was too small to tell them where it hurt, or what was wrong. He was too small to answer when they bent over his crib and asked how their big boy was doing. He was too small, period. He wasn't growing fast enough, and he had trouble breathing. He was almost a year old, but he looked half his age. When it became clear that something was wrong with Henry, my folks reacted differently. My dad was stoic. My mom nervously chattered. It didn't matter what the subject was, she just felt better talking. That summer took something out of them that they'd never get back.

I awoke with a start and stared at the ceiling until I realized where I was. There was a shaft of moonlight shining through the window and I could almost make out the titles on the spines of the books on the shelves above my desk. It took a few moments for me to focus on what had awakened me. Voices. A chair scraped on the wood floor of the kitchen and I could hear hushed voices.

I crawled out of bed and walked as quietly as I could toward the sound of people talking. I heard my father's voice but couldn't make out what he was saying. A second man's voice answered, but again they were speaking too softly for me to hear. As I reached the doorway to the kitchen, I heard a single word from the second voice, which by now I recognized as Dr. Heintz.

"Hypoxia," he had said.

I didn't hear any other talking, but I could hear my mother quietly sobbing. Afraid to listen any longer, I hurried back to my room and got into bed. I pulled the covers tight against my chin and silently cried. I didn't know what "hypoxia" meant, but I had heard my mom crying. There was no good reason for the doctor to be in our kitchen so late, and whatever he was telling them, it was clearly bad news. I cried for my mom. My mom cried for Henry, but I cried for her.

My parents and the doctor stayed in the kitchen whispering for a while longer, and then I heard my dad coming out of the kitchen and I caught the end of a sentence that had started before the door opened.

"...will pack you a suitcase," he said.

I heard drawers sliding open and closed, and I heard feet shuffling on the floor in my parents' bedroom. The next voice I heard was the doctor.

"No need to wake Michael," he said, "I can take you and the baby, and your husband can bring Michael along in the morning."

I wanted to jump up and tell them that they didn't have to worry about waking me. I wanted to run out and ask what was wrong. I had a million questions, but I was too scared to move. I just lay in bed and listened as my folks took Henry out to the doctor's car. My dad came back into the house alone. Reaching the front stoop, he stood in the open doorway. I heard the doctor's car start and the tires crunching over the gravel in the driveway. I heard the hinges on the screen door squeak and the click as my dad gently pulled the door closed. I stared into the moonlight as my dad's footsteps creaked across the old wooden floor, and then it was quiet. For a long time, I strained to hear, but it was quiet. Then I heard a sound I'd never heard before – my father sobbing.

I'm not sure how long I'd been sleeping when I felt my dad's firm grasp on my shoulder.

"Morning, Mike," he said, in a cross between a rasp and a whisper.

I blinked my eyes open, afraid that he'd be able to tell that I had been crying, but he was already taking some clothes from my dresser drawers and laying them out on my bed.

"We need to get dressed, pal," he said in a surprisingly strong voice, "Henry had to go to the hospital last night, and Mom's up with him. Let's get dressed and we'll go see them."

When I got to the kitchen, my breakfast was on the table. My dad told me to have breakfast while he shaved. There was a bowl of cereal and a glass of milk. I climbed up onto the chair and grabbed the spoon but then stopped. My dad had filled my glass with milk…and poured orange juice over the cereal. I drank the milk and poured the cereal and orange juice into the sink. I wasn't really hungry anyway.

"All set?" my dad asked, an almost cheerful tone in his voice.

I nodded without answering and followed him out of the door and into the driveway. We climbed into my dad's car, a powder blue Plymouth Valiant. I cranked the window open, because it was already getting uncomfortably warm in the car. My dad slid behind the wheel and turned the key. The engine sputtered once and came to life. We backed out of the driveway and headed off down the street without saying a word.

"Is Henry really sick?" I asked when I could summon up the courage to talk out loud.

"I'm afraid he is," my dad answered quietly.

"Is he going to die?" I blurted out. The distance between a six year-old's brain and his mouth is shorter than it is for an adult.

My dad took a minute before answering. When he did, it was in a gentle, reassuring tone of voice.

"Not today, Mike," he said.

If he was able to elaborate, he elected not to. I think he was probably afraid that if he tried to explain things to me, he'd break down. Either way, he drove the rest of the way to the hospital with one hand on my shoulder but he didn't say another word.

I've never really managed to get the medicinal smell of hospitals out of my head. When we walked into the hospital, I immediately smelled some of the same smells that had invaded our house since Henry took ill. To this day, whenever I walk into a hospital and smell the smells, I think of Henry.

We rode the elevator up three floors with an old man in a wheelchair who was being pushed along by a guy who looked like he must be his son. The old man was here to visit someone, but he looked like he should stay. They got off of the elevator on the second floor and the younger man eased the wheelchair into the corridor and said, "C'mon Dad, Mom will be so glad to see you."

The elevator doors closed; when they opened again, we stepped out and everything looked white. The nurses wore white dresses, white stockings, white shoes with thick white rubber soles, and little white cardboard hats pinned into their hair. The walls were white, the fluorescent lights were bright white, and the sheets on gurneys lined along the hall were all white. The first burst of color in this white landscape was my mother's sundress as she sat next to Henry's bed, holding his tiny hand in her fingertips.

Henry had tubes attached to needles stuck into his arms and a gas mask taped over his nose and mouth. He looked even smaller than usual in the big metal bed. If Henry looked half his age, my mom looked twice hers. She was humming a lullaby to Henry when we came in. She looked up at my father and smiled, but it wasn't a happy smile. My dad gave her a hug, and he reached over to pat Henry and when he did, she turned and opened her arms toward me. I ran to hug her and she held me tighter than she had ever held me before. She kissed the top of my head and squeezed even tighter, not saying anything.

When my mom spoke, she was talking to my dad, and she was reciting numbers and telling him things that the nurses had told her, none of which sounded like English to me. They stood together holding hands next to Henry's bed and I sat down in my mom's chair. After a few quiet moments, the door opened, and in walked a man I had never seen before. He was dressed differently, but he didn't look like a doctor. He smiled at my parents as he extended his hand toward my father.

"I'm Father Tim," he said.

My parents took Father Tim out into the hall, where they talked for a long time. He had a gentleness about him that was apparent even to a child. As he stood with my parents outside the open door, I noticed something about him that I would later come to realize was his way – he listened more than he talked.

When my father spoke, Father Tim stood erect, occasionally nodding. When my mom talked, Father Tim leaned forward, holding her hands in his, smiling reassuringly. After a long conversation, they came back into the room and Father Tim walked over to where I was sitting. Crouching down to get to my eye level, he introduced himself, reaching out to shake my hand.

"I understand you'll be coming to school at St. Basil's this fall," Father Tim said, more of a statement than a question. I nodded my head, more of a reflex than an answer.

"How about we take a few minutes to get acquainted?" he suggested, adding, "I'm brand new to St. Basil's too, and I could use a friend."

I looked over to my mom, who smiled and nodded, saying, "We'll be right here, honey; we need to talk with the doctor."

Father Tim gently put his hand between my shoulders and we walked together to the elevator, past the white sheets, the white walls, and the white uniforms of the nurses. We rode the elevator back downstairs and stepped out on the main floor.

"How old are you, Michael?" Father Tim asked.

"Six," I answered.

"Are you excited about starting first grade?" he smiled.

"No," I answered. I didn't know him well enough yet to lie.

"Why not?" he asked, turning the corner as we walked.

"I don't like school." I'd never really been to school except for kindergarten, which was mostly coloring and learning to play with modeling clay without eating it.

"What was your favorite part of kindergarten?" he asked.

"Nap time," I said, without a hint of sarcasm.

"I think you'll like first grade," Father Tim reassured me, "you have a brand new teacher – you'll be her very first class."

Somehow it didn't make me feel better knowing that my first grade teacher had never taught before. I didn't have any idea about what went on in school, and now it seemed neither did my new teacher. If she was supposed to be teaching us, who was teaching her? Father Tim seemed to think it would all work out fine.

We walked a little farther down the hall and passed the hospital chapel, without going inside.

"Let's go outside for some fresh air," Father Tim suggested, "I can't get used to the way hospitals smell."

We went outside, and it was already getting hot again. We crossed the street and sat down on a bench in the shade of an elm tree, one of the few that had survived the Dutch Elm Disease that killed most of the oldest trees in town. A short way off, a group of teenagers was playing a game of touch football. Father Tim took off his jacket and draped it over the back of the park bench.

"Things have been pretty tough around your house, haven't they?" he said, again not really asking a question.

I nodded quietly, not sure what to say.

"Your brother's illness has been hard on your mom and dad, hasn't it?"

"Yes," I replied. I was working my way toward phrases. Sentences would come later.

"What's been the toughest part?" Father Tim asked, strategically phrasing a question that couldn't be answered with a nod or a syllable.

"Everyone's scared all of the time," I answered.

"Are you scared?" he asked.

I nodded.

"What scares you the most?" he probed.

"That things will never go back to the way they used to be," I replied.

It's interesting that it didn't occur to me at that moment to say that I was afraid that Henry would die. I had never known anyone who died, and to a six year-old, death is an abstract concept. What I knew for sure was that things were no longer normal, and my biggest fear at that moment was that they never would be again. Father Tim did not seem surprised by the answer. He didn't even hesitate before he answered.

"It's OK to be afraid, Michael. Everyone is afraid sometimes. Moms and dads can be afraid. Even policemen and firemen can be afraid. There's nothing wrong with being afraid sometimes."

Father Tim sat quietly for a minute of two, careful not to say too much too fast. I swallowed hard. I wanted to ask him a question, but it wouldn't come out.

"Is there anything else that scares you?" Father Tim asked quietly.

I nodded again, and tried to swallow, but my mouth was dry. Father Tim just sat quietly, giving me time to get the question out.

"Is Henry going to die?" I asked.

"The doctors are doing everything they can for him," Father Tim answered, "but he's very sick. Henry has a hole in his heart, Michael. It makes it very hard for his heart to pump the blood around inside his body. He doesn't get enough oxygen, which is why he has trouble breathing, and his little heart has to work too hard trying to catch up."

"Can they fix it?" I asked.

"They can give him medicine to help his heart to work a little easier. If he grows a little bigger, the hole might even close itself, or his heart could get big enough to work a little harder to make up for it."

"How long will he be sick?"

"For a while yet," Father Tim answered, "it takes a long time."

"But he'll get better?"

"We hope so, Michael, we hope so."

"If he dies, my mom will be so sad."

"She loves Henry very much," Father Tim whispered, "and she loves you very much, too. Be patient, Michael, and don't worry if it looks like your mom is paying more attention to Henry right now – she is, but she loves you and she needs you more than ever."

I sat quietly. The touch football game became blurry as tears welled up in my eyes. My mom was crying for Henry, but I was crying for her.

"Do you know what a hero is, Michael?"

I didn't answer. I was listening, but no words were coming.

"A hero is someone who acts bravely when they're afraid," Father Tim continued. "You can tell a lot about a person by the way they act when they're afraid. When the time comes, Michael, you'll be a hero."

Henry did not die that summer. He came home and he got stronger. He even put on a few pounds before the start of the school year, when I first joined Father Tim at St. Basil's. I had no way of knowing as we sat together on that park bench that Father Tim would have a profound impact on my life.

The football rolled under the bench and one of the teenagers called from the field, "Hey Father, how about a little help?"

Father Tim grinned and jumped up. He was young. He didn't look much older than the kids playing ball. He almost seemed glad to have the chance to throw the football with them. He reached beneath the bench and came up with the ball. Turning back toward the field, he pointed over the head of the teenager and called out, "Go out for a long one…a real Hail Mary."

Chapter 2

11:39 A.M.

As I TURNED INTO THE parking lot of St. Basil's, I was struck by how little the place had changed. The saplings that we planted in third grade to commemorate the death of Cardinal Blanchard had grown into a dense canopy of trees with trunks a foot across, but the circle drive still led you to the massive front doors of the old church, their stained glass allowing rays of colored light to fall onto the marble basins holding holy water in the vestibule.

I didn't stop in front of the church, because the hearse would be parking there, followed by the cars driven by the Knights of Columbus, who would stand guard in their plumed hats, holding silver swords in their white-gloved hands. I continued past the statue of St. Basil, standing as he had for decades in a small grove of evergreen bushes carefully pruned by the women of the Holy Rosary Society.

Instinctively, I drove to the end of a row in the parking lot, selecting a space with a curb on one side, eliminating the possibility of a door ding on at least one side of the car. It wasn't even my car, but old habits are hard to break. As I reached into the backseat for my jacket, I realized that without thinking of it, I had dressed in navy blue pants, a white shirt, and a dark blue necktie, the uniform we wore at St. Basil's...all I needed was a bright red sweater.

I was in no particular hurry to arrive in the church. It was early, and I worried that I would run into too many people who I hadn't seen in years. While there were people who I looked forward to seeing, there were many more who I had not seen on purpose. Glancing at my watch, I decided to take a detour through the school. In the middle of the summer, it was a good bet that the school would be empty.

As I climbed the stairs to the front doors of St. Basil's School, I found myself following the curved indentations in the stone steps, worn smooth by thousands of small footsteps. Reaching for the door, I remembered the first time that I reached up over my head, pulling on the brass handle that seemed so high back then. Opening the door part way, I leaned around, poking my head into the dark entryway, subconsciously worried that one of the nuns who had been gone for years might be lurking inside.

Satisfied that the coast was clear, I stepped inside, allowing the heavy door to click closed behind me. It took a few moments for my eyes to adjust to the dim lighting. As I stood in the hallway, faintly familiar smells conjured memories that I didn't know I had. The corridor, with the familiar inverted white milk glass light-fixtures suspended from the ceiling, led to a moderately sized room with a high ceiling that doubled as a gymnasium and the school library. Those two functions may seem to be mutually exclusive, but they weren't when we were in school. During the day, metal carts with wobbly wheels held books that had been donated by parishioners. There was a thirty-five year-old world atlas that showed Europe as it appeared immediately after World War I, a complete set of the *Encyclopedia Britannica* (except for missing the volumes for "M" and "R"), and an assortment of classic literature, including 285 pages of War and Peace and most of Huckleberry Finn.

Folding chairs and old wooden card tables, which one disassembled by unscrewing the legs, were scattered throughout the library during the school day. When St. Basil's hosted a basketball game, the folding chairs were pushed against the wall to serve as the players' benches, and the wooden tables were stacked in the hall, their unscrewed legs piled beside them. The metal carts with our treasure of the Great Books were pushed, rattling and shaking, down the hall into an empty classroom. The library was too small to be a real gymnasium, and the gymnasium was too large for the pitiful collection of donated books, but it was all we had. There were no locker rooms. After practice or games, you pulled your navy blue pants and white shirt over your basketball uniform and went home to take a bath.

Walking back toward the main entrance, I saw a familiar sight. Recessed into an indentation in the wall was a statue of the Virgin Mary. Perched atop the statue's head was a tiny wreath of dried flowers. I couldn't help smiling at the realization that the students still celebrated the "May Crowning" of the Virgin Mary. The miniature wreath of dried flowers had been fresh roses just a couple of months ago, placed on the statue by one of the eighth grade girls. In our time, the selection of a girl to crown the Virgin Mary was based on an essay expounding the virtues of a religious vocation and the amount of money raised for the "Pagan Babies".

I've never known anyone who has ever actually met a "Pagan Baby". Pronounced as one word, "Paganbabies" was the major fundraising initiative every year at St. Basil's. Beginning shortly after the start of the school year and continuing for what seemed like months, "Paganbabies" was a major undertaking by the good sisters. Armed with photos of underprivileged infants from third world countries, the nuns let it be known that the road to Heaven was paved with loose change donated to "Paganbabies". Kids would turn the cushions of their couches inside out, scrounging for pennies and nickels to drop into the glass jar on Sister's desk at school. Sitting behind her desk looking at you over the top of the "Paganbabies" jar, the only thing that the nun was missing was an accountant's green eyeshade.

Moving past the Blessed Virgin, I made my way to the classroom at the far end of the hall. Reaching for the light switch as I entered the room, I found myself standing in front of eight rows of ancient wooden desks, the kind with the hinged tops that lifted to reveal storage space inside. It was my old first grade classroom.

If you tilted your head just right, and closed one eye, Sister Thomas Aquinas actually looked like a girl beneath her white habit and wire-rimmed glasses. When I heard that my teacher for first grade would be Sister Thomas Aquinas, I wasn't sure what to expect. I'd never seen a real nun before, but Sister Thomas Aquinas seemed like a contradiction in terms.

Sitting in my first grade classroom that first day of school, my eyes darted along the cardboard strip that extended from the door to the window, with the entire alphabet in upper and lower case letters. Running my fingers along the ancient wooden desk in front of me, I saw many of the same letters gouged into the wood, but hadn't a clue what they spelled, which was just as well. It was the early 1960s and parents had not yet become obsessed with teaching differential calculus to pre-schoolers in the hopes of impressing Yale, so I (like every other first grader at St. Basil's) was able to tie my shoes and recognize my name, but reading would come later.

The door flew open and what looked like a ghost raced into the room, stopping thirty-five six year-olds in mid-shout. A mysterious clacking accompanied the spectre, and the entire class stood riveted in place as the phantom faced the wall and reached up to make a hideous, blood-curdling scraping sound that would stay with us for the rest of our lives.

Apparently oblivious to the fact that seventy tiny eyes behind her could make no sense of the scrawling, the ghost traced out a series of the letters that appeared on the cardboard strip above her head. "Sister Thomas Aquinas" she had written, and – turning around – she squinted through her wire-rimmed glasses at the collection of gaping mouths and furrowed brows in front of her.

"Good morning boys and girls, my name is Sister Thomas Aquinas, and I will be your teacher this year." It was at that instant, with my head tilted just so, with one eye closed, that I thought I saw a girl beneath all of those white robes and clacking beads.

St. Basil's Catholic School had stood on the spot where it presently creaked and groaned since 1917. A two-story stone building with one enormous stairway that led to...well it led to somewhere that the first and second graders had never seen. Both first and second grades were taught together in the single classroom on the ground floor. If you survived to third grade you climbed those stairs...and no one really knew what was up there.

Sister Thomas Aquinas taught first and second grade. Not exactly at the same time, but in the same room. She would teach the first graders how to trace the letter "G", reminding us to use the "big G" when writing letters to God, then leave us to write "G" four hundred and eighty-seven times while she stepped to the rear of the room and taught the second graders that squares had four sides. Being a nun was apparently less attractive an occupation in the 1960s than it had been during the Great Depression. There were not enough nuns to go around anymore, so our first and second grade classes had to share Sister Thomas Aquinas.

No one who has never lived in a convent can say for sure that there are training programs in torture and corporal punishment, but anyone who has ever attended Catholic school believes such programs exist. Not unlike the military, there seems to be an order of hierarchy among nuns – the pleasant ones languish in entry-level positions while the good sisters who would make a Marine drill sergeant flinch rise to the position of school principal.

The principal at St. Basil's was four feet tall, wore government-issue wire-rimmed glasses (most Catholics are convinced that nuns with 20/20 vision wear wire-rimmed glasses with clear lenses), and she never went anywhere without her leather gloves. It could have been 95 degrees and Sister Pius would have her black leather gloves. The reason Sister Pius kept her gloves at the ready became clear on the third day of school.

Sister Thomas Aquinas was helping the second graders count the sides of a square while the first graders diligently began our letters to God, carefully scrawling capital "G" across our papers, when Sister Pius stormed into the room.

"Sister Thomas, may I borrow your classroom for a moment?" asked the diminutive principal, not waiting for an answer.

"Of course," replied Sister Thomas Aquinas, as if she had a choice in the matter.

With that, Sister Pius reached out into the hall and pulling her arm back through the doorway, brought Kevin Dagan into the room by the ear. Kevin tried to keep up, almost running with his head cocked following the beet-red ear on which Sister Pius had such a firm grasp.

"Mr. Dagan...please tell the younger children why we are here."

Everyone stopped what they were doing and stared at Kevin Dagan, in part because we had never actually seen a third grader before, let alone had one talk to us. Third graders disappeared up the stairs never to be seen again, and it was rare indeed to find one of the species so far from their natural habitat.

"Mr. Dagan, we're waiting..."

It's not clear whether Kevin Dagan was unsure of the question or just reluctant to make matters worse, but for whatever reason, he stood perfectly still, looking like someone who hoped to go unnoticed. It was way too late for that, however, and Sister Pius had nearly exhausted her notoriously limited supply of patience.

"Mr. Dagan, were we running on the stairs?"

It would not occur to a third grader to point out the absurdity of that question, as clearly Sister Pius had not run on any stairs, these or others, in decades. It was obvious to everyone, even the six year-olds in the room, that Sister Pius was not really including herself in the "we"...

Kevin Dagan looked like a death row inmate facing the warden as he nodded his head in response to the Spanish Inquisition over running on stairs. In a movement reminiscent of gunslingers in the old west, Sister Pius yanked her black leather gloves out of their holster and cracked Kevin Dagan across the face with a slap that could be heard all the way at the top of the third grade stairs.

"We do not run inside the school, Mr. Dagan, now return to your class."

With that, Kevin Dagan fled from the room, presumably slowing to a walking pace before reaching the stairs, to return to his classroom. Sister

Pius then turned to face the class, her eyes magnified four times their normal size by the fishbowl lenses in her wire-rimmed glasses.

"Children, it is important to always follow the rules," said Sister Pius, turning on her hob-nailed boots and rattling out of the room, her rosary beads leaving an echo in her wake. Clearly, the entire Kevin Dagan incident had been the grammar school equivalent of public executions in medieval England. Before the masses had an opportunity to plot an overthrow of the throne, Sister Pius was determined to make an example that would quell any civil unrest for the foreseeable future.

Sitting across the aisle from me in first grade was a peculiar looking kid named Walter. Undoubtedly named for a great-grandfather who lived in the era when parents named their children Walter, when automobiles had crooked crank handle starters protruding from their front grills, he didn't go by "Wally" or "Walt"...he answered only to Walter.

Walter had ears that protruded from his head like two open car doors, so that kids sitting two rows behind him had to crane their necks to see the blackboard. His hair stood up in every direction, as if he had stuck his head into an electric fan before leaving for school. His necktie (all boys at St. Basil's wore white shirts, blue pants, blue neckties, and bright red sweaters) was always cockeyed, with one of the plastic flaps that held the pre-tied neckwear in place jutting out of his shirt collar.

It was Walter who first learned one of the basic tenets of a Catholic education the hard way. Sometime during the first week of school, in the middle of one of Sister Thomas Aquinas's lessons differentiating venial sins from mortal sins, Walter thrust his hand in the air unexpectedly. Unprepared for an interruption at such a crucial time in the curriculum, Sister Thomas Aquinas ignored Walter and continued lecturing the six year-olds on our fate should we commit a mortal sin or a collection of venial sins sufficient to accrue equivalent wrath from a benevolent Creator.

Walter kept his arm raised overhead, alternating between his right and left hands, always using the other to prop up the raised arm. Finally Sister Thomas Aquinas interrupted her fire and brimstone and asked, in an exasperated tone, "Walter, what is it that can't wait until after our lesson?"

"I gotta pee," answered Walter.

"Do you mean you need to visit the lavatory?" asked Sister Thomas Aquinas.

"No, I gotta pee," replied Walter.

"Well, you'll have to wait until recess," said Sister Thomas Aquinas, adding, "Boys and girls, the time to use the lavatory is before or after school, not during our lessons."

No one had ever heard the word "lavatory" before, but having heard Walter twice say that he had to pee, we connected the dots. Walter just frowned, lowering his arms and crossing his legs, and began rocking back and forth, repeating under his breath, "I gotta pee…I gotta pee…" over and over.

While Sister Thomas Aquinas described the differences between hell, purgatory, and a completely incomprehensible heavenly freight elevator called "limbo", Walter continued his mantra. It was impossible to concentrate on just how serious a crime you had to commit to graduate from purgatory to hell with Walter muttering "I gotta pee," while rocking rhythmically from side to side, his toes pointing inward and his cheeks turning red.

When it seemed like I couldn't stand listening to him for one minute longer, Walter fell completely silent. His rocking stopped, and he folded his hands on his desk in front of him. I looked across the aisle and saw Walter smiling. It wasn't a happy smile as much as a mildly contented upturn of his mouth at the corners. The front of his navy blue pants was two shades darker than the rest. It wouldn't be until fifth grade that I would drink so much as a glass of water before leaving for school in the morning.

Across the aisle on the other side was a Mexican kid named Anthony Suarez. Sister Thomas Aquinas called him "Anthony", his family called him "Tony", and we all called him "Spic". I don't remember how Spic got his nickname. Most likely, the open-minded parents in the neighborhood had given it to him.

"Oh, that Spic is out in the backyard again."

"Doesn't that Spic have a home of his own to go to?"

"I told you when those Spics moved in that there'd be trouble."

Whenever Tony Suarez came around, it seemed like everyone always called him "Spic", and the name just stuck. Now, when Tony met anyone for the first time, he said, "Just call me Spic."

Spic's sister was also in our class. She was almost a foot taller, an oddity for twins. If you saw them together, you wouldn't even guess that they were related. It would be some time before we realized that Spic's sister was two years older, and that this was her third year in first grade.

One day toward the end of first grade, the weather had warmed up and everyone had spring fever. The nuns wanted a break, so they announced that the next day would be "career day". Kids in each class nominated their fathers to come in to describe their jobs to the students, presumably to give the little geniuses ideas as to what they wanted to be when they grew up. It would be twenty years before anyone would think to invite mothers in to talk about their jobs. A career was a rather abstract concept to a first grader. For most of us, jobs were something your dad had, and most of us didn't even know what our own fathers did for a living. Nevertheless, the nuns were growing tired of trying to hold our interest, so they invented career day.

I was careful not to volunteer my dad. He never talked about his job at home, so I figured he didn't want to talk about it in front of my class. Five hands shot up when Sister Thomas Aquinas asked for volunteers. After a brief interrogation of the volunteers, Sister Thomas Aquinas was satisfied that no one was bringing in a mobster or an ex-convict. We ended up with a dentist, a construction worker, a janitor, an engineer, and a genie.

Rebecca Slotkowski's father was a dentist. Dr. Slotkowski was an unusually thin man with a large Adam's apple and very thick eyeglasses. He wore a white jacket that made him look like the high school kid who worked at the drugstore but without the pimples. Dr. Slotkowski brought a giant plastic tooth and a three-foot long toothbrush to demonstrate proper brushing technique. Since most of us had much smaller teeth, we ignored the brushing lesson.

Dr. Slotkowski also brought a bottle of pink tablets. He gave one tablet to each student and told us to chew the tablets up. While everyone was chewing, Dr. Slotkowski explained that the pink color would stick to spots on our teeth that needed brushing. After chewing the tablets, if we looked at out teeth, the pink would show us places we had missed with our toothbrushes.

Within a minute or two, the classroom had turned into a circus. Everyone was grinning at one another with pink slime coating their teeth and gums and running down their chins. It was obvious that the pink tablets had been created by a toothbrush company. The pink stain stuck to everything – teeth, gums, tongue, clothes, everywhere. There was a brief intermission following Dr. Slotkowski's presentation to allow the class to go to the bathroom and gargle away the pink dye.

Vinny Lorenzo's dad was a construction worker. He built roads and bridges. His job was to run the jackhammer that broke concrete into little pieces so it could be hauled away before the new road or bridge was built. Mr. Lorenzo walked into the classroom wearing his hardhat, work boots, and heavy gloves. His hands were shaking, and at first we thought he was nervous. Then we realized that both hands were shaking at the same time, and they were shaking up and down just like they would if he was holding a jackhammer.

Mr. Lorenzo stood in the front of the class, his hands still shaking, and began to describe his job. He startled us at first, because he was shouting at the top of his lungs.

"RUNNING A JACKHAMMER IS AN IMPORTANT JOB," Mr. Lorenzo shouted. "WITHOUT A JACKHAMMER, YOU COULDN'T PICK UP CEMENT WITHOUT GETTING A HERNIA," he continued. Mr. Lorenzo then got sidetracked on a tangent that might have been better addressed by a kid's dad who was a doctor.

"I KNEW A GUY WHO HAD A HERNIA ONCE," Mr. Lorenzo screamed. "HE TRIED LIFTING A HUNK OF CONCRETE BEFORE I JACKHAMMERED IT, AND HE FELL OVER AND HAD TO GO TO THE HOSPITAL."

Sister Thomas Aquinas looked at her watch and decided that it was a good time to thank Mr. Lorenzo and move on to the next profession. She waited for Mr. Lorenzo to stop shouting, then politely said, "Class, let's thank Mr. Lorenzo for coming in to share his very important job with us." Mr. Lorenzo never heard a word that Sister Thomas Aquinas had said. He just continued shouting.

"ONCE YOU GET A HERNIA, YOU CAN'T LIFT CONCRETE ANYMORE OR YOU'LL GET ANOTHER HERNIA, SO IT'S SMART TO WAIT UNTIL I JACKHAMMER THE CONCRETE BEFORE YOU YANK YOUR GUTS OUT LIFTING IT."

Sister Thomas Aquinas moved toward Mr. Lorenzo, thinking that he might hear her if she was closer. "Thank you for a very important lesson about jackhammers, Mr. Lorenzo," she shouted; Mr. Lorenzo still didn't hear her, but he did see her moving toward him. He turned and looked at her.

"Huh?" he grunted loudly.

"We're very glad to have you here," said Sister Thomas Aquinas, now elevating her voice even more.

"FEAR? NO I DON'T HAVE NO FEAR," said Mr. Lorenzo. He was deaf as a post from years of jackhammering concrete so that guys wouldn't get hernias lifting it.

Not sure how to get Mr. Lorenzo out of there, Sister Thomas Aquinas began clapping her hands, nodding to the class to join her. We all began applauding and Mr. Lorenzo got the message that he was finished. He smiled politely and shouted at the top of his voice, "I HOPE YOU LEARNED HOW IMPORTANT JACKHAMMERS ARE TO YOUR DAILY LIFE!"

As Mr. Lorenzo shuffled out the door, his hands were still going up and down in the staccato motion of a vibrating jackhammer. Vinny just sat with his hands folded, beaming with pride.

Joseph Alessio Sr. was known around the neighborhood as Joey "Chits", the "chits" referring to favors, which Joey Chits traded like currency. Joey Chits was involved in local politics, but not as a politician. He was a guy who got things for politicians, like votes, and in turn he got things from politicians, like a well-paying no-show job at a city sewage treatment plant. He got up in the morning, drove down to the sewage plant, punched in, then drove home and watched television or took a nap. Later, toward the end of the day, he drove back to the sewage plant, punched out, and drove home. It irritated him to have to make two trips.

When Joe Alessio Jr. volunteered his father for career day, he figured it would be no problem, since his dad would be sitting around the house watching T.V. When Joey Chits heard about career day, he mistook it for a real job, so he didn't show up. When Joey Chits no-showed for career day, Sister Thomas Aquinas went to Ike, the school janitor, to fill in. Reasoning that a sanitation inspector and a janitor must have a lot in common, Sister Thomas Aquinas thought Ike would make a suitable replacement.

Ike walked in with a mop and a broom. He held the mop out in his left hand and the broom out in his right. Raising the mop, he said, "This is a tool for cleaning up yer wet spills, like milk, juice, ink, or puke." Turning to the broom, he added, "This here is a tool for cleaning up yer dry spills, like pencil shavings, paper scraps, potato chips, or the oatmeal stuff that soaks up puke." Ike didn't wait for questions. He turned and walked out the door and down the hall.

For a week before career day, Carol Malone had been telling everyone that her father was coming in and that he was an engineer. Everyone was looking forward to Mr. Malone's visit; we all loved trains and couldn't wait to talk to someone whose job was driving them.

When Mr. Malone came in, he didn't look anything like what we expected. He didn't have any striped overalls. He didn't wear a floppy hat. He didn't have a red handkerchief. He didn't even have a pair of gloves. He wore a short-sleeved white shirt, brown pants that were two inches too short, and black shoes with spongy soles. In his shirt pocket was a plastic pouch that folded over the outside of the pocket. In the plastic pouch were several pencils, sharpened to needle-sharp points, two ballpoint pens and a small plastic ruler. It turns out that Mr. Malone was something called a "hydraulic engineer", which we soon learned had nothing to do with driving trains.

Mr. Malone took out a wooden contraption with a section in the center that slid back and forth. It had a glass window over its edges with a red line painted on the glass. Along the surfaces of the wooden slats were tiny markings and numbers. Mr. Malone tried to explain that you could solve any mathematical formula or problem by simply sliding the wooden slats back and forth, lining up the red stripe on the glass window, and reading the answer to the problem. He called it a slide rule.

It seemed a little hard to believe that you could get the answer to your arithmetic homework from the three pieces of wood and a tiny piece of glass. But Mr. Malone was a smart guy and if he said he could do it, we figured he probably could. He reached into a cardboard box and carefully lifted out something that he had wrapped in tissue. He gently unwrapped the tissue, cradled the object in his hands, and gingerly laid it on the corner of Sister Thomas Aquinas's desk. It looked like a miniature bridge.

Mr. Malone said that he had used his slide rule to calculate how to build a tiny bridge completely out of toothpicks that could hold one hundred pounds. He was very proud of his toothpick bridge, and went on to say that he was entering it into a national contest for toothpick bridges, where the winner would receive a fifty-dollar savings bond and a fountain pen.

He invited us to come closer to look at the bridge, but asked us not to touch it. He was very nervous about the national contest. You could tell that he had a spot reserved in that plastic pocket pouch for a new fountain pen. The class took turns crouching down and looking at the miniature masterpiece. Every toothpick had been carefully glued into place, one by one. It must have taken months to build.

Sister Thomas Aquinas asked Mr. Malone again how much weight his slide rule had calculated that the bridge could support. "One hundred pounds," Mr. Malone proudly exclaimed, turning his back on the bridge and beaming at the nun, who was standing near the door.

Lou the Screw had been doing a bit of arithmetic in his head, without the benefit of a slide rule, or for that matter, any real familiarity with arithmetic. He calculated that since he weighed just about exactly two hundred pounds, if he stood on one foot he would weigh one hundred pounds.

While Mr. Malone was basking in the attention given by Sister Thomas Aquinas, Lou the Screw sprang from his seat, grabbed the toothpick bridge and laid it on the floor. Carefully standing on only one foot, Lou the Screw stepped up onto the bridge. The tiny structure immediately exploded, sending shards of toothpicks in every direction.

Mr. Malone turned back just as the splintering sounds signaled the end of the toothpick bridge. He stood with his eyes wide and his mouth hanging open, staring in disbelief. Tears welled up in his eyes. He gasped and muttered a few words but couldn't string them into a sentence.

"You…it…why…too heavy…never…fountain pen…"

Mr. Malone was in a state of shock. Feeling badly, Lou the Screw bent down and started picking up the toothpicks one by one. Lou cupped one hand collecting the toothpicks, while crawling along picking them up with the other. Mr. Malone just stared straight ahead, sputtering.

Ike walked past the door, heard Mr. Malone, and then saw Lou the Screw crawling along, picking up toothpicks. Grabbing his broom, Ike rushed into the room showing an air of importance. In a loud voice, Ike said, "This here's one of yer dry spills," and began sweeping up what was left of Mr. Malone's toothpick bridge.

The last guest on career day was Alba, the garage door genie. He wore a striped turban made out of a table cloth with gold thread that shined when the light hit it. He had a goatee and wore a leather vest with no shirt beneath it. His arms were wrapped in aluminum foil. He wore bedroom slippers that came to a point in the front.

Alba wasn't anyone's father. In fact, none of us had ever seen him before. If we had, we would have remembered it. Sister Thomas Aquinas said that Whitey's father had to go out of town, but he offered to get his brother-in-law to come into class in his place. It turns out that Alba was married to Whitey's dad's sister.

Alba's real name was Alan. His brother's name was Barry. Together, they owned the Al-Ba Garage Door Company. The genie outfit was just something that Whitey's uncle came up with on the spur of the moment.

Alba played a game where he tried to guess what kind of car your parents drove. He would ask you your name, then your address, carefully writing the information on a clipboard that he carried. When he had your name and address, he would guess what kind of car your parents drove.

It was ten or eleven kids before we realized that he always guessed the same kind of car. He would write down your name and address, then close his eyes as if he were trying to see your parents' car in his head, then invariably he would say, "Studebaker."

If the kid actually knew what kind of car his parents drove, he'd correct Alba and Alba would write the answer down. Then Alba would ask the kid if his parents had a garage. If the kid said yes, Alba moved on to the next kid. If the kid said no, Alba made another mark on his clipboard.

When Alba had guessed every kid's parents' car, and made all of his marks on his clipboard, he told us that he had a special treat for us. Alba the garage door genie said that he could make a person disappear. Everyone scooted forward on their seats, anxious to see the magic trick.

Alba asked us to choose one person for him to make disappear. Hands shot up all over the classroom. Everyone volunteered to disappear. Sister Thomas Aquinas was the only one without her hand up. She was standing between Alba and the door, with her arms folded in front of her. Alba looked at the hands waving frantically in front of him, then looked at Sister Thomas Aquinas, then at the door behind her.

"Who would like to see me make Sister Thomas Aquinas disappear?" Alba asked in a deep voice.

The classroom erupted in applause and laughter. Sister Thomas Aquinas, being a good sport, moved away from the door and over closer to Alba the garage door genie. Alba took a wrinkled silk scarf out of his pocket and waved it flamboyantly through the air. Handing the scarf to Sister Thomas Aquinas, Alba asked her to face the class and hold the scarf out in front of her face. He then instructed the class to be very quiet and to close our eyes. He said that it was very important that everyone count backwards from ten down to zero and only then to open our eyes. The trick would only work if we all counted backwards together. With our eyes closed, we counted backwards, starting at ten.

"...five, four, three, two, one, zero!"

When we reached zero, we opened our eyes. Sister Thomas Aquinas was still standing right where she'd been, holding the silk scarf in front of her face. Alba the garage door genie had disappeared.

Spending first and second grades in the same classroom with the same nun made time seem to blur together. The only clear difference was that the first graders sat in the front of the classroom and the second graders sat in the back. Memories could only be associated with either first or second grade by recalling whether we were sitting in the front or the back of the room when something happened.

One thing that separated first from second grade was the fact that in second grade Walter always wore a sweater. From the first day of school, when the temperature was still near 90 degrees, through the fall and winter, and right on through the last day of school, when it again approached 90 degrees outside, Walter wore his sweater. He would walk into the classroom every morning, his hair exploding in every direction, his clip-on necktie askew, and his bright red sweater buttoned up to his neck. By the middle of the day, almost without fail, his sweater would be wrapped around his waist, the arms tied together, like a Scottish kilt covering the entire front of his navy blue trousers.

About halfway through second grade, Father Tim took over teaching our Religion Class. Three days a week, Father Tim walked over from the rectory and Sister Thomas Aquinas took the first graders out to the playground, leaving the second graders in the classroom. Father Tim sat on the desk, his legs dangling over the edge, opened his arms wide, and invited us to move up toward the front of the room near him. Having recently "graduated" to the rear of the classroom, we weren't in a hurry to go back to the first grade desks, but we were in Catholic school and when the priest said move, you moved.

Everyone shuffled forward, taking seats in the front of the classroom, but no one sat in the very first row. Father Tim smiled, pulled one of the front row desks around, and sat in it facing the rest of us.

"This is a very special year," Father Tim said.

"This year, you will make your first Holy Communion," he added.

"Who knows what Communion means?" Father Tim asked.

Without hesitation, Leonard Felch raised his hand. Leonard wasn't the dumbest kid at St. Basil's, but if they organized a "dumb Olympics", Leonard would be assured of at least a bronze medal. Pointing at Leonard, not knowing what he was in for, Father Tim said, "Yes, young man?"

Paraphrasing the geopolitical discussions he had heard at home, Leonard blurted out, "Communion is what the pinkos in Russia do," a smile spreading across his face like a beaming light of pride.

Father Tim tried not to laugh, but the harder he tried, the more he shook. The rest of us, not even trying to avoid it, broke into hysterical laughter...everyone, that is, except for Walter. Walter just rocked from side to side, smiling.

Pulling himself together, Father Tim corrected Leonard, explaining that, "Communion is a blessed sacrament in which you eat the body and blood of Jesus..." which silenced the rest of the room as quickly as if an atomic bomb had gone off. No one had thought much about Communion, even though we had seen our parents walk up to the railing in the front of the church, kneel down, and wait for the priest to come along with a gold cup and place something into their mouths while saying something in a foreign language. Never in our wildest dreams (or worst nightmares) did we imagine that the priest had body parts in that chalice. All of a sudden, Leonard Felch's Russian communists didn't seem so funny anymore.

It took Father Tim almost two weeks to convince us that Holy Communion was some sort of "miracle" in which Jesus turned his body and blood into a thin sliver of crisp bread, and that we were not destined to a life of religious cannibalism. Just about the time that everyone calmed down about the sacrament of Holy Communion, Father Tim dropped the second nuclear bomb on us: Confession.

Father Tim explained that it was impossible to receive Holy Communion until we had been absolved of all of our sins by completing the sacrament of Confession. Confession was a scary process by which seven year-olds sought forgiveness for their sins by kneeling in a dark closet and whispering into a screen to a priest seated on the other side, who served as a sort of United Nations translator for God. Not surprisingly, no one was very enthusiastic about the prospect.

As the time for our First Communion approached, we began spending more and more time in church practicing. For such a solemn event, it would be absolutely necessary for everyone to follow the choreography precisely. To increase the precision, the nuns used crickets.

Crickets were small metal contraptions that fit easily into the palm of the hand. When held between the thumb and forefinger, a cricket could be squeezed and released, resulting in a loud popping sound as the metal snapped back into its original shape.

As our class processional made its way up the center aisle of the church, Sister Thomas Aquinas would wait until just the right moment, and then squeeze her metal cricket.

"Clickitt"...the sound echoed throughout the church.

Hearing the signal, everyone stopped where they were.

"Clickitt, clickitt"...two chirps signaled time to genuflect, which involves dropping one knee to the floor for an instant, then returning to a standing position; the two rows of second graders dutifully genuflected in unison, hands folded in front of them and eyes straight ahead.

"Clickitt"...the next chirp told us to proceed into our pews and face forward. Talking or fidgeting was strictly forbidden...breathing was allowed if done quietly.

On the Friday before our First Communion, we had our last rehearsal. As the procession inched its way up the aisle, we heard the familiar "clickitt" of Sister Thomas Aquinas, and everyone stopped on cue.

Upon hearing the double "clickitt, clickitt," everyone genuflected as instructed. It was then that all hell broke loose. Unknown to Sister Thomas Aquinas, Eddie Wilkins had pilfered a spare cricket from her desk drawer, and had smuggled in into rehearsal.

Before Sister Thomas Aquinas could signal the class to enter the pews, Eddie double-clicked his cricket.

"Clickitt, clickitt" echoed through the church, causing the entire procession to genuflect a second time. Sister Thomas Aquinas, caught off-guard, hesitated momentarily...that was the opening Eddie Wilkins needed. Eddie let loose with a series of double clicks, sending the long line of seven year-olds into a fit of genuflecting, up, down, up, down, up, down...

Sister Pius sprang into action, sensing immediately that things had run amok. Moving as quickly as possible without actually running ("we don't run in the Lord's house"), Sister Pius moved abreast of the procession, her head cocked slightly as she listened for the source of the rogue clicking.

Timing his clicks perfectly, Eddie kept the procession line bouncing up and down in the aisle while avoiding Sister Pius's detection. Her fuse burning as she paced up and down the aisle, Sister Pius instinctively reached to her holster for her black leather gloves. Eddie waited for her to pass, and then clicked his cricket two more times. Seeing Sister Pius rush past in an enraged blur, Eddie counted silently in his head, and then clicked his cricket.

Unfortunately, like a bat in a dark cave, Sister Pius had been closing in on the sound and she now stood directly behind Eddie as he squeezed the metal cricket. Before he could get the second click away, Sister Pius wound up and cracked him in the back of the head with her black leather gloves. She hit him so hard that the cricket flew from his hand and clattered down the aisle, coming to rest silently at the feet of Sister Thomas Aquinas, who bent down and scooped it into her hand. Hearing only the first of Eddie's final clicks, the procession obediently made its way into their pews, facing forward quietly. With our backs to Sister Pius and Eddie, no one noticed as she dragged him out of the church by his ear.

On the afternoon before our first Holy Communion, we were led over to the church like a bunch of convicts on the chain gang. It was time for us to make our first Confessions. You made your First Confession the day before your First Communion in order to leave as little time as possible for you to commit a seven year-old sin in between.

In preparation for our day in court, each of us had dutifully made a list of our sins. Even though the confessional was as dark as a moonless night, we all carried little scraps of paper with our sins written down. There was no chance of reading them in the confessional, but carrying the lists around with us somehow made us feel prepared.

Skinny Boggs moved into the neighborhood from someplace in South Carolina at the beginning of the summer before second grade. For the first few months after he moved in, we all thought his first name was Skinnyboggs, because that's all his mother ever called him. Mrs. Boggs had a voice that sounded like a scalded cat, and she would stick her head out of the screen door and screech, "Skinnyboggs, you git yourself home this minute!" or, "Skinnyboggs, when yer daddy gits home, heez gunna tan yer hide!"

Skinny Boggs' dad was a prison guard. Named for Forrest Bedford, the Confederate general and originator of the Ku Klux Klan, Forrest Boggs worked at the state penitentiary. He walked with a limp and one eye drooped, making him a scary looking guy when he came out of the house in his prison uniform.

Everyone in the Boggs family spoke with a drawl that made it almost impossible to understand a word that they said. Skinny Boggs cussed like a longshoreman, the profanity being the little bit of what he said that we could make out. He couldn't explain where the name "Skinny" came from, but then he spoke with such a drawl that he had difficulty explaining anything. One thing that needed no explaining was Skinny's collection of filthy magazines.

The Boggs house was the Library of Congress of pornography. Stacks and stacks of the dirtiest magazines any of us had ever seen filled the basement and half the garage. In spite of the fact that we couldn't understand most of what he said, Skinny Boggs was one of the most popular kids in the neighborhood almost from the day he arrived.

As I knelt in the pew memorizing my lines, a movement out of the corner of my eye caught my attention. It was Skinny Boggs making his way down the pew, stepping over the backs of legs as he approached several of us at the end of the row. Skinny was carrying something heavy under his arm and about halfway down the pew, he stumbled over an outstretched leg and dropped a sheaf of papers, scattering pages and pages of hand-written sins beneath the pews.

There was no time to enjoy the moment, because I felt a tap on my shoulder and saw the door to the confessional standing open, with no one between me and the darkness. Looking down, I saw my feet betray me, one in front of the other walking into the confessional. My feet disappeared when the door closed with a hushed whoosh and everything was black.

Swallowing hard, I tried to recite the words I had memorized in rehearsal, but the first three times that I opened my mouth, nothing came out. Finally, on the fourth try, I was able to stammer, in a cracking voice, "Bless me Father, for I have sinned. It has been fill in the blank since my last confession."

In fact, I had never before been in confession, but the card they gave us said we should say, "Bless me Father, for I have sinned. It has been – fill in the blank – since my last confession"...and in Catholic school, following the rules precisely is everything. Without waiting for a response from the priest, I launched into my list of sins.

"I don't always clean my room."

I had never cleaned my room, so technically I was committing another sin by lying in church, which was probably going to be more than a misdemeanor venial sin.

"I took a piece of candy from the drugstore and didn't pay for it."

Actually, I had dropped the candy in my nervous panic leaving the store and had not even eaten it, but to be on the safe side, I confessed it anyway.

When I finished my list, I concluded with a recitation of the Act of Contrition. Then I held my breath waiting for the priest to tell me whether purgatory was in my future and to hand down my penance. I waited and waited, but there was no response from the priest.

I began to think that my list of sins had so overwhelmed the priest that he was speechless. In all his years listening to sinners, he had never heard such a list of misdeeds. He was having difficulty adding up the years that I would spend in purgatory.

At that moment, an invisible door slid back, letting in a faint shaft of light from the other side of a screen that I had not realized was only inches in front of my face in the dark.

"Hello, my child, please proceed," whispered the priest.

In weeks of rehearsals, they had never told us that the priests actually sit between two confessionals, alternating between the two, leaving each penitent alone while listening to the other. I had just confessed my sins to an oak panel, behind which the priest had been listening to someone else's confession.

Relieved that my sins had in fact not doomed me to centuries of fiery inferno, I began again…

"Bless me Father, for I have sinned. It has been fill in the blank since my last confession."

Hearing a quiet chuckle from the other side of the screen, I recognized the laugh as Father Tim's.

"It's ok, Michael…take your time," he reassured me.

Instead of a recitation of memorized sins and fourteenth century prayers, my first confession turned out to be more of a conversation. Father Tim would ask me questions, listen patiently, and give advice gently. When we finished, he asked how my mom and dad were doing. He asked how Henry was, and how I was feeling. I'd been worried about Confession for nothing. It wasn't a scary voice coming from behind a curtain in a dark place. It was Father Tim, and we talked just like old friends sitting on a park bench.

I stood up and turned to leave, feeling the weight of the world lifted from my shoulders. As I opened the door, the brightness of the light outside the confessional made me squint involuntarily. As my eyes readjusted to the light, I saw Walter stepping into the confessional on the other side, his red sweater wrapped around his waist, a demented smile on his face.

Chapter 3

HENRY DIED IN THE SUMMER before I started fifth grade. There were a lot of technical terms for what went wrong, but in the end, his heart just wore out. The hole never closed, and the extra work was just too much. On his next birthday he would have been five.

Henry had been in and out of the hospital since he was born. He was always small for his age, and frail. He was smart, and funny, but he never got strong enough to run or jump or climb trees. When he was doing a little better, he shared a bedroom with me. When he was doing a little worse, he slept with my parents so that my mom could listen to him breathing. The house was always quiet. A purposeful quiet that made it easier for my mom to listen and worry.

That summer, Henry was back in the hospital twice. He was having trouble breathing again, and his lips were almost always a purplish blue. About a week before he died, they brought Henry home. The doctors had done as much as they could, and everyone knew that Henry would be more comfortable in his own home. A hospital is the worst place in the world to die.

If it was possible, the house got even quieter after Henry came home from the hospital. The doctor was coming to the house twice a day now, on his way to his office, and again on his way home. One of my parents was with Henry all of the time. He stayed in their bedroom, and my dad brought in a small television set with a metal antenna that he called "rabbit ears". The room glowed with a flickering blue light day and night. I think the television was for my mom and dad, who took turns sitting awake with one hand on Henry's chest, feeling him breathe now that it was hard to hear him breathing.

Henry slept almost all of the time toward the end. I think they were giving him medicine to help him sleep. There were no tubes, no machines, no needles. Just the flickering of the television screen and the creaking of my mom's rocking chair. His sheets had horses and cowboy hats, not the sterile white bedding of the hospital.

Whichever of my parents was not with Henry was with me. They tried to make things as normal as possible, but I was too old now to pretend that everything was alright. I knew that something was seriously wrong. No one spoke of dying, but somehow the hope had leaked out of my parents. They touched hands as they traded places, one going in to be with Henry, the other coming out to be with me. They waited until I went to bed to have any long conversations. They put up a good front, but I could see in their eyes that the fight had gone out of them…and out of Henry.

In the four years since Henry first became seriously ill, he had turned into a kid. When he was an infant, he was something to look at, but when he didn't die that first summer, he turned into my little brother. We had spent the last four years getting to know each other, becoming friends. Now, lying in my parents' bedroom in that flickering blue light was a friend of mine. When I was six, I cried for my mother. My mom cried for Henry. Now that I was ten, I cried for Henry. And my mom cried for me.

It's funny. If Henry had died that first summer of his life, I would have been sad for my mom and dad, but I don't think I would have known how to miss him. Now, when I thought of him being gone, I had trouble catching my breath. It was like I was the one with a hole in my heart.

It was still dark outside when I was awakened by a sound that shattered the silence of the house. I sat up in bed and listened. The sound wasn't loud – it was a whimper. My mom was making the saddest sound that I have ever heard, before or since. I ran into her room because I didn't know what else to do. She was kneeling beside Henry's bed, and her rocking chair was still rocking back and forth, empty. Her head was lying on Henry's chest, her eyes closed tightly.

My dad scooped me up in his arms and pressed his hand between my shoulders, pulling me close. I could feel the whiskers on his cheeks and his tears were moist against my skin. No one said anything. It was as though everyone knew what everyone else was thinking and no one felt the need to speak. Henry just lay still; he looked like he was sleeping. The raspy sounds of his labored breathing were quiet now. The blue light from the television threw shadows against the walls. The house was completely quiet.

My dad put me down in the rocking chair and kissed my forehead. He turned and wrapped his arms around my mom's shoulders, still not saying anything. He held her for a few minutes, then he stood and brushed

Henry's hair from his forehead and patted his cheek. When he turned back toward me, my dad looked old. His eyes were tired and his hands were shaking like the old man I had seen in the hospital elevator with Father Tim four years earlier.

My dad bent down and whispered something to my mom that I couldn't hear. She nodded her head and patted his hand and he reached over and picked me up again. He carried me out to the living room and we sat down on the couch. It took my dad several minutes to say anything. It was the first time any of us had spoken out loud.

"Henry fought for as long as he could," my dad explained, "but his heart just got tired."

I nodded, unable to formulate any words right away.

"He's in a better place now, Mike – he won't be sick any more."

"Is Mom ok?" I asked.

"She'll be fine. She's sad right now, but she's been getting ready for this. She didn't want Henry to be sick anymore."

"Are you ok?" I asked, looking into his tired eyes.

"I'll be just fine, too," he smiled, "we all will."

We sat together without talking for a few minutes. Neither of us knew what to say, but neither of us minded the quiet.

Finally, my dad rumpled my hair with his hand and said, "Your mom will need you to be brave, Mike."

I don't think he meant what he said. I don't think that my mom needed me to be brave, and I don't think that my dad thought that she did. I think he believed that it would help me get through this if I thought my mom needed me to be brave. Maybe he was right, but I didn't feel brave. I felt sad and scared.

I don't know whether it was right then or later on that I remembered Father Tim telling me about heroes. Heroes were people who did brave things when they were afraid. On the park bench beneath the elm tree he had told me that when the time came, I'd be a hero. I wiped my eyes and stood up. Turning toward my parents' bedroom, I could hear my heart beating. I stopped outside the door and looked in. My mom was rocking in the chair, holding Henry in her arms. I took a deep breath, and felt my chest ache. I gritted my teeth and stepped into the bedroom.

About a week after Henry's funeral, Father Tim knocked on our front door. When I opened the door, he was standing on the porch, smiling at me through the screen. Behind him on the sidewalk was a bicycle. It was a girl's bicycle with a wire basket on the front and a little silver bell that you rang with your thumb. The paint was mostly gone, and the seat had holes in the cover where tufts of stuffing poked out. He grinned at me and said, "How about you get your bike and let's take a ride?"

I didn't know what to say, so I just went to the garage and got my bike. When I got back to the sidewalk, Father Tim was on the dilapidated girl's bike and was peddling off down the sidewalk. I fell in behind him, but I had trouble riding slowly enough to avoid running into him. As he peddled, the front tire of his bicycle wobbled, making it hard for him to ride in a straight line.

We rode through the neighborhood and stopped at the corner market, where Father Tim abruptly jumped off of his bike, running alongside it until it wobbled to a stop. Among its many deficiencies, the ancient bicycle had no brakes.

"Wait here," Father Tim called over his shoulder after leaning the bike up against the brick wall of the store front. I pulled to a stop and waited for him to return. In a few minutes, Father Tim came out holding two bottles of orange Nehi soda. Reaching out to hand me one of the bottles, he said, "Thirsty?" He had a knack for questions that didn't really need answers.

We sat on the curb with our feet in the street and drank our Nehi sodas. Father Tim drank half of his soda before turning to ask me a question.

"How are your mom and dad doing, Michael?"

"Okay, I guess. Dad doesn't say too much, and mom tries not to cry, but she still does sometimes."

"She'll cry for a long time," Father Tim said, "but it's ok to cry, Michael...in fact, it's good to cry."

"She tries not to cry in front of me," I said, "but I see her wiping her eyes on her apron sometimes."

"She's trying to be strong for you," Father Tim observed.

"I don't need her to be strong for me. It's ok with me if she cries."

"Have you told her that?" Father Tim asked.

"No."

"Well, you should. It would help her to feel better."

I took a long drink of soda. It gave me an excuse not to talk. Father Tim watched me for a minute before continuing.

"How are you doing, Michael?"

"Okay," I lied.

"It's ok for you to cry too, you know."

I didn't say anything. I just tried not to start crying right there on the curb.

"It's ok to be sad, Michael…it's ok to be sad and it's ok to cry if you feel like crying."

I was running out of soda. Pretty soon I'd have no excuse not to talk, so I decided to just go ahead and say it.

"I'm sad sometimes…and sometimes I'm mad."

"Mad at who?" asked Father Tim.

"God."

"Do you think God made Henry die?" he asked quietly.

"Who else?" I asked, less a question than an answer.

"God doesn't make people die, Michael, He allows them to die when it's their time to go to Heaven."

To a ten year-old, the subtle nuances of theology are indiscernible shades of gray. I was angry at God and no philosophical hair-splitting by Father Tim was going to get God off the hook.

"Then I'm mad at God for letting Henry die," I said, with as much indignation as I could muster.

"That's ok," Father Tim reassured me. "It's ok to be mad…mad is sometimes healthier than sad…and God can take it."

I hadn't really talked about how I was feeling with anyone since Henry died. I talked to my parents, but we seemed to step gingerly around the hard stuff like we were stepping over porcelain or glass. We talked about everything and anything except how we were feeling. It felt good telling Father Tim that I was mad at God. I was afraid Father Tim would be upset, but he wasn't. He just kept telling me that God was tough, that He knew that I still loved Him, and that He'd be waiting for me when I felt better about things.

After Henry died, my parents withdrew from life just a little. They didn't do it on purpose, they just sort of got lost in their sorrow. Henry's passing left a hole in their lives. I found myself looking at that empty place where Henry had been and feeling alone. Something that Father Tim told me that day sitting on the curb meant more to me later, when I was old enough for it to sink in.

"It's alright to feel alone sometimes, Michael. Some things just can't be shared – they're too big to get your arms around, so you just have to live around the edges."

I thought about that a lot over the years. From time to time things happen that can only be handled alone. Sometimes living around the edges is all that you can do. Sitting there with Father Tim, I found the courage to ask him a question that had been bothering me more than I realized.

"Do you think Henry was afraid?" I asked.

"Do you?" Father Tim answered with a question.

"I don't know. He slept a lot when he came home from the hospital, but whenever he was in the hospital, he never acted afraid."

"I don't think Henry was old enough to be afraid of dying," Father Tim explained, "and your mom and dad did a great job of making him feel safe."

"They were afraid, though," I whispered.

"Who?"

"My mom and dad."

"Did they tell you that they were afraid?"

"No, but I could tell."

"How do you feel about that?" he asked.

"Proud," I said.

"Proud?" he asked, puzzled.

"They were brave even though they were afraid. They were heroes."

"That's just what they said about you, Michael."

I didn't feel like a hero. I felt sad, and mad, but I didn't feel like a hero. Still, it felt good to know that my parents thought I was. Maybe it was too hard for them to talk about yet. Maybe it was only something that they could tell to Father Tim. Either way, it made me feel better to hear it. I felt a little less sad, a little less mad.

A faint roll of thunder rumbled in the sky and raindrops began splattering on the sidewalk. Father Tim glanced at the clouds and said we'd better be heading home. He asked if I wanted him to ride back to my house with me, but I knew that I could go much faster without him. I told him that I'd be fine, and I got onto my bike.

"Come and see me before school starts," Father Tim said, squinting through the raindrops as he climbed back on his battered bicycle. "We'll toss the football," he said, pushing away from the wall with a wave of his hand.

I turned toward home and rode a short way before I stopped and looked back over my shoulder. I watched as Father Tim wobbled down the sidewalk, peddling home through the rain.

Chapter 4

12:01 P.M.

THE PARKING LOT WAS STILL empty when I stepped back outside the old school. The funeral Mass wouldn't begin for another couple of hours, so despite the heat, I decided to take a walk around the old neighborhood. So much had changed, but I was hopeful that a few familiar sights might trigger happy memories of a place and people long gone. I hooked a finger into the collar of my suit jacket, draped it over my shoulder, and walked back three decades.

About a block from St. Basil's, I turned a corner and crossed the street in the middle of the block. There was no traffic on the street, just a truck from the city's department of sewer and water parked in the shade of a tree. A barricade was set up around an open manhole and three city workers were standing around the barricade smoking cigarettes. One of the three was holding a plastic Coca-Cola cup that was just slightly smaller than an oil drum. Another was drinking Starbuck's coffee, which seemed like torture on such a hot day. The third guy was reading the sports page of the morning newspaper. Every few minutes a barrage of obscenity would come bellowing out of the manhole and the three guys would start laughing and shouting even worse epithets down into the hole in the street. Everything looked normal for a union job.

I couldn't help smiling as I walked past the three guys standing around the manhole wasting time. Some things may have changed, but one thing was still the same. The city never sent one guy to do a job that three guys could watch. If Pinhead Griffith's dad was still alive, he'd have been proud.

Pinhead was my best friend. He was a foot taller than the rest of us, and he was all elbows and knees. His shoulders were as bony as the rest of him, and all of those sharp edges made his head look like it had sunk between his shoulder blades. Nobody knew who gave Pinhead his nickname – it may have been his mother – but he'd been Pinhead for as long as any of us had known him.

Pinhead was a natural leader. He was so much taller, it gave him the illusion of looking older. He was always calm under pressure. He was the guy who we could always count on to think before we leapt. He wasn't the smartest guy in school, but he was smarter than most. What really made Pinhead a leader was the strength of his character. He was honest and reliable. He cared about people, and they knew it. He was the nicest guy any of us knew. And from the time we were six years old, he was my best friend.

Pinhead's dad was a garbage man. He had worked his way up to driving the truck, a real promotion from the job of hanging off the back of the truck with your face in the garbage all day. Mr. Griffith would rumble through the neighborhood, sitting up in the cab of the truck waving at kids and honking the horn. You could hear Pinhead's dad coming from a block away. If the wind was just right, sometimes you'd smell him coming before you actually heard him.

One of the fringe benefits of being a garbage man was the stuff they brought home. Three-legged coffee tables, lamps with no cords, the occasional set of snow tires with enough tread left for another winter. Several times each summer, Pinhead's dad would have a garage sale and pile all of the junk he'd amassed out in his driveway. People would come by and pick through the piles like it was a department store.

The merchandise was all defective, but the prices were cheap. You could buy a toaster with no knobs for a quarter. A tennis racket without strings went for a nickel. A full set of left-handed golf clubs cost three dollars. A woman once paid Mr. Griffith $1.50 for a Nativity set that was missing the baby Jesus. She said she'd put it out until Christmas Eve, when the manger was empty anyway.

Pinhead's dad gathered up run-down furnishings and broken odds and ends, hoarded them in his garage for a month or two, then sold them back to the folks in the neighborhood at bargain basement prices. He was years ahead of his time as a recycling environmentalist.

Pinhead loved to tell anyone who hadn't heard it – and most of us had – how his dad and the other garbage men scammed the city. At the city dump, there was a big scale that they used to weigh the trucks. It wasn't that the city cared how much the garbage weighed, it was a way to keep the garbage men from sleeping on the job. By weighing each truck as it arrived at the dump, the city could be sure that the trucks weren't half-empty.

Pinhead's dad and the other garbage men would pick up the trash in one or two alleys, then drive to an out-of-the-way place where they dragged a hose out to the truck and pumped water in along with the garbage to fill up the truck. Since water is a lot heavier than the garbage, it didn't take much time with a hose to do a day's work.

Once they'd pumped enough water into the garbage truck, they drove off and parked under a highway overpass where they could sit in the shade and play cards or sleep. When enough time had passed to make it look good, they returned to the dump and sloshed onto the scales to be weighed.

From the time we were young, Pinhead always liked school. Most of us looked at school like a jail sentence…something to be endured. Pinhead was always in a good mood. He almost never missed school, even when he was sick enough to fake it the rest of the way. He answered questions in class and even asked a few. We didn't hold it against him. We just never knew what he liked about the place. No matter – Pinhead liked everyone and almost everyone liked him.

I stopped a few doors down from the open manhole and stood in front of a house that I barely recognized. I counted the driveways starting at the corner, running the names of the old neighbors through my head as I went along, to be sure that I had the right house. When I was sure that it was the right house, little things started to look familiar again. The funny peak in the roof of the porch that didn't match the rest of the roof lines, because the porch had been added long after the original house was built. That it was still standing, albeit leaning a little, after all these years was a tribute to the builder, Danny Noonan's mother. Not his dad – his mom.

Danny Noonan wore his hair in a crew cut. The very front of his hairline was waxed straight up with a concoction called "Butch Wax". A comb coated with Butch Wax would keep a crew cut standing at attention all day. On hot days, Butch Wax attracted flies, but it never gave up its shape.

Danny was a little guy, but tough. You had to be tough growing up in the Noonan house, because Danny's mother was constantly yelling at someone. If she wasn't yelling at his father, she was yelling at Danny. If you walked past Danny's house, you would think that everyone was hard of hearing, because Mrs. Noonan was always shouting at the top of her lungs.

Mr. Noonan wasn't hard of hearing, but he acted like he was. When Danny's mom launched into one of her tirades, Mr. Noonan would just sit in his armchair, usually in his underwear, staring straight ahead. There was no television in the room, and he wasn't facing a window, but he'd just stare. The louder Mrs. Noonan got, the harder Mr. Noonan stared, until she became hoarse from shouting and resorted to belting him in the back of the head with her broomstick. Mr. Noonan had decided long ago that a broom handle to the back of the head was better than trying to talk sense to Danny's mother.

One spring Mrs. Noonan decided that their house would be more of a home if it had a front porch. She began every morning shouting at Mr. Noonan that the front stoop needed a covered porch, and she ended every day with a solid thwack to the back of his head. Finally, she realized that he wasn't going to build a porch, so she built one herself. Mr. Noonan was careful not to get too close to her whenever she was holding a hammer.

Standing in front of the old Noonan house, I couldn't help wondering what it must have been like growing up with all of that hollering and screaming all of the time. Our home had been so quiet – too quiet – for so many years that sometimes I wished someone would shout, or at least raise their voice.

The side yard between the old Noonan house and the house next door was completely fenced in now. A six-foot high chain link fence separated the two houses and a locked gate faced the street. I wondered what could be in the back yard that was so valuable that it needed a locked security fence. Nothing in the neighborhood looked very valuable from the street. I walked closer to the gate, curious to see what might be behind the run-down house. Maybe an expensive car.

When I was within a foot of the gate, a large brown dog rushed the fence, its teeth bared and spittle flying from its jaws. Its tiny ears were almost flat against its head and it was making a growling sound that emanated from somewhere in its intestines. The dog jumped against the fence with pure hatred in its eyes. I immediately recognized it as a pit bull and instinctively jumped back. My heart was pounding as I stumbled and back-peddled toward the sidewalk. The dog barked and growled, shook its powerful shoulders as it tossed slobber into the air, and jumped vertically in an effort to clear the fence.

I had run half a block before I was brave enough to stop and catch my breath. Bravery actually had nothing to do with it. If I hadn't stopped running, I would have collapsed. I stood bent over, with my hands on my knees, listening. When I didn't hear growling, I knew that the dog hadn't escaped its pen. That was when I realized that my knees were shaking beneath my hands.

It took several minutes for me to catch my breath, and all the while anger was replacing fear, so I never really did completely calm down. I straightened up and looked back down the street. Everything looked normal. I wanted to stay angry, but I couldn't. Sadness pushed the anger aside as I realized that things had changed and that there was nothing that I or anyone could do to stop it.

Danny Noonan had a dog when we were kids. It was a mutt, part beagle, part greyhound, and part St. Bernard. It was a friendly dog, but clumsy. It was always knocking something over or falling down the stairs. Mrs. Noonan took to calling the dog "dumbass". After about a year of her calling the dog dumbass, the name stuck.

Danny Noonan would be out walking with his dog and people would ask, "What's your dog's name?"

"Dumbass," Danny would reply.

More than a few people gasped in horror at what they thought was a derogatory term directed at them. A few guys took a poke at Danny, thinking he was being a wise guy.

When the dog followed Danny to school, he would walk along, turning over his shoulder and shouting, "Go home, dumbass!" Girls walking behind the dog burst into tears.

One afternoon on the way home from school, Danny's dog left the sidewalk and wandered into old Mrs. Leahy's garden. Danny couldn't see Mrs. Leahy kneeling among her rose bushes, but he did see his dog digging mischievously in her flower beds.

"Get out of those flowers, dumbass!" yelled Danny.

Standing up, Mrs. Leahy sputtered, "Well, I never…" and stomped off toward her house. Danny just grabbed his dog by the collar, and shaking his head continued toward home.

It was Danny Noonan's mother who gave Joe the Bum, another of our friends, his nickname during a Christmas blizzard when we were about twelve years old. Mrs. Noonan, who might generously be described as indelicate, but was more accurately described as coarse, had a nickname of her own – "Duke". It's uncommon for a mother to have a nickname, and even less typical for it to be "Duke", but in the case of Mrs. Noonan, the name fit. She clearly wore the pants in the family, and she had a vocabulary that would peel paint.

One Christmas Eve, Mrs. Noonan set off for the corner store to pick up a few odds and ends. It had snowed the night before, so she had awakened Danny early and saw to it that he shoveled a path from the front door to the sidewalk and cleared the walk in both directions in front of their house. She then gathered her pocketbook and set off on foot for the market on the corner. She had gone a short way, passing several houses with their sidewalks cleared of snow, when she came to an abrupt stop in front of Joe's house – the only house on either side of the street with its sidewalk not cleared of snow. Standing out in the cold, Duke Noonan was confronted by a wall of snow that reached almost to her knees.

Joe's dad had left early to drive down to the sewage treatment plant to punch in and not work. Not working on Christmas Eve paid time and a half. He had not shoveled the drive or the sidewalk, because he never did. The politicians who he helped get elected had always arranged for city crews to clear the walk and the driveway. It sometimes took a while, but if he was patient, his driveway always got plowed.

Duke Noonan was furious as she contemplated stepping through knee-deep snow. She looked into the picture window and there was Joe, movie star looks and all, waving to Mrs. Noonan who was scowling at him from the street. Muttering something about patronage workers and lowlife deadbeats, Duke Noonan waded through the snow, cursing and gesturing obscenely at Joe in the window. She finally made her way through the snowdrift and on to the corner store.

On her way back home with a bag of groceries in each arm, Duke Noonan expected to see Joe out shoveling the walk. To her amazement and fury, Joe had not made so much as a move to clear any of the snow. The wind, which had been at her back on the way up the street, was now howling in Mrs. Noonan's face. Reaching Joe's driveway, Mrs. Noonan stopped and looked toward the picture window, where Joe stood as if he hadn't moved since the last time she was here. Unable to deliver an obscene gesture while holding two sacks of groceries, Duke Noonan unleashed a verbal barrage that would embarrass a dockworker.

Joe pretended not to understand, smiled even wider, and continued waving. Mrs. Noonan stormed into the snow, turning her head toward the window for emphasis with each new burst of profanity. About halfway across Joe's driveway, Duke Noonan slipped and went down, her sacks of groceries flying into the air. When the bags landed, groceries scattered everywhere, sinking into the snow where they fell. Dragging herself up, Duke Noonan was now beyond furious...she was seething. She picked up as many groceries as she could find, placed them into the paper sacks, which were now wet from the snow, and bear-hugged them to her chest as she stomped toward home.

Kicking open the door, Mrs. Noonan dropped the groceries to the floor and began shouting at her husband as if he had done something to contribute to the disaster. The louder Duke Noonan shouted, the harder Mr. Noonan stared. It was a cold day, so he was sitting in his long johns in his favorite armchair. Danny Noonan heard his mother screeching and, calculating that trouble was brewing, he poked his head from the kitchen and asked what was wrong.

"What's wrong?" screamed Duke, "I'll tell you what's wrong...that dirty bastard down the street with the no-show city job didn't clear his sidewalk and I nearly broke my ass."

"Didn't Joe come out to help you?" Danny asked hopefully.

"Come out to help me? That good-for-nothing bum? He just stood in the window waving at me, grinning like a goddamned idiot. He's just like his old man, Joe the Bum."

Mr. Noonan may have coughed, or then again he may have done nothing out of the ordinary to attract Duke's attention to the back of his head. Either way, she reached for her broom, still cussing Joe the Bum.

I wanted to take a look at our old house before returning to St. Basil's, so I started walking again, checking over my shoulder occasionally to make sure that the pit bull was not following me. At the corner of the next block, I saw the old bakery where we used to buy day-old donuts for a penny. The windows, which years ago had been filled with cakes, pies, and pastries, had been converted to those small cubes of glass that look like ice – too opaque to make out anything but light and shadows on the other side. The door, which had always been open when I was a kid, allowing the sublime aroma of freshly baked bread to waft out into the street, was closed. A hand-painted sign screwed into the door on a slightly crooked angle read "Loans". I didn't want to think about what would happen if you borrowed money and couldn't repay it.

On the second floor of the building, accessible by an exterior stairway that looked more like a fire escape, was a small apartment where the Coolacks had lived. Mr. Coolack was a baker. He learned the craft from his father, who in turn learned it from his father. In the Ukraine, the Kulakovric men had been bakers for five generations. Around the turn of the century, Stanislav Kulakovric grew fearful of the changes that were making his native country a dangerous place. He took his life savings and booked passage on a steamship to America. When he landed at Ellis Island, an over-tired, tone-deaf immigration agent heard "Kulakovric" and wrote "Coolack" on his clipboard. With the stroke of a pen, the Kulakovric family tree was pruned and Stanislav Kulakovric, the Ukrainian baker, became Stan Coolack.

Stan's grandson, Alexander, ran the corner bakery in our neighborhood. He always had flour in his hair and a smile on his face. He made his living by kneading dough hours before the sun came up, sweating in front of a brick oven in the early hours of the morning, and making small talk with the neighborhood ladies as he wrapped their rolls and bread for dimes and quarters. He lived in the tiny apartment upstairs with his wife and their three children, the youngest of whom was our friend Cuckoo.

Cuckoo Coolack wore thick black plastic glasses. He looked like Buddy Holly, only goofier. Cuckoo was always looking at things a little crooked, and it wasn't because of his eyesight. He was left-handed, and his brain was wired backwards. His nickname just happened, because it sounded good with his last name, but for Cuckoo, it fit. He had a knack for asking questions that no one else would have ever thought of, and for seeing things that everyone else missed. Joey Chits once described Cuckoo as being "half a bubble off plumb". It was like Cuckoo had changed time zones but forgot to reset his watch. But there was nothing he wouldn't do for you if you were in trouble.

Cuckoo had a problem with his glasses. They were always getting in the way of flying balls or swinging elbows. At any point in time, Cuckoo had three or four pieces of adhesive tape holding his glasses together. When he wasn't breaking them, we were. Whether the game was baseball, or football, or basketball, the fact that Cuckoo's glasses would get broken was certain... the only questions were how long it would take and how it would happen.

In the days before one-hour eyeglasses, getting a new pair involved waiting a week or longer and cost more than most families could afford. A new pair of glasses meant a lot of freshly baked bread and rolls, so Cuckoo's mother was constantly nagging him to be more careful. After a game of basketball or baseball, Cuckoo would walk home, climb the wooden stairs alongside the bakery, and try to sneak into the apartment, but it was no use. The door would close and from the sidewalk we could hear Mrs. Coolack scolding, "You broke your glasses... again!"

The bakery was one of our favorite hang-outs. Mr. Coolack would set aside the donuts that had gone un-sold the day before and gave them to us for a penny. It wasn't that he was trying to make money by selling them to us. He was losing money by charging us only a penny, but he wanted to teach us an important lesson. He wanted us to get into the habit of paying for what we wanted, so he asked us for a penny.

The only member of our circle of friends who could eat a dime's worth of penny donuts was Fat Peter. He had a head that looked like an anvil and a body shaped like a pear. His face was always red because breathing was an aerobic exercise for Peter – walking was an adventure. In order to find pants with a waist big enough to go around him, his pant legs were always a foot too long. His mother refused to waste the fabric by cutting them, so his cuffs were always rolled up and folded several times. His mom was frugal, and she wouldn't take up the hems in his pants. She said he would grow into them. The problem with that logic was that Peter was growing horizontally, not vertically.

We could have been criticized for giving Fat Peter an unflattering and some would say mean-spirited nickname, but we didn't do it. His dad's name was also Peter, and he was about six feet tall and thin as a rail. His dad had always been called "Skinny Pete", so to make things easy around the house, his mother nicknamed him Fat Peter. If she was mad at one or the other of the two men in her house, she would shout "Skinny Pete" or "Fat Peter" to clarify who was in trouble at the moment. When we heard his mother call him Fat Peter, we were only too happy to do the same.

Fat Peter complained a lot. He had more aches and pains than a grandfather, and he was absent from school more than anyone else in the group. He was also a worrier. No matter how well things were going, Fat Peter was always worrying that something terrible was about to happen. While the rest of us were thinking of ways to get into trouble, Fat Peter was worrying that we would. Most of the time, we figured that he was making stuff up, because he was sick a lot on days when we had math or science tests. One time, however, Fat Peter had an iron-clad excuse to miss school when he ended up in the hospital. He was the only kid we ever knew who had kidney stones.

We decided to sneak into the hospital to see him, because back then kids were not allowed to visit anyone except their own relatives. I wasn't anxious to go see Peter, because I hadn't been in a hospital since Henry was sick, and I was in no hurry to go back. The rest of the guys talked me into going, however, and we headed off right after school let out on a Friday afternoon. Pinhead, Danny Noonan, and I were elected as the visiting party.

We needed a plan, because there was no way that three of us could just walk through the hospital without being noticed and stopped by security. When we arrived at the hospital, we sat in the waiting area and watched as people came and went. There was a guard in a green uniform sitting behind a desk just inside the main door. People would stop and ask for the room number of their relatives, then wait while the guard looked their name up in a three-ring binder.

Pinhead got an idea. He'd go first, and Danny and I would follow. We agreed to meet at Fat Peter's room. Pinhead took a deep breath and walked up to the security guard.

"Excuse me officer," Pinhead said without making eye contact. "My brother has kidney stones. If a kid had kidney stones, where would they take him?"

"Pediatrics is on the third floor," the guard replied, "but you can't go up without your parents. Are they here with you?"

Pinhead hadn't thought past his first question. The rest of his plan was still waiting to be thought up. He paused for a moment, then grabbed his stomach and bent over.

"I think I caught kidney stones from my brother," Pinhead faked, "I need to go to the bathroom."

The security guard peered over the edge of the desk, not sure what to make of Pinhead doubled over and moaning about needing to go to the bathroom.

"The restroom is over next to the elevator," the security guard gestured.

Pinhead stood up and thanked him. He walked toward the restroom without as much as a limp. Pinhead took his time walking toward the restroom. The security guard was distracted by an elderly couple asking for a room number in a very loud voice. As the guard picked up his binder to check the room number for the old people, Pinhead bypassed the washroom and stepped into an empty elevator, pressing the number three. He smiled and waved at us as the elevator doors slid closed.

A few minutes later, I walked up to the desk and asked the guard if there was a washroom nearby. He looked at me for a long time, then pointed toward the elevators.

"It's next to the elevators," he said. "Another kid just went in there. If he's still there, tell him there's no loitering."

I wasn't sure what loitering was, but since the guard thought Pinhead was doing it in the bathroom, it couldn't have been good.

"I'll tell him to hurry it up," I promised, and walked away as quickly as I could without actually running. I walked into the restroom and stood there for a few minutes, hoping that the guard wouldn't follow me in. After a little while, I opened the door a crack and saw a woman standing at the security desk holding a bunch of helium balloons. It was a perfect cover. When she walked to the elevator, I stepped out and kept the balloons between me and the guard. We entered the elevator and the woman pressed the button for the third floor. I stayed next to the balloons.

Danny Noonan knew that going to the bathroom was not an option. If he asked the guard about the bathroom, we'd all get caught. He waited until he saw his opportunity, and then he sprang into action. A florist van pulled up outside the entrance, and a delivery man pulled a large bouquet from the rear doors and started toward the main door. Danny held the door open for the man, who smiled down at Danny and nodded. When the man with the flowers passed through the doorway, Danny sprinted to the truck and pulled out another bouquet.

The delivery man stopped at the guard desk to check on the room number of the patient whose flowers he was carrying. Danny, moving much quicker than the delivery man, eased through the hospital doors and stood behind him. The security guard checked his list, told the delivery man the room number, and paid almost no attention to the unusually large clump of flowers moving past his desk.

When they reached the corner near the elevators, Danny set his bouquet down gently on a table and scooted around the delivery man just as the elevator doors opened.

"Which floor, mister?" Danny asked helpfully.

The delivery man looked down at Danny with his arms loaded with flowers and said, "Six," then smiled again, commenting on how polite Danny was.

Danny pressed the number six and the number three. When the elevator stopped on the third floor, Danny stepped out, telling the delivery man to have a nice day. The doors closed and Danny smiled, turning his attention to finding Pinhead and me in Fat Peter's room.

When we arrived at his room, Fat Peter was sitting up in bed looking perfectly healthy. None of us knew what kidney stones were, but whatever they were they sounded bad, and Peter didn't look like he had anything bad at all. He smiled and waved as we walked into his room, a little like a convict surprised to see his old cronies inside his jail cell.

Since Fat Peter seemed healthy enough, we offered to take him for a ride – in a wheelchair. He climbed out of bed, his hospital gown covering the front of him, but not his backside. Sitting in the wheelchair, Fat Peter looked content, until his head snapped back and his hospital gown shot up as we screeched out into the hall, the three of us pushing the wheelchair as fast as we could run.

We headed away from the nurse's station and down the long hallway. The floor was polished so brightly that light reflected off of it from the window at the far end of the corridor. Rushing past rooms with machines and monitors and blinking lights and beeping sounds, we made a beeline for the end of the hall. As we neared the end of the corridor, we tried to make a left turn, but the floor wax was so slippery that we all fell in different directions, leaving Fat Peter and the wheelchair to crash head first into the wall.

The noise attracted the attention of the nurse, who, seeing three hooligans and a patient all sprawled on the floor beside an overturned wheelchair, probably thought the worst. She called for security just as we picked up the wheelchair, re-situated Fat Peter in the cockpit, and started off down the hallway to the left. We had nearly completed one lap around the hospital floor when a security guard steppedout ahead of us, held up his hands, and said, "Stop right there." Like a cops and robbers movie, we reversed direction and retraced our steps, being more careful to make the turn at the end of the hall as we heard the security guard's footsteps behind us.

As we rounded the corner and headed back toward Fat Peter's room, we saw a nurse and the security guard from the front desk downstairs approaching from that end of the hall. Now boxed in, there was no place to go. We kept heading for Fat Peter's room, but the security guard cut us off and we stopped suddenly, dumping Fat Peter head first out of the wheelchair and across the shiny-waxed floor. Fat Peter slid through his doorway and into his room, his exposed rear end peeking through his hospital gown. Scrambling into his bed, Fat Peter now looked more like a guy with kidney stones, or some other awful disease. We left the wheelchair between us and the security guard, ducked through a metal doorway, down the stairs and out the front entrance of the hospital. I'd never had a good day in a hospital before that visit to Fat Peter. It was the first time I realized that I might not hate hospitals as much as I thought I did.

Standing in front of the old bakery, looking at the crooked loan sign on the door, I couldn't help feeling sad. If I closed my eyes, I could see a kind Ukrainian baker, collecting pennies from the neighborhood kids, and handing out stale donuts. When I opened my eyes however, I was standing in front of the loan shark, who handed out pennies to the neighborhood and collected more than they could afford. You can't go through life with your eyes closed, but sometimes it would be nice if you could.

I made my way down the block to the alley and turned left. Every house in the old neighborhood had a small front yard facing the street. The homes were long and narrow, standing like a row of soldiers shoulder to shoulder. They had larger back yards and detached garages that faced the alley. Rather than using valuable space by running driveways between houses, the alleys provided a common driveway for two blocks of houses. The streets were paved. The alleys were made from crushed cinders.

I walked down the alley past garages that once housed DeSotos and Hudsons, cars made by companies that had died decades ago. None of the two or three car garages common in newer houses today. Just single car garages barely wide enough to fit an average-sized car. Families only had one car when we were kids. The garage doors were reminiscent of old barns. Hinged on their sides and latched in the center, the old garage doors swung open into the alley. No electric door openers, no remote controls. Drivers parked in the alley, got out and opened the swinging doors, then returned to their cars to pull inside.

Beside each garage were garbage cans, waiting for the garbage trucks that still rumbled down the cinder alleys. Molded plastic garbage cans, some with small plastic wheels, had replaced the dented sheet metal cans that our parents had used. The plastic cans lasted longer, and they didn't rust, but you lost something when garbage cans no longer had metal lids with hammered metal handles. In the summer, those old metal garbage can lids were the shields of medieval knights. In the winter, they were saucers for sledding.

Just past the fifth garage on the right was an old rusty gate in an old rusty fence. Stopping at the gate, I got my first look in thirty years at my old backyard. The first thing that hit me as I looked over the fence was how small the yard was. In my mind's eye, the backyard was a broad expanse of grass where my dad had pitched baseballs to me and where I had hit towering home runs over the then-new fence into the alley. Looking at it now with older eyes, it was a cramped patch of ground hemmed in by the neighbor's garage on one side and our garage on the other. The towering home runs had traveled less than sixty feet, about the distance between home plate and the pitcher's mound on a regular baseball diamond. The only thing now holding together the wires of the fence that had been brand new back then was the rust.

The clothesline where my mom had hung Henry's sheets and my dad's shirts out to dry was gone. In the corner of the yard where the clothes had rustled in the breeze was a satellite television dish. The lawn, always green and freshly mown when we were kids, was overgrown with weeds. When I had decided to come back for Father Tim's funeral, I wondered whether I wanted to see the old house again. Wondering was a waste of energy, because there was never any question that I would come back to the house. Now, standing in the alley looking over the fence, I was wondering again. Wondering how the time had gone by so quickly. Wondering how my parents could have been so happy here. Wondering how they pulled themselves together and went on after Henry died. Wondering just when it was that you stopped seeing the world through a child's eyes... and when you stopped looking forward and started looking back.

I turned back to the alley and started off toward St. Basil's. I was in no particular hurry, but I had seen what I came to see. When I reached the sidewalk, I stayed on the side of the street that was shaded by trees. About a block from our old house, I heard a familiar sound. The scraping of tennis shoes on cement. The staccato echo of a bouncing ball.

I stopped outside a chain link fence and watched a group of teenagers playing basketball. The jockeying for position, the grunts and gasps, and the good-natured trash talking all brought a smile to my face. They were playing a half-court game with a white metal backboard. The rusting rim had no net. It was the first thing in a while that made me smile.

Basketball. Back in our hey day at St. Basil's, we were hoopers.

Chapter 5

THE FIRST DAY OF FIFTH grade basketball practice was during the week of Thanksgiving, so in addition to rolling the rickety metal carts loaded with books out into the hall, we had to move about two hundred boxes of canned goods that had been collected for the less fortunate. It was during the process of moving the food pantry that we first realized that Lou the Screw wasn't like the rest of us.

Lou the Screw was always bigger than the rest of us. Even back at St. Basil's, he was almost six feet tall and weighed more than 200 pounds. It wasn't just his size that set Lou apart, though. Lou the Screw was just different. Lou's parents came from someplace called the "old country". We looked it up in the atlas in our gym/library, but we couldn't find "old country" anywhere on any of the maps. They spoke only broken English in public, so we figured they must have spoken "old country" at home.

No one knew how old Lou was, or what grade he was in. For as long as anyone could remember, Lou was a student at St. Basil's. He would attend classes with the eighth graders one day and the sixth graders the next. He never asked or answered questions in class, so it was hard to tell what he knew and what he didn't. The nuns talked differently to Lou, the way you'd talk to a very young child.

Years later, when we were older and began driving cars, Lou was the only one who never qualified for a driver's license. He walked everywhere. Morning or night, there would be Lou, hands in his pockets, walking. Lou's inability to get a driver's license probably stemmed from the real reason that even as a kid, he was different... Lou occasionally had fits.

No one knew what triggered Lou's fits. Without warning, Lou would crouch down on his hands and knees, rock back and forth, and make weird growling or moaning noises. The first time we saw one of Lou's fits, it was scary. After a while, we began dealing with our uneasiness the way kids do – with wisecracks.

In the movies, just before giving the propeller of an old airplane a crank, the pilot would shout "contact". The engine would sputter to life and the propeller would make a high-pitched whining noise. Lou's fits sounded a little like an airplane propeller starting with a low groan and winding up to a higher pitch. When we stopped being afraid of Lou's fits, someone would always shout "contact" whenever one of his spells started.

While groups of two or three guys worked together, lifting boxes of cans onto the growing stacks at the end of the gym, Lou the Screw picked up two boxes at a time, raising them over his head with apparently very little effort. Another difference between us and the Screw was the fact that we were moving the boxes up against the wall, while Lou was unstacking them and moving them back to where we'd started.

"Lou, what are you doing?" Father Tim asked as he walked into the gym.

"Moving the boxes," replied the Screw, undoubtedly curious as to why Father Tim couldn't see that for himself.

Sensing that Lou lived life on the edge of control, and not wanting to do anything to push him over the edge, Father Tim smiled and asked in a quiet voice, "Do you think you could move the boxes backwards, Lou?"

Lou stood perfectly still, as if he was thinking about Father Tim's question, then he grinned and said, "Sure." With that, Lou walked over to the stack of boxes against the wall, took two boxes from the top of the stack, and walking backwards, moved them out into the middle of the gym floor.

When we finally got all of the boxes moved, Father Tim blew his whistle and called everyone around him. There was a mad dash across the gym floor, with guys pushing and shoving to get choice spots nearest Father Tim, several employing baseball slides across the hard wood floor, the sound of their exposed skin screeching on the floor echoing in the rafters.

"How many of you have played basketball before?" asked Father Tim.

Almost everyone raised his hand. Heck, we had all played basketball at recess or in the parks – we were hoopers. Taking us at our word, seeing so many raised hands, Father Tim made the mistake of thinking that he had an experienced squad of roundballers.

"Great, then let's get started with some dribbling drills."

We lined up at the far end of the gym and Father Tim handed each of three guys at the head of each line a basketball, telling them to dribble the length of the court. When he blew his whistle, the three guys took off like they were shot out of a gun. One carried the basketball under his arm like a football, dropping in on the floor every six or seven steps as he ran. The second bounced the ball off the floor so hard that it came straight up and hit him in the face. The ball ricocheted off of his face and out the door into the hall. He immediately went to the back of the line, his shirt pulled up and pressed against his nose, which was bleeding steadily.

The third dribbler was a blur of feet, hands, and bouncing ball. He ran as fast as he could, head down watching his hand slap the ball up and down. He never even slowed down before crashing full force into the stack of boxes of Thanksgiving canned goods, landing on the seat of his pants as the ball rolled harmlessly into the corner.

Father Tim blew his whistle again, and believing that he was moving to a safer drill, told us that we would work on our defense. Pointing to Cuckoo Coolack and Pinhead Griffith, Father Tim said, "You two guys will be on offense." Putting his hand on Lou the Screw's shoulder, he said, "Lou, you stop them from scoring."

"Now boys, we're going to learn how to defend against the fast break," said Father Tim.

None of us knew what a fast break was, let alone how to defend against one, but we were all too ashamed to admit it, so we just nodded like we understood.

"When you're back on defense alone," said Father Tim, "you have to stop the man with the ball. If you stop the man with the ball, your teammates can get back to help you with the trailer..."

None of us lived in fancy homes, but nobody lived in a trailer, either, so again we were at a loss as to what Father Tim was talking about. Still afraid to convey our complete ignorance, however, we continued nodding solemnly.

"Ok, let's give it a try," said Father Tim, tossing the ball to Coolack and blowing his whistle.

Lou the Screw stood flat-footed near the free throw line as Cuckoo dribbled toward him, not veering left or right but headed straight for the basket.

"Stop the dribbler," shouted Father Tim.

Anxious to comply, Lou the Screw (without moving his feet) stuck out his arm and caught Cuckoo in the throat, stretching him out as if he'd hit a clothesline while riding a bicycle. A roar of laughter erupted from the rest of us, even before we had verified that Cuckoo was still alive.

"No!" Father Tim shouted, running toward Cuckoo, who was lying on his back, toes pointing straight up, arms not moving at his side. Kneeling next to Cuckoo, Father Tim lifted his head gently and asked if he was ok. Cuckoo didn't say anything. It's almost certain that he couldn't, but he blinked his eyes a few times and sort of nodded his head. His glasses were in three pieces scattered around the free throw line.

"Get a drink of water and walk it off," advised Father Tim.

It's not clear where the practice originated, but down through the ages, coaches have told athletes to "walk off" injuries ranging from simple bruises to multiple fractures. Somehow they think that if they can drag you to your feet and get your legs moving, everything will be fine. So Cuckoo got a drink of water and walked it off, though not in anything approximating a straight line.

"Lou, you can't stick your arm out and hit a player," explained Father Tim. "You have to move your feet and keep yourself between the other player and the basket. If he moves left, you move left – if he moves right, you move right...defense is all about footwork Lou, ok?"

The Screw nodded, but it wasn't clear that he had any more conviction in his nodding than we had in ours. Father Tim tossed the ball to Pinhead Griffith, and told Danny Noonan to join Pinhead on offense. Danny gave Lou the Screw a wide berth as he made his way onto the court. Father Tim blew his whistle and Pinhead passed the ball to Danny.

Danny looked at the basketball like it was radioactive and immediately passed it back to Pinhead. Pinhead took one look toward the basket and at Lou the Screw and passed the ball back to Danny. Neither player took a step toward the basket; they just stood out in the middle of the floor throwing the ball back and forth.

Growing impatient, Father Tim shouted to Pinhead, "Take the ball to the basket!" Pinhead reluctantly started toward the free throw line, weaving back and forth like he was in a minefield.

When Pinhead went left, Lou took a step to the left...when Pinhead weaved right, the Screw moved right...and when Pinhead reached the free throw line, Lou the Screw tackled him, the two of them crashing to the floor in a tangle of arms and legs. The ball rolled to Danny, who, even with Lou the Screw lying on the floor, passed the ball to Father Tim.

Running out of patience, Father Tim helped Pinhead to his feet and began shouting at Lou the Screw. "Basketball is not a CONTACT sport, Lou! It's a game of finesse, it's a game of speed, it's not a game of CONTACT!"

With the last word "contact" echoing in the gym, Lou the Screw went into one of his spells. He began bouncing on his toes and turning in circles, occasionally squatting down like a catcher, then dropping onto his hands and knees, rocking back and forth, all the while, making some low moaning sounds. Everyone began shuffling their feet away from Lou, an ever-widening circle opening around him. Everyone except Father Tim.

Father Tim bent down and grabbed hold of Lou, not the way you would if you were mad at someone, but more the way you would if you were hugging someone. While Lou rocked back and forth and moaned, Father Tim rocked along with him, speaking softly into his ear. We couldn't hear what Father Tim was saying, but whatever it was, in a few minutes, Lou settled down.

Father Tim sat in the middle of the floor holding Lou the Screw for a long time before he looked at the rest of us and said, "It's ok, boys, everything will be ok now. Let's call it a day."

As we gathered up the basketballs and moved the library furniture and rare book collection back into the gym, Father Tim sat on the floor, still holding Lou. They were still there when we left, our school uniforms half-buttoned over our practice clothes. We were sure that we had seen the last of Lou the Screw on the basketball team, but next practice, there he was. Father Tim never said a word about Lou's spell, but we noticed that he rarely shouted at practice after that, and never at Lou.

Our first real game was against a public school far enough away that we didn't know anyone who went there. Our school had no buses, so we met at the circle drive in front of the church and climbed into Father Tim's car for the trip to Samuel L. Gompers School. These were the days before seatbelts and plaintiff's lawyers, so we jammed four guys in the back seat and three in the front seat next to Father Tim.

On the way to Gompers School, Father Tim tried to prepare us for what we would encounter when we got there.

"These kids don't have a lot," Father Tim said.

"They don't all have houses of their own, and many of them don't have great situations at home. We should be grateful for everything that God has given us," Father Tim said as we pulled up to the entrance to Gompers School.

Nothing Father Tim could have told us would have prepared us for what we saw as we walked into the main entrance. The place was enormous – the hallways seemed to stretch for miles in every direction. As we were led to a staircase to go down to the locker rooms, the area surrounding the stairs was encased in a chain link fence. Looking up, you could see that the fencing extended up the entire open stairwell, two stories up and one down. Everything was loud. Voices echoed in the hallways, footsteps echoed on the stairs. As we changed into our uniforms in the basement locker room, there was a strange rumbling sound above our heads.

The stairs leading from the locker room to the gymnasium were narrow and steep. As we climbed the stairs in single file, the rumbling overhead got progressively louder. When we reached the top of the stairs and opened the door, a shaft of light illuminated the narrow stairwell and a deafening sound filled our ears. Running out onto the basketball court, it was immediately apparent that the rumbling was the crowd noise, something completely foreign to St. Basil's. Bleachers reached from courtside to the ceiling and there were hundreds of people there to see the game. Another realization quickly came to us – counting Father Tim, we were the only eight white people in the gym.

Overwhelmed by the atmosphere, it took us a few minutes to become acclimated enough to glance at the other end of the court to see who we would be playing. When we did, our eyes nearly popped out of our heads. The shortest player on the Gompers team was a foot taller than Father Tim. Their tallest player stood beneath the basket flat-footed, reaching up and grabbing the bottom of the net. One of the Gompers players came over to retrieve a ball that had rolled to our end of the court. As he bent down to pick up the ball, I noticed that he had a goatee.

I don't remember the score of the game, but I do know that the only time that we got to handle the ball was after they scored a basket. Every other pass, every rebound, every jump ball went to Gompers. I'm sure we didn't score more than ten points, and I'm not sure they scored fewer than one hundred. As we climbed back into the car to return to St. Basil's, Father Tim's pre-game homily came back to me… "We should be grateful for everything that God has given us," he had said. I'm sure that Father Tim was right, but at that moment, I would have been grateful if God had given us a few taller players.

About a week after getting trounced by Samuel L. Gompers, we had our first game against another Catholic school, and one named after a girl, at that. St. Anne's School was located in a predominantly Hispanic neighborhood. Hispanic was not a word used back then – when we were in school, we thought it was a Mexican neighborhood. In any case, we knew enough about bigotry to know that Mexicans were shorter than Negroes, and we thought we had a chance against St. Anne's.

St Anne's School looked more like St. Basil's than Gompers had. Like St. Basil's, St. Anne's lacked locker rooms, so we wore our uniforms underneath our street clothes on the ride over there. We changed our shoes in a hallway and entered the gym carrying our clothes under our arms.

After a few passing drills and some warm-up shooting, the referee blew his whistle and both teams took their seats on folding chairs along the concrete block wall. Lou the Screw, being almost a foot taller than the rest of us, walked out to center court for the jump ball to start the game. As the players took their positions around the center circle, I sat at the end of the bench watching the cheerleaders from St. Anne's. One of the girls looked older than the rest, and strangely familiar. Just as the referee prepared to toss the ball in the air, I caught the eye of one of the St. Anne's players. It was Tony Suarez!

"Hey, it's Spic!" I shouted without thinking.

"Spic, hey Spic!"

Tony smiled and began to wave, as I stood up from my chair and waved.

It soon became obvious that Tony was no longer known as "Spic" in his new neighborhood. The gym fell silent for a moment, until the full effect of what I had shouted set in. The St. Anne's fans began shouting and pointing; more than a few threw hats, paper cups, and one tossed a half filled bottle of Coca-Cola onto the floor.

The referee took the ball and hurried off the court, while the angry mob began moving down the bleachers toward the court. It's likely that an ugly riot may have broken out had Lou the Screw not chosen that precise moment to go into one of his spells. All of the shouting, the flying debris, and the impending disaster had pushed Lou over the edge, and he dropped to his hands and knees and began rocking back and forth.

Seeing Lou on the floor, Fat Peter instinctively shouted, "Contact!" and everyone stopped what they were doing and looked. Thinking that Lou the Screw was searching for a lost contact lens, the St. Anne's players began crawling around trying to help. Father Tim seized the opportunity to calm things down by joining the players, moving on his hands and knees over to Lou, where he draped his arm over Lou's shoulder and calmed him down. Spic Suarez took the opportunity to explain to his teammates that I hadn't meant to be as offensive as my well-meaning outburst clearly was.

Things finally quieted down enough to start the game, which we did without the referee, who had bolted out the door and into his car when he heard the first "Spic". We lost the game, but the score was much closer than the Gompers game had been. Father Tim shook the other coach's hand, leaned forward and whispered something that caused the other coach to smile and nod, then whisked us out of the gym and out to the car, still in our basketball uniforms and carrying our clothes.

We hadn't won a game all season when Father Tim called us together at the end of practice to say that we had just added a final game to our schedule. We would be playing the Joseph P. Kennedy School. Joseph P. Kennedy, the older brother of President John F. Kennedy, was a pilot during World War II. He was killed when his plane exploded on a mission over Europe. As we prepared to play a game against the Joseph P. Kennedy School, however, the only thing that mattered to us was that we had one more chance to win a game before the season would be over.

Standing in the center of the court with the rest of us sitting around him, Father Tim began a speech that sounded more like a history lesson than a pep talk. He began with the explanation of who Joseph P. Kennedy was, going on to tell us that President Kennedy also had a sister who was mentally retarded (that's what it was called back then) and who had lived most of her life in institutions. None of Father Tim's efforts to enlighten us were having much effect until he said that the Kennedy family had established residential schools for profoundly handicapped children and had named the schools after the World War II pilot, Joseph P. Kennedy. It was at that moment that a dim, flickering light appeared in our own marginally functional heads. Knowing glances were exchanged around the circle surrounding Father Tim. A couple of guys even smiled. We were going to play a basketball game against a team of mentally retarded players. Father Tim was a genius! We had been thrashed by public school players and narrowly defeated by every Catholic school we played. Finally Father Tim had found a team we could beat.

The week leading up to our last game of the season seemed like it would never end. We couldn't wait to get to the Joseph P. Kennedy School to experience what the Wide World of Sports announcer mysteriously referred to as the "thrill of victory". Up until now, we had experienced only the "agony of defeat".

The day of the big game finally arrived. It was a long ride to the Joseph P. Kennedy School. It was located out in the country someplace, where grass and trees replaced asphalt and buildings. As we passed through stone gates, a large bronze plaque welcomed visitors to the "Joseph P. Kennedy Residential School for the Mentally Retarded". The grounds were like a park – wooded lawns, winding roads, and a collection of brick buildings with large white pillars. A number of the buildings had rows of narrow windows, too small to climb through, just large enough to let in fresh air and light…looking back now, those were dormitories.

Father Tim pulled the car up in front of a building that looked a little like a hangar at the airport. Its roof was rounded and it was longer than it was wide. A painted sign over the doors read "Athletics and Recreation". This was the first school we had ever seen that had an entire building dedicated to its gymnasium; not even Samuel L. Gompers School could say that.

As we changed clothes in the locker room, there was a strange mix of anticipation and apprehension in the air. The anticipation of our first victory of the season was almost too much to suppress. Danny Noonan was counting backwards, simulating the end of the game, "five, four, three, two, one…"; when he made a buzzer sound, everyone jumped into the air, slapping each other on the back, imagining how they would feel after actually winning a game. Mixed with the anticipation was a bit of apprehension. None of us had actually ever seen retarded people; there were more than a few guys at St. Basil's that we suspected might be, but this was different – these were kids who had been sent off to live away from home, with windows too narrow to climb through. None of us knew what to expect when we went out on the floor.

We also began wondering if we would feel bad about beating a team of retarded players. What if they started crying or something? How would we go home and brag to our friends that we won our first game…against a school for the mentally retarded? We decided that they were probably used to losing and that this would just be another in a long line of drubbings; no need to worry about how they'd react. As for our bragging rights, we would just say that we'd beaten the Joseph P. Kennedy School – none of our friends would ever come this far from the city to see the place for themselves. Having resolved our apprehensions, we lined up to go out onto the court for our first win.

Unlike the Samuel L. Gompers School gymnasium, the Joseph P. Kennedy School gymnasium was quiet. There was no crowd – in fact, there were no spectators at all. Obviously, families did not visit the Joseph P. Kennedy School on weeknights, and the rest of the students must have been back in their dormitories. The quiet was so loud you could hear it.

The players on the Kennedy team did not look like the kids we were used to seeing. Several had facial features characteristic of Down's Syndrome, a gentle smiling countenance unfamiliar to those of us who grew up in the city. Two of the players had mustaches; they looked as if they were at least thirty years old. The notion of grown people still being in a school was one that we were unprepared for. The idea that it might feel bad to beat these guys started to return.

The game began as all games do, with a jump ball at center court. Lou the Screw, who had more in common with the players from the Joseph P. Kennedy School than any of us, walked out to take the tip-off for us. The center for the Kennedy School was very tall, but he appeared not to be paying attention when the referee prepared to toss the ball into the air. As the ball went up, Lou the Screw jumped and swiped his arm at the ball, missing it as it continued up beyond his reach. The center for Joseph P. Kennedy, without so much as rising to his toes, swung his arm at the ball like a hammer, knocking it on a straight line the length of the court and into the wall at the end of the gym. It took the referee a second to put his whistle back into his mouth, which was hanging open in disbelief, and to award the ball to St. Basil's.

Fat Peter threw the ball inbounds to Pinhead, who dribbled the ball up the court, ready to start the landslide that would end in our first victory. What happened next would be repeated throughout the rest of the game, and the result would be a blowout that would make us forget all about that early season embarrassment at the Samuel L. Gompers School.

Pinhead held the ball high above his head, and the shorter player guarding him had no chance to steal it from him. Pinhead passed the ball to Lou the Screw, who did just what Father Tim had drilled into us all week in practice. Lou held the ball, keeping his body between the other team and the ball, and waited for Danny Noonan to come streaking past him for a short pass and a lay-up.

Just as Father Tim had drawn it on the chalkboard in practice, Danny ran in a wide arc around the pack of players who were bunched around Lou the Screw. With perfect timing, Lou flipped the ball to Danny, who dribbled once and let the ball roll perfectly off of his fingers and up against the backboard. It was like a ballet.

When the ball reached the backboard, the center from the Joseph P. Kennedy School again seemed not to be paying attention. Apparently he was, however, because he reached up and plucked the ball from mid-air, then turned without hesitating and threw the ball the length of the court to another Kennedy player, who caught the ball beneath their basket and laid it in for a score.

That pattern repeated itself with alarming regularity throughout the game. As the fourth quarter wound down, "...five, four, three, two, one..." there was no celebration. No one jumped in the air, no backs were slapped – no one had imagined how it would feel if we actually lost this game. Curiously, the Joseph P. Kennedy School players were not jumping around either. It was as if they didn't even realize that they had won. A few of them smiled, one hugged their coach, but in general, there was none of the celebrating that we had envisioned for ourselves had we won.

We started back toward the locker room in a stunned silence. It was bad enough that we had ended the season without winning a game, but how were we going to explain that we had lost to a team of mentally retarded players? It was the kind of thing that kids at home would hold over our heads for years...maybe forever. When we reached the locker room, Father Tim did something that he had never done before or after a game...he shouted.

"Everybody gather 'round," he called. Then he lowered his voice.

"Boys, you learned an important lesson tonight. Throughout your lives, the most dangerous times will be those when you think you can't lose. When you underestimate the task at hand, you set yourself up for disappointment."

What we hadn't known was that Father Tim knew all along that we were likely to lose to the Joseph P. Kennedy School. For a week leading up to the game, Father Tim had quietly watched us practice our congratulatory celebration, never saying a thing – just watching quietly. All week, we had thought that Father Tim had looked everywhere for a team that we could beat. Standing here now, he wasn't upset that we'd lost, but only that we had been so sure that we'd win. It was almost like he'd planned the whole thing.

"As you get older, boys, there will come times when you think that you've got it made. Everything will be going your way. That's when you need to be the most careful, boys. That's when something can happen to make you lose everything. When you begin to feel over-confident, remember this game, boys."

When Father Tim finished, Cuckoo Coolack raised his hand. Father Tim looked at Cuckoo and raised his eyebrows.

"Father, how come those guys weren't more excited about winning? If we won our first game, we'd have been a lot happier."

"For those kids, it's not about winning, boys. It's about playing. Winning a basketball game won't change their lives, any more than losing one will. Playing the games changes their lives."

Father Tim stood up and started toward the door. Turning the knob, he stopped and turned around.

"For the record, boys, this wasn't their first win. They haven't lost any games this year, and they didn't lose any last year either."

With that, Father Tim closed the door behind him.

Chapter 6

12:43 P.M.

AFTER LEAVING THE PICK-UP BASKETBALL game, I walked several blocks back to St. Basil's. If it was possible, it felt like it was actually getting hotter. Before making my way to the church, I decided to walk around the school grounds. It was a testament to my reluctance to face the funeral that I chose a tour of the grounds in the sweltering afternoon heat. Walking away from the circle drive in front of the church, I followed the sidewalk around the corner of the old school.

The sidewalk was of the same vintage as the school. It had been poured in the days when sidewalks consisted of large squares of concrete separated by evenly spaced lines of tar. The construction technique was based on the tendency of concrete to expand when heated. If poured in one continuous run, sidewalks would buckle on days as hot as this. The tar served as a sort of shock absorbing cushion between slabs of concrete.

Bending down, I did something I hadn't done in thirty years. I poked my finger into the soft tar between two sections of sidewalk. I felt a little silly and hoped no one would come along and find me up to my knuckle in molten tar. We used to dig the tar out of the cracks in the sidewalks with sticks, then roll the tar into balls and carry them around in our pockets. There were railroad tracks running along the back of the schoolyard, and when freight trains would rumble past, we would throw the tar balls at the passing boxcars, where they would stick with a loud splat. If there were no trains passing, we would start "tar ball fights" which resembled snowball fights without the charm. Guys would grab the lids of trash cans, which in those days had convenient aluminum handles in their centers; we used them as shields while pelting each other with balls of tar. As the tar cooled, it hardened, and the clatter of tar balls denting garbage can lids could be heard everywhere.

Standing in the old schoolyard, I marveled at how much bigger it felt when we were kids. The Holy Wars of Tar seemed like they were fought on an immense battlefield. Looking around now, I wondered how everyone even fit in the schoolyard, let alone how we all ran around like Philistines hurling tar at one another. I wondered whether the students who attended St. Basil's today had tarball fights anymore. It seemed unlikely. The thrill of catching a guy looking the other way and nailing him in the side of the head with a fistful of tar probably paled in comparison to the virtual reality video games that enabled kids to actually turn their opponents into pools of molten tar.

Much of St. Basil's property that had been playgrounds and makeshift ball fields had been paved and was now used for parking on Sundays. Fifty years ago, families had one car and most walked to Mass on Sunday. Parking was the least of the parish's concerns back then. Today, people came from farther away, everyone seemed to drive their own car, and parishioners wanted their cars parked off of the streets.

There used to be an area where the youngest kids would play on equipment that today's parents would outlaw. There were shiny silver aluminum slides with narrow, slippery metal stairs about two stories high. Once at the top, you threw your feet out in front of you and raised your hands into the air. On days like today, the surface of the slide would heat up to about four thousand degrees, and what began as shouts of excitement quickly changed into shrieks of pain as you got third degree burns from the hot metal slide. Today, playground slides are made of laminated plastic, and rarely get more than six feet off the ground.

In the corner of the schoolyard, there were long wooden "teeter-totters". For some reason, word never seemed to pass from one generation to the next, so that every year the same scene was repeated on or shortly after the first day of school. Two kids would be rocking gently back and forth on the teeter-totter when a thundering herd of older kids would charge the ramparts of the castle, seize the catapult, and (displacing one of the two riders) slam the end of the teeter-totter down, launching the remaining rider into the air. Insurance companies undoubtedly outlawed teeter-totters years ago, because in the spot where they once stood is now a brightly-colored assortment of large plastic squares, stacked in geometric shapes with round holes for climbing.

The centerpiece of a small child's playground was always a merry-go-round, though there rarely seemed anything particularly merry about it. A circular wooden platform with galvanized pipes for handles, the merry-go-round turned on a central pole when pushed by a group of children. Invariably, the ground surrounding the platform was worn into a rut from years of repeated circling and pushing. Depending upon the age of the contraption, it was not uncommon to see the pushers from only their knees up as they labored in the rut.

The attraction of the merry-go-round was never clear to me, even as a child. It was impossible to revolve on one for longer than a few seconds without becoming completely sick to your stomach. More than once someone became ill and ejected the contents of their stomach into the air, the circular motion and centrifugal force distributing it evenly among those toiling in the rut. With few places to hold onto, merry-go-round riders were regularly launched into the air, tumbling head over heels across the playground.

You start to think of old playground equipment as a risk instead of an adventure just about the time that a passing freight train changes from a rolling tarball target to a traffic nuisance. The worst part of growing up is the trading in of wonders for worries. My wife Annie and I grew older together, but only I grew up. Wiser than me, Annie knew better than to let worries push their way in. In a way, she had found Neverland, and she had stubbornly held onto her enthusiasm and her sense of wonder.

The first time that I met Annie, I thought she was a nun. I went to college at Notre Dame. Like virtually every other Catholic school within one hundred miles of the campus, St. Basil's sent a busload of boys to visit Notre Dame every September. We toured the academic buildings, ate in the dormitories, listened to speeches about the Four Horsemen and George Gipp, and left with the tune of the Notre Dame Victory March ringing in our ears. The advertising agencies on Madison Avenue could learn a thing or two by taking a campus visit to Notre Dame.

I arrived in South Bend in 1967, having literally dodged a bullet when my birthday was chosen 363rd in the military draft lottery. Fate had smiled on me; my future called for long hours in the library instead of endless nights in the rice paddies of Vietnam.

It would be a year after I graduated before Notre Dame first admitted women, so it was no surprise that an hour and a half after arriving on campus, my roommate and I were on our way over to Saint Mary's College, the all-girls school located just across the street. Founded just before the Civil War, Notre Dame and Saint Mary's were run by the Fathers and the Sisters of the Holy Cross, respectively. I had only been on Saint Mary's campus for a few moments before learning a thing or two about the Sisters of the Holy Cross.

The entrance to Saint Mary's is marked by two stone pillars, which form the gateway to a beautiful tree-shaded entry drive known as "The Avenue". Stately maple trees line each side of The Avenue like sentinels. The canopies of the trees grow together, forming a shady tunnel in the summer that turns red and gold each autumn. At the far end of the Avenue stands Holy Cross, a picturesque stone dormitory built at the turn of the century. Just inside the entry doors of Holy Cross is a twin staircase, winding up and around a white marble statue of the Blessed Virgin Mary, from whom the school takes its name. Halfway up those stairs is where I first met Sister Harriet Louise. More precisely, it is where I met Sister Harriet Louise's cane.

My college roommate's name was Francis Donlon, but everyone called him Mudshark. We had spoken by telephone only once before arriving at Notre Dame, so the first time that I met Mudshark – in fact the first time I saw him – was when I walked into our room on move-in day. My arms were loaded with boxes and I fumbled with the key while trying to open the door. Hearing a chair scrape against the ancient wood floor and a frantic scuffing of feet from inside the room, I quickly realized that my roommate had already arrived.

When I finally got the door open and backed into the room, Mudshark was sprawling across his desk, pulling a corner of his bed sheet over something that he obviously did not want anyone to see. Looking back over his shoulder, he grinned sheepishly and said, "You alone?" I nodded, too busy straining to see what Mudshark was trying to hide to actually respond. Seeing no one behind me, Mudshark relaxed and settled back into his desk chair.

"Man, that was close," he sighed, "I didn't know whether your parents were with you."

"My folks are parking the car," I replied. "They'll be up in a few minutes."

With that, Mudshark sprang back into action, scooping loose marijuana leaves into his desk drawers, moving a small scale from his desk to his closet, and reaching for an aerosol can of room freshener. I just stood there, staring. I had seen people smoke marijuana, but I had never seen so much of it one place, and I was just putting the pieces together in my mind, realizing that Mudshark was planning to open up shop as a businessman.

"You sell that stuff?" I asked incredulously.

Mudshark looked at me out of the corner of his eye, one eyebrow raised as if he was surprised by the question.

"You know what the tuition is here?" he asked.

I had never thought to ask. My parents never talked about how much college would cost. They always talked about grades. When the time came to choose a school, money was never mentioned. I was caught off guard by Mudshark's question, and I was a little embarrassed to realize that I did not know how much the tuition was.

"It's more than my dad makes in a year," Mudshark snorted, not waiting for me to answer. "I gotta help out with the costs, and I ain't washing dishes. You can't pay for college with a paper route," he counseled.

"But you can go to jail for selling pot." I sounded like the narrator on one of the film loops that they used to show in high school health class.

"Not if everyone stays cool," Mudshark reassured me. "The people who buy the stuff sure aren't going to tell anyone, so if we keep our mouths shut, no one will ever know."

"I can't stand the smell of the stuff," I complained. "If you're going to be smoking dope, I need a new roommate."

"Relax," Mudshark waved his hand, "I don't smoke it. It gives me a headache and I can't sleep. This is strictly business. Cash business. That's it."

I was sure that Mudshark's cash business was going to be a problem. I was sure that he'd get arrested and I didn't want to be standing nearby when that happened. I was sure that I needed a new roommate, but for now I was also sure that my parents would walk in any minute. If they saw marijuana, they'd call the police themselves. For the time being, I would introduce Francis Donlon to my parents, kiss my mother goodbye, and deal with Mudshark later.

It took only fifteen minutes for my parents to move my things into the dorm room, but it took an hour of small talk before my mom was reluctantly ready to leave. On the way downstairs, my mom gave me a lifetime's worth of instructions on everything from laundry soap to first aid. My dad said very little; when he did speak, he talked about the upcoming football season. Parting was just not a topic of conversation for my father.

When we reached the car, I hugged my mom. She tried to let go three times before she actually did. Tears ran down her cheeks and she dabbed at her eyes with a handkerchief in a futile attempt to stem the flood. I gave her another hug and kissed her softly on the cheek, reassuring her that I would be home soon. She opened the car door and slumped into the front seat, telling me that she would bake a pie and mail it to me. I couldn't help smiling at the thought.

I shook my father's hand and thanked him. I didn't specify exactly what I was thanking him for, but I know that he knew. He opened his mouth to speak, but for a long moment, no words came. He swallowed hard, and I saw his eyes glisten. Then he pulled me close and wrapped his arms around me, his hand finding its usual place between my shoulder blades.

"Make us proud," he whispered into my ear.

"I will," I croaked, barely able to speak myself.

"You always do," he said, and then he turned and opened his door without another word.

I stood on the curb and waved as they drove away, feeling homesick already even before they had driven out of view. Almost forty years later, I still see the left turn signal of my dad's car blinking as he rounded the corner and was gone.

My parents had been gone for less than ten minutes when Mudshark grabbed his room key and started for the door.

"C'mon, Mike, let's head over to Saint Mary's," he said, reaching for the doorknob.

"What for?" I asked, my feet propped up on my desk.

Mudshark looked at me like I was speaking a foreign language. "What for? Girls, you idiot."

I had always been clumsy around girls, and the thought of just wandering onto a campus full of them without knowing anyone made me break out in a rash. On the other hand, the prospect of sitting in our room watching Mudshark weigh small plastic bags of pot held no interest, so I decided it was better to follow him over to Saint Mary's.

We crossed the quad, walked past the Main Building, its golden dome shining in the sunlight, and continued on past Sacred Heart, the neo-gothic church that would be elevated to Basilica status by the Pope twenty years after I left Notre Dame. We followed a winding path down a steep hill to the Grotto, a replica of the shrine of Our Lady of Lourdes, where the Blessed Virgin appeared to a French peasant girl in 1858. From the Grotto, we followed the edge of the lake that separates Notre Dame from Saint Mary's.

"What do we do when we get there?" I asked, struggling to catch my breath after scrambling down the steep stairs.

"Improvise," responded Mudshark without slowing down.

We reached the stone gate at The Avenue late in the day. The sun was filtering through the leaves of the trees, dappling the long walkway ahead. We walked briskly, aware that two unaccompanied guys would draw suspicious stares from the nuns who ran Saint Mary's. As we approached Holy Cross, Mudshark scampered up the stone stairs, taking two steps at a time. Gesturing for me to follow, he pulled open the massive oak door and slipped into the dimly-lit foyer inside. Stepping into the dark, my eyes had not yet adjusted when Mudshark started up the right side of the double staircase.

"You take the left side," he whispered, pointing to the other set of stairs.

Blindly following orders, I started up the left staircase, still waiting for my eyes to adjust to the dim lighting. I had just reached the portion of the stairs where the wooden banister curves to the right when everything suddenly looked bright.

I instinctively grabbed my forehead, a searing pain penetrating my skull, when I realized that the bright lights were stars caused by a sharp thwack to my face by Sister Harriet Louise's wooden cane. I staggered backward, grabbing the banister to keep from falling, and was just sufficiently aware of my surroundings to refrain from unleashing the torrent of profanity that was running through my head, looking for a way out.

"Just where do you think you're going, young man?" Sister Harriet Louise rasped in a venomous voice.

I didn't reply right away. As a matter of fact, I didn't reply at all. Somehow, telling the nun that my pot-selling roommate and I were skulking about hoping to meet girls didn't seem like the right answer. Not having a plausible alternative, I quickly decided that keeping my mouth shut was the safest thing to do.

"Unescorted men are not to be in the dormitories of Saint Mary's," Sister Harriet Louise continued, waving her cane at me in a menacing fashion.

Had Mudshark not turned and run out the door upon hearing Sister Harriet's cane smash into my forehead, we may have stood a fighting chance against the diminutive four-foot six-inch bantam in the habit. Standing alone, however, I was no match for her. I was about to turn and run myself when a voice from behind the good sister said, "I'm sorry, Sister, he's with me."

As my vision returned to normal and my eyes re-focused so that I was no longer seeing double, I looked beyond Sister Harriet to see a beautiful girl silhouetted against a stained glass window. In her hand, she carried a rosary, leading me to believe that she was another nun, or a nun-in-training at the very least. Sister Harriet Louise looked at me suspiciously, then looked back at my rescuer who was now halfway down the stairs.

"Hello, Edward," the younger woman said, looking directly at me. "Sorry I'm late, but you know you're not supposed to come in without an escort."

For a moment, I thought she was talking to someone else, but then it occurred to me that if I wanted to get out of here alive, for the next few minutes, my name was Edward.

"I'm really sorry," I said, which was the God's honest truth – I had never been more sorry about being anywhere in my life.

Sister Harriet, apparently buying the ruse, lowered her cane and turned her attention to the younger woman, who was now standing on the same step as the little nun.

"Very well, Annie. Just be sure this doesn't happen again. Now, put him on a leash and walk him back to Notre Dame."

With that, Sister Harriet Louise climbed the rest of the stairs and disappeared. Her tiny feet were invisible beneath her flowing habit, creating the illusion that she was floating. She never went anywhere without her cane, even though she never actually needed it for walking.

Looking at the ugly welt on my forehead, Annie said that I should get some ice on it when I got back home, then she opened the door to let me out. I stepped out onto the porch, expecting her to follow. Annie just stood in the doorway, looking at me.

"Aren't you going to walk me back?" I asked.

"Don't you know the way?" she replied.

"I thought I needed an escort. If I get caught alone, I could get another cane to the head."

"And you'd deserve it," Annie retorted.

Deciding that I had caused enough trouble for one day, I turned to start back to the campus. As I stepped down from the porch, I mustered the courage to thank her.

"Thanks for saving me back there, sister."

"I'm not a nun," Annie replied with a chuckle.

"Sorry. The rosary fooled me," I said awkwardly.

"We say the rosary with some of the older sisters, those who are getting on in years and are a bit frail."

"Frail like Sister Harriet?" I asked, gingerly touching my throbbing forehead.

Annie laughed. "No, Sister Harriet Louise can take care of herself."

"So why did you cover for me back there?" I asked.

"You looked pitiful," Annie replied, capturing in three words my only hope of appealing to girls.

"Are you a freshman?" I asked hopefully.

"I'm a first year," Annie corrected, using the term adopted by all-girls schools.

"Can I call you?" I asked, amazed that I got it out without stuttering.

"Sure," Annie said. "But for now, you'd better get some ice on your head."

I reached for my forehead, feeling the knot that was now about the size of a golf ball.

"I guess you're right," I said, with a bashful smile. "I'll call you tomorrow."

I started back down The Avenue toward Notre Dame, not sure whether the light-headedness that I was feeling was from the beating that I had taken or from my infatuation with Annie. I had gone only a short way when I heard Annie's voice from the stairs of Holy Cross.

"How will I know you when you call?" she grinned.

I realized that in my stammering and bumbling I had forgotten to tell her my name. I turned back toward where she was standing and called, "For now, I'm Edward."

Then I waved and headed back up The Avenue, one eye out for nuns.

I did call Annie the next day, and the next day and the day after that. Our first few "dates" were spent shouting at each other; we went to football games and pep rallies together and had to shout to be heard over the crowd noise. By the last game of the football season, I finally summoned the courage to ask Annie to go steady with me, a term now reserved for dinosaurs and those of us who went to college in the sixties. In spite of my newly found courage, things still did not go exactly as I had planned.

We'd been yelling at each other throughout the game, and it was well into the fourth quarter. Knowing that it was now or never, I straightened my back, turned toward Annie, took her hand in mine, and started to shout. At that precise moment, Notre Dame fumbled the ball and the entire stadium went silent. My voice seemed to be bouncing off of the scoreboard and returning in a series of echoes.

"I'd like you to go steady with me!"

The hushed crowd turned toward the sound of my voice and a rumbling roar rose from the bowels of the stadium. I got a louder ovation than the Fighting Irish had received when they ran out onto the field.

Annie didn't shout a reply. I think she was too stunned by the question, and she probably had a foreshadowing of the lifetime of embarrassment that lay ahead if she spent very much of it with me. She leaned over and kissed my cheek, her eyes saying everything I hoped to hear. As I walked her back to Saint Mary's that afternoon, I noticed a peculiar mannerism as I held her hand. For some reason, our fingers interlocked just so, and I straightened her ring with my finger to make room. Today, thirty-eight years later, the same thing happens every time I hold her hand.

Over the next three years, Annie and I spent more and more time together and falling in love just sort of snuck up on us. Annie lived in California, so we went months without seeing each other during the summers. There's no way of knowing, but I think missing each other helped us stay together. By our junior year, we began talking about the future as if we would spend it together. We didn't discuss marriage directly, but more and more we found ourselves talking about life after college and during those conversations, "we" were still "we".

In the spring of our sophomore year, Annie joined the Saint Mary's choir and they sang every Sunday morning at Sacred Heart. I went to Mass occasionally to hear the choir and to avoid the questions from Annie about why I had drifted away from religion and what deep psychological meaning that might have. I couldn't wait for Annie to stop taking psychology classes, but in the meantime I just went to Mass – it was easier.

In time, I realized that I felt better after an hour in church and I began looking forward to Sunday mornings. What had been an obligation for all of those years growing up became an opportunity when I was on my own and making my own decisions. I enjoyed the routine. I found the few moments of quiet introspection that the church provided to be a source of comfort. And it made Annie happy.

A week before Christmas during our junior year, right in the middle of final exams, I called Annie and asked her to meet me at the Grotto. She asked if everything was alright. I told her that we needed to talk. I could tell from the tone of her voice that she suspected that something was wrong, but she didn't press for an answer. Annie never pressed. She always knew when to step back and leave room. She promised to meet me in half an hour.

It snows a lot in South Bend, because of its location at the very southern tip of Lake Michigan. This night there was already a foot of snow on the ground and more was falling. I put on the parka that I had bought at the Army surplus store and trudged through the snow to the Grotto. Set back inside the cave were rows and rows of flickering votive candles. Anyone who needed solace or felt the need to ask God for a favor covered their bets by stuffing a dollar into the donation box and lighting a candle. Judging from the number of tiny flames flickering in the Grotto, God had been fielding a lot of requests.

I sat on a wooden bench looking out over the frozen lake that separated the campuses and waited for Annie. From time to time a student would quietly step up to the railing inside the Grotto, drop a few coins into the slotted box, and light a candle. I couldn't help wondering how many of the candles represented desperate pleas for passing grades with it being the second day of final exams.

Annie materialized from the shadows like a ghost. One minute I was sitting all alone and the next she was sitting beside me. She wore a knit hat with a matching scarf and mittens, all cream colored wool. Her dark brown overcoat was cashmere. Everything about Annie was elegant. She came from a wealthy west coast family. Her great grandfather was born the year that the Transcontinental Railroad was completed, and his father had made a fortune in land speculation, buying property just ahead of the expanding railroad and re-selling it to settlers who built the towns once the track was laid. Her father was a newspaper publisher. His father played football with Knute Rockne at Notre Dame.

Annie came from money, but she didn't act like it. In fact, she almost seemed embarrassed by it. For the first year that we dated, I was very self-conscious about our difference in social classes. She was the third generation of her family to come to school in South Bend. I was the first member of my family to go to college. From the very beginning, however, Annie put me at ease. She didn't have to work at making people feel comfortable around her, it came naturally.

"Is everything ok?" Annie asked as she slid closer to me on the bench.

I nodded. The candlelight from the Grotto behind me reflected in her eyes, making them sparkle. The air was cold enough for clouds of condensation to form whenever one of us spoke. Annie looped her arm through mine before stuffing her hand back into the pocket of her coat.

She sat patiently, quietly, waiting for me to say what I'd come to tell her. I struggled to remember the exact words that I had practiced saying out loud before she arrived, but they were all jumbled in my head. I was freezing, but beads of perspiration broke out on my forehead. Annie must have thought I had a fever.

"I've been thinking about what it would be like if we had never met," I began, "it was hard but I was thinking about it."

All the way over to the Grotto, I had practiced saying, "It's impossible for me to even think about life without you…", but somehow the words spilled out of my mouth in the wrong order. A flicker of alarm flashed across Annie's face, but she remained quiet, waiting for me to elaborate. Having taken the first step of a wobbly stagger, I continued with my soliloquy.

"You could probably have your choice of guys if we weren't together."

It was getting worse. I had meant to say that I always wondered why she was satisfied with me when she could have her choice of any guy she wanted. In my nervous stammering, everything was coming out all wrong.

"Mike, are you trying to tell me something?" Annie asked, with more than a little trepidation in her voice.

Thinking that she was asking a simple question, I gave a simple answer.

"Yes."

Connecting the wrong dots in her head, Annie started to cry. Everything that I was saying sounded like a clumsy attempt to end our relationship and Annie responded accordingly. Seeing tears welling up in her eyes, I panicked.

"I didn't mean to make you cry, Annie. This is very hard for me to say, and it's coming out all wrong."

"You don't have to spell it out for me, Mike," Annie said, removing her arm from mine and edging away from me on the bench.

The light bulb finally went off in my head and I realized that Annie thought I was breaking up with her. I saw a look of pure sadness come over her face. Then I saw my life flash before my eyes. Then I finally did the smartest thing I had ever done in my life. I shouted.

"Annie, I want you to marry me!" The words echoed off of the walls of the Grotto and out over the lake.

It took a second or two for the gears inside Annie's head to stop, reverse direction, and re-engage. It was the longest few seconds of my life. I thought she had to think about it, which is never a good sign after a proposal. When the shock of my ineptitude wore off, Annie's eyes spoke before she did.

I suddenly remembered that I had planned to get down on one knee, like you see in old black and white movies, and in my dazed state of mind I lurched forward off of the bench to kneel down. Unfortunately, there was a patch of ice directly in front of the bench, and I lunged forward, falling face first into a snowdrift.

If Annie ever answered me, I never heard it. My head was buried in snow and my feet were slipping and sliding on the ice as I struggled to get back up. When I finally pulled myself out of the snow bank, Annie was laughing too hard to say anything at all. Elegance came naturally for Annie, but not for me.

We stood in the snow holding each other for a long time without saying anything at all. The first thing that I remember Annie saying was that she loved me. If I had been struck deaf and never heard another sound for the rest of my life, I had heard everything I ever needed to hear.

The ring that I gave to Annie that night had the largest diamond that I could afford, which is to say it was tiny. The women in Annie's family wore earrings with larger diamonds, but Annie reacted like it was the most beautiful ring she had ever seen. I couldn't help apologizing for its size, but Annie would have nothing of an apology. She made me feel ten feet tall, something she would do for the rest of our lives together. On our twentieth wedding anniversary, I suggested to Annie that we replace the diamond in her engagement ring. She wouldn't hear of it.

Sitting in the snow that night, neither of us had any idea where life would take us, but we trusted each other enough to believe that it would be better together. Life looks different when viewed over your shoulder than it does from a wooden bench when you're twenty. That said, looking back, Sister Harriet Louise had no way of knowing the favor she was doing when she brained me that day with her cane.

We sat together for another hour, sometimes talking about the future, sometimes laughing about the past, but mostly just sitting quietly, enjoying the unspoken comfort of knowing that the other was there, and always would be. I learned something about Annie that night at the Grotto, something that would stay with me for the rest of my life. She always seemed to know exactly what to say, even when that meant not saying anything at all.

Chapter 7

We graduated within a few days of each other, Annie from Saint Mary's and me from Notre Dame. Standing with my father in front of the golden dome, my ceremonial mortar board perched atop his head, the tassel hanging in front of his face, was the proudest moment of my life. We smiled as my mother fumbled about, trying to take our picture with the lens cap stuck on the camera. I felt my dad's arm around me, his hand firmly pressed between my shoulder blades, and I cried.

We lingered for a long time on campus, soaking in the moment, burning the sights into our minds, none of us certain how long it would be before we returned. None of us had been college graduates for longer than an hour, so we had no way of knowing for sure, but we all suspected that it would never be quite the same again. We would all come back as alumni, we'd go to Mass at Sacred Heart, we'd visit the Grotto, and we'd have a drink or two before and after a football game, but we would be visitors. There would be homecomings, but Notre Dame would not be home anymore. In many ways, the same thing had happened to our parents' houses over the last four years.

As we made our way across the quad for the last time, Annie walked with my mom, leaving me to follow behind with my dad. We talked about almost everything except what lay ahead. In a few weeks, we would all take a train to California where Annie and I would be married. I had been accepted to medical school at Stanford in Palo Alto, about an hour from Annie's home. We had already picked out a tiny apartment near the campus. Annie would be teaching special education in a small school two hills west of Stanford. Had we accepted an offer of financial help from Annie's father, we could have afforded a bigger apartment, but we wanted to make it on our own.

Walking across the Notre Dame campus, my dad avoided any discussions about California or my leaving. Instead, he told me how proud he was of what I had done, and what I was going to do. He was a simple man who had never lived farther than six blocks from where he was born. He was happy for me, and he wouldn't want me to stay, but he was going to miss me when I was gone. Four years of college only softened the pain of saying goodbye, it didn't make the pain go away. So, like always, we talked of everything else.

Before leaving, my mom stopped at the Grotto to light a candle, as she always did when she came to campus. My dad and I stood in the shade of a tree while my mother knelt at the rail beneath the statue of Mary. I'm not sure what made me say what I was thinking out loud – it just tumbled out of my mouth before I could stop it.

"I wish Henry was here."

"I've wished the same thing every day for twelve years," my father answered quietly.

"I wish he was going to be here for mom when I have to leave."

"Wouldn't make it any easier to say goodbye to you," he murmured.

"I always wondered how you and mom went on after he died."

"Not going on was not an option." A simple answer from a simple man.

"Things were never the same, though, were they?" I asked.

"A big piece of your mom stayed behind with Henry. I suspect she'd say the same about me."

There was a pause while my father seemed to struggle silently to summon the words.

"It's funny," he continued, in a voice even quieter than it had been, "but it seems like every time you say goodbye to your child, a little of you stays behind."

At that moment, I suddenly saw my father differently. I started to see why he never talked about partings. I'd always thought that he was avoiding it, somehow hoping that if he didn't talk about it, he wouldn't have to think about it. But he thought about it a lot. I guess he figured that the more he talked about it, the bigger the piece of him that would stay behind.

We stood without talking for what seemed like a long time, but it could only have been a moment or two. When I turned to say something, it was too late. He had already started over toward my mom. When he reached her, he quietly took her elbow and helped her up. They began walking toward the car. I stayed behind, watching them, just as I had while standing in the doorway of St. Basil's the day before I left for college. It had only been four years, but they looked older now, each parting having taken its toll. Without saying anything, Annie slipped her hand into mine, our fingers interlocking just so. I moved her ring with my fingertip to make room, and we slowly started off down the path behind my parents.

Carmel-by-the-Sea is one of the most beautiful places in the world. Nestled into the Monterey Peninsula south of San Francisco, its craggy shoreline rises up from the Pacific Ocean into sheer bluffs on the way to the foothills of an inland mountain range. Perpetually windswept, the cypress trees that jut out of the rocky soil grow twisted trunks that give way to soft green canopies whose tops are all flattened, looking more like clouds sheared off by the relentless westerly breezes. Everything about Carmel looks like a watercolor painting, the edges muted and softened by changing light, fog, and sea mist.

Ocean Avenue runs through the center of the quaint little town, down a steep hill, lined on both sides with art galleries, boutiques, and restaurants. At the foot of the hill, the narrow road widens into a cul-de-sac that marks the end of the continent. A horseshoe-shaped bay defines the waterfront of Carmel. The sunsets are so exquisite that local residents drag lawn chairs down to the beach every evening to watch the show one more time.

The water is too cold for swimming, which is just as well, as the ocean in that area is well-known as being shark-infested. Seals and sea lions sun themselves on rocks just off-shore, and where there are seals, there are sharks. Sea otters float amid the kelp that covers the surface, balancing stones on their bellies against which they crack open mollusks that they pry from the ocean floor. The view from the foot of Ocean Avenue is one of the world's great vistas.

Halfway down the hill, in a little shop with a window of stained glass, Annie was going over the last details with the florist who was handling everything for the wedding. Annie's folks lived an hour north of Carmel, and her father had rented an entire hotel that sat perched on a bluff overlooking the ocean. Family members from both sides, bridesmaids and groomsmen, and a few very close friends all had rooms for the weekend.

The ceremony itself was to take place in a white gazebo at the edge of the cliff. Annie's dad prevailed on the priest, who grew up as a tree-hugger from Oregon, to proclaim the bluff "God's Cathedral", thereby making an exception to the usual requirement that the wedding take place in a church.

Annie's family had more money than Fort Knox, but they never flaunted it. Her parents stayed in the smallest room in the hotel, insisting that the guests have the best accommodations. They made everyone feel welcome, especially my parents, who had never been farther from home than St. Louis. Everything was impeccable, but nothing was ostentatious. It was easy to see how Annie had remained so down to earth.

The weather cooperated, and the ceremony – like the bride – was beautiful. An orchestra played throughout the afternoon reception. After dinner, Annie and I prepared to leave. We were driving up the coast to San Francisco, where we would spend the first few days of our honeymoon before driving on to Lake Tahoe. There were still two hours of daylight left, which was just about right for the trip up the Pacific Coast Highway. Wrapping around the edge of the cliffs between Carmel and San Francisco, the drive was romantic in the early evening. After dark, it could get treacherous.

Pinhead relished his role as best man. He had given a remarkable speech during dinner, bringing tears to the eyes of every woman in the audience and many of the men. Seeing me getting ready to leave, Pinhead jumped up and offered to bring our car around to the front of the hotel. Annie kissed her parents and excused herself to run upstairs and change out of her wedding dress for the drive up the coast.

I stayed behind to thank Annie's parents and to say goodbye to mine. It would be difficult to see my folks more than once or twice a year during medical school. They promised to come out for Christmas, and I said we would try to come back during the summer. We all knew that life was changing.

I held my mom for a long time. I didn't let go until I felt her loosen her grip on my shoulders. There was nothing that I could say to keep her heart from aching, so I didn't try. I just kissed her on her cheek and told her that I loved her. Then I asked her to mail me a pie.

My dad stood patiently waiting while I said goodbye to my mom. He looked uncomfortable in his tuxedo, but not from the clothes. I reached to shake his hand, but he pulled me close, wrapping his arms around me. I tried three times to say something, but nothing came out. My dad whispered in my ear, his breath warm against the skin behind my ear.

"Be happy, Michael."

I finally gathered myself enough to say what I had started to say but never did back on graduation day at Notre Dame.

"Dad, I'm glad that saying goodbye means a part of you stays behind, because I'm gonna need it."

My dad put his hands in his pockets and let what I had said sink in for a moment. Then the slightest hint of a smile came over his face.

"You have everything you need, Michael. Remember what you're feeling right now. It won't be that long before you're standing here with your own children. Just try to leave a little of yourself behind every day. Don't wait for goodbyes."

I hugged him one last time and turned without saying a word. I didn't need to say anything, which is lucky because I wouldn't have been able to. I'd walked a few steps when I stopped and turned around. He was right where I left him, hands in his pockets, wisps of his thinning hair lifted by the steady breeze. He smiled again and nodded silently. At the moment of my life when I needed him the most, he had never stood taller.

Annie was waiting for me at the front of the hotel, wearing blue jeans and a grey sweatshirt with STANFORD MED in cardinal letters. She carried a small duffel bag and her purse. The suitcases were already in the car. She stood on her toes to kiss me when I reached her.

"Everything ok?" she asked.

I nodded. "Everything's great."

Long after Pinhead should have arrived with the car, he came around the corner of the building half walking, half running, out of breath, and clearly bothered by something. When he saw us standing in the circle drive, his shoulders slumped.

"Hey guys, we've got a slight problem," Pinhead called from across the manicured lawn.

"What kind of problem?" I asked, starting to worry.

"Well, I was backing your car out, and you know those brick pillars holding up the patio where the band is playing?"

Fearing the worst, Annie blurted out, "Did you knock down the patio?"

"Not all of it," Pinhead answered.

Annie started toward the entrance of the hotel, expecting a catastrophe, but Pinhead stopped her.

"Everything's fine," he assured her, "the patio's fine, just a chunk taken out of a few bricks. Your car's kind of a mess, though."

Relieved that the orchestra wasn't lying in a heap of rubble, Annie relaxed and came back to where Pinhead and I were standing.

"How bad is it?" I asked.

"Well, it'll run, but the bumper's creased and the trunk popped open and won't close."

We were stuck. We couldn't drive two hours along the coast with our trunk flying open, and we couldn't leave the car in San Francisco the way it was. I was about to go and ask my dad for the keys to his rental car when Pinhead said he had an idea.

"Annie's dad gave me the keys to his car when he needed me to move it to make room for the band to unload their equipment." Dangling the keys between his thumb and forefinger, Pinhead suggested that we take Annie's father's car.

"You've got to be nuts," I said, shaking my head.

"I think he's right," Annie said, "My dad would offer us his car if he knew what happened. There are enough relatives here that he'll have no problem getting home tomorrow. We'll bring him his car when we come back from the mountains. Besides, it's a great car."

In spite of my better judgment, I went along with the plan. Pinhead helped us move our suitcases from the dented trunk of our eight year-old Pontiac Catalina into the back seat of Annie's dad's Mercedes roadster. The trunk was too small for all of our luggage because the convertible top folded down into what would have been trunk space. Pinhead promised to explain everything to our folks, then he hugged Annie and shook my hand. He was still waving when he disappeared from my rearview mirror as I turned onto Highway 1 and headed north to begin our honeymoon.

For the first hour we sang along with the radio and watched the sun sink lower in the sky, casting shadows in the hillsides that made the landscape change colors every few minutes. The roadster hugged the road as we wound back and forth through an endless series of hairpin curves, tracing the irregular shape of the coast. Heading north, we were tucked against the side of the cliffs while the oncoming cars edged along with only of few feet of loose gravel separating them from a ninety foot drop to the beach.

About halfway to San Francisco, we noticed the first wisps of fog coming ashore. The sun was well above the horizon, but it was blocked by a blanket of fog several miles out to sea. The temperature was dropping, making it easier for the fog to hang together in the valleys between hilltops. It would be dark in less than an hour, but it was the fog and not the dark that worried me. It is rather easy to follow the coastal road in the dark, especially heading north, with the rock walls next to the car. In the fog, however, curves came along unannounced, making it much too easy to miss a turn and drive off the edge of the mountain. Unless the wind picked up and blew the fog away, it would be very dangerous for us to continue for much longer.

I glanced down at the dashboard and immediately knew that we needed to change course. The gas gauge had moved into the red warning zone near empty. Not anticipating that his daughter and new son-in-law would steal his car, Annie's dad had not bothered to fill the tank. Halfway between Carmel and San Francisco on the Pacific Coast Highway, on a ten foot wide strip of asphalt between the mountain and the sea, there are no billboards, no road signs, no exit ramps, and no gas stations.

"I need to turn off at the next opportunity and head inland to get gas," I explained to Annie. "We should probably continue east from there and take the interstate the rest of the way to San Francisco."

Annie nodded and changed the station on the radio. Another ten minutes went by and the fog had become so thick that I could only see about fifty yards ahead of us. I slowed down and strained to see the places where the road curved right or left, focusing on the white line painted along the inside edge of the road. It had been more than forty minutes since a car passed us going in the opposite direction, telling me that visibility must be even worse ahead, since no one in their right minds was venturing out onto this treacherous stretch of road in the fog. I slowed down even more. I tried flipping the high beam headlights on, but the glare made it even harder to see, so I clicked back to the regular headlights.

We were in no man's land. If we tried to turn around and head back to Carmel, we'd be driving in the outer lane of the road, perilously close to the edge. If we stopped, anyone coming behind us would have no way to see us before it was too late. We had no choice but to continue on, desperately looking for an intersection with a road heading inland and away from the fog that was rolling in off the ocean at an alarming rate.

We slowed to a speed only slightly faster than we could walk, feeling our way around the curves as the road wound down to one of the few places where it was close to sea level. The sun had set somewhere beyond the fog, and in the dark everything took on a ghostly appearance. We could hear the surf breaking just to our left, so we knew that we were at the bottom of another hill. Annie saw the gravel road before I did. It appeared out of the fog on her side of the road like an apparition.

I slowed to a crawl and eased the car onto the narrow gravel road that was actually little more than a path. We had no way of knowing where the gravel road would take us, but since it was heading away from the ocean, at least we knew that we wouldn't drive off of the cliff. If we had to, we could sleep in the car and wait until the fog lifted in the morning. For now, we decided to follow the road for a while in the hope that it would lead to a small town or at least a gas station.

Without pavement to reflect our headlights, and with no white lines painted along the edge of the road, we had a hard time seeing more than a few feet in front of the car. Annie hung out of the right side of the car staring down at the edge of the gravel, and I watched the left side of the road. Whenever we strayed off of the rutted path, Annie would shout "left" and I would pull the wheel back. We continued driving by the Braille system until Annie suddenly yelled, "Stop!"

The gravel road came to a dead end. To our surprise, there was a crossroad at the end of the gravel that was almost paved. It had been paved at some point long ago, but the asphalt had crumbled over the years. Nevertheless, it was a road. The gravel service road that we had been following connected the main Pacific Coast Highway with this long-forgotten country road that ran parallel to Highway 1.

There was no sign of civilization in either direction, so we turned left onto the broken pavement, reasoning that we were better off moving north. We followed the country road for a mile or so. We were getting discouraged, afraid the road had been abandoned, when we saw a dim light not too far ahead.

I drove toward the light and as we got closer we saw that it was actually the reflection of a single light bulb off of a wooden sign. The gooseneck light fixture was rusty and barely hanging from the top of the sign. The sign had been painted sometime during the Truman administration. The letters were badly faded, and several had worn away completely. The letters that remained read "THE LO_E _UT". A faded arrow pointed down an intersecting road that was as dark as a coal mine. Our only reason for following the arrow was the lone bulb burning in the rusty fixture over the faded sign. Someone was still bothering to change the bulb.

About a quarter of a mile down the intersecting road was another dimly lit billboard, this one with all of its lettering intact. "WELCOME TO THE LOVE HUT", the sign said. In smaller letters, the sign advertised "GAS and LODGING". The gas pumps looked like something from a Norman Rockwell painting from the 1940s, and the ramshackle building that was once a mechanic's garage had been converted into a motel. A crooked sign over a screen door said "LOBBY". I took a deep breath and went inside. There was no one in sight. On the counter was one of those silver dome bells with the little tapper on top. I rang the bell but no one came. I was about to ring it again when a voice rang out.

"I'm not deaf, you don't gotta ring it again."

I leaned over the counter and looked down to where it sounded like the voice had come from. A midget with a cigar clenched in his teeth was climbing up onto a stool. Hauling himself up and standing on the stool, the midget looked me in the eyes...sort of. His left eye was looking at me, but his right eye seemed to be looking at the door. I decided to stare at his left eye in an effort not to be rude.

"Welcome to the Love Hut," the midget said, without removing the cigar from his clenched teeth. "You want the room for an hour, two hours, four hours?"

"Pardon me?" I replied, not making the connection yet.

"We got a rate for an hour, for two hours, or for four hours. How long you gonna be?"

The light bulb finally went on over my head, and I stammered, "Uh, actually I'd like to spend the night."

The midget's eyebrows arched and he winked the eye that was aimed in my general direction. "Honeymoon, James Bond?" he asked with a lascivious smile. The eye that drifted off to the right was watching Annie as she bent over in her tight blue jeans to pump the gas into the car. I didn't like the way he was looking at Annie, but in spite of his size, he scared me for some reason.

The midget's smile turned to a scowl. He shifted his gaze so that both eyes were aimed out the door and at my car. I was still wearing my tuxedo, which must have seemed odd, seeing Annie's backside in blue jeans. Combining that with the Mercedes roadster, I must have looked like a kid out for a joyride after his high school prom, driving his father's car. Returning one eye to me, he said, "We don't allow no funny business here."

"No need to worry, I assured him. "We're on our way to San Francisco and just need a place to sleep for the evening."

He seemed convinced, or at least indifferent. Paperwork was evidently not the order of business, because he made no effort to have me check in.

"Thirty bucks," he muttered, "plus the gas."

I knew better than to ask if he accepted credit cards, so I just handed him fifty dollars in cash. He didn't even check the gas pump. He just stuffed the $50 into his pocket, making no movement to give me change. I decided not to argue. He reached over to a series of hooks on the wall. There was a row of keys, each attached to a chain and a block of wood. In order, the wooden blocks said "Men", "Women", "Room 1", "Room 2" and "Bridal Suite". He grabbed the block of wood that said "Room 1" and slid it across the counter toward me.

Surveying the blocks of wood chained to keys hanging on the wall behind the midget, I pushed the key to room 1 back toward him and said, "I think we'll take the Bridal Suite." I had no illusions that it would actually be a bridal suite, but under the circumstances, it was worth a shot. The midget put his hands on his hips, cocked his head to one side, and looked at me like I'd just asked him to solve a calculus problem.

"Sorry, Romeo, the Bridal Suite is occ-u-pado," he smiled.

"But the key is right there," I said, pointing over his shoulder.

"It's reserved, Casanova. You can't just walk in dressed like Frank Sinatra and expect the best room in the house. This ain't no Red Roof Inn."

I could see that I wasn't getting anywhere with the room upgrade, so I reached across the counter and grabbed the key to room 1. A little annoyed, I decided to ask for my change from the fifty dollars I paid for the room and gas. At 65 cents a gallon, the gas couldn't have cost more than $10. I had at least $10 coming to me, and now that he had stiffed me on the bridal suite, not to mention the crack about Frank Sinatra, I wanted my money.

"I think I have some change coming to me," I said, trying to lower the timber of my voice for dramatic effect.

The midget didn't even blink. Either eye. He bit down harder on the stub of his cigar, his jaw muscles visibly tightening, and gave a curt two-word reply.

"Service charge."

"Service charge?" I asked.

"Yeah, service charge...I provide service, you get charged."

"But you didn't provide any service."

"I checked you in."

"No, you didn't. You didn't fill out a form, you didn't write anything down, you just gave me a key."

"Exactly," the midget said, quite pleased with himself.

"Exactly what?" I asked, feeling particularly brave with the counter separating us.

"I gave you the key. Ipso Facto, service charge."

"How would you like it if I called the Better Business Bureau?" I asked. I wasn't sure that there really was anything called the Better Business Bureau, but you always heard people say they were going to call it.

"How would you like to spend the rest of the night tryin' to stop yer nose from bleedin'?" the midget threatened.

Convinced that I had made my point, and not interested in punctuating it with bloodshed, particularly my own, I reached for the key and started for the door. With one hand on the flimsy screen door, emboldened by knowing that I could run if necessary, I turned to give him one more piece of my mind, but when I looked back at the counter, the midget was gone.

Annie had finished pumping gas into her dad's car. The amount due was displayed on the Depression-era gas pump with numbers on little plastic wheels that seemed to float in some viscous liquid inside a thick glass ball that magnified the numbers into a blurry streak. The three wheels were not quite synchronized, resulting in the digits failing to line up in a precisely straight line. According to the pump, Annie had either put $9.85 or $98 worth of gas into the car. The midget had ripped me off. I would deal with that in the morning, hopefully with the day shift.

I pushed open the screen door and stepped outside. The door slammed shut with a loud "thwack". I squinted in the darkness and tried to get my bearings. An old vending machine that still dispensed glass bottles of Coca-Cola leaned up against the building at the end of the sidewalk. I helped Annie get the suitcases out of the back seat and we put the convertible top up and locked the car. We followed the sidewalk around the corner of the building and made our way along the row of wooden doors with peeling paint.

The first door that we came to had no number affixed to it. There was, however, the outline of the number one that was a shade darker than the surrounding area, suggesting that at one time there had been a number there. I tried the key in the lock and the door creaked open. Reaching inside, I groped for the light switch. Feeling it with my fingers, I flipped the switch on. Nothing happened. At least at first I thought that nothing had happened, but after a minute or two, I realized that the room was the slightest bit less dark than before.

Stepping inside, I noticed that the switch operated a table lamp, which had a black light in it. An eerie purple glow illuminated an area about three feet around the lamp. Shuffling my feet, I inched around in the dark until I found two more lamps, one a floor lamp, and the other on a table across the room from the first. I turned both lamps on, only to find that every bulb in the room was a black light. The room looked like a giant bug zapper. Annie stood in the doorway, afraid to step into the room.

I finally found a normal light fixture in the bathroom, so I left the door open to allow a shaft of light to cut into the shadows. There was an odd reflection of the bathroom light that disoriented me until I realized that there was a mirror on the ceiling over the bed. I grabbed the bags and helped Annie find her way through the dark until we reached the edge of the bed. We waited for our eyes to adjust to the eerie lighting, then looked for the television, figuring that even if there was nothing on to watch, it would lend more light. I found the television, but when I tried to turn it on, nothing happened. Bolted to the nightstand next to the bed was a metal box with a slot for coins. On the side of the box it said, "Magic Fingers – 25 cents". I'd heard of vibrating beds before, but I never believed the stories. Unable to resist seeing one for myself, I dropped a quarter into the slot. The bed didn't move, but the television came to life in the corner of the room.

The room took on a blue glow as the television threw shadows into the corners. On the screen, two naked women rode horses along a beach, bouncing along with ridiculous smiles on their faces. The picture was snowy, fading in and out as if one of the wires had come loose from the back of the television. The production value of the movie was poor, and the producer obviously saved money on the models. It was hard to tell their rear ends from those of the horses. After only a few minutes, the television snapped off and the room was dark again. Some entrepreneur had hot-wired the television to the Magic Fingers vending machine and was selling dirty movies for about ten dollars an hour.

I was beside myself. This rundown roadside den of iniquity was no place to spend our wedding night. I turned to apologize to Annie, only to find her smiling.

"What's so funny?" I asked, involuntarily smiling myself.

"You couldn't make this place up," she chuckled.

"It's no place to spend a wedding night, let's get out of here," I said.

"Where would we go in that fog?" Annie replied, in more of a statement than a question.

"We can find another place, or sleep in the car," I offered.

"It'll be ok," Annie reassured me, "as long as you keep your shoes on."

"We're supposed to be in San Francisco," I complained, "with champagne, and room service, and a view of the Golden Gate Bridge..."

"We have the rest of our lives, Mike, don't worry about one day."

"This isn't just any day, Annie."

"It's just the first day, Mike. We have the rest of our lives together."

"Well, this is a hell of a place to start the rest of our lives."

Then Annie said something that has stayed with me since. Something I have thought about more than once over the years since she first said it.

"You start the rest of your life every day, from wherever you find yourself."

That summed up Annie's approach to life better than anything. She was a glass-half-full optimist, with a gritty determination to make the best of whatever life threw at her. I tended to bitch about the glass being half empty, but Annie always saw possibilities.

We never unpacked on our wedding night, never even got undressed. Neither of us was too keen about crawling between the sheets of the bed, vibrating or not, so we laid down on top of the bedspread, with our shoes on. Annie laid her head in the crook of my arm and I ran my fingers through her hair, breathing in the faint scent of Carmel. I told her that I loved her, but I don't think she heard me. Her breathing was a little heavier than a moment before – she was fast asleep. I couldn't help thinking that this was something we'd laugh about some day... a story to tell our kids. Annie was right. We had the rest of our lives together.

Chapter 8

1:15 P.M.

I MADE MY WAY AROUND St. Basil's School to a bench that was shaded by a large maple tree. I didn't remember a tree in that spot, but that's probably because it would have been a sapling when I was here last. I draped my suit jacket over the bench and took a seat, thankful for the shade. Looking out across a small patch of grass, I realized that this cramped little square is where we spent so many recesses chasing each other or a ball, a different game for every season. The place looked so small now, but back then it felt like you could run forever.

We would fit whatever game we were playing to the patch of green by rotating the field. Football was played horizontally across the playground. Baseball was played corner-to corner. By placing home plate in one corner of the field and playing diagonally, the playground turned into a diamond. The craziest game that we invented needed no particular orientation on the playground. It was an amorphous bit of felonious mayhem that we called "maul ball".

The rules of maul ball were straightforward – there weren't any. There were no teams in maul ball, no scoring system, and no time limits. No one ever won a game of maul ball, but then again, no one ever lost one either. The only way to tell whether a game had just begun or was about to end was to examine the clothes of the participants, looking for the tell-tale rips, tears, grass stains, blood stains, and general disrepair.

Maul ball was played by as many as twenty or thirty guys at a time. It generally involved a football, but if a football was not handy, any ball, or for that matter, any object easily carried under one's arm, could be substituted. The game began as the doors to the school opened for recess and the guy with the ball ran off like a bat out of hell with the remaining twenty-nine players in hot pursuit. The ball carrier ran as far and as fast as he could, shifting direction constantly to confuse his pursuers. When the chase culminated with the ball carrier being caught, he was tackled and immediately buried when everyone else in the game piled on top.

Players than unpiled and formed a circle around the fallen ball carrier, much like wolves surrounding their captured prey. The ball carrier then dragged himself to his knees and had the option of tossing the ball to anyone in the circle. When the ball was thrown to another player, he was required to catch it. Missing the ball intentionally resulted in considerably more vigorous piling on by other players than a normal chase and tackle. A player catching the ball would bolt off in a desperate sprint for survival, running in an erratic pattern around the property until he was buried under the combined weight of the remaining players.

An observer watching from a distance would be left with the unmistakable image of a gazelle on the Serengeti being pursued by a pack of jackals. The only difference in maul ball was that the jackals were accompanied by lions, elephants, giraffes, and every other creature in Noah's ark...and when the gazelle was brought down, all of the other animals hurled themselves onto the growing pile of arms and legs.

No one ever threw the ball to Lou the Screw. The few times that Lou got the ball by mistake, he lumbered around the schoolyard with six or seven guys draped over his shoulders and back trying to haul him down. No one was foolish enough to try to tackle the Screw by grabbing his legs. Tackling Lou the Screw was a little like stopping a cement mixer rolling down a hill by stepping out in front of it.

One day, Whitey Shelton did something that would earn him a place in the maul ball hall of fame forever. Whitey had the ball as we left class and was tossing it into the air and catching it as we made our way down the long corridor to the door that led to the maul ball field. About a foot shorter than everyone else in the class, Whitey Shelton went through life doing crazy things to make people forget how small he was. He was fearless...he was as dumb as a bag of hammers, but he was fearless.

When we reached the end of the hallway, Whitey pushed open the door and bounded down the stairs two at a time, tucking the football under his arm. Hitting the bottom of the stairs, Whitey was off like a shot, sprinting across the field before most of us had even left the school. Whitey got his name from the color of his hair, which ordinarily stuck up from his head like he had just gotten out of bed, but now, running at top speed across the playground, Whitey's hair was all blown straight back.

Taking advantage of his quick start and the fact that most of his pursuers were still piling out of the school, Whitey ran around like a banshee for what seemed like half of the recess period. Whenever anyone drew close to him, he darted off in another direction, shifting the ball from arm to arm as he ran. It seemed like no one would ever catch him when Whitey Shelton made a tactical mistake. He would glance furtively over his shoulder from time to time to see how close his pursuers were. About twenty minutes into his run, he looked back and saw only half of the usual thundering herd following him. He concluded that the rest had been left behind, and he envisioned them off somewhere gasping for air and holding their sides. As Whitey watched the pack behind him losing ground, he gave in to the urge to shout back over his shoulder in a taunting tone of voice.

In fact, the rest of the posse was not off somewhere gasping for breath – it had split off from the larger group and had circled around the school to set an ambush. Had Whitey not been preoccupied with taunting his winded pursuers, he may have eluded the ambush, but with his head turned, he ran smack into the outstretched forearm of Lou the Screw. Whitey's head was at the level of Lou the Screw's chest, and when he hit the Screw's forearm, his feet joined his head at that height as he momentarily stretched out, perfectly horizontal to the ground, before dropping like a sack of flour. Everyone was so tired from chasing Whitey that they only half-heartedly fell on him in a pile-up that looked more like the stacking of cordwood than an actual mugging.

When everyone unpiled and formed the customary circle around Whitey, he just laid there for a few minutes trying to focus his eyes. After a few more minutes went by, Whitey worked his way up to his knees and began looking around the circle. He squatted over the ball and turned in a complete circle, making eye contact with each of the now-exhausted jackals. As Whitey turned around the circle, everyone wondered who he would sentence to be next. That's when Whitey Shelton made his hall of fame move. He jumped up and ran off with the ball again himself. In the history of maul ball, no one had ever kept the ball to run again after being mauled. No one tackled Whitey as he broke through the circle, because no one had ever seen this happen before. Everyone was caught completely unprepared for such an audacious and ill-conceived move by Whitey.

It took only a moment for everyone to realize what had happened and to tear off after Whitey again, but that moment of hesitation was all he needed. He was back up to full speed again and he was gone. The chase was now on, but realistically, there was no chance that anyone would run down Whitey, not with the head start that he had. Whitey looped back and forth across the playground, jumping over kids down in the rut of the merry-go-round, weaving between kids on the swings, and ducking beneath the scalding aluminum ladder, all the while evading capture by the dwindling number of us who had the stamina and attention spans to keep up pursuit.

At the end of recess every day, one of the nuns would step out of the school doors and ring a brass bell on a wooden handle. The pitch of the bell and the vigor with which the nuns shook it would immediately stop everyone wherever they were and signal the end of our recreation time. Whitey had avoided capture for the remainder of recess and was still well ahead of his nearest pursuers when Sister Thomas Aquinas stepped out and rang the bell. At the clang of Sister Thomas Aquinas's bell, Whitey turned instinctively and saw her standing on the stairs. He knew that he had done what no one had ever done in the glorious history of maul ball...he had retained possession of the ball for an entire recess period.

Also hearing the bell signifying the end of recess, one of the second graders stood up from his seat on the teeter-totter and started toward the doors, as he had been taught to do. With no weight on one end, the teeter-totter shot up and caught Whitey Shelton just below his chin as he ran past. The sound of the wooden teeter-totter cracking Whitey Shelton in the jaw was slightly louder than Sister Thomas Aquinas's brass bell, and everyone on the playground stopped and stared at Whitey, who for the second time that day, was flying through the air horizontal to the ground.

Whitey skidded to a stop in the pea gravel beneath the swing set, wearing only one shoe. The other shoe had flown off and was lying on the merry-go-round, which was turning slowly as it lost its momentum. Still firmly tucked under Whitey's arm was the ball. Dragging himself to his feet, his eyes now hopelessly unfocused, Whitey started toward the stairs where Sister Thomas Aquinas now looked on with a mixture of deep concern and disbelief on her face. Completely unaware that he was missing a shoe, Whitey hobbled like a pirate with a wooden leg up the stairs and into the school.

Whitey weaved from side to side down the hallway, no longer in attempt to avoid pursuit, but now because he was unable to walk in a straight line. He tossed the ball into the air just as he had on his way out earlier, but this time when the ball came down, Whitey was no longer standing in the same spot and the ball fell behind him. He continued his peg-legged stagger, oblivious to the ball that was wobbling along on the floor. Outside, the merry-go-round finally came to a stop, with Whitey's shoe still lying right where it had landed.

Sitting beneath the shade of the tree, I could almost see Whitey dashing across the playground, his hair blown back, the ball tucked squarely under his arm. My gaze wandered across the old playground to the school. Looking up at the windows of the classrooms of St. Basil's, my mind drifted back almost nineteen years, to an autumn day when I stood outside of Erin's pre-school, leaning against a different tree, looking up at the windows of another classroom.

Chapter 9

ON HER FIRST DAY OF school, Erin had a bout of homesickness and she spent much of the morning in tears. For the next few days, I walked Erin to school, then stood outside in plain view from the windows. Erin would come to the window and peek out, make eye contact with me, and wave. The time that it took for Erin to come to the window varied, but once she was reassured that I was out there, she was fine for the rest of the morning and I would leave. After a week, she stopped coming to the window altogether.

Sitting alone on the bench, I realized how much I missed my kids. Not just today, but every day. It's not that they're gone, but they're going. Erin graduated from college in May. Emily is a sophomore and she just left to spend the summer semester studying in England. Erin went along and is staying in London for two weeks – it's her graduation present. Annie flew over with the girls and will return with Erin – that's Annie's graduation present. I keep glancing over my shoulder, staring behind me, wondering where the time went.

Every summer when the girls were small, we spent a long weekend in Saugatuck, Michigan. It was a little more than four hours north of our home, which was just outside of Indianapolis. For the first few visits, we stayed in several of the bed and breakfast inns that were so prevalent in the small town. When we became more familiar with the area, we found a house that sat on a high bluff overlooking protected wetlands. We rented that little house in the woods each time we returned thereafter.

Saugatuck is situated at the mouth of the St. Joseph River, where it empties into Lake Michigan. On one side of the tall sand dunes that define the town's boundaries is the lake. On the other side sits the quaint little artists' colony, with its streets lined with art galleries, specialty shops, ice cream parlors, and inns. The river divides the town, and the only way across the river was on a turn-of-the-century chain ferry.

Little more than a floating barge, the ferry was attached to a large metal chain that lay along the riverbed, stretching from one side to the other. In the early 1900s, the chain was attached to wooden wheels that were cranked by hand to pull the ferry from one riverbank to the other. By the time we visited Saugatuck, the hand-cranks had been replaced by motorized winches, making the crossings less dependent upon the availability of barrel-chested stevedores.

Every summer, when we arrived in Saugatuck, we would make a point to stop at a little white farmhouse on the outskirts of town. At a picnic table set back from the road, a wisp of an old lady sold sweet corn, tomatoes, and vegetables of all shapes and sizes. We loaded the car with fresh produce and headed off to the house on the bluff, where we cooked a feast and ate overlooking the wetlands and the river off in the distance.

From the backyard of the house a winding set of stone steps descended the face of the bluff, leading to a landing alongside a creek that weaved through the marsh on its way to the river. Floating in the creek, tied to a wooden post, was a canoe that came along with the house. The marsh extended for several miles, its creek curling into and around the reeds and cattails, doubling back on itself every few hundred yards.

As soon as we unloaded the car, the girls would help Annie shuck the corn and get a pot of water boiling. They would then take me by the hands and we would gingerly climb the stairs down to the landing to launch the canoe. Annie always made an excuse to stay up on the bluff. It wasn't that she didn't want to go for a ride in the canoe, but she wanted to stay behind, anxious for the adventure to be something that the girls shared with their dad. I always knew how hard it was for Annie to step back to make room for "daddy time", as she called it. She knew what it meant for girls to spend time with their fathers, and she always made sure that ours did.

I would snap the girls' life jackets on, lift them carefully into the canoe, then step in and take my seat in the rear. Erin sat in the front, her paddle occasionally reaching the water enough to make a ripple. Emily sat on the floor of the canoe between us, one hand on either side, her eyes barely high enough to look over the edge. We paddled out into the marsh and stopped to look back up to the top of the bluff. There was Annie, binoculars in her hand, waving from the deck of the house. I'll never forget Annie standing alone on that bluff year after year, waving. She always knew when to hold on tightly, and when to let go.

The best advice I ever got about raising girls came from a patient who I treated about a month after Erin was born. Seventy-seven years old,

Otto's daughters had daughters. He had complications from diabetes – his eyesight was nearly gone, his kidneys had failed, and his circulation was so poor that he could barely walk. He needed what we call a cut down procedure to provide vascular access for dialysis. I had been called in to do the procedure, which took only a few minutes to perform. While I was in the room, Otto overheard one of the nurses say something about my new baby girl and his ears perked up immediately. He knew a little something about bringing up girls, and what he said to me that day stayed with me forever.

"I have two beautiful daughters," he beamed proudly, "and four granddaughters even more beautiful than their mothers."

I didn't say much. I didn't have to. He was clearly happy to talk about his daughters, and I was only too happy to listen.

"They're grown now, my daughters," he went on, "but I get to talk to them almost every day. They call just to see how I'm doing. They don't have anything special on their minds most days, but they call to see how I'm doing. They're busy, I know that for sure, but darn if they don't call anyway."

"Do they live nearby?" I asked.

"Couple hours away," he answered absent-mindedly. It was almost as if my question had disrupted his chain of thought, so I kept my questions to a minimum.

"When they were little, the smartest thing I ever did was to take them on dates." His eyes softened as his mind took a trip back to another time. "We did a lot of things together as a family," he continues, "but I always made sure I set aside time to take each one of the girls on dates all alone. Time just for them. Time to talk about what was important to them. I only had one rule…the restaurant had to have cloth napkins. They could pick any place they wanted, as long as it had cloth napkins."

I couldn't help smiling. Here was a guy who looked like he'd be more comfortable in a diner than a fancy restaurant. His rough hands told even a casual observer that he had worked hard all of his life, doing hard work. He was weathered from long days spent working outside in the elements. Money couldn't have been easy to come by for him. I smiled at the thought of this guy with the calloused hands, sitting across a table from his little girl, carefully unfolding his cloth napkin and putting it in his lap.

"As the girls got older, we kept going on dates," he continued. "Even after they got married, every month or two, I would meet them for dinner, just to talk about what was important to them. It's hard now that they live so far away; we don't have dinner any more, but they still call me. They called their mother every day until she passed. Now, they call me. I know they're busy, so I try not to keep them too long, but it sure means a lot just to hear their voices. They got a million things going on, but still, they call."

"You're a lucky guy, Otto."

"Don't I know it?" he replied. "That's the thing about having daughters. Daughters never leave you. Sons go off and get wrapped up in their own lives – think about when was the last time you called your mother – but daughters, they stay close, even when they're far away."

I took note of what he said, but it would be some time before I would really appreciate it. It's like everyone always telling you to enjoy your kids when they're young, because they grow up so fast. When you're young yourself, you nod politely and acknowledge the comment with an almost dismissive wave of the hand. Then fifteen years go by and you find yourself wondering where the time went. Then you're the one telling the twenty-something parents to enjoy their children, because they grow up so fast, but you know that they're only half-listening to you.

I don't know what ever became of Otto. It's a part of being a surgeon that they don't talk about in medical school. You see patients for a brief episode of their lives, and if all goes well, they and you move on. I never saw Otto again, though I wish I had. He was a guy I would have liked to get to know. I only saw him once, for about an hour, but he changed my life.

As the girls grew up, no matter how busy I was, or how busy they were, we always made time for dates. Little snippets of time set aside just for us. When they were young, we might sit out on a wooden pier feeding bread crumbs to bluegills in a pond not far from our house. Or hold hands walking home from the ice cream parlor, trying to stay one lick ahead of the melt. When they were a little older, it might be a baseball game, or the ballet. When they went off to college, each of them one hundred miles from home in opposite directions, I would drive to campus after work, take them out to dinner for a break from dorm food, then head back home to Annie. I never instituted the cloth napkin rule, but I never forgot Otto's lesson about raising daughters.

When Emily was eleven years old, she announced that she wanted to play hockey. Not field hockey with girls, but ice hockey against the boys. Emily is left-handed, and her brain is wired backwards. I gave up trying to understand her long ago, when I realized that it was much easier to just enjoy her. I only had one question when she said that she wanted to play hockey.

"How important do you think it is for a hockey player to know how to skate?" I asked.

"Huh?" Emily responded with a confused look on her face.

"Well, you don't know how to ice skate," I explained as gently as I could.

"How hard can it be?" she asked.

"Well, the first time I tried, I fell on the back of my head and got a concussion," I cautioned her.

"They have helmets now," Emily replied, matter-of-factly.

Three weeks after her first lesson, Emily skated out to take her first shift as right wing on the junior hockey team. She wasn't just the only girl on the team, she was the only girl in the league. She weighed a little over eighty pounds, but twenty pounds of that was equipment and tape. What she lacked in size, she more than made up for in grit. If she got knocked down, which happened every time one of the bigger kids hit her, she scrambled back up and jumped back into the play.

It was midway through the second period of the last game of the season. Emily had not scored any goals, but then almost no one else had either. At that age, most of the players skated in a rugby-like scrum, most likely leaning on each other to avoid falling down. Emily was smaller than all of the other players, but she was also smarter. She avoided the scrums, looking instead for open ice, where her speed made up for her diminutive size. I walked along the glass, following the puck, in part to see the game more closely and in part to get a little circulation going in my feet, which were almost frozen.

Emily watched the thundering herd scuffle along the boards, everyone flailing at the puck amid skates and sticks. She staked out a patch of open ice in front of the net and waited patiently while the other players inched along like a street sweeper. Suddenly, the puck shot out of the huddle and slid directly toward Emily. Timing her swing perfectly, she redirected the puck past the goalie, who stood motionless like a guard at Buckingham Palace, and into the net. My arms shot up along with hers. I would have cried if my eyes weren't frozen open.

Emily's last shift of the season was another memory for a lifetime. She was skating across the rink at center ice, chasing the puck, when she disappeared beneath a kid who had clearly been held back several grades in school. At almost two hundred pounds, he hit Emily like a cement truck running over a bicycle. They both went down in a heap, but not a single shred of Emily's uniform color was visible. The puck was somewhere beneath the two of them, so the whistle blew to stop play. When Baby Huey got up, Emily reappeared, reminiscent of Lazarus rising up from the dead. She adjusted her helmet, if not her teeth, and skated wobbly in the general direction of the bench. I made my way around the rink to the glass behind the team bench. I watched Emily, looking for signs of distress, but all she was doing was smiling at one of her teammates. I rapped on the glass to get her attention. She turned and smiled at me. I mouthed the silent words, "Are you alright?" and she gave me a gloved thumbs-up sign and nodded.

Emily's season and career ended that day, not as a result of the collision, but perhaps because of the goal. She had done it. She had set her sights on learning to skate and on playing a game ordinarily reserved for guys. She had ignored the sideways glances from parents who long ago forgot that sports are about the playing, not the trophies. She had earned the respect of her coaches, and she had shown what she was made of. I was happy for her when she made the goal, but I was proudest of her when she got up after getting run over by a freight train. Life is easy when you're up. What's important is how you respond when you get knocked down.

Erin had none of her younger sister's interest in playing sports. Each autumn, when the air was heavy with the musty scent of burning leaves, Erin would play football with me in a quiet corner of our yard. She would catch the ball, barely able to wrap her arms around it, then run straight at me, giggling. There were none of the evasive moves that put Whitey Shelton into the maul ball hall of fame. Erin made a bee line toward me and shrieked gleefully when I caught her in my arms and tumbled to the ground cradling her and the football. When it was my turn to carry the ball, I scooted along on my knees, pretending to evade her tackles, and she would jump up onto my back, her hands holding onto anything she could grasp, until we crumpled into a heap again, laughing. As far as Erin was concerned, the game would have been just as fun without the ball.

When Emily was barely old enough to walk, she joined Erin and they teamed up to score touchdowns on the backyard gridiron. Erin quickly took on the role of the first child. She carried the ball just long enough to draw my attention, then handed it to Emily, who had a lot of Whitey Shelton in her. Emily would run in all directions, struggling to hang onto the ball, which was almost as big as she was. Like Whitey, Emily got up after being tackled and took off running. She would have been a natural maul baller.

On another autumn evening, nearly ten years after our last backyard football game, Erin and I were walking together in the bluish glow of her high school football field's halogen lights. Erin played the flute in her school's marching band, and we were heading back to the car after the game. Annie and Emily had driven separately, and they were on their way home to make sandwiches for the crowd of band kids who came to the house after every game.

The stadium was empty, the last trickle of fans making their way through the gates as the clean-up crews already started their work. Erin had been in high school for a little over a month, just long enough for me to know that my fears of having her grow up were without merit. When the girls were young, I thought I wanted to make time stand still. I was afraid that if they grew up, I would lose them. As it turned out, I found myself enjoying each phase of their lives a little more than the last. It's funny. Until it happens, you can't imagine anything being better than right now. But girls have an uncanny ability to grow up without growing away, and every new stage of their lives makes you wonder what you were worried about.

Walking together on that crisp October night, Erin and I were doing what we so often did. We were talking. We always had that kind of relationship. She would talk to me about everything. Things that made her happy. Things that made her sad. I always knew that if she needed to, she would come to me and we could talk. So I should have been prepared for what was coming, but I wasn't. Like a deer in the headlights, I never really saw the truck until it hit me.

"Dad, if I tell you something, will you get mad?"

Trying to hide my uneasiness over the question, I replied in a confident voice, "Of course not, what's up?"

"Well, a boy in the band asked me to go out."

I thought that I'd been preparing for this moment for most of Erin's life. When she was little, I envisioned myself like some cartoon character, sitting in a rocking chair on the front porch, holding a shotgun. I had rehearsed a number of responses, but they always sounded like things you'd say to someone who was trying to rob you. So it was a bit of a surprise when I opened my mouth and heard not a hysterical rant, but a soft and steady voice.

"Is he a nice guy?"

"Yes," replied Erin, "he's really nice."

"Is he respectful?" I asked, feeling like I was making progress.

"Very."

That's when I should have stopped. If I had, I would never have exposed myself as the Neanderthal that I was. But I didn't stop. Instead, I asked what I thought was the next logical question, having heard Erin say that the boy had asked her to "go out".

"Where does he want to go?"

Erin did an admirable job of keeping herself from laughing out loud. She smiled patiently and explained that I may have missed the meaning of the term "go out".

"I think in your day, you would have called it 'going steady'," Erin explained.

Despite feeling a rush of embarrassment wash over me, I tried to maintain what little bit of poise I had left. I put my arm around Erin and chuckled.

"Sorry. I guess I'm a little out of practice. Well, if you're going to 'go out', will you promise me one thing?"

"Daddy!" she exclaimed, reading more into the question than I had intended.

"No, no..." I smiled. "Will you promise to come and talk to me if your heart gets broken?"

Erin relaxed and grinned, "Sure, Dad."

We drove home that night in the silence that only good friends can comfortably share. Erin came to talk to me often over the next eight years, but never with a broken heart.

A few days before Christmas during her senior year of college, Erin came home and we sat up late talking like we had done so often over the years. She was student teaching that semester, and she had story after story about the kids. She was as happy as I ever remember seeing her. After telling another story, Erin took a sip of water and leaned forward.

"Daddy, if I tell you something will you get mad?"

The question took me back to the high school parking lot, with Erin in her marching band uniform. I looked at her and smiled.

"I doubt it, what's up?"

"Well, a boy in the band asked me to marry him."

I thought I'd been preparing myself for this moment for the last eight years. This time, when I opened my mouth, a soft but somewhat less steady voice emerged.

"Is he a nice guy?" I whispered.

Erin brushed a tear from her eye and laughed out loud. With a catch in her voice, she said, "Yes, Dad, he's really nice."

"Is he respectful?" I asked, now choking up a bit myself.

Erin started to answer, but no words came out. She just nodded her head. I moved over to the couch, sat beside her, and held her tightly in my arms. I kissed her forehead and whispered into her ear, "Be happy."

At that moment, I realized that I had learned one of life's most important lessons. It was something that Annie knew long before I did. I had learned when to hold on tightly, and when to let go.

Erin asked Emily to be her maid of honor, and they immediately decided that it would be fun to look for their dresses in London. Annie must have seen the stricken look on my face, even thought I hadn't said a word. She pulled me aside and reminded me that it was Emily, not Erin, who had an eye for expensive fashion. It was right about then that I heard Emily exclaim, "Remember that dress that Diana wore when she married Prince Charles?" and I knew that I was finished.

In the two months since Erin's graduation, wedding plans had taken on the scope of the Allied invasion of Normandy. Eisenhower made fewer decisions conquering a continent than seemed to be involved with organizing a three-hour dinner party for two hundred people. The wedding was planned for next June, almost a year away. With June 6th falling on a Saturday, I said it would be entirely appropriate to choose D-Day. I felt like a German looking out over the English Channel…I wasn't sure when, but the invasion was coming.

Flowers went from white to yellow then back to white. Centerpieces would be cut flowers, then silk flowers, then seedlings that could be transplanted to create a rain forest. A white limousine became a black limousine, then like a scene from Cinderella, it was transformed into a white carriage drawn by gray houses. An eight piece jazz ensemble gave way to a 1940s era big band, which in turn was dumped in favor of a twenty-five-member orchestra, complete with strings. At one point, I even thought I caught Emily looking at the website for the New York Philharmonic.

Less than a week ago, the plans changed rather suddenly. Instead of a date sometime next June, the wedding is now set for this Christmas. Annie said it would be a wonderful Christmas present. She even suggested that I wear a red tie with my tuxedo. How I would look escorting Erin up the aisle was a big topic of conversation when the wedding was moved up to Christmas.

Next June had seemed like a long way off. In one sense, it was too long, because with every passing day, limousines changed into horse-drawn carriages and ice sculptures changed into topiary gardens. There seemed to be no limit to what the girls could dream up with a year to think about it. So when the wedding was moved up to Christmas, part of me was relieved. The rest of me hopes that I make it until then.

Chapter 10

1:43 P.M.

I PICKED UP MY SUIT jacket and slung it over my shoulder as I left the bench and walked across the old playground toward the church. People would be arriving soon, and it was too hot to spend much more time outside in the sun. As I rounded the corner of the school, I noticed that there were a few more cars in the parking lot. The church wouldn't be full for Father Tim's funeral, but at least it wouldn't be empty.

Entering the church, I was immediately struck by how really beautiful old churches are. The center aisle stretched out for what looked like a quarter of a mile. The pews were dark, with years of varnish built up on the hand-carved wood. The ceiling was arched, three or four stories high, with heavy wooden beams reaching up each side, meeting in the middle.

The ceiling of St. Basil's was pale blue, but it gradually worked its way to a rich royal blue over the sanctuary and altar. High on the back wall of the church was a wooden crucifix, carved one hundred years ago by an artist more interested in immortality than money. Along each of the sidewalls were a series of stained glass windows, each one depicting one of the twelve stations of the cross. The glass was stained in deep colors that resonated when the sun dropped low in the sky and cast its light directly upon them. There is no such thing as a good place to be dead, but as a place for Father Tim's send off, St Basil's was magnificent.

The floor was tile, and no matter how softly you walked, your footsteps echoed, for the church was always very quiet unless Mass was underway. If you walked halfway to the altar and turned around to face the rear of the church, you were overwhelmed by the massive pipe organ in the loft overhead. A pipe organ is the dinosaur of the music world. Bigger and more powerful than anything that came before or after it, the pipe organ will stop you in your tracks when you see or hear it. Not many exist in the modern world; they have been replaced by smaller electronic organs, which are less costly to purchase and easier to maintain. Electronic organs would satisfy you entirely if you had never heard a pipe organ.

Pipe organs work by using large bellows to force air through pipes of varying length and diameter; the taller and wider the pipe, the lower the sound. The smallest pipes (making the highest notes) are only a few inches long and about the diameter of a soda straw. The largest pipes reach from the floor to the ceiling and are difficult to wrap your arms around. The wall of sound created by a ninety pound grandmother sitting at the keyboard of a pipe organ is overwhelming.

I dipped my fingertips into the porcelain bowl of holy water and made the Sign of the Cross. The theology of holy water was lost on me a long time ago. Symbolically, the water is meant to represent a cleansing of one's soul or conscience, a form of renewing your baptism. I studied science after leaving St. Basil's and scientists often find blind faith difficult to accept. We are trained to observe, measure, and analyze. There is nothing scientific about holy water. If you put it beneath a microscope, tested it chemically, or measured its boiling point, you would conclude that it was indistinguishable from ordinary water. Yet Catholics, both scientists and artists alike, dip their fingertips into holy water and trust that their souls or their consciences will be cleansed. On this trip back to St. Basil's, I felt like there was no downside to believing.

The church was largely empty. There were thirty or forty people scattered throughout the pews, but such a small congregation in such an immense space was easily swallowed up and virtually disappeared. About a dozen pews back from the altar, off to the left side of the center aisle, I recognized the silhouette of a familiar figure – it was Pinhead. I made my way as quietly as the tiled floor would allow, genuflected at the edge of the pew, slid in next to Pinhead, and sat down.

He turned and smiled widely when he saw me, then without saying a word, he stuck out his hand. My hand disappeared into Pinhead's as we greeted one another for the first time in over twenty years. The last time I had seen him was at my father's funeral. Pinhead was living in one of the Dakotas back then, but when he heard of my father's passing, he came immediately. I felt bad about losing touch with the guys from the neighborhood, but none more so than Pinhead. He left for a job in the Dakotas while I was in medical school and we just eased away from each other. If my mother hadn't called to tell me of Father Tim's passing, I would have never known. When I decided to come back for the funeral I wondered who might be here. I hoped Pinhead would make it back, still thinking he was off in the Black Hills somewhere.

Pinhead whispered, "How've you been, Mike?"

"Fine, Pinhead, how about you?"

"I've been great. Got a new job teaching P.E. and coaching basketball at Gompers Junior High."

He smiled when I looked at him with my eyes as wide as saucers. I never would have guessed that Pinhead would move back to the old neighborhood to teach, but then I never would have bet against it either.

"How long have you been back?" I asked.

"Two years. I got tired of clean air and crickets, so I came back to car horns and cockroaches."

"Married?"

"Nah, no one would have me."

Pinhead told me that he had spent a lot of time with Father Tim in the two years since he'd come back. He volunteered as a mentor to kids who Father Tim thought needed a strong role model. As Father Tim's health had begun to fail, Pinhead began stopping by for meals now and then, and to sit with the old priest in the evenings when it could be lonely for someone who was dying.

"How was he toward the end?" I asked.

"He never let on that things were bad, but you could tell they were," answered Pinhead. "He still had his sense of humor right up until the very end."

"Did he seem afraid to die?" I asked.

"No. He was in no hurry, but he wasn't afraid at all. He said he'd irritated nearly everyone he'd hoped to down here, and he was now ready to irritate St. Peter."

"Was he alone when he passed away?" I asked.

"I think so," Pinhead replied. "I had dinner with him that evening, and he seemed a little more tired than usual. We talked a bit, but he would get quiet and close his eyes between stories. When it seemed like our visit was keeping him from resting, I patted his hand and told him I'd see him next week. I thought he was asleep when I got up to leave, but when I got to the door, he called out in a quiet voice 'Walter' – it caught me by surprise, because he almost never called me by my real name – I stopped in the doorway and turned back. Father Tim asked 'do you think the boys knew how much I enjoyed coaching basketball?'. I didn't know how to respond, so I said, 'Yes, Father, I think they did...but I wish we would have won a game for you'. He smiled and said 'Basketball wasn't the real game, Walter – that was never the real game'. I smiled back and said, 'Goodnight, Father', and he whispered 'God bless you, Walter'. That was the last time I saw him. He passed quietly in his sleep that night."

I sat for a while without saying anything. Pinhead and I just sat there together, neither of us saying anything for several minutes.

"Do you think any of the other guys will come?" I asked.

"I don't think so," replied Pinhead. "It's not that they wouldn't want to, but they've scattered."

One by one, Pinhead told me what he knew of the whereabouts of the old gang.

"Joe the Bum's father lost his job at the sewage treatment plant when the mayor lost his re-election campaign back in 1979. They moved out to California where Joe's uncle owned a car dealership. Joe's dad got a job selling cars but talk is he did the same thing he did here – he drove back and forth a lot but didn't do much work...only now he always drove a new car."

"What about Joe?"

"He met a girl who was almost as pretty as him, and her old man was loaded. He owned a string of transmission repair shops that specialized in vintage cars – cleaned up on the rich guys with the movie star cars."

"Did he marry her?"

"Absolutely. He got a job working for her father. He started out working on cars, but you know Joe. Work gives him a rash. So now he drives around between shops and tries to stay out of the way. Mostly, I think he takes daddy's daughter to movie premieres and parties."

"The apple doesn't fall far from the tree," I grinned.

"Remember the crush Fat Peter had on Wendy McGinnis?" asked Pinhead.

"Remember the four foot rabbit on Valentine's Day?" I answered.

Fat Peter had a crush on Wendy McGinnis in eighth grade. Wendy was a very cute girl who had beautiful red hair that fell down to her shoulders in spiraling curls. She was as nice as she was cute, and it seemed like everyone had a crush on her. Fat Peter wanted to do something romantic for Valentine's Day because he was trying to compete with Francis Gandolini, the son of the neighborhood butcher.

Francis Gandolini was disturbed. He had been "held back" twice so he was nearly sixteen and was about to become the first kid to drive himself to school at St. Basil's. The nuns had flunked Francis twice, once because he was stupid and once because they were convinced that he was a lunatic. They apparently thought that they could protect the rest of the world from Francis if they just kept flunking him so that he could never leave.

In seventh and eighth grades, it was a popular pastime for guys to catch flies in their bare hands. If a fly landed on your desk and you cupped your hand behind it and swept your arm forward rapidly, aiming not at the fly but just above it, where it would go when it saw your hand with it's beady little compound eyes, you could snatch it out of mid-air. When the weather turned warm, every time the nun turned her back on the class, twenty guys would be flailing at their desks, trying to catch flies. You couldn't be certain that you caught a fly, because there's no weight in your hand to feel. If you didn't see or hear it fly away, you would hold your closed fist up to your ear to see if you could hear the fly buzzing inside.

So the classroom looked like a ballet every time the nun turned to write on the blackboard. Twenty arms would swing forward in unison, and then twenty fists would be raised to the sides of heads. If you caught a fly, the best thing to do with it was to turn to one of the girls and hold out your arm. Turning your closed fist upward, you opened your fingers slowly and released the fly over the girl's desk. Since prehistoric times, men have set forth in pursuit of big game and returned to the women of their villages with their catches.

Francis Gandolini was particularly adept at catching flies. It's probably because he had so much practice hanging around his father's butcher shop. It wasn't his prowess catching flies that set Francis apart, however, it was what he did with them after he caught them. Francis would snatch a fly from the air and stand up at his desk and fling the fly down onto his desktop. The fly would hit the desk before it could take off, and the collision would temporarily stun it. It would lie on Francis' desk as if it was dead but then after a moment or two it would begin walking around and eventually fly off. No studies have been done to verify that flies have headaches, but it would stand to reason that hitting a wooden desk at the human scale equivalent of 200 mph would have a fly looking for an aspirin when it finally staggered to its feet and flew away.

Watching Francis hopping out of his seat and hurling flies at his desk several times a day was disturbing in itself, but he got everyone's attention when he went one step further. It happened one day when a substitute teacher sat in for Sister Benedict, who was having a wisdom tooth pulled. A substitute teacher at St. Basil's meant a neighborhood volunteer who came in and sat at Sister's desk all day while the class shot spitballs through straws and sailed paper airplanes through the air like a busy afternoon over an airport.

Francis began by taking a length of red thread that he had unwound from one of the buttons on his sweater and stretching the thread out across the top of his desk. He then waited patiently for a fly to land in his vicinity. Scientists could confirm that flies do not communicate by noting that they continued landing on Francis's desk. If flies had even a rudimentary form of communication, the airspace over Francis's desk would have been designated as a no-fly zone.

Creeping up behind the fly, Francis swiped his hand forward and in one single motion, rose to his feet and hurled the unsuspecting fly against the top of his desk. Predictably, the comatose fly lay still while Francis quickly grabbed the red thread, made a loop, and encircled the fly's abdomen, gently tugging the thread into a knot around the fly's midsection. Francis then sat patiently, the end of the thread pinched between his thumb and forefinger, and waited for the fly to wake up. In a few minutes, the fly began walking unsteadily across Francis's desk, turning each time it reached the end of the thread.

After several more minutes, the fly regained its senses sufficiently to launch itself into the air, to the delight of Francis. As the fly became airborne, it flew in tight circles, held in check by the thread. Heads began to turn and whispers turned into snickers as the class watched Francis sitting at his desk with a "fly kite" buzzing in a circle over his desk. Distracted by his newfound celebrity, Francis let go of the thread and the fly buzzed off, trailing the length of red thread behind it. It buzzed back and forth overhead, probably trying to clear its head from the coma. With each pass, the fly dragged the thread behind it and Francis began lurching and grasping in an attempt to recapture his circus act.

Had Sister Benedict been in the classroom and not in a dentist's chair, the mayhem would have ended quickly. With Kenny Baldwin's mom sitting at the teacher's desk with her mouth hanging open, however, Francis hopped from desk to desk trying desperately to snag the thread each time it flew past. Finally, the fly's compound eyes must have focused, because it flew in a straight line for the window and with a final bank of its wings in a salute to Francis, it was gone. Francis returned to his desk and began fumbling around with the only remaining button on his sweater.

Wendy McGinnis was not interested in Francis but neither Francis nor Fat Peter knew that. As Valentine's Day approached, Fat Peter was desperate to do something to let Wendy know how much he liked her. He pestered us to ride the bus with him to a place where he had heard you could buy a four foot stuffed rabbit; he was sure he could win Wendy's heart with the over-sized rodent. Complaining the entire way, Pinhead and I had accompanied Fat Peter to a run-down store in a rough neighborhood where neither of us would have agreed to go had we known where he was headed. Emptying his pockets, Fat Peter bought the bright yellow rabbit, which, when you counted its ears, was nearly as tall as he was.

Standing at the bus stop, Pinhead said we should take the bus that made a connection but took a route through safer neighborhoods. Fat Peter complained that he had barely enough money to make it back on the bus we had come on...he didn't have enough for a transfer. Pinhead and I had enough for transfers, but not enough to cover Fat Peter. Rather than leave him behind with his stuffed rabbit, we decided to ride through the rough part of town with him.

When the bus came, we all climbed on. Fat Peter laid the rabbit on the seat beside him, next to the window. Pinhead sat across the aisle and I sat down behind Fat Peter. We had only gone a few blocks when we came to a stoplight and I noticed three gang bangers on the sidewalk pointing at the window where Fat Peter's rabbit ears stuck up above the seat. No one called them gang bangers back then, because the crime was not yet organized, but these guys were bad news. Sensing trouble, I told Fat Peter to put the rabbit on the floor. He refused, saying it would get the rabbit all dirty. Another block and another stoplight and things went from bad to worse. The three guys had run up the street alongside the bus and now a fourth guy had joined them. They were laughing and pointing at the window next to Fat Peter's seat.

Halfway up the next block was a bus stop. When the driver opened the door, one of the thugs stepped in and began digging in his pockets, acting as if he was searching for the fare to pay the driver. A second co-conspirator slid behind the first and walked straight over to where Fat Peter sat. Saying nothing, he looked at Fat Peter, then at the rabbit. He reached across Fat Peter's seat and grabbed the rabbit by the ears. Without a word, he returned to the front of the bus and stepped back out onto the sidewalk. His partner in crime mumbled something to the driver and stepped off the bus as the doors closed. Just that quick, without so much as a word being said by any of us, the rabbit had been kidnapped and was on its way down the sidewalk in the opposite direction.

On Valentine's Day, Fat Peter explained what had happened to Wendy, but he was sure that he had lost out to Francis, who had brought her a valentine package wrapped in white butcher paper. Francis confidently walked up to Wendy and handed her his package. She opened the stiff white paper and unwrapped the package to find a sheep's heart that Francis had brought from his dad's butcher shop. Wendy screamed, dropped the "valentine", and asked Fat Peter to walk her home.

"What ever happened to Wendy?" I asked Pinhead.

"She married Fat Peter," he replied. "Fat Peter went to law school out east somewhere and he's a judge now in Virginia or North Carolina."

"Justice served," I said.

"After Duke Noonan passed away, Danny sold the old house and invested the money in a McDonald's franchise. In order to get a franchise, he had to take one out in Idaho. He now owns six of them and makes about three quarters of a million dollars a year."

Pinhead paused before continuing, almost as if he was reluctant to say what he was thinking. He lowered his voice even further and continued.

"Terrible thing that happened to Whitey."

"What happened?" I asked, a sick feeling growing in the pit of my stomach.

"He had relatives in Oklahoma," Pinhead explained. "He went out there after high school and got a job working for the government. Had something to do with Indian reservations, I think. Anyway, he had done pretty well, had an office job, and was supervising a whole lot of people."

"So what happened?" I repeated, feeling myself getting more and more nervous.

"He died when that asshole blew up the Oklahoma City Federal Building."

We sat in silence for what felt like a very long time.

"Ever hear anything about Lou the Screw?" I asked, trying to change the subject.

"Father Tim talked about him a lot," said Pinhead. "Always had a soft spot for Lou ever since he had that fit in basketball."

"Is Lou alright?" I asked, fearing the worst.

"He lived with his parents until they both died. Then he went to live for a while with an aunt or a cousin out west. I heard he's living in one of those group homes where you go when you need someone to look after you."

We hadn't talked about Cuckoo, and I was almost afraid to ask. Accident prone from the first day I met him, Cuckoo was the one I had been most worried about. Pinhead always had a knack for knowing what I was thinking. Now was no exception.

"He's ok," Pinhead said in a quiet voice.

"Who's ok?" I replied, turning my head.

"Cuckoo. He's ok."

"Who said he wasn't?"

"I know you were worried."

"I wasn't worried."

"He's ok."

"What's he up to?"

"He got a scholarship. Went to Georgetown. Got a degree in anthropology or archaeology or something."

"What the hell do you do with a degree in archaeology?"

"He went on to school. He's an optometrist."

"An OPTOMETRIST??!" I said, much louder than I intended.

"Yeah, an optometrist. Now Cuckoo makes money whenever some kid breaks his glasses."

Pinhead and I laughed out loud, then sat back in the pew and spent a few minutes not saying anything at all. The news of what had become of the guys and the reality that Father Tim was dead took a few moments to sink in. As we sat together without talking, a faintly familiar scent wafted past my nostrils. It was a sweet smell, almost too sweet a smell. I turned and looked at Pinhead and he turned and looked at me. We had both smelled it at exactly the same time.

We smiled at each other and both whispered simultaneously... "incense".

Chapter 11

WEDDINGS ALMOST ALWAYS COME ON Saturdays, which must explain where the custom of tipping altar boys came from. People felt bad about making two juvenile delinquents come in on a Saturday to serve Mass, so they came up with a little something for the effort. It was customary for the best man to slip five dollars to each of the altar boys after a wedding Mass. If it wasn't guilt over ruining a Saturday, it might have been attempted bribery, hoping to discourage us from doing something completely insane to ruin the solemn occasion. Whatever the reason, five dollars was a lot of money to a kid in seventh grade, and even though we'd have liked to be playing rockball with the guys, Pinhead and I knew where our bread was buttered.

We were serving Mass for a wedding on the hottest day of the summer. Father Tim told Pinhead to prop open the back door to the sacristy, which is the vestibule behind the altar out of view from the congregation where the priest and altar boys don their robes. It is also where the church keeps its supplies for Mass.

In the cabinets of the sacristy were candles of all shapes and sizes and wicker baskets on long wooden poles that the Knights of Columbus used to collect donations from parishioners during the offertory portion of the Mass. From a theological perspective, the offertory portion of the Mass refers to the section of the liturgy during which the priest "offers up" to God the bread and wine in the hope that God will see fit to convert it into the body and blood of Jesus...not literally, of course. That may have been where the "offertory" section of the Mass originally came from, but in the real world, "offertory" meant that the Knights of Columbus stuck those wicker baskets on long wooden poles in your face as you sat in the pew to see what you personally had to offer financially. If you were a little short that week and didn't put anything into the basket, the Knight of Columbus might bean you with the basket on his next pass. Some guys tried faking the donation, making a motion toward the basket with their hand as it passed without actually putting anything in. The Knights of Columbus must have gone through some wicker basket basic training though, because they could tell when you faked a toss. Then they would pause, holding the basket in front of you for long enough so that everyone could see that you weren't coughing up...it was better to just take your beaning like a man.

Between the candles and the wicker collection baskets in the sacristy cabinet were a box of charcoal and a metal canister of incense. For special occasions, like Christmas or Easter Mass, or for weddings and funerals, Mass included ceremonial blessings involving incense. The priest held a golden urn that was suspended from a heavy chain. The urn was comprised of two halves; the top separated from the bottom and slid up the chain, allowing the altar boys to sprinkle incense onto hot charcoal, causing the incense to smolder. When the two halves of the urn were re-coupled, sweet smelling smoke escaped through holes in the top of the urn.

The priest would move about the church or the altar carrying the smoking urn, swinging it back and forth, reciting incantations from the twelfth century. It was quite a production. No one understood the incantations, because they were all in Latin, but the solemnity of the moment was not lost on anyone. When the incantations were completed, the priest handed the still-smoking urn to an altar boy, who carried it out through the sacristy and emptied its contents outside behind the church, where the remainder of the smoldering incense could burn away harmlessly. Once he had safely disposed of the sacramental smudgepot, the altar boy returned to the sanctuary to rejoin the proceedings.

The wedding that hot day in June was Pinhead's first time preparing the incense and disposing of it afterward. In the sacristy before the ceremony, Pinhead carefully placed the charcoal squares into the golden urn, and filled the small companion bowl with granular incense. As the organ music began, Pinhead grabbed the urn and the incense bowl and followed Father Tim out toward the altar.

The church was nearly full, as both the bride and the groom were from the neighborhood. The bride made her way up the long center aisle of the church while the groom fidgeted nervously at the altar with Father Tim. Standing confidently alongside them was Pinhead, urn in one hand, incense in the other. When the bride reached the altar, Father Tim read a long passage in Latin from an enormous leather-bound book that I held while standing in front of him. Closing the book, Father Tim turned to Pinhead and took the urn containing the charcoal, which was glowing red inside. Father Tim slid the top of the urn up the chain and held the urn out so that Pinhead could sprinkle incense onto the coals.

Ordinarily, the small golden incense bowl has a small golden spoon in it. The spoon is smaller than a teaspoon, and is used to extract just a tiny amount of incense to sprinkle over the glowing coals in the urn. Whether the oppressive heat had distracted Father Tim or he just had his mind on something else, he didn't notice that Pinhead had the incense bowl but no spoon to dip into it. Pinhead wasn't aware of any spoon. He had never done this before. So when Father Tim slid the top of the urn up the chain, Pinhead dumped the entire contents of the incense bowl onto the coals. Immediately, a large cloud of gray smoke billowed out of the urn. Father Tim stared dumbstruck before gathering himself and moving away from the groom and the bride, who was now coughing like a tuberculosis patient.

Father Tim fairly ran around the altar, an expanding cloud of sickeningly sweet smoke following behind him. He cut his incantations short and handed Pinhead the urn, which was Pinhead's cue to remove it outside. Pinhead just stood there, forgetting that he was supposed to leave or perhaps just overcome by the smoke. Father Tim took Pinhead gently by the shoulder, turned him slowly toward the sacristy door, then gave him a shove between the shoulder blades that made Pinhead's head jerk back.

Pinhead left the altar, stumbled into the sacristy and staggered toward the back door. He then compounded the comedy of errors with one more miscue. Instead of emptying the coals and incense onto the ground, Pinhead merely set the intact urn on the sidewalk just outside the back door that Father Tim had propped open when we arrived. Because Pinhead had dumped enough incense onto the coals for ten weddings, the urn just kept billowing smoke. With the door propped open, a strong breeze was blowing into the sacristy, and it carried the noxious fumes right along with it. Pinhead returned to the church, where the smoke had thinned out just enough that you could barely make out the figures of the bride and groom standing at the altar. He flashed a confident look at Father Tim and gave him a "thumbs up" signal.

Right about then, the cumulus cloud of incense smoke from the back door rolled out of the sacristy and into the church, triggering another spastic fit of coughing by the bride, whose white dress was now a pale shade of sooty gray. Saying nothing, Father Tim raced off the altar, his robes flowing, and ran into the sacristy at a full sprint. He fought his way through the smoke, found the urn, and knocked it over into the gravel behind the church. Removing the prop that was holding the door open, he closed the back door and made his way back to the altar.

I have never seen Father Tim marry two people as quickly as he did these two once he got back to the altar. When the groom kissed the bride, Father Tim motioned frantically to the organist up in the choir loft, who began playing the recessional march at twice its normal tempo. Outside the church, neighbors had lined the steps holding handfuls of rice to throw in celebration. When the large wooden doors of the church opened, smoke billowed out and the people lining the steps dropped their rice and covered their noses and eyes. The bride and groom took the steps two at a time, ducked into their waiting car, and were gone before the first row of guests had exited the church.

You learned to be an altar boy when you reached fifth grade at St. Basil's. Father Tim would gather all of the fifth grade boys together and take them over to the church to learn the choreography of the Catholic Mass. There was much to learn…when to stand, when to sit, where to be when, how to pour water and wine into the chalice without dumping it onto the floor…and then there was the Latin.

Prior to Vatican II, a global conference of bishops convened in 1962 for the purpose of bringing Catholicism out of the Dark Ages and into the seventeenth century, the entire Mass was conducted in Latin. To make matters even worse, the priest said the Mass facing an altar set against the back wall of the church, so that his back was turned to the congregation the entire time. It was hard to feel intimately involved in the proceedings when the priest faced away from you and chanted in a language that no civilization had actually spoken for a thousand years.

In order to serve Mass, altar boys had to learn the prayers in Latin. You learned them phonetically, so that you could say something that sounded religious in response to the priest. No one ever bothered to learn what any of the words in Latin actually meant. The first time I served Mass it was with Fat Peter. At the beginning of the service, the priest and the altar boys knelt down facing the altar and recited a series of mysterious Latin incantations. The priest would say something and the altar boys were supposed to repeat it back to him.

"Kyrie Eleison," cantered Father Tim.

"Kyrie Eleison," answered Fat Peter.
"Christie Eleison," offered Father Tim.
"Christie Eleison," replied Fat Peter.
"Kyrie Eleison," concluded Father Tim.
"Caveat emptor," said Fat Peter, a confused look on his face.

Catholics have an inordinate number of saints. Saints are people who were singled out for some miraculous achievement during their lives and who became destined to have churches or days off school named in their honor. Some saints are household names, like St. Peter or St. Patrick. Others are more obscure, like St. Aloysius. Patron saints have their names associated with particular groups of people or causes. St. Joseph is the patron saint of carpenters and St. Jude is the patron saint of lost causes.

St. Christopher was the patron saint of travelers. When we were kids, nearly everyone's parents had a little plastic statue of St. Christopher with a tiny magnet in its base that they used to stick the statue to their dashboard. It was not uncommon to see a broken down car being towed away, with a St. Christopher statue still standing vigil in the windshield. The tow truck had fuzzy dice or a lady's garter hanging where the St. Christopher statue should have been.

Sometime in the last twenty years, the Catholic Church revoked St. Christopher's halo. He was originally canonized because he had performed a miracle, saving a child by carrying him on his shoulder across some dangerous body of water. I never heard exactly why they threw Christopher out of the saints' club. It may have been that someone found out that the water that he crossed was only a foot deep, or that too many cars that his statues were blessing needed to be towed by trucks with ladies' garters hanging from their mirrors.

Once each year, we would celebrate the feast of one of the Church's most obscure saints, who was the patron of one of the most obscure causes: St. Blaise, the patron saint of choking. It would seem more appropriate (or at least more optimistic) if St. Blaise was the patron saint of NOT choking, but something may have been lost over the centuries in translation.

It seems that somewhere in the eleventh or twelfth century, St. Blaise (presumably known to his friends simply as "Blaise" at the time) stumbled across a child who was choking on a fishbone. Eight hundred years before

Dr. Von Heimlich perfected his "maneuver", St. Blaise slapped the choking victim on the back and dislodged the fishbone from his throat in the nick of time. Apparently, villagers were so awestruck by the miracle (evidently up until that time anyone swallowing a fishbone invariably died) that they carried Blaise around the town square on their shoulders and subsequently named a church after him. From that point on, school children were allowed to stay home on the anniversary of the day when the fortunate victim coughed up the fishbone.

Nearly nine centuries later, parishioners at St. Basil's lined up to have their throats blessed on the feast of St. Blaise. Over time, as the risk of choking on a fishbone diminished but people partial to St. Blaise still wanted to celebrate his day, the blessing of the throat was credited with everything from preventing cancer to curtailing profanity. Desperate to have holy Adam's Apples, devout observers lined the aisles of the church once each year.

The blessing of throats involved a symbolic apparatus that consisted of two holy candles crossed in the shape of a "V". They were tied together with holy ribbon and sprinkled with holy water. An altar boy would slide the candles along the outsides of the parishioner's neck, bringing the point at which the candles crossed into contact with the person's throat. Father Tim would recite a prayer that went something like, "may the blessing of St. Blaise, patron saint of chokers, descend upon you and prevent you from wedging food or other airway obstructions into your windpipe now and forever." The person with the newly blessed throat would dutifully answer, "Amen".

Whenever one of our friends knelt down to receive the blessing of St. Blaise, we would jam the candles against their throats so tightly that if they got out an "Amen" at all, it was two octaves higher than normal. Father Tim knew what was going on, because he would occasionally stifle a chuckle when he heard Joe the Bum's voice crack on his "Amen". Something told us that Father Tim was as amused by the feast of St. Blaise as the rest of us.

In the sacristy cabinets, along with the candles, the wicker baskets, the charcoal, and the incense, was a five-gallon jug of red wine. Before it was turned into the blood of Christ during Mass, the wine was just wine. One afternoon after school, Joe the Bum, Pinhead, and I were hanging up the cassocks that had just come back from the dry cleaners when Joe spotted the jug of wine.

"Hey guys, look," he whispered.

Before we realized what he was up to, Joe had taken the jug down from the cabinet and was rummaging around looking for paper cups near the sink.

"Let's try some," said Joe, pouring wine into three paper cups.

There was no one around, so we figured it couldn't hurt to satisfy our curiosity. One sip of the wine and we all grimaced. It was bitter and tasted like you would expect wine to taste when it came in a five-gallon jug with a metal screw cap. No one was very anxious to finish their paper cup of vinegar, so we started toward the sink to pour the rest down the drain. Before we reached the sink, Sister Pius walked into the sacristy carrying an armload of cassocks on hangers. Seeing us holding paper cups, her eyes darted to the counter and to the open jug of wine. Her face clouded over and she laid the cassocks down on a small table. Without saying anything, she took the cups from our hands, held one up to her nose and went straight to the sink, where she poured the contents and ran the faucet. Barely able to contain her anger, Sister Pius took Joe and Pinhead by the elbows and pulled them with her to a group of chairs near the door.

"Sit here and do not move," she growled. "I am calling your parents and they will come to get you."

She turned toward me and pointed to an empty chair.

"You too."

We sat there for almost an hour before Sister Pius returned. She was carrying a dripping umbrella. It was pouring rain. Riveting Joe the Bum and Pinhead with her stare, she said, "You two boys come with me. Your parents are in my office." Stopping at the doorway, she turned to me and said, "I was unable to reach your mother, Michael; you will have to see Father Tim."

I wasn't sure whether I felt worse about my parents finding out or Father Tim. My parents would be angry...Father Tim would be disappointed. Sister Pius, Joe the Bum, and Pinhead left through the side door of the sacristy and headed toward the school. Sister Pius walked ahead of Joe and Pinhead, who half walked and half ran, in part to keep up with Sister Pius and in part to avoid the rain. It was another half hour before I heard the door creak open and saw Father Tim standing outside in the rain holding an umbrella.

"C'mon Michael, I'll walk you home."

I stood up and felt my legs wobble. Taking slow, deliberate steps, I made my way to the door, preparing myself for the scolding that I knew was coming. Father Tim leaned forward, bringing the umbrella closer, and pulled the door closed behind me. We started walking down the sidewalk toward the gate, Father Tim taking small steps to be sure the umbrella covered me.

"How have things been going in school?" Father Tim asked.

"Okay, I guess," I answered, wondering if it was a trick question.

"Have you thought of what you'd like to become when you're older, Michael?"

"Not really, Father."

"Well, it's not so important that you know just yet. Whatever it is that you decide to do, Michael, you'll do it well."

We walked a bit further toward my house, moving to the side of the pavement to avoid a puddle. Father Tim put his hand on my shoulder, in part to pull me under the umbrella, and in part as a gesture of reassurance.

"What do you think your parents would say about today?"

"I don't think they'd say anything," I answered tentatively.

"Nothing?"

"No. I just think they'd start belting me."

Father Tim chuckled and tousled my hair. We turned the corner and walked the half block to my house. All the way home I had hoped that my folks would be gone when we got there, but I knew that wouldn't happen... they were always home at this time of the evening. When we reached the steps to my front porch, Father Tim paused. Instead of climbing the stairs and ringing the doorbell, Father Tim just stood in the rain holding the umbrella, silhouetted against the streetlight behind him. Beads of water fell from each spine of the umbrella's frame.

"Do your homework, Michael."

"Father?"

"It's getting late. Be sure that you do your homework."

"Aren't you going to talk to my parents?"

"I talked to you."

It was true, he had talked to me all the way home, but he hadn't said a word about the wine except to ask me how my parents would take the news. I was completely unprepared for Father Tim to leave without telling my parents what had happened.

"Father, why aren't you mad?"

"It's impossible never to do anything wrong, Michael. What's important is that you recognize wrong when you see it."

Leaving me standing beneath the roof of our front porch, Father Tim backed out into the rain, now able to hold his umbrella comfortably over his own head. He gave me a smile and said, "We'll see you tomorrow, Michael. Tomorrow's another day."

He turned and walked through the soggy front yard to the sidewalk and started back up the street from where we had come. I turned to go into the house, but stopped when I heard his voice.

"Michael..."

"Yes Father?"

"Did you think that the first time I ever tasted wine was when I was saying Mass?"

Not waiting for an answer, Father Tim gave a brief wave of his hand and disappeared into the gloom. There would never be another rainy night when I wouldn't think of him.

Chapter 12

3:55 P.M.

SMELLING THE INCENSE, I WAS about to make a crack about Pinhead smoking the bride and groom out of their wedding back when we were kids, but I was interrupted by a quiet commotion at the back of the church. Turning to look over our shoulders, we could see two men in black suits wheeling a casket into the church from outside. A third man, also wearing a black suit, was escorting an elderly lady up the long center aisle toward the altar. She walked slowly, with one hand looped through the man's arm and a cane in her other hand. She looked vaguely familiar, but I couldn't place her as any of the ladies from the old neighborhood. A few wisps of silver hair swept across her forehead. She was tall and graceful, even though her gait had been slowed by age. I glanced at Pinhead to see if he recognized this mysterious older woman. He seemed to be struggling as much as I was.

When the couple drew within a few rows of pews from the spot where we were sitting, I immediately recognized the soft features behind the simple gold-rimmed eyeglasses. It was Sister Thomas Aquinas. The last time I had seen her, she had been in her early thirties. It's funny how we somehow expect to see people the way we last saw them, making no mental adjustments for years or even decades in between. Sister Thomas Aquinas had aged gracefully, but watching her make her way up the aisle with a cane stood in stark contrast to memories of her playing softball on the playground, holding the pleats of her habit in her hands as she ran the bases.

Sister Thomas Aquinas was our first teacher at St. Basil's. Since we had Sister Thomas Aquinas for both first and second grades, we got to know her better than any other teacher we ever had. Sometimes it seemed like Sister was more of a kid than a nun. She would join in games at recess, tell corny jokes, sing in class, and generally act more like us than like the older nuns. It was as though someone had forgotten to tell her that she was supposed to be mean to us.

As we got older, Sister Thomas Aquinas seemed to stay interested in how we were doing. She would stop us in the halls or on the playground and ask us how we were doing in fourth or sixth grade. There was something special about the way she asked – you could tell that she really cared. My last memory of Sister Thomas Aquinas was of something that happened just before we graduated from St. Basil's.

In eighth grade, we had a spelling bee. Everyone lined up around the perimeter of the room, leaning against the walls. Sister Catherine, our eighth grade teacher, would read a word and if it was your turn, you repeated the word, spelled it, then repeated it again. If you were correct, you remained standing. If you were wrong, you sat down. Like the gunfight at the O.K. Corral, the last one standing won.

Things started out innocently enough. Several kids spelled their words correctly, a few made mistakes and sat down. When Sister Catherine reached Cuckoo, she pronounced his word: "refraction". Cuckoo just stood there staring at Sister through his twisted, taped-up glasses. He had no idea how to spell the word. A strategy during spelling bees when you didn't know how to spell a word was to ask for a definition. The definition never helped you spell the word, but it bought you time to think. So Cuckoo smiled and said, "Sister, can you give me the definition?"

Sister Catherine obliged, telling Cuckoo that "refraction is the process whereby light waves are bent, altering the focal point at which multiple rays of light converge, thereby changing the perception of the light or images created from it." Cuckoo never moved. He had ice water in his veins. Without so much as a flinch, Cuckoo (who had understood not a single word of the definition) fell back on the second strategy for spelling bees… "Sister, would you please use the word in a sentence?"

Running low on patience and knowing that Cuckoo was the equivalent of a drowning victim requesting a glass of water, Sister Catherine dryly replied, "The manner by which eyeglasses correct your vision involves the process of refraction." Cuckoo's calm demeanor disintegrated before our eyes. At the mention of eyeglasses, Cuckoo's face went white and he swallowed twice before responding. "Thank you Sister," he said; then he walked to his desk and sat down, without uttering a single letter.

The spelling bee continued for another six or seven rounds with kids falling by the wayside as it progressed. When Whitey Shelton spelled "centrifugal" with an "s" and without a "u", there were only two of us still standing. Pinhead was leaning against the wall near the door and I was across the room beneath a photo of Pope John XXIII.

Sister Catherine announced to the class that now that there were only two students remaining, the spelling bee would end with the first misspelled word. As soon as someone made a mistake, the other student would be the winner. She went on to add that the winner of the St. Basil's spelling bee would advance to the regional spelling bee to be held at the Samuel L. Gompers School. The regional spelling bee would be held one week from Saturday.

Chills ran down my spine. The thought of spelling words in front of my classmates was harmless enough, but going back to Gompers School and spelling words in front of a bunch of public school kids, not to mention parents, was a nightmare. As if that wasn't bad enough, you had to waste a Saturday doing it. I looked at Pinhead and I could tell by the frown on his face that he was no more interested in going to Gompers School on a Saturday than I was. He seemed preoccupied when Sister Catherine said in a loud voice, "We'll start with Mr. Griffith."

Pinhead returned his attention to Sister Catherine as she pronounced his next spelling word: "Bred". Knowing that the word could be spelled two ways, depending upon its meaning, Pinhead cleverly asked Sister Catherine for a definition.

"It is the past tense of the verb 'breed'."

Taking no chances, Pinhead asked Sister Catherine to use the word in a sentence. He wanted to be absolutely certain that he knew which version of the word he was being asked to spell. Impressed by Pinhead's earnestness, Sister Catherine went on, "The ranchers bred their cattle to produce the strongest steers possible."

Now certain that he knew which form of the word Sister Catherine meant, Pinhead cleared his throat and said in a confident voice,

"Bred"

"B-R-E-A-D"

"Bred"

Pinhead was halfway to his seat before Sister Catherine could tell him that his answer was not correct...he didn't need her to tell him that he had just expertly misspelled the word. He was grinning at me from ear to ear as he settled into his seat and clasped his hands behind his head in a gesture of pure satisfaction. After Sister Catherine announced that I would represent St. Basil's at the regional spelling bee one week from Saturday, Pinhead rushed over to congratulate me. I wanted to belt him.

When Sister Thomas Aquinas heard about the regional spelling bee, she decided that she would like to accompany the first of her students to carry the flag of St. Basil's off into the Nerd Wars. As I was climbing into my dad's car one week from Saturday, my mom uttered the words that made me shiver, "Sister Thomas Aquinas was nice enough to come to the spelling bee, and your father is giving her a ride."

I might have passed out, I can't say, but if I did, when I awoke, I found myself jammed into the back seat of my dad's car with a nun, whose habit would attract only slightly less attention from the public school kids than my bright red uniform sweater. It seemed like it took hours to drive the mile or so from St. Basil's to Gompers School. In the car on the way to Gompers, Sister Thomas Aquinas talked about everything but the spelling bee. She asked me what sports I might play in high school, whether I would be taking algebra, and if I had given any thought to what I might study in college. Looking back, she knew that I was nervous and was steering the conversation as far away from Gompers School as possible.

When we entered the gymnasium, where the spelling bee would take place, my parents patted my shoulder and wished me luck. Sister Thomas Aquinas lingered a moment, just long enough to whisper, "I before E, except after C" with a wry smile and a twinkle in her eye. It was just like her to make you laugh when you felt like crying.

As it turned out, my red sweater may have distracted at least one of the public school kids. The first contestant stepped up to the microphone, looked over at me and said,

"Xylophone...S-W-E-A".

I spelled a few words correctly before exiting the competition by spelling "geranium" with two "N"s. Unlike Pinhead, I was actually trying to get it right. When I returned to my seat, feeling somewhat embarrassed, I was afraid to look over to where Sister Thomas Aquinas was sitting. I was afraid she would be disappointed. When I finally worked up the courage to look, she was looking right at me; she had been waiting for me to look. As soon as she made eye contact with me, she winked. Then she smiled. Then she silently mouthed the words, "I'm proud of you."

I've never felt better about losing at anything, before or since. Until I saw her coming up the aisle of St. Basil's, walking slowly with a cane, my last memory of Sister Thomas Aquinas was as a thirty year-old, eyes twinkling behind her gold-rimmed glasses, telling me that she was proud of me, even if I had misspelled "geranium".

Reaching the front pew on the opposite side of the aisle from us, Sister Thomas Aquinas bowed at the waist and stepped into the pew, sitting down by herself. The man in the black suit made his way back down the aisle toward the rear of the church. That's when I realized that he was from the funeral home and that Sister Thomas Aquinas was indeed alone. I patted Pinhead on the shoulder and whispered, "I'll be back." Then I crossed the aisle, genuflected, leaned toward her, and started to introduce myself. Before I could say anything, Sister Thomas Aquinas smiled, her eyes twinkling behind her gold-rimmed glasses, and said, "Michael, I wondered if you boys would come back."

I stood with my mouth open for a moment, struck dumb by the fact that she had recognized me. I couldn't keep myself from asking her how she remembered all of us after so long.

"I don't remember everyone, but you never forget your first class, Michael."

I slid into the pew and sat down beside her.

"It's great to see you," I whispered. "Are you still at St. Basil's?"

"No, we've been gone for almost fifteen years now. There aren't enough of us to go around these days, so we've had to make some difficult choices about where we can be."

"Where do you live now?" I asked.

"In Arizona. Our Mother House is in Tucson, so most of us are now in small towns throughout the Southwest. We've had to concentrate on areas where teachers are scarce."

"What grade do you teach?"

"I don't have my own classroom anymore. I had a mild stroke a few years ago, so it's hard for me to be as active as I used to be. Whenever one of the teachers has a child who needs individual attention in a subject or two, I help them."

"St. Basil's can't be the same without you."

"Times are different, Michael. It's very hard to find young women who are prepared for religious vocations."

"Too many distractions?" I suggested.

"Too few families...that, and religion has gone out of style."

"It seems like you have to give up so much," I replied. "Kids today have so much that it must be hard to interest them in a vocation. Do you ever have second thoughts yourself?"

"There are things I sometimes wish I could have done. It would have been nice to travel. And I miss having close friends of my own. I love the people where I am, but it's different somehow, than having a group of lifelong friends. I've never wanted to marry anyone, but sometimes I wish I had that one companion to share things with. I wouldn't trade my life for anything. If I had the chance to go back and choose another path, I wouldn't. I love what I do, but the religious life can sometimes be lonely. How about you, Michael...do you have a family?"

"Yes. My wife and I have two daughters, Erin and Emily. They're wonderful. Erin just graduated from college. She begins her first job as a schoolteacher in a couple of weeks. Emily oscillates between wanting to be an astronaut and a foreign correspondent. She left earlier this week for a summer of study in England. We tried to have kids for a long time before we were able to…we are thankful now that they came when they did; they won't grow up and leave home while we're still young. I would miss them terribly."

"Are you happy, Michael?"

"That's an interesting question, Sister. Most people would ask what my job is, but you asked if I was happy."

"I'm more interested in the latter", she said with a smile.

"Yes, I am happy, Sister. I have a terrific family and a rewarding job."

"In that order?" she asked, tilting her head.

"Absolutely," I replied. "I've even begun thinking of spending less time at work and more time at home."

"And what is it that you do?" she asked.

"I'm a surgeon, Sister."

"A doctor," sighed Sister Thomas Aquinas. "How wonderful. How exciting."

"It has its moments, I guess, but it's not as exciting as it looks on television. In fact, it's more tiring than anything else. It's exhilarating when you have an emergency. It sounds odd to say it, but it's even a little exciting when something goes wrong. But most of what we do is very routine, which is what you'd want if you were the patient."

"It's hard to imagine surgery being routine," Sister Thomas Aquinas said, almost to herself.

"It's why we play music in the operating room," I explained.

"And your life, Michael, if you had it to do over again, would you take the same path?" she asked.

"Sure," I replied without stopping to actually think about it. "I wouldn't want to go through the training again, and I have made a lot of trade-offs in the course of being a doctor, but it's a part of who I am, I guess."

"You've put your finger on what a vocation really is," Sister Thomas Aquinas replied, "Religious for me, medicine for you. In either case, your life is defined by your role in the lives of others. You can always wonder what would have been, had you taken the road less traveled, but in the end, if you have enriched another life, you have made a difference."

I was uncomfortable talking so much about myself, and even more uncomfortable thinking about the decision that I was close to making to cut back on my practice. Anxious to change the subject, I asked, "Why do you think that you were always so much closer to the kids than all of the other nuns?"

"I was younger than most of the other nuns," she replied.

"But you were singing when they were shouting," I laughed.

"They got tired."

"Did you get tired?"

"Not yet," she smiled.

The two men in the black suits wheeled Father Tim's casket past our pew and positioned it in the center of the aisle. It was draped in a purple cloth and had a spray of flowers resting on it. They retraced their steps and took places in the pews toward the back of the church.

"How did you hear about Father Tim out in Arizona?" I asked Sister Thomas Aquinas.

"He was very good about keeping in touch with us after the order had to withdraw from the parish. For a number of years we had a reunion each summer and as many of us as could make it back would come. The reunions became smaller and smaller, the victims of distance and age, until finally they stopped altogether."

"But you still kept in touch?"

"Yes. We exchanged letters and cards until computers came along, and then we used e-mail to keep in touch. When Father Tim became ill, he never told any of us. His secretary sent us a message about six months ago telling us that he was failing. When he passed, she sent us a message along with a photo of him taken a year or so ago saying Mass at Easter."

"Are you the only one who made the trip back?" I asked.

"I think so. As I say, distance and age have taken their toll."

"What made you come back?"

"I grew up here. For most of the nuns, this was just one of many places where they lived. For me, it was home."

"The parish will miss Father Tim," I observed.

"More than you know," she nodded. "It's unusual for a pastor to stay in one place for so long. They often have ambitions to move on and up. Other times they wear out their welcome. Father Tim loved it here at St. Basil's. He had many opportunities to go to newer churches in much bigger parishes. He passed up all of the moves that would have given him powerful roles in the church. He always said that this was his home. When I heard that he was sick, I took comfort in knowing that he was in the one place where he always wanted to be."

"Will you miss him?" I asked, the question catching in my throat.

"I already do."

There was one question that I wanted to ask Sister Thomas Aquinas, but I was afraid to. I was afraid that she might take it the wrong way. I almost decided not to ask, but like she had always done when we were young, she made me feel like I could ask her anything. So I did.

"Sister, are you ever afraid you'll run out of time before you do everything you wanted to do?"

"Actually, Michael, I'm sure that I'll run out of time before I do everything that I want to do, but that's the wonderful part of living. If you have filled your days so that you are afraid that night will fall...if you have done so much that you long to do just a little bit more, then yours is a life well-lived."

Before I could respond, the organist opened the bellows and the church was filled with music. The new pastor of St. Basil's, with an altar boy flanking him on either side, appeared in the doorway of the sacristy. He looked so young, about the age that I remembered Father Tim. One of the altar boys carried a heavy leather book, its pages gilded at their edges. The other held the familiar incense urn.

I don't remember much about Father Tim's funeral Mass. I spent the hour quilting together tiny fragments of memories. The sound of his voice booming across the basketball court. The sight of him holding Lou the Screw and whispering in his ear after one of Lou's fits. The street lights reflecting the rain as it rolled off of his umbrella on my parents' front lawn...the sight of him disappearing into the shadows. My attention was drawn back to the church as the Mass came to an end. I placed my hand beneath Sister Thomas Aquinas's elbow and helped her to her feet, the floor of St. Basil's vibrating as the pipe organ played Amazing Grace.

Chapter 13

NOBODY WANTED TO SERVE AS an alter boy for funeral Masses. As we got older, we always made sure that we got the weddings, but we left the funerals for the younger kids. The reason was simple: nobody tipped the altar boys at a funeral. Unlike weddings, which were usually happy affairs and were almost always planned in advance, funerals came on short notice and no one was in the mood to dig a sawbuck out of their pocket for the altar boys.

The oddest funeral I ever served was for a crooked used car dealer named Little Shit Pendleton. That couldn't have been his real name, but it's what everyone called him. He had sold so many junk cars to people that broke down a week after they bought them, that everyone referred to him as "that Little Shit Pendleton". Nearly everyone in the neighborhood wanted to kill him. When he died peacefully in his sleep, everyone who ever bought a car from him felt cheated for a second time.

Little Shit Pendleton didn't have any friends. He never came out of his ramshackle shed on the car lot long enough to make any. He rubbed everyone the wrong way. People with no money to spare spent too much on his broken down heaps. The rich folks who never had to buy a used car hated Pendleton Autos because it was an eyesore. They were constantly threatening to sue the old man because his car lot looked like a junkyard... and in a literal sense, it was. He just kept on parking dented old rust buckets out on his lot, thumbing his nose at the bankers and lawyers who were complaining.

Little Shit Pendleton had a wife who couldn't stand him and a son who once got into a fistfight with him over a bet that the old man lost and refused to pay. Two weeks after Pendleton died, when his money stopped coming in, his wife ran off with a Merchant Marine. Two weeks after that, Pendleton's house caught fire in the middle of the night. It would have been the biggest fire in town for years except for the fact that his used car lot was on fire at precisely the same time.

Pendleton's son was brash, you had to give him that. He was also as dumb as a fence post. As the firemen were spraying water on his parents' house, he walked up the sidewalk acting surprised. Approaching the fireman who seemed to be in charge, Pendleton stuck his hands into his pockets and tried to act nonchalant.

"Big fire, huh?" he said, sidling up next to the fireman. "Think it'll be a total loss?"

Even from a few feet away, the fireman caught a whiff of what smelled like kerosene on Pendleton's clothes. When he took a step closer, the smell got stronger. Smelling kerosene as well as a rat, the fireman looked over Pendleton's shoulder and caught the eye of a nearby policeman who was standing in the glow of the burning house. Raising his eyebrows and tilting his head toward Pendleton, the fireman let the cop know that he thought something was wrong. The cop started toward Pendleton, his hand instinctively moving to the nightstick in his belt. When he got within a few feet of Pendleton, the cop smelled the kerosene, too. Making eye contact with the fireman, the cop tapped his nose and looked to the fireman for confirmation. The fireman nodded almost imperceptibly.

Reaching out and placing his hand on young Pendleton's shoulder, the cop said in a quiet but firm voice "Why don't we let the fireman get back to his job and we can take a walk over here to talk?" Without waiting for a response from Pendleton, the cop started moving him away from the fireman and toward his waiting squad car.

"How come you're out walking in the middle of the night?" asked the cop.

"I wasn't out walking. I was driving my car," answered Pendleton.

"Where is your car now?" the cop asked suspiciously.

"Uh, I parked it up the block. I didn't want it clogging up traffic when I noticed the fire engines outside the house."

"You live here?" asked the cop.

"It's my old man's place", replied Pendleton, his hands in his pockets again.

"You spill something on yourself?" the policeman asked suddenly.

Pendleton shifted his weight from one foot to the other, avoiding eye contact, a frown on his face.

"I uh, I'm going on a trip in the morning. I uh, was filling up my car so I can get an early start, and the nozzle shot gasoline onto my shoes."

"Why don't I just drive you to your car?" suggested the policeman, not a hint of hospitality in his voice.

"Uh, maybe I should stick around here, in case they need me for anything."

"I think they've got things under control here. Why don't we go make sure nothing happens to your car. I'd hate to see anything get in the way of that trip you have planned."

The cop took Pendleton by the arm and led him over to the squad car. As they approached, the radio in the police car crackled and the voice of the dispatch officer came over the air.

"Unit seven, this is Dispatch, please respond, over."

The policeman looked at Pendleton and told him to stay put. He opened the driver side door, never taking his eyes off of Pendleton, and sat down in the front seat of the squad car. While talking into the microphone in his squad car, the cop smiled over at Pendleton and nodded. After several minutes, he put the microphone back in its cradle, got back out of the car, and walked over to Pendleton.

"Are you Brian Pendleton?" the cop asked.

"Yes."

"Do you drive a blue Plymouth sedan with the license plate CR4327?"

"Yes. Did they locate my car?"

"Yeah. It's over at your father's used car lot. On fire."

Brian Pendleton went to jail for three years for burning down his father's house and used car lot. He did it for the insurance money. The widow Pendleton married the Merchant Marine and moved to San Diego. The city condemned the property after the used car lot burned and the bankers and lawyers turned it into a park.

If we had known how Little Shit Pendleton's wife and son felt about him, we wouldn't have been as surprised as we were by his funeral. Three days after the old man died, Danny Noonan and I were in the sacristy with Father Tim preparing for his funeral Mass. I had just finished buttoning my cassock when there was a knock at the back door. Standing outside was a funny looking little man with a wrinkled up face. He was wearing an old baseball cap that was flattened on top of his head. Stitched into the fabric of his faded jacket was the name "Ned".

I looked over Ned's shoulder and saw a white panel van. It had spots of brown where the rust was rotting through from the inside. One of the rear tires was almost flat and the truck had only three hubcaps. The mirror on the passenger side was dangling from the door, hanging by one screw. The rear doors were standing open as if Ned had recently loaded something into or out of the truck.

"I got the deceased," mumbled Ned.

"Huh?" I replied.

"The dearly departed is in the back 'o the truck."

"The coffin?"

"You don't think we'd just throw the body in the truck, do ya? 'Course it's a coffin."

Every minute or two, Ned would make a strange hocking sound, turn his head slightly, and spit on the ground.

"Where's the hearse?" I asked.

"Hearse costs extra...family didn't spring for it," Ned explained.

"Geez..." was all I could manage. I'd never seen a dead person dropped off at the back door of a church in an old rusty van before.

Eyeing my black robe, Ned squinted at me and asked "You the priest?". It was obvious that he didn't spend a lot of time around churches.

"No. I'll go get him," I said, closing the door and walking over to where Father Tim was writing something in a spiral notebook. I told Father Tim about Ned, and he went over to the back door.

"Can I help you?" asked Father Tim.

"Casket's here," said Ned. "I'm supposed to wait until after the service and then drive it over to Holy Trinity Cemetery."

Looking past Ned to the dilapidated van, Father Tim looked puzzled. Evidently he hadn't seen too many dead bodies dropped off at the back door of a church in a beat up panel truck either.

"Do you have the widow with you?" Father Tim asked, craning his neck, trying to see into the passenger window, which was cracked in two places and held together by duct tape.

"Widow? Nobody in the truck but the guest of honor," choked Ned, spitting on the gravel. "Boss told me to give you this," Ned added, handing Father Tim an envelope.

Father Tim opened the envelope, which contained a crisp $100 bill wrapped inside a folded slip of paper. On the paper, in scrawling penmanship, was a note:

To Whom It May Concern:

Enclosed please find $100 to cover the cost of committing the soul of this no good son of a bitch to the hereafter. Please forward his remains to Holy Trinity Cemetery, where he bought himself a gravesite, no doubt right after selling one of his wretched cars to some unfortunate soul. If the $100 isn't enough for a *full funeral, just say $100 worth of prayers… he never spent a day of his life in church, so he'll never know the difference.*

The note was unsigned. Father Tim turned the paper over in his hands, looking for any sign of its author, but there was none. It was the first time that I ever remembered seeing Father Tim totally speechless. After standing motionless for a few minutes, Father Tim turned back to Ned.

"I never met the man. I usually speak with someone who knew him to get an idea of how to approach the eulogy. Did you know him?"

"I only met him once, Padre, and I don't think you could repeat anything I'd have to say about him in church."

"Why not?"

"Because he sold me this truck."

Father Tim followed Ned over to the van and helped him drag the casket out of the back of the truck. Instead of the rolling cart that the funeral directors used when they brought a casket in a limousine hearse, Ned had a battered old hand dolly, the kind you saw in warehouses or on loading docks. To our amazement, he tilted the casket on end, balanced it on his dolly, and wheeled it with Little Shit Pendleton standing upright through the back door, across the sacristy, and out into the church.

Danny Noonan had the incense urn ready. I grabbed the leather prayer book and we joined Father Tim in the doorway of the sacristy. With Ned hocking and spitting outside, we walked through the door and into the church. There we were greeted by two sights that stopped Father Tim dead in his tracks. First, the casket was still on end, leaning up against the altar. Second, there was no one in the church. No family. No relatives. No one. For the second time that morning, Father Tim was tongue-tied.

"Wait here, boys," said Father Tim.

He walked over to the casket, raised his arm and extended his open palm. He spoke in a quiet voice, concluding with the traditional priestly blessing in the Sign of the Cross. Returning to us, he put an arm around one of each of our shoulders and led us back to the sacristy. As Danny went out the back door to empty the urn of its coals, Father Tim held the door open and called to Ned, who was leaning up against the van, spitting.

"All set, Ned."

Ned seemed startled for a moment, surprised that the ceremony was over so soon, but he recovered quickly with an indifferent shrug. He retraced his steps with the hand dolly, propped the casket up, and wheeled it back out to the van. Leaning the casket against the rear bumper, Ned squatted down, grabbed one of the casket handles, and slid it back into the truck. He slammed the back doors and climbed behind the wheel. The starter made a loud grinding noise as Ned pumped the gas pedal trying to coax the engine to life. After several attempts, the engine coughed and sputtered. With a loud clanking, it finally started. Holding one foot on the brake while revving the engine, Ned dropped the truck into gear and lurched away, catching the dangling side mirror on the corner of the church. The mirror sheared off of the truck, dropping to the ground with a thud. As Ned veered out of the driveway without even slowing down, the back doors flew open, banging against the sides of the van as it rumbled down the street and out of sight.

After changing clothes, Danny Noonan and I walked home. On the way, Danny shared a thought that had been rattling around in his head.

"I learned something today, Mike."

"What's that?"

"No used cars for me. When I buy a car, it's going to be a brand new Cadillac."

Cars were a big deal in our neighborhood; when we left St. Basil's for high school, they became an obsession. Joe the Bum used to work on cars in his father's garage. Guys who didn't have the money for a real mechanic, or who didn't want to spend it if they did, brought their cars to Joe the Bum. Joe's garage floor was littered with engine parts that he had removed from cars but couldn't remember how to put back.

Joe the Bum's dad got him a second-hand car with a faulty carburetor. The engine knocked so badly that the car would shake and run for five minutes after you turned off the key. Joe the Bum would never admit that he had no idea how to fix something. One Saturday afternoon, he decided to replace the carburetor once and for all. Joe had the car in his dad's garage with the hood up when we arrived. He was leaning over the engine holding a flashlight in one hand and a screwdriver in the other. He had removed the old carburetor but had not yet installed the new one. When he heard us come in, he asked Cuckoo to get into the car and start the engine.

Pinhead had once watched his dad work on the engine of the garbage truck and seemed to remember that the carburetor had something to do with the amount of air that got mixed with the gasoline. Pinhead was also taking chemistry in school and knew that gasoline, air, and a spark were dangerous. He asked Joe the Bum whether it was a good idea to start the car with the carburetor removed and the fuel line and an open-air pipe leading into the engine. Joe the Bum ignored Pinhead and made a circling motion with his hand toward Cuckoo, indicating that he should start the engine.

When Cuckoo turned the key, flames shot straight up out of the engine. When he saw the fireball erupt under the hood, Cuckoo jumped out of the car and slammed the door. The flames were nearly reaching the wooden rafters of Joe the Bum's garage.

"Turn off the key!" shouted Joe.

Cuckoo looked at him like has was nuts. There was no way that Cuckoo was getting back into a burning car. Joe the Bum opened the car door and turned off the key. Nothing happened. The flames kept shooting into the air. The engine kept belching fire as it sputtered and knocked, refusing to shut down.

Sensing that the garage was in danger, Joe shifted the car into neutral and hopped out, shouting to everyone to help push the car out into the alley. Pinhead, Joe, and I started pushing the car out of the garage. Cuckoo just stared, the flames reflecting off of the lenses of his glasses. He was no more anxious to push a burning car than to drive one. We shoved the car out into the alley, the flames shooting even higher than before. Unfortunately, with no one in the car to apply the brakes, the momentum that we created by shoving the car out into the alley kept it rolling...across the alley and right into the neighbor's garage, the door of which was standing open.

The neighbor's garage was jammed with rakes, shovels, bicycles, a lawn mower, and cardboard boxes stacked along one entire wall. When the flaming car rolled into the garage, there was no room on either side of the car for us to get inside to push it back out. The rafters caught fire and one of the cardboard boxes ignited, then spread to the entire stack of boxes lining the wall. In less than a minute, flames were shooting up through the roof shingles as the garage turned into an inferno. The fire department came and kept the fire from spreading to the neighbor's house or any of the surrounding garages. The blaze burned until there was nothing left but the charred remains of Joe the Bum's car and the concrete slab that used to be the floor of the neighbor's garage.

Joe the Bum's dad was scheduled to work at the sewage treatment plant that day, which meant that he was home watching television. When he heard the sirens, he came out of the back door to see what was going on. Seeing the neighbor's garage smoldering, Joe's dad went over to the neighbor to offer his condolences, unaware that it was Joe's car that started the fire.

"Tough break, Jim. Is there anything I can do for you?" Joe's dad asked the neighbor. Pulling strings with the city to make things happen was his specialty.

"Actually, there is," replied the neighbor.

"You name it," boasted Joe's dad, acting as if no favor that the neighbor might ask could be too big.

"You can have what's left of your kid's car towed off my property."

Joe's dad made a few phone calls and the next morning a city work crew showed up with a truckload of wood and building supplies. Over the next two days, they built the neighbor a brand new garage, bigger than the old one. Joe's dad drove down to the sewage treatment plant each morning to punch in, then returned home to supervise the neighborhood garage construction until late afternoon, when he returned to the sewage plant to punch out. Joe's dad put an end to his home auto repair business. With no money coming in from working on cars, Joe resorted to selling the engine parts lying around his garage that he had never been able to put back into the cars he was fixing.

Earl's Chicken Shack was a neighborhood fixture while we were growing up. It was an old stone building with rounded ramparts at the top. When it was originally built, which must have been in the 1920s, it was home to a bank. The architecture was designed to look like a fortress, an appealing visual image for a bank. In 1929 the banks failed, and the building sat empty for a number of years. It changed hands several times before Wilhelm Guenther converted it into Earl's Chicken Shack in the late 1940s.

The stone edifice was as far from a shack as a building could be, and Wilhelm Guenther's middle name was Klaus, not Earl. It was the late 1940s, however, and World War II was still too fresh in everyone's memory to open a restaurant named "Wilhelm's" anything. Mr. Guenther figured that people would think that chicken cooked by someone named Earl would be good, and that someone named Earl would probably sell chicken from a shack, not a castle. Besides, Earl's Chicken Fortress didn't have much of a ring to it.

Fat Peter got a summer job at Earl's Chicken Shack. His main job was to drain the chicken fat and cooking grease out of the deep fryers and to pour the oily liquid into five gallon buckets. He would leave the buckets out behind Earl's Chicken Shack for a day or two, where the chicken fat would harden into a paste. Fat Peter then took the buckets to a dumpster, turned them upside down, and pounded on them with his fist until the greasy chicken fat plopped into the garbage bin. There were always two or three thousand flies buzzing around the dumpster.

Dominic Lorenzo was five or six years older than us. He had been a student at St. Basil's until he was expelled in fourth grade for starting fires. Dominic started his first fire in a wastebasket in the boys' bathroom. He was caught when Sister Pius, smelling smoke, looked into the bathroom and found the wastebasket smoldering. A trail of toilet paper stretched across the floor from the burning wastebasket to the stall where Dominic was hiding, the toilet paper stuck to his shoe.

Dominic started his second and last fire using a can of spray paint and a match. He was lighting matches, then spraying the aerosol paint at the match, where the gases ignited and created a miniature flamethrower. He was doing this outside on the playground when he got the paint can too close to the match and the aerosol can exploded. Miraculously, he wasn't killed or even badly hurt, but the explosion attracted Sister Pius, who found Dominic standing on the playground, all of the hair singed off of one arm, and the fingertip of his other hand bright yellow from the spray paint.

Dominic left St. Basil's that day, and finished grade school at Samuel L. Gompers. He spent two years in high school before dropping out and getting a job in the steel mills. He worked the night shift, which meant that he went to work at midnight. Every evening, between nine o'clock and eleven-thirty, he made a nuisance of himself driving around the neighborhood in his pride and joy hot rod.

Dominic drove a GTO, a car cherished by gearheads everywhere for its speed. The engine of a GTO sounded like a jet fighter – extremely powerful and unbearably loud. Show-offs like Dominic modified their GTOs by removing all equipment designed to muffle sound. They jacked up the rear ends of the cars so that the back of the car was three feet higher than the front, giving the impression that the car was always speeding downhill. The driver could only see a foot in front of the hood.

Dominic loved his GTO. He washed it every afternoon when he woke up. Every night while it sat outside the steel mill, a thin layer of soot from the smokestacks settled over the car. Every afternoon, Dominic washed it, drying it with towels so that he could see his reflection in the metallic blue paint. Then he would drive it way too fast up and down the streets of the neighborhood, terrorizing kids on bicycles or elderly pedestrians.

Every night for an entire summer, Dominic would pull up to the corner where we were pitching pennies while we waited for Fat Peter to get off work at Earl's Chicken Shack. He'd sit there revving his engine, smirking at us, and then stomp on the accelerator. His wide tires would spin so fast that they smoked on the pavement, then they would grab the asphalt and propel the car forward like a bullet shot from a gun. Gravel and grit from the street would spray out behind him, most of it hitting us in the face.

We'd had enough of Dominic and his hot rod when we decided one hot August night to fix him once and for all. It was eight forty-five and Dominic would be pulling up in about fifteen minutes if he kept to his usual timetable, which he always did. Pinhead ran across the street to Earl's Chicken Shack. Peering in through the windows from the sidewalk, he made eye contact with Fat Peter. Pinhead nodded his head deliberately and pointed at his wristwatch. Fat Peter nodded back and disappeared into the kitchen.

We were at our usual corner, pitching pennies as if nothing was unusual. Pinhead and Fat Peter appeared from behind Earl's Chicken Shack, running in low crouches. Pinhead carried a five- gallon bucket in each hand. Fat Peter had a bucket in one hand and a push broom in the other. They were breathing hard when they got to the corner. Pinhead set his two buckets down on the sidewalk, then reached over and took the remaining bucket that Fat Peter was holding. Carefully selecting buckets that had been put out behind Earl's the evening before, Pinhead and Fat Peter had fifteen gallons of partially hardened greasy chicken fat. Working quickly, Pinhead emptied the three buckets of chicken fat onto the pavement at the corner while Fat Peter carefully spread the oily paste with the push broom. When they were finished, a one inch thick layer of greasy chicken fat coated the street.

Pinhead stacked the buckets and Fat Peter ran them back to Earl's Chicken Shack. Admiring his handiwork, Pinhead turned quickly and said, "We've got a problem." The streetlight was shining straight down on the corner and the light was reflecting off of the chicken fat. Pinhead worried that Dominic would see the shiny surface and know that something was wrong.

Bending down, Pinhead gathered a handful of stones and began throwing them at the streetlight twenty feet overhead. On his third toss, Pinhead hit the bulb in the streetlight and a shower of broken glass rained down on the sidewalk as the corner was thrown into darkness. Just then, we heard the familiar rumble of Dominic's GTO coming up the street from two blocks away. We pretended to be pitching pennies when Dominic rolled to a stop at the corner, right on schedule. He sneered at us through his open window, too stupid to even wonder why we were pitching pennies in the dark.

"Still no wheels, pedestrians?" taunted Dominic.

"Shove it, Dominic," responded Joe the Bum.

"Need a ride to the bus stop?" continued Dominic, sniffing as if he smelled something peculiar.

"Your engine sounds a little slow tonight, Dominic," Pinhead called out, knowing that would infuriate Lorenzo.

"You think so?" snarled Dominic, revving his engine louder than usual.

"Didja change gasoline Dominic? Sounds like a lawn mower," Pinhead needled.

"Eat my dust," shouted Dominic, popping his clutch and burying the accelerator all the way to the floor.

The tires of the GTO spun out of control on the greasy layer of chicken fat. The rear end swung left, then right, and then left again. Dominic just kept his foot jammed on the accelerator, watching the neighborhood sweep back and forth across his windshield. The GTO shot forward as the tires spun through the grease and made contact with the pavement, but the car was pointed at the sidewalk on the other side of the street.

As soon as the GTO gained enough speed to do any damage, the rear tires advanced just far enough to hit an undisturbed patch of chicken fat and Dominic was sliding sideways through the intersection. When the car reached the dry pavement in the center of the intersection, the tires regained traction and the GTO shot across a lane of traffic and slammed into a telephone pole, creasing the blue metallic hot rod into the shape of a "V".

We gathered up our pennies, kicked the broken glass off of the sidewalk, and started off in the direction of Dominic's car, which had sent a plume of steam up through the hood. We walked up the block on our side of the street past the accident scene, then crossed over and started back toward the wreck. As we got within earshot, we could hear Dominic sputtering and whining that the accident wasn't his fault.

The policeman made Dominic touch his index fingers to the tip of his nose, then drew a chalk line on the sidewalk and told Dominic to walk along it...another cop was walking slowly around the car, examining the damage. As we passed the policeman, we heard him mutter, "It's the damnedest thing...the car smells like fried chicken."

Public school kids learned to drive in school. Catholic school kids learned to drive at the Vernon Mulrooney Driving Academy. We spent the time that public schools devoted to driver's education in theology class. Catholic schools concentrated on saving our eternal souls. If we wanted to learn to drive, we were on our own.

Vernon Mulrooney was an insurance salesman in the neighborhood. Two evenings a week and every other Saturday he taught the Catholic kids how to drive. It was no coincidence that no kid ever graduated from the Vernon Mulrooney Driving Academy until their parents bought auto insurance from the Vernon Mulrooney Insurance Agency. Old Vernon wasn't much of an educator, but he was a shrewd businessman. He knew how to turn one dollar into two. No one knew for sure how old man Mulrooney got a license from the state to teach driver's education. Joe the Bum's dad said that Mulrooney had "greased some palms", and if anyone knew about slippery palms, it was Joe the Bum's dad.

About a year and a half after the chicken grease incident with Dominic Lorenzo, Pinhead, Joe the Bum, Danny Noonan, Cuckoo and I enrolled in the Vernon Mulrooney Driving Academy. Fat Peter's birthday fell in a month with no "R" in it, so he had to wait for the next class three months later.

There was nothing remotely academic about the Vernon Mulrooney Driving Academy. The state required that all driving students complete a certain amount of "classroom" work before actually setting off in on-the-road mayhem. Vernon Mulrooney had no classroom, so he improvised. For our first day of "class" we were instructed to meet at a neighborhood gas station and auto repair garage called "Grimey Mike's".

The proprietor of "Grimey Mike's" was actually a guy named Butch, but he thought that "Grimey Mike's" had a better ring to it than "Grimey Butch's". Vernon Mulrooney paid Butch a few bucks and looked the other way on the occasional questionable insurance claim in exchange for the use of Grimey Mike's garage for the "classroom" portion of our instruction. The class was held at night, since we had to be in school and Butch needed the garage during the day. On the evening of our first drivers' education class, not sure exactly what to expect, Pinhead, Joe, Danny, Cuckoo, and I started off on foot for Grimey Mike's garage.

"You think you'll pass the driver's test on your first try, Pinhead?" asked Cuckoo, more to break the tension than anything else.

"I dunno," mumbled Pinhead, only half-listening.

"I could pass the test today," bragged Joe the Bum, "I been driving cars since I was twelve."

"Sitting in your old man's driveway rolling the windows up and down and honking the horn don't count," chided Danny Noonan.

"Doesn't count," corrected Pinhead.

"What?" asked Danny.

"Sitting in your old man's driveway doesn't count...not don't count," Pinhead elaborated.

"It's drivers' ed...it ain't English class," Danny sniffed.

"I heard they blindfold you and make you drive around pretending it's dark and your lights don't work," said Cuckoo, his voice raising an octave.

Before anyone could answer Cuckoo, we rounded the corner and were standing in the driveway of Grimey Mike's Garage. The large overhead door to the repair garage was half open, and we bent over at the waist and ducked inside. The garage was dingy, with a single bare light bulb casting shadows into the four corners of the cinder block walls. A row of folding chairs was lined up against two of the walls, and an old beat up jalopy was parked over the grease pit with its hood open and one door lying off of its hinges.

"C'mon in boys," invited Vernon Mulrooney, holding a clipboard in his hand. He asked our names and checked us off of his list, pointing toward the metal chairs along the wall.

"Grab a seat, we'll get started in a minute."

Vernon Mulrooney was an enormous man with a face that was perpetually beet red. He weighed over 400 pounds and his hair was always slicked down from perspiration. He wore a necktie that ran out of fabric halfway down his belly, and his pants were cinched tight with a thin belt that made him look like he was wearing a mailbag. His sleeves were rolled up to his elbows, and he looked like he might explode at any minute.

There were three other kids already sitting on folding chairs when we got there, and several more drifted in after we arrived. When Vernon Mulrooney had checked the last name off of his list, he laid his clipboard down, clasped his hands together, and sighed with a long raspy breath.

"Before we go out on the road, we'll cover the fundamentals of operating a vee-hickle here," he wheezed.

Moving to the front end of the jalopy, Vernon nodded his head toward the open hood and said, "In here you gotcher motor...it's what makes the loud noise when you stomp on the gas."

Joe the Bum looked over at us with a smirk. Clearly this was not going to be a class in nuclear physics. Pinhead and Danny Noonan were looking at the only girl in the class, not even hearing Vernon Mulrooney. On the other side of Joe the Bum, Cuckoo was feverishly taking notes. Joe the Bum's sense of security turned out to be misplaced when Vernon Mulrooney reached into a toolbox and removed two wrenches. He squinted at the wrench in his left hand and read aloud to the class, "Five thirty-seconds of an inch."

Turning to the wrench in his right hand, he read aloud, "Three eighths of an inch...can anyone tell me which wrench is larger?"

Everyone in the garage raised their hand – everyone except Joe the Bum. The smirk on Joe's face changed to a frown. Seeing all of the hands in the air, Mulrooney looked directly at Joe the Bum, who looked away, hoping to avoid eye contact in an effort to become invisible.

"Joe, how about you?" asked Mulrooney.

"Hey, nobody said there would be math," protested Joe.

We met twice a week in Grimey Mike's Garage for three weeks, learning how to change flat tires and how to pump gas into the tank. Mr. Mulrooney brought his own car in on the night when we learned to pump gas. He had everyone take a turn until his gas tank was completely full. Joe the Bum asked if we could learn how to "hot wire" a car, in case we ever lost our keys and needed to drive an old lady home in an emergency. Vernon Mulrooney smiled for one of only two times during the three weeks, but just shook his head.

After the "classroom" portion of our studies, it was time for actual driving lessons. We divided into groups of three for our on-the-road lessons. Vernon Mulrooney sat in the passenger seat while we took turns driving his car. The two guys not driving rode in the back seat, where they could learn from the things that Mulrooney was yelling at the driver. In Grimey Mike's Garage, Vernon Mulrooney had always talked in calm tones, occasionally even sounding almost pleasant. As soon as we got into his car, however, he changed from Dr. Jekyll to Mr. Hyde. It may have been because he was afraid of dying, or that he was terrified that we would wreck his car, but for whatever reason, whenever someone was driving, Mulrooney punctuated virtually every sentence with "goddammit".

"Turn right at the next corner...slow down — not so fast, goddammit!"

"Wait until it's clear in both directions before pulling out into – watch out for that truck, goddammit!"

"How did you ever make it past the sixth grade when you can't read street signs, goddammit?"

One afternoon Cuckoo was driving and Pinhead and I were riding in the back seat. Cuckoo was talking a mile a minute, which he tended to do when he got nervous. As we drove through the same intersection where we'd chicken greased Dominic's hot rod, Cuckoo glanced out the window and saw Earl's Chicken Shack. Figuring that anyone the size of Vernon Mulrooney must like chicken and anxious to make a good impression, Cuckoo turned away from the windshield, pointed out the rear passenger window, and said with a smile,

"Mr. Mulrooney, you can get some really good chicken in there."

As he turned and pointed, Cuckoo's left hand tugged at the steering wheel and the car bumped over the curb and up onto the sidewalk. We careened down the sidewalk for half a block, scattering pedestrians and knocking down an awning in front of the florist shop. Vernon Mulrooney grabbed the steering wheel and wrenched the car back over the curb, shouting, "You're on the sidewalk! You're on the sidewalk! The road has the line painted down the middle, goddammit!"

When you signed up for the Vernon Mulrooney Driving Academy, your parents had to promise to take you out to practice driving. Old Vernon spent as little time as possible actually teaching people to drive, so that he'd have more time to sell them insurance for the times when they smashed their cars into each other. Mulrooney knew that they'd hit something sooner or later, and he wanted them to be driving their own cars when they did.

Pinhead's dad figured Pinhead would scrape some paint as he learned to drive, and he wasn't any more anxious than Old Man Mulrooney to have the paint scraped off of his own car. That's why Pinhead learned to drive in the garbage truck. There was no garbage pickup on Sundays, so we were surprised to hear the unmistakable roar of a garbage truck rumbling up the alley one Sunday afternoon. Joe the Bum stepped out into the alley and looked in the direction of the noise. His face broke into a wide grin and he began gesturing to us to hurry over to where he was standing.

The roar of the garbage truck's motor came in erratic spurts, punctuated by periodic clanking, grinding, and metallic screeching as Pinhead tried to locate the next gear. The truck careened from one side of the alley to the other, narrowly missing garages and occasionally flattening a garbage can that had been left out by one of the neighbors. Behind the truck was a wake of garbage strewn across the alley - four or five flattened garbage cans, and half of an old sofa, surrounded by tufts of stuffing floating in the air. We scampered back out of the alley as the truck approached, and stood well away from the path of the clanking, grinding behemoth. As they approached, we could barely hear Pinhead's dad shouting over the noise of the transmission, "...in third gear, I told you to keep it in first gear!"

Pinhead saw us as he veered away from the back of the garage across the alley, and he grinned out the window and waved. We stood in the backyard making that "pulling on a chain" motion that was the universal signal that kids used to ask a truck driver to blow his horn. Pinhead recognized the gesture and nodded as he roared past, reaching up above his head and grabbing a metal handle that he thought was the horn.

Pinhead's dad's voice was now clearly audible despite the noise of the motor and the gears.

"...'snot the horn, don't pull that lever!"

As they rumbled past, Pinhead yanked on the metal handle that he thought would blow the horn. No horn sounded, but the entire back of the garbage truck began to rise on a huge piston beneath the section that held the garbage. Pinhead kept grinding through the gears and veering wildly from one side of the alley to the other, as the rear of the truck kept rising until garbage began tumbling out everywhere. Half a truckload of garbage and fifty thousand gallons of water dumped into the alley as Pinhead made his way to the corner. With his left turn signal flashing, Pinhead turned right at the stop sign, the back of the truck fully extended into the air. With the fading sound of metal grinding on metal, the garbage truck turned the corner and was gone.

Each student of the Vernon Mulrooney Driving Academy received a form on which they and their parents were to keep track of their driving practice. In the days before photocopy technology was invented, people used mimeograph machines to churn out copies. The duplicates came off of the machine wet and smelled from the chemicals used to create the image on the paper. At our last class in Grimey Mike's Garage, Mr. Mulrooney handed everyone a mimeograph copy of the driving practice form. We walked all the way home taking deep breaths while holding the copies over our faces. The chemicals made you dizzy if you smelled them long enough.

When you practiced driving with your parents, you were supposed to write down on the form the amount of time spent, where you drove, and the prevailing weather conditions. You could not get your driver's license until you had practiced for fifty hours, and your parents had to sign the form each time that they took you driving. Joe the Bum and his dad sat down at their kitchen table on the night that Joe got home with the form and began filling in all of the blanks. Joe's dad had a Farmers' Almanac that predicted the weather, and they sat hunched over the Almanac making up practice sessions and weather reports. Joe's dad carefully changed pens and occasionally used a pencil to make the forgery look legitimate. When he had filled in every line of the form, Joe the Bum's dad wrinkled the paper, then re-straightened it, and carefully pressed his coffee cup on the corner of the page, leaving a perfect cream and sugar circle. Holding the form up to the light like a jeweler examining a precious stone, Joe the Bum's dad chuckled and said, "masterpiece".

Vernon Mulrooney handed out the driving practice forms late in the evening on a Tuesday. Joe the Bum turned in his completed form, carefully documenting fifty hours of driving practice, on Thursday afternoon of the same week. Old Man Mulrooney looked at the form when Joe handed it to him and placed it beneath the metal clip on his clipboard. It made no difference to Vernon Mulrooney that Joe the Bum turned in his form swearing to having had fifty hours of driving practice less than thirty-six hours from the time he got the form. A form was a form and Vernon dutifully placed a check mark next to Joe's name on his list.

Danny Noonan's dad offered to take him out to practice driving, but Duke Noonan would have none of it.

"You can't teach him to drive," she bellowed, "you can't even drive yourself."

No one had ever seen Mr. Noonan driving the family car. For that matter, no one had actually seen Mr. Noonan even riding in the family car. Duke Noonan drove everywhere that Danny needed to go, and she would be the one who took Danny to practice. The first time that Duke Noonan took Danny driving, she sat in the passenger seat and held the steering wheel with her left hand. Danny drove around the neighborhood for an hour, but Duke never let go of the wheel. When they returned home, she yelled at Danny all the way into the house, telling him that he was over-steering.

One afternoon, Danny was driving and Duke was sitting in the passenger seat while we were out in Joe the Bum's driveway. Danny's car went up and down the street twenty or thirty times, and every time they went past, we heard snippets of Duke shouting obscenities at the top of her lungs.

"...didn't slow down, son-of-a..."

"...the hell were you looking at?"

"...worse than your father, for Crissakes."

Cuckoo's dad couldn't take time away from the bakery, so his mother had to take him out driving. Mrs. Coolack was a nervous lady, and the prospect of taking Cuckoo out in traffic was more than she could take. Instead of practicing on city streets, Mrs. Coolack took Cuckoo over to the football field, which had a cinder track running around it. Mrs. Coolack drove the car onto the running track and pulled to a stop. She stepped out of the car and made her way around to the passenger side, changing places with Cuckoo. For several hours at a time, every Saturday for six weeks, Cuckoo drove the car around the running track, while his mom held onto the dashboard with both hands, her eyes closed tightly, saying Hail Marys. Cuckoo eventually logged his fifty hours of practice, but for the first three months after he got his driver's license, he could only make right turns. Wherever he went, if he needed to go left, he had to make three right turns to do it.

If Vernon Mulrooney thought that teaching kids how to drive was dangerous, he was totally unprepared for the harrowing experience of teaching nuns. For no apparent reason, Sister Pius decided that she wanted to learn how to drive. The convent at St. Basil's had no automobile, so no one could figure out why Sister Pius wanted to know how to drive, but she did...and when she decided to learn, she called Vernon Mulrooney. Vernon Mulrooney came to St. Basil's to teach Sister Pius the classroom portion of the program. Not even Vernon Mulrooney could imagine Sister Pius ducking beneath the garage door at Grimey Mike's. When it was time for Sister Pius to actually practice driving, Mulrooney had no alternative to using his own car.

On the first day of actual driving practice, Sister Pius talked Sister Thomas Aquinas into coming along. Sister Thomas Aquinas wasn't really interested in learning how to drive, but she thought it might help Sister Pius to have someone along for moral support. Sister Pius promised to get Mr. Mulrooney to let Sister Thomas Aquinas drive a bit while they were out. Vernon Mulrooney arrived at St. Basil's to pick up Sister Pius and Sister Thomas Aquinas just as the two nuns were stepping out of the convent door. He pried himself out of his car. His stomach was jammed against the steering wheel so tightly that he honked the horn when he moved. Bowing graciously, Mulrooney held the doors open as the two nuns climbed into the car. Squeezing himself back in behind the wheel, Mulrooney started to pull away from the curb when Sister Pius stopped him.

"Mr. Mulrooney, may we please stop by the rectory so that Father Tim can bless the car?"

Mulrooney didn't know what to say. No one had ever asked him to have his car blessed before. He couldn't think of a good reason to refuse, so he muttered, "sure, Sister" and pulled up in front of the rectory. Father Tim was out in the yard leaning on a rake as Sister Pius rolled down the window and motioned for him to come over. Obliging, Father Tim approached the car, the rake still in his hand.

"Father, we're going driving, would you bless the car?" asked Sister Pius.

A momentary twinkle in his eye and an almost imperceptible smile suggested that Father Tim had never been asked to bless a car before either. Equally unable to think of a good reason to refuse, Father Tim smiled at Sister Pius and said, "sure, Sister."

Holding the rake in one hand like a shepherd's staff, Father Tim raised his right hand in the familiar Sign of the Cross and said in a loud voice,

"May Almighty God look with favor upon this motor car, protect its passengers from harm, and return them safely at the close of their journey, in the name of the Father, and of the Son, and of the Holy Spirit, Amen."

As Sister Pius pulled her head back into the window and turned the hand crank, Father Tim caught Mr. Mulrooney's eye and winked. Mr. Mulrooney put the car in gear and pulled away from the curb, waving to Father Tim as he left the rectory. He pulled out into traffic and headed off toward the Immaculate Conception Cemetery, where he knew the roadways would be quiet and no one could get hurt.

Along the way, Sister Pius sat in the passenger seat beside Mr. Mulrooney and tried to watch everything he did to make the car start and stop. As she absentmindedly shuffled her feet, her right foot settled into a deep rut that had been gouged completely through the carpet and down to the bare metal. It was from Vernon Mulrooney jamming his foot into a brake pedal that wasn't there, in his mind's eye trying to slow or stop the car as student driver after student driver scared the wits out of him. When they arrived at the cemetery, Mulrooney followed the paved roadway toward the back of the graveyard and slowed to a stop along a stretch of level ground with no one in sight.

"Shouldn't be any traffic back here..." Mulrooney reassured Sister Pius, adding with a smile, "and we shouldn't bother any of the tenants."

Mulrooney screwed himself back out from behind the wheel, making room for Sister Pius to slide into the driver's seat – in fact, he made so much room that Sister Pius and Sister Thomas Aquinas could have both slid into the driver's seat at the same time. The seat was so far from the steering wheel that Sister Pius could barely reach the wheel with her arms fully extended. Reaching the pedals with her feet was out of the question.

The front seat of Mulrooney's car was a "bench seat" which meant that he and Sister Pius had to be the same distance from the dashboard. In order for Mulrooney to fit into the seat, Sister Pius sat so far from the pedals that her short little legs wouldn't reach. Seeing that Sister Pius could not touch the brake with her toes, Vernon Mulrooney reached down and pulled a lever on the side of the seat. He slid forward gingerly, sucking in his breath in a painful effort to wedge himself close enough to the dashboard for Sister Pius to be able to drive.

With Mulrooney shoehorned into the seat beside her, Sister Pius peered out beneath the arc of the steering wheel, too short to have an unobstructed view through the windshield. Bracing himself against the dashboard and turning sideways toward Sister Pius, Vernon Mulrooney said in his calmest voice:

"Ok, Sister, when you're ready, shift the car into first gear and gently press the accelerator."

Bypassing first and second gears, Sister Pius shifted the car straight into third gear and stomped on the accelerator like it was a bug on the kitchen floor. The car lurched forward, throwing Mulrooney back into the seat with such force that all of the air rushed out of his lungs with an audible hiss. All that Sister Thomas Aquinas could manage to say as her head snapped back was a soft "oh my...."

Sister Pius gripped the steering wheel tightly in both hands, squinting through her thick glasses trying to make sense out of the landscape that was rushing past her through the tiny slit between the steering wheel and the top of the dashboard. Mr. Mulrooney managed to reinflate his lungs through a series of raspy gasps.

The car rocketed down the single lane blacktop road, gaining speed as Sister Pius pressed the accelerator all the way to the floor. Just ahead, the cemetery road bent to the left and continued up a small hill. Reaching the curve, Sister Pius stared straight ahead, oblivious to what she could not see ahead of her. Holding the steering wheel perfectly still, Sister Pius drove the car off the road and onto the grass. Vernon Mulrooney's eyes followed the curve of the road, expecting the car to begin its turn at any second. When the road turned but the car did not, he stared at Sister Pius with his eyes bulging. His mouth was moving but no words were coming out.

Aside from the bumps as they shot across the cemetery lawn, Sister Pius had no way to know that they had left the roadway, since all that she could see through the gap in the steering wheel was sky. As they sped along between two rows of graves, tombstones whizzed past the windows like the pickets of a fence.

Vernon Mulrooney thought back to Father Tim winking at him with the rake in his hand. He silently hoped to himself that Father Tim hadn't faked the blessing. His mouth was still moving, but only sounds, no words, came out. Sister Thomas Aquinas watched the scenery scream past the window. Too polite to complain, she whispered pleasantly,

"Well, if you're going to kill us, you've picked a convenient place."

Mulrooney had been on his best behavior all day, holding doors for the two ladies and bowing graciously and all, but he was watching his life flash before his eyes along with the tombstones that were whistling past. Finally, he found his voice, and when he did, the old Mulrooney came bursting forth in full force.

"Jesus H. Christ, Sister, if you don't stop this car, you're going to kill us all, goddammit!"

Nothing else had managed to wrest Sister Pius's attention away from the tiny patch of blue sky that she'd been staring at, but Mulrooney's outburst did the trick. Lifting her foot from the accelerator and turning sideways in the seat to face Vernon Mulrooney, she gave him the look that had struck fear into the students of St. Basil's for two decades. As the car coasted to a stop, Mulrooney began to calm down. When the car stopped moving, Vernon realized that he would survive the ordeal after all. He sheepishly smiled at Sister Pius and apologized.

"Sorry Sister, I got a little excited back there...didn't mean to startle you."

Sister Pius softened her glare and released her grip on the steering wheel. She turned to Vernon Mulrooney and asked, "Well, Mr. Mulrooney, how did we do?"

Momentarily thinking of what it would be like to accompany Sister Pius on enough lessons to actually teach her to drive, Mulrooney summoned up all of the bravado that he could muster and said in a loud voice,

"Fan-damn-tastic, Sister, you pass!"

Sister Pius's face brightened, and she thanked Mulrooney profusely. Then she turned to Sister Thomas Aquinas in the back seat and said, "Sister Thomas Aquinas, it's your turn to steer."

Without a moment's hesitation, Mulrooney blurted out, "No! Er, I mean, she passes too!"

Danny Noonan eventually did get his brand new Cadillac. It happened a few years after Little Shit Pendleton's funeral, and it almost involved a funeral for Danny in the process. Lester Griggs was Danny's cousin. Duke Noonan had a sister who married a doctor, which probably contributed to Duke's persistent feeling that life was unfair. Dr. Griggs was a wealthy surgeon who had more money than time for Lester. Duke's sister was even uglier than Duke, and she spent more time in the plastic surgeon's office than she spent keeping an eye on Lester. As a result, Lester Griggs had the two things that spell trouble for a teenager: too much money and idle time.

Lester lived in a big house out in the suburbs. The Griggs' property was heavily wooded and had a pond and a gazebo. It looked like something out of a movie. Doctor Griggs and Duke's ugly sister had "his and hers" Mercedes Benz sedans. Either of the two cars cost more than most of the houses in our neighborhood. From time to time, Lester would come by to show Danny whatever new extravagant purchase he had made. For guys like Lester, having money was only fun if you could parade it around in front of guys who didn't have any. Lester's showboating bothered Duke

Noonan a lot more than it bothered Danny. Danny knew how to handle guys like Lester.

One autumn afternoon, Duke Noonan's sister brought Lester over to Danny's house for a visit. What she really came for was to show Duke Noonan her latest mink coat. It was only November and the weather was still mild, but Mrs. Griggs drove into the Noonan's driveway and stepped out of her Mercedes wearing a full-length mink coat. Duke Noonan stepped out onto the porch with a scarf in her hair holding about seventy-five curlers.

Mrs. Griggs got out of the car and started parading up and down the driveway like she was in a fashion show. She whirled around making the new mink coat twirl around in the air. The coat was mostly black except for a streak of lighter colored fur down the middle of the back. Duke Noonan smirked, saying that it looked like a skunk.

We were out on the sidewalk, enjoying the late fall weather playing cards when Lester and his mother drove up. Lester always tried to hang around with us on his visits to the neighborhood. He saw us out on the sidewalk and made a beeline toward us when he got out of the car.

"Hey, gents," greeted Lester. 'Gents' was obviously a term used only out in the suburbs where rich people had ponds and gazebos. In our neighborhood, the only time you saw the term 'Gents' was on the men's room door of some dump that was trying to act like a real restaurant. We kept playing cards without even acknowledging that Lester was there.

Lester stood watching, trying to figure out what game we were playing. Pinhead was the dealer and he would deal two cards to each player, the cards laying face up on the sidewalk. Each player would then decide whether to bet or not to bet, and Pinhead would decide whether to accept their bet or not. If they agreed to the bet, Pinhead would deal the player one more card. Depending on that one card, either Pinhead or the player would start whooping and celebrating, while the other would pay up on the bet. It was not immediately apparent to Lester how the players determined who won. He continued watching for a while longer, but still couldn't grasp the rules of the game. Having money in his pocket and desperately wanting to be one of the guys, Lester was bursting at the seams to get into the game. Finally, unable to stay on the sidelines any longer, he asked, "What are you guys playing?"

"Between the sheets," answered Pinhead without looking up.

"How do you play?" asked Lester.

"You get two cards. Your third card has to be between the other two for you to win. Say you got a six and a jack. If your next card is a ten, you win, because a ten is higher than six and lower than the jack. If you get a three or a queen, you lose."

"How do you bet?" asked Lester.

"The farther apart your first two cards are, the more likely you are to have your third card come in between them, so the more you bet. You'd bet a lot more if you had a four and a queen than you would if you had an eight and a ten. For the dealer, it's the opposite. He's betting that you'll get a card outside of the first two. So he'll bet more if your cards are close together and less if they're far apart."

"Can I play?" Lester asked, already taking his money out of his pocket.

"Sure, sit down," invited Pinhead.

Pinhead dealt Lester a five and a queen. Lester bet a quarter. Pinhead accepted and dealt Lester a seven. Lester grinned and Pinhead handed him a quarter. Next, Lester got a seven and a ten. He bet a nickel. Pinhead wanted to bet a dollar, but Lester would only bet a dime. Pinhead dealt Lester a nine. Lester slapped his forehead.

"I should have bet you the dollar," he said to Pinhead.

"I'm glad you didn't," replied Pinhead, giving Lester a dime.

The game went on for a while, with Lester winning a few quarters and losing about as many. Then Pinhead dealt Lester the "between the sheets" equivalent of a full house in poker...a two and a king. Forty of the remaining fifty cards would be winners for Lester. Everyone started talking at once.

"Oh man, you got the deuce-king!" cried Cuckoo.

"Bet it all!" shouted Joe the Bum.

"How much money do you have?" asked Danny Noonan.

Lester's eyes darted from face to face as everyone shouted encouragement to him. He could hardly contain his glee as he dug into his pockets and took out all of his money to count it. When he had tallied up his bankroll, Lester proudly announced that he had five dollars and seventy-five cents, a fortune in our circles.

Danny Noonan said, "Heck, that's not enough for a deuce-king...you better go over to the house and get some more money from your Ma."

Lester looked at Pinhead, then said, "Should I?"

"We'll wait," answered Pinhead.

Lester scrambled to his feet and ran across the lawn and up the porch steps to Danny Noonan's house. The screen door banged loudly as Lester threw it open and ran into the house. While he was gone, Pinhead held the deck of cards in his hands, running his fingers around the stack. Catching Danny Noonan's eye, Pinhead smiled. Without saying a word, Danny smiled back and nodded his head. A few minutes later, Lester came running back across the street with a huge smile on his face. He plopped back down and pulled a crisp ten-dollar bill out of his pocket. Laying it down next to the rest of his money, Lester looked squarely at Pinhead and said, "I bet fifteen dollars and seventy-five cents."

Pinhead said "okay" and turned over the top card on the deck. It was the Ace of Spades. Lester's face melted like a candle next to a bonfire. He stared at the three cards with his mouth open. He was frozen, unable to move as Pinhead reached over and scooped up the fifteen dollars and seventy-five cents.

"Tough break," consoled Joe the Bum.

"Man, an Ace dagger…" said Cuckoo, doing everything that he could not to burst out laughing.

"Never would have thought it could happen," lamented Fat Peter.

"Gotta go. Game's over," said Pinhead, standing up to leave.

"You better head back to the house, Lester," suggested Danny Noonan.

We left Lester sitting on the sidewalk contemplating his rotten luck and headed off. Even split six ways, almost sixteen dollars was a lot of money. After another five minutes of staring at the pavement, Lester got up and crossed the driveway toward his mother's Mercedes. He was looking at his feet and shaking his head.

"Man, the Ace dagger…" he said to himself, still clueless as to what had happened.

When Lester got his driver's license, he couldn't wait to drive his mother's new car over and pick up Danny Noonan. He wanted to rub Danny's nose in it. The fact that Lester was not yet insured on the vehicle was neither here nor there. When one of his mother's friends picked her up to go shopping, Lester grabbed her car keys. He was in a big hurry to show off the car in our neighborhood. Danny Noonan was standing in his front yard when Lester drove up in a new Mercedes convertible with the top down. Lester waved as he turned into the driveway, coming to a stop with two wheels on the pavement and two in the grass.

"Wanna go for a ride?" asked Lester.

"Your mom know you're driving her car?" answered Danny.

"She's out shopping – it's no problem," replied Lester.

Danny didn't have anything to do, so he climbed into the front seat and closed the door. He didn't bother buckling the seat belt because back then no one did. He looked around the interior of the car, marveling at the leather upholstery, which was much nicer than any of the furniture in Danny's house. Lester put the car into reverse and backed out of Danny's driveway, leaving tire tracks in the grass along the way. They started off down the street, with Lester steering in a slightly erratic back and forth manner. When they came to the corner, Lester put his left turn signal on…then turned right.

They had been cruising the neighborhood for about half an hour when a dog ran out from between two parked cars, dragging a leash behind it. Ordinarily, a dog running out into the street would just be something to avoid running over, but this dog was different. Too inexperienced to make the connection, Lester missed the one clue that would have avoided disaster: the leash. A dog dragging a leash means that moments before there was someone holding that leash. In this case, that someone was a small child, just tall enough to be too short to see among the parked cars. A second or two behind the dog came the child, running into the street, chasing the leash. Lester was focusing on the dog, trying to make sure that he didn't hit it. It was Danny who saw the child.

"Watch out for the kid!" Danny yelled.

Danny diverted Lester's attention from the dog to the child in the nick of time. Lester wrenched the steering wheel to the right, swerving just enough to miss the child by inches. In his panic, however, Lester jammed his foot down on the gas instead of the brake. The car shot forward and sideswiped a parked car with a sickening scraping noise. Lester overcompensated and jerked the steering wheel back to the left, his foot still pressing the accelerator.

Now the car rocketed across both lanes and ricocheted off of two more cars parked on the other side of the street. The mirror on Lester's side of the car sheared off and the car bounced back into the middle of the street, now a danger to cars in both lanes. A bread truck was approaching and Lester's car was straddling the centerline. The truck driver blasted his horn and Lester swerved back to the right for the last time. He bounced over the curb with such a force that he and Danny both rose up off of their seats. Lester's hands flew off of the steering wheel and the car plowed across the sidewalk, which by an act of God was empty. Going nearly thirty miles an hour, Lester's convertible slammed into a fire hydrant and stopped instantly, throwing Danny Noonan up and over the windshield. Danny sailed through the air for about forty feet before crumpling in a heap on the sidewalk in front of the barbershop. Lester sat stunned in his car, a geyser of water shooting up in the air from the fire hydrant that had snapped off beneath the Mercedes. Three men rushed out of the barbershop shouting for someone to call an ambulance. Danny wasn't moving.

My parents and I were sitting at the dinner table in our kitchen when there was a loud banging at the back door. I went to see who was there. When I opened the door, Pinhead was standing on the porch looking like he'd seen a ghost.

"Danny was in an accident. They took him to the hospital but somebody from the barbershop said they think he was dead."

I just stared at Pinhead. I couldn't even comprehend the thought of Danny being dead. Guys our age didn't die.

"What are we going to do?" I asked.

"Mom says no visitors are allowed in the hospital emergency room, so the guys are meeting at the rectory. Father Tim's at the hospital and he told my mom to have us wait for him at the rectory. He said he'd let us know about Danny as soon as he knew something."

I went back to the kitchen and grabbed my jacket from its hook. My parents were looking at me like they thought that I was going out to goof off. Before they could yell at me for leaving the dinner table, I told them what was going on.

"Danny's hurt," I said. "He's at the hospital, and they say he might be dead. Father Tim told us to come to the rectory."

I followed Pinhead down the back stairs and we ran together to the rectory at St. Basil's. All the way there, neither of us spoke a word. Joe the Bum and Fat Peter were already at the rectory when Pinhead and I arrived. Fat Peter's mother had gone to the hospital to be with Duke Noonan. There was no news yet. We sat in Father Tim's living room talking about almost everything except what had happened to Danny. About an hour after we arrived, Cuckoo knocked on the front door.

"Any news?" he asked as he came through the door.

We just shook our heads. For the next few hours, there were long stretches when no one said anything. We just sat and waited for Father Tim. It was almost ten o'clock when we heard footsteps on the front stairs. Father Tim came in looking very tired. No one was brave enough to ask.

Father Tim put down his black leather bag, which we all knew contained everything that he needed to administer last rites.

"Danny's going to be all right boys," said Father Tim, who was clearly as relieved to tell us as we were to hear it. "He'll be in the hospital for a long time, but the doctors said he was out of the woods now."

There was a collective sigh of relief from the five of us, and everyone began chattering. All of the tension that had been bottled up inside everyone came flooding out now that we knew that Danny wasn't going to die.

"Why did someone say he was dead?" asked Cuckoo.

"He was unconscious for a long time," explained Father Tim. "When they found him on the sidewalk, he was not moving and someone jumped to the conclusion that he was dead."

"How bad is it?" asked Fat Peter, the only one of us with first-hand experience at being a patient in the hospital.

"He broke both arms and one leg, and he has a cracked vertebra in his back," said Father Tim. "He'll be in a cast for almost two months, then he'll have to have a lot of therapy to get his strength back...he was very lucky."

It didn't sound very lucky to us. We could tell that Father Tim was very tired, and since there wasn't anything that we could do, as long as we knew that Danny was going to be OK, we left for home. It was almost two weeks before we could go to the hospital to visit Danny. When we did, we were not prepared for what we saw. He was in a cast from his ankle to his shoulder. One leg was attached to a chain that hung from a bar above his bed. His left arm was held above his head by another chain hooked to a bar next to his shoulder.

Sitting next to Danny's bed was Duke Noonan. She seemed to be awfully cheerful for someone sitting next to their son in a hospital. Standing next to her was a guy who we had never seen before. He wore a brown plaid suit with black shoes and a striped tie. The collar of his shirt was frayed at the edges. He was holding a stack of papers in one hand and a vinyl briefcase in the other.

"Well, I think that's about it for now, Mrs. Noonan," said the guy in the bad suit. "I'll file these papers and then we'll see where we go next." He eased his way around the end of Danny's bed and slid past us and out the door. As he disappeared down the hallway, I noticed that one of his shoes was untied.

Duke Noonan looked up and seemed genuinely happy to see us. "Come in, boys," she invited, "Danny will be so happy to see you." She then leaned over Danny and patted the hand that was not covered in plaster. "I'll go get a bite to eat and let you spend some time with your friends." Then she did something that none of us could ever remember seeing her do…she smiled. She thanked us for coming as she left the room carrying her purse.

"How's it going, guys?" Danny asked as we moved closer to his bed.

"Better for us than for you, it looks like," said Joe the Bum, not trying to be funny.

Danny spent a few minutes telling us what had happened. He didn't remember anything after hitting the curb and bouncing off of his seat. He told us that the rest of the story he had heard from the police, who in turn got it from the guys at the barbershop who had seen what had happened. The cops had left out the part of the story where Danny was dead. We talked about how long Danny would be in the hospital, and how it might be the rest of the school year before he came back. He would have tutors to teach him at home. Then he said something that caught us all by surprise.

"When I get fixed up, I'm getting a Cadillac."

"What?" asked Joe the Bum.

"That guy who just left is a lawyer. He was driving behind Lester the day of the accident and he saw the whole thing. When they brought me here in the ambulance, he followed them in his car to make sure that the hospital knew that it wasn't my fault. He explained what had happened, and next thing my mom knows, we've got this private room with a television and a telephone."

"What's that got to do with a Cadillac?" asked Joe the Bum, his eyes narrowing.

"The lawyer talked to the cops and found out that Lester's old man is loaded. He says we can sue my uncle and aunt for medical costs and that we can also get a pile o'dough for 'pain and suffering'. When my ma heard that she could sue her sister and her rich brother-in-law, it was like she had just heard a good joke…she started laughing and slapping the lawyer on the knee. She said putting up with her sister since she married that doctor had been nothing but pain and suffering."

"You're nuts," said Joe the Bum. "No insurance company is gonna pay you enough for hospital bills and a new Cadillac."

If anyone should know about what insurance companies would or wouldn't pay for, it was Joe the Bum. His dad had pulled almost every scam there was, and when it came to knowing what you could and couldn't get away with, Joe the Bum was something of an expert.

"That's just it," said Danny. "Lester wasn't covered on his mother's insurance. The lawyer says that Lester's parents are on the hook to pay, and that they have almost as much money as the insurance company. He told Ma that the Griggs would pay almost anything we asked for to make sure that they get to keep that house with the pond and the gazebo…I told my Ma to ask for a brand new Cadillac."

"I still think you're nuts," said Joe the Bum.

"We'll see…" answered Danny.

It was almost six months before Danny Noonan was back to normal. He moved a little funny sometimes; he said it was because he had a metal plate in one ankle and some screws in his other leg. For the most part, however, if you didn't know that he'd almost died, you'd never guess it from looking at him. One afternoon in September, with the air just beginning to turn cool in anticipation of autumn, my mom came home from the store and said something that should have set off an alarm in my head, but didn't.

"I just saw Mrs. Noonan at the market," my mom said as she put her groceries down on the kitchen table. "She was wearing the most beautiful mink coat I've ever seen...and such an unusual color…it was almost all black but it had a streak of lighter colored fur down the middle of the back. If I didn't know better, I'd think it was a skunk."

I didn't immediately make the connection between Duke Noonan wearing a fur coat that looked like a skunk and the lawsuit against Dr. and Mrs. Griggs. Obviously, Duke Noonan had come into a considerable sum of money – her sister's money – but it wasn't until Pinhead appeared at the screen door on our front porch that it hit me. Standing outside with his hands cupped around his eyes to help him see inside through the screen, Pinhead called to me, "Hey Mike, c'mon. Danny got his car."

For months all we had heard from Danny was how he was going to get a new Cadillac. He'd been saying it for so long that we had just started to ignore him whenever he brought it up. Now here was Pinhead, hollering through my screen door that Danny Noonan's ship had come in. I went out the front door and followed Pinhead down the steps and up the block toward Danny Noonan's house. When we got there, sure enough, there was a candy apple red Cadillac convertible with white leather interior. The top was down and the car was parked along the curb across the street from Danny's house.

The whole neighborhood was out looking at Danny's new car. Everyone was standing a few feet away from the car peering into the white interior. No one got close enough to touch it, almost as if it was radioactive. Danny was leaning up against a telephone pole, holding court. He was telling everyone who would listen exactly how much the car had cost. He added that the convertible was even more expensive than an ordinary Cadillac, emphasizing the word "ordinary" as if any brand new Cadillac could be ordinary.

Joe the Bum came walking up the sidewalk, an admiring smile on his face. He hadn't believed Danny when he said he would get a new Cadillac, but coming from a long line of schemers, Joe the Bum admired a good scam artist when he saw him. "I never thought you'd pull it off," said Joe.

"If you like the car, you'll love that..." Danny said, tilting his head in the direction of his driveway. Joe looked in the direction that Danny had nodded and saw a brand new motorcycle parked in Danny's driveway.

"Are you telling me that you got a new car AND a motorcycle out of this deal?" asked Joe, his eyes portraying his disbelief.

"Yep," answered Danny proudly.

"Unbelievable," admired Joe. "Let's take the car for a ride."

"Nah, I don't want to get the interior dirty," said Danny, "but we can ride the motorcycle if you want to."

Joe the Bum didn't need to be asked twice. He hurried over to the motorcycle and climbed on. Danny came over and climbed on behind Joe, wrapping his arms around Joe's waist. Joe jumped on the starter and twisted the throttle and the motorcycle engine roared. With each twist of the throttle, the engine got even louder. We could see Joe and Danny leaning toward one another, each saying something to the other, but it was impossible to hear exactly what they were saying over the roar of the motorcycle's engine.

"Is first gear up or down?" shouted Joe, who had never driven a motorcycle before.

"Sure," yelled Danny, having no idea what Joe had said.

"No...which way do I shift...up or down?" Joe asked without turning his head.

"Blue," answered Danny. Clearly, he could not hear Joe over the roar of the motor.

Joe shrugged and guessed that first gear was one notch up. Clicking the clutch once, he twisted the throttle. He had guessed wrong...the engine shifted into third gear and as he accelerated, Joe the Bum and Danny Noonan shot forward like they were fired out of a cannon. The front wheel of the motorcycle rose off of the ground and it was everything that Joe and Danny could do just to hang on. They roared down the driveway and across the street on one wheel, then slammed into the side of the candy apple red Cadillac going full speed. When the motorcycle smashed into the car, Joe the Bum pitched over the handlebars, somersaulted in the air, and landed on his back in the white leather front seat. Danny Noonan sailed over the top of the Cadillac and landed in the bushes in front of the neighbor's porch. Joe the Bum sat up slowly, cleared his head, and saw the motorcycle wedged into a crease that it had made in the side of Danny's new car. A young kid rushed over to where Danny lay motionless in the bushes.

"I think he's dead!" shouted the kid, seeing Danny's eyes closed and assuming the worst.

Danny's eyes blinked open. He looked left and right without moving his head. In spite of the fact that he could move, he made no effort to do so. He just sighed and said in a dejected tone of voice, "Not again..."

The motorcycle was a total loss. They repaired the Cadillac, and almost matched the new paint to the original shade of red. If you didn't look too closely, you might never know that it had been wrecked, but Danny knew...and it was never the same.

Chapter 14

5:17 P.M.

Amazing Grace, whether played on a magnificent pipe organ or on a lone bagpipe, stirs the spirit. Its strains invariably conjure up emotions, and today was no exception. I walked back down the center aisle of St. Basil's with Sister Thomas Aquinas, careful to take small steps so that she wouldn't struggle to keep up. I brushed a tear from the corner of my eye. I was mourning the passing of youth as much as I was the death of a kind and thoughtful old priest. As we neared the back of the church, the bright sunlight streamed in through the open doors that awaited Father Tim's casket. It was a powerful visual image – moving from darkness toward the light. The new pastor and the two altar boys had led the procession up the aisle, and they now stood silhouetted against the sunlight ahead of the casket.

Two of the three guys in black suits were wheeling the casket toward the doors. The third made his way over to us. He smiled and nodded politely without saying anything to me. To Sister Thomas Aquinas he extended his arm and said softly, "Sister?" Sister Thomas Aquinas patted my arm and whispered, "I'll see you at the cemetery, Michael," then moved off with the funeral director toward his car. As he helped her into the passenger seat, I couldn't help smiling...it was a Cadillac.

I turned to look for Pinhead. He had followed the casket out of the church and was helping the two black suits slide it back into the hearse. He hadn't told me that he was a pallbearer, and it hadn't occurred to me to ask. Considering how many evenings he had spent with Father Tim in the two years since he'd taken ill, however, it made perfect sense. I had planned to offer Pinhead a ride out to the cemetery, but he would be accompanying the casket. I lingered in the vestibule of the church for a while after everyone had gone. I was in no hurry to leave, in part because St. Basil's had always been a safe place for me and for some reason right now I felt like I needed to be in a safe place. The other reason for my lagging behind was that I dreaded the thought of going out to the cemetery.

Growing up, I always wondered why the Catholic Church was so stubborn about making changes. It took them one thousand nine hundred and sixty years to allow Catholics to eat meat on Fridays except in Lent. The liturgy was virtually the same as it had been six hundred years ago. The hymns were written in Gregorian monasteries before the turn of the first millennium. Today, standing here in the vestibule, at least part of the reason for centuries of Catholic stubbornness came to me. It was the sameness that made you feel safe. It was the familiarity that made me reluctant to leave at this very moment. It was the fact that you could be away from the church for years – for decades – and when you decided to come back, it was there waiting for you, almost just as it was when you left it.

From the time when I first arrived at St. Basil's as a six year old, until I left the neighborhood for college and forgot to ever come back, this had been home. I attended Mass every day until I was in sixth grade. Then we dropped down to twice a week plus Sundays. Two thousand, five hundred times while growing up, I walked into St. Basil's Church for Mass. It had now been more than twelve thousand days since I left, but the minute I walked through the doors, I was back home. Now, faced with the prospect of going back outside, I was taking my time. Where I had to go could wait. Just a few more minutes back home…

They had closed the rear doors of the hearse and Pinhead was sliding into the back seat next to the black suits. In a moment, the parade of cars would begin, all of their headlights on in the middle of the day. I disturbed the surface of the holy water with my fingertips and instinctively made the Sign of the Cross as I left St. Basil's to return to my life.

If it was possible for it to have become even hotter, it felt like it had. Heat waves rippled the air above the pavement, creating the optical illusion of standing water. I took off my jacket again and slung it over my shoulder. Beads of perspiration collected on my forehead before I reached the Lexus at the far end of the parking lot. I chuckled at having parked it so far from the entrance, worried that it would get a dent. The inside of the car was like a furnace. I opened all of the windows, turned the air conditioner on full blast, and then stepped back outside for a few moments until the super-heated air was blown out of the car. I got back in just as the hearse began to pull out of the circle drive. The black Cadillac with Sister Thomas Aquinas pulled in behind the hearse and the rest of the cars in the parking lot followed suit. While we had been inside, someone had placed a bright orange placard that read "funeral" beneath the windshield wipers of each car.

The funeral procession inched its way through traffic. We didn't stop for red lights, but the traffic between blocks was still heavy enough to create gridlock. Even though the car was new, I kept looking at the temperature gauge, worried that the engine would overheat with the air conditioning blasting away in traffic.

Staring at the sunlight reflecting off of the trunk of the car in front of me, my mind went out for a short wander. I thought about Pinhead coming back to the old neighborhood to teach. He had always been my best friend, and behind the wise cracks, the pranks, and the tough exterior, I always knew there was a serious side to him. If any of us was likely to realize that there was nothing far away that you couldn't get at home, it was Pinhead. I wondered what kind of a basketball coach he was. Remembering him sprawled on the court all tangled up with Lou the Screw, I couldn't help smiling. I wondered if Pinhead spends as much time as Father Tim had spent teaching his kids how to be good basketball players, not just how to play good basketball. I bet he does. I hoped I would be able to make it to one of his games in the fall.

After all those years of scraping together dimes and nickels for spending money, pooling our money to share a basket of chicken and fries at Earl's, Danny Noonan was a hamburger tycoon. I wondered what it was like to be one of the richest guys in town – surely making three quarters of a million dollars a year had to make Danny one of the city fathers in rural Idaho. I bet he never let a kid go without a burger and fries just because they were a little short.

I couldn't help wondering what it was like for anyone who was in trouble for the first time when they stood in the courtroom looking up at Fat Peter. His altar boy cassock had never fit him quite right, and I wondered if his black judge's robe fit any better. Always fair and slow to judge anyone in the neighborhood, even when they deserved it, the Honorable Peter Supinski now held people's futures in his hands. I almost felt sorry for any doctor who came before him accused of botching a case of kidney stones.

It was hard to imagine Cuckoo being called Dr. Coolack. Dr. Cuckoo was easier to believe. I wondered what Cuckoo told mothers who dragged their kids in with broken glasses, bitching about how money didn't grow on trees. I bet he pulled the kids aside, out of earshot of their mothers, and whispered reassurances to them that he could fix their glasses up as good as new. If he thought of it, he would show them a picture of himself as a kid, his eyeglasses held together by half a roll of tape.

The most difficult thing to accept was Whitey Shelton being gone. He was always the kid in the middle of everything. A foot shorter and twenty pounds lighter than everyone else his age, Whitey always made up for his diminutive size with bravado. I wondered what Whitey was thinking the day the ground shook in Oklahoma City. I wondered if he had time to think of anything at all. I bet that if he did, he was on the move when the walls came down.

The traffic started moving and my attention snapped back to the car ahead of me. The funeral procession weaved through the neighborhood on its way to Immaculate Conception Cemetery, where we would say our final goodbyes to Father Tim. Halfway up the block on the left was Bailey's Hardware Store. At least when we were kids, it had been Bailey's Hardware Store…now it was a generic Ace Hardware store, undoubtedly no longer owned by the Bailey family. It was at Bailey's Hardware Store that I witnessed one of the boldest acts of larceny since the Great Train Robbery. We were sitting on the stoop of a house across the street from the hardware store. We had been wandering around for most of the morning, not doing much of anything at all. Cuckoo was talking about a movie that he had seen the night before.

"…so this kid swipes a wristwatch in a department store and starts to walk out of the place when the store clerk yells for him to stop…next thing he knows, he's at Boys Town and Father Flanagan is reading him the riot act."

"That's because the kid was an amateur," said Joe the Bum.

"Of course he was an amateur, he was a kid," replied Cuckoo.

"He didn't know what he was doing," Joe answered, impatiently.

"You do?" asked Pinhead.

"Sure," said Joe. "You gotta have a plan. You can't just stuff something down your pants and try to sneak out. That's exactly what they're watching for."

"What kinda plan?" asked Fat Peter, out of curiosity, not professional interest.

"I'll show ya," said Joe, getting up and starting across the street toward Bailey's Hardware Store. We sat and watched as Joe crossed the street and entered the store. He was gone for five or ten minutes, then he appeared at the front door of the store carrying a big cardboard box on one shoulder.

When he reached the street, he turned and walked slowly down the sidewalk. He turned his head only slightly, made eye contact with us, and smiled. He was carrying a toaster oven.

We held our breath waiting for someone to come running out of the hardware store chasing Joe the Bum, but no one did. Joe turned the corner at the end of the block and disappeared and still no one was following him. We started walking down the block on our side of the street, still watching the front of the hardware store for pursuers. Joe the Bum kept walking with the toaster oven, down the sidewalk a block and a half away. He was heading home. Keeping a safe distance in case Joe got ambushed by the cops, we followed him all the way to his house. He made it all the way home without so much as a second glance from anyone who saw him.

"How'd you do that?" asked Cuckoo.

"Simple," answered Joe, "the secret is to take something so big that you can hardly carry it. They're watching everyone who touches something small enough to swipe, but no one believes you'd just walk out the front door with a toaster oven on your shoulder if you hadn't paid for it...if you could lift one, you could walk a refrigerator out the front door."

"What're you gonna do with a toaster over?" asked Fat Peter.

"I'll just put it in the garage and wait until I do something to get my ma mad, then I'll give it to her as a present."

"Aren't they gonna ask you where you got the money?" Fat Peter tried to apply logic to Joe the Bum's household.

"Nah, with my dad's friends, stuff is showing up all the time...who's gonna notice a toaster oven?"

It wasn't hard to imagine Joe the Bum out in California, with some no-show job and married to a girl whose father was a wheeler-dealer. Joe had been training his whole life for just such an opportunity.

With only a few blocks left before reaching the cemetery, the funeral procession came to a stop. The flashing red lights at the railroad crossing told us that we'd be delayed by a passing freight train. The four engines at the head of the train told us that we would be stuck for a while. I snuck another look at the engine temperature gauge, but the needle was safely below the red zone. I pressed a button on the dash to display the outside temperature. It was down to 85 degrees. The temperature had fallen almost fifteen degrees just since we had left the church. I watched the cars of the freight train roll by, almost wishing I had a tar ball to throw. About thirty cars into the train was a boxcar that looked like one of those auto carriers, but this one carried boats. Bright metallic paint jobs...a dozen brand new bass boats...it brought back memories of the nearly fatal fishing trip.

Pinhead and I had been planning the trip for weeks. His parents were taking the train to a cousin's wedding and would be gone all weekend. When Pinhead asked if he could use the car to go with me on an overnight camping trip, his folks must have calculated that he could do less damage in a tent with me than in his house with the whole gang. Choosing the lesser of two evils, they said that he could use the car.

About two hours from home was a campground called Christmas Tree Lake. You brought your own tent, cooked over a campfire, and went to the bathroom in the woods. The campground didn't have any amenities, but it had something much more important – boats with outboard motors. We had been to the place with our parents, but this would be different. Just the two of us, roaring around the lake in our own boat. There was only one problem... Pinhead couldn't swim.

We got up while it was still dark and packed our gear into the trunk of Pinhead's parents' car. We were on the road before the neighborhood woke up, and we got to Christmas Tree Lake by mid-morning. We stopped at a little shed that leaned to one side of the entrance to the property. Behind the counter was a scraggly looking guy with a tooth missing right in the front. He was wearing an eye patch.

"Mornin' fellers," he drawled. We had never heard anyone with a southern accent in the neighborhood, and we were a little confused because Christmas Tree Lake was actually northwest of home.

"What can I do ya for?" he smiled, exposing the cavernous gap between his teeth.

"We'd like to rent a campsite," I said.

"And a boat," added Pinhead quickly.

"Y'all old enough ta drive?" asked the caretaker.

We looked around us to be sure that he was talking to us. Our car was parked directly in front of his open door and we were the only ones within a mile of his shed, but we figured it wasn't in our best interest to ask him how he thought we'd gotten there.

"Yessir," Pinhead replied, handing him his driver's license.

Squinting at the license, the caretaker frowned. It wasn't clear whether he'd found something that troubled him or if he was just struggling to read. Holding the license up to the light, he raised his eye patch and then smiled, nodding his head. Replacing the eye patch, he said, "Sometimes I have to use my good eye. That'll be three dollars fer the camping and four dollars fer the boat. If you want an anchor, that's another dollar."

I looked at Pinhead and he looked at me. We'd never taken a boat out on our own, so we weren't sure whether we needed an anchor. Figuring that it couldn't hurt to have one, we gave the caretaker eight dollars. He punched a button on an ancient cash register and the drawer opened. He put six dollars into the cash register and stuffed two dollars into his pocket.

"Yer in campsite number eleven," he said. "Yer boat is number three… it's tied up at the dock."

We started to leave when the caretaker called us back. He reached behind the counter and pulled out a length of rotting rope. As he pulled on the rope, we heard a banging noise as he dragged out an old chunk of a car transmission tied to the end of the rope. He handed the transmission to Pinhead.

"What's this?" asked Pinhead.

"Yer anchor," grinned the caretaker.

We followed the rutted gravel road around the perimeter of the lake, looking for campsite number eleven. We passed a series of empty campsites, watching the battered wooden signs increase in number…eight, nine, ten. We pulled into campsite eleven and turned off the car. As we got out, we were greeted by an unexpected sight. After passing ten empty campsites, we found ourselves no more than twenty yards from our neighbors in campsite number twelve. Looking beyond our neighbors, we saw a long string of vacant campsites continuing down the gravel road. The caretaker had assigned the only two occupants in the entire camp to adjacent plots.

Our neighbors weren't camping in a tent. They had an old battered mobile home trailer. We had the impression that they had been there for a while. There was a clothesline stretched from the trailer to a tree with underwear blowing in the breeze. A dog was sleeping in the shade under the trailer. A closer look revealed that the trailer wasn't sitting on tires…it was resting on concrete blocks. The final clue that they were doing more than camping was nailed to a post in front of the trailer – it was a mailbox.

We set about pitching our tent and unloading our fishing poles and groceries, trying to ignore the racket that was coming from the trailer next door. There were shouts and the sound of breaking glass, then laughter. We were glad that we had a boat. When we had the tent up and our sleeping bags tucked inside, we began to untangle our fishing poles and prepared to head off to the boat. That's when we noticed a young kid standing ankle deep in the water, his pants rolled up to his knees, where he rested his hands as he bent over at the waist peering into the lake.

He was a strange looking kid. He had his hair clipped so short that at first glance he looked bald. His teeth were all twisted and when he looked over at us, it became apparent that his eyes were crossed. He returned his gaze, such as it was, to the surface of the water. He stood perfectly still for a long time, then he jumped out of the water and landed in the mud at the edge of the lake. Cupping his hands around his mouth, he turned to face the trailer and began shouting at the top of his lungs.

"Ah jist seen thuh dawgfish!...Ah jist seen thuh dawgfish!"

There was another round of shouting from inside the trailer, another sound of shattering glass, then more laughter. But no one appeared in the doorway.

Pinhead and I just laughed and started off for our boat. We walked down to the dock and found boat number three. At one time, perhaps during the Eisenhower presidency, the boat had been red. Now the wood was both the color and consistency of newsprint. Pinhead stepped gingerly into the bow of the boat and tied the transmission anchor to the steel eyelet on the keel. I stepped into the stern near the motor; when I sat down on the wooden bench, my feet were submerged in oily brown water.

It took seven or eight yanks on the starter before the outboard motor sputtered to life. By twisting the throttle, I could keep the motor running. The entire rear transom of the boat shook from the turbulence caused by a badly bent propeller shaft. Oblivious to the questionable seaworthiness of the vessel, Pinhead and I shoved off and headed out toward the middle of the lake.

Christmas Tree Lake was formed when a series of strip mines filled with water. Generations of coal miners had dug deep gouges into the earth, extracting the coal that fueled the steel mills that built American cities. When they dug too deep, they hit the water table and then it was time to abandon that mine and start another. The water filled the deep coal mines, creating lakes that often had sheer drop-offs that were as much as one hundred feet deep. Pinhead and I found a spot near a sheer rock wall and began fishing. In a very short time, the wind had blown our boat up against the rock wall. We moved to another spot where we could see the rocky bottom twelve or fifteen feet below the surface. Pinhead dropped the transmission overboard, playing out rope until the anchor hit bottom.

We fished for a while longer before the wind kicked up even stronger. With the anchor wedged in the boulders at the bottom of the lake, we began turning in circles, blown by the wind. Just off the left side of the boat was a jagged boulder that protruded above the surface of the lake. Each time the wind blew us around again, we slammed into the nearly submerged rock. Unable to swim, Pinhead was getting more nervous each time the flimsy hull banged against the jagged rock. He pulled at the anchor rope as hard as he could, but the anchor was hopelessly lodged in the boulders at the bottom of the lake. The wind wasn't dying down. In fact, it felt like a storm might be brewing. We debated whether or not to cut the anchor line, afraid of what the one-eyed pirate in the caretaker shed would say when we came back without his transmission. It didn't take long for Pinhead to become more frightened of drowning than he was of the caretaker, and he pulled out his pocketknife. Once the anchor was cut loose, we started the motor and aimed the boat back toward the dock.

Since neither of us had any experience piloting a boat, we weren't quite sure how to dock the skiff. Pinhead leaned out over the bow as I maneuvered the boat toward the dock. About ten feet from the dock, Pinhead shouted, "We seem to have too much momentum." If he had shouted "Stop!" we might have fared better. I turned off the motor, but the boat was going way too fast. We hit the pier head-on and Pinhead pitched over the bow and into the lake. Seeing Pinhead disappear into the water, I rushed forward, knowing that he couldn't swim. When I got to the bow, Pinhead was flailing in the water, his arms splashing as he gasped for air. He was churning the water into a froth trying to keep his nose and mouth above water. I was about to jump into the lake when I stopped and looked more closely.

"Pinhead!" I shouted.

He continued to struggle.

"Pinhead!" I shouted again.

He twisted his head and looked up at me, still thrashing his arms in the water.

"Stand up!"

Pinhead stopped waving his arms and stood up. The water was only waist-deep. He grinned sheepishly and walked to shore. I tied up the boat and lugged our fishing gear up onto the dock. We each grabbed two armfuls of stuff and walked back to campsite number eleven. Pinhead walked slightly ahead, water dripping from his hair and clothes, an empty fish stringer dragging behind him in the dirt.

When we got back to camp, the Beverly Hillbillies were still laughing and breaking glass in the trailer next door. The little bald kid with the wandering eye was now sitting in the mud along the shoreline holding a fishing pole. There was a little girl just outside the trailer, about twenty yards away from the cross-eyed bald kid. She looked like she must be his younger sister. She was cute, but filthy. She looked like she was about seven or eight years old. She had curly hair and very pleasant features in between smudges of dirt. The most striking thing about her was her vocabulary. She punctuated almost every sentence with profanity.

"Billy, momma says not to sit in the damn mud."

"Billy, momma says to bring the damn garbage out."

"Billy, momma says you better not come in smelling like no damn fish."

From the sounds of it, "damn" was the only adjective that she knew. Billy just sat in the mud ignoring her. He made no move to bring out any garbage, and from the looks of him, the odor of a fish might be an improvement.

We gathered some branches and kindling to start a fire. Pinhead was wearing the only clothes that he had brought, so we needed to get him dried out. We chose a spot a safe distance from the tent and started making a pile of wood.

I glanced over at Billy just as his fishing pole began to twitch violently. Scrambling to his feet, Billy gripped his fishing pole tightly and began yelling, "Whoa! Whoa!" His sister heard the commotion down by the water and walked halfway to the lake to see what was going on. Seeing Billy struggling with his fishing pole bent in half, she turned and ran toward the trailer, hollering,

"Momma, come look. Billy caught the damn dawgfish! Billy caught the damn dawgfish!"

Billy never even tried to turn the handle on his fishing reel. It was as if he didn't know what it was for. He just started walking backward from the muddy shoreline toward the trailer, with about thirty feet of taut fishing line stretching between him and the fish. He kept backing up until he was only a few steps from the front door of the trailer. It was then that the fish rolled out of the water and into the mud where Billy had been sitting a few moments before. When the fish was on dry land, Billy ran down to the edge of the water and began struggling to lift it in his arms.

The screen door of the trailer opened and a heavyset woman emerged. She staggered down to where Billy was wrestling with his fish, grabbing it in both arms only to have it slip from his grasp and land with a thud back in the mud. His mother surveyed the scene, then put her hands on her ample hips and said disgustedly,

"That ain't no damn dawgfish...that's a damn carp...don't you track that damn mud up here with you, Billy, and jump in the lake – you smell like a damn fish."

She turned and waddled back to the trailer. Pulling the screen door open, she turned sideways to squeeze through the doorway, then disappeared inside. The squeaky door slammed shut behind her. A moment later there was more shouting, then the sound of breaking glass, then laughter.

The end of the freight train passed the crossing. There was no caboose. It's too bad that most freight trains don't have cabooses anymore. There was always something nice about seeing the little red car at the end of a long train. It signaled the end. We would wave to the guy sitting in the caboose, and he would wave back from his open window. It's not the same without the caboose. The end comes unexpectedly, and there is no one to wave goodbye.

When the gates went up, the funeral procession resumed the trip across town to the Immaculate Conception Cemetery. Just across the railroad tracks, halfway up the next block on the left hand side of the street, was Tulley's Funeral Home. The Tulley family had owned the neighborhood funeral home for 87 years. Winthrop Tulley was a gentle, kind man who genuinely cared about the families whose relatives he buried. He was a source of great comfort for my mother and father when Henry died. He would have been a comfort for my mother and me when my father passed away, but by then we were a thousand miles away.

Chapter 15

The series of events that led to my father dying in Boston began at Point Reyes, a rocky spit of land jutting out into the Pacific Ocean an hour north of San Francisco. It was the beginning of my last year of medical school, and Annie and I had driven up to spend a Sunday afternoon watching the whales migrate south from Alaska now that summer was over. Point Reyes sits atop a cliff with breathtaking views up and down the coast in either direction. In the early fall and late spring, the humpback and gray whales pass by, their rhythmic spouts of expelled air mixed with water visible on the horizon. We packed a picnic lunch and a pair of binoculars and set off for the day.

The wind is a constant at Point Reyes. It buffets you as you make your way along narrow walking paths worn into the ice plant that clings to the inhospitable rocky soil. Conversations must be conducted in slightly elevated voices in order to be heard. The Pacific is cold there, so there is almost always a chill in the air. Annie wore a cream colored Irish knit sweater over blue jeans. Her hair was pulled back in a pony tail to keep the wind from whipping it in her face.

The way medicine works is that fourth year medical students decide what specialty they would like to pursue, presumably by reflecting back on their rotations through the various clinical specialties during their education. More than one medical student has based their choice of specialty on the price of the cars in the parking lot belonging to their respective faculty mentors. Whether passionate or economic, the choice of a specialty is the biggest decision a medical student will ever make.

Most people think that prospective doctors choose their specialty and that's the end of it. In fact, it's much more complicated. At the same time that medical students are trying to decide what discipline to specialize in, residency programs run by medical schools and teaching hospitals are evaluating the students, deciding which students are likely to make the best specialists. It is entirely possible, perhaps even common, for a medical student to aspire to one specialty but to be accepted into a residency in their second or even third choice. Not everyone who wants to be a brain surgeon is cut out to be one.

Through a complex matching process, part blind dating and part job interview, students make lists of specialties and training programs that would make them happy while hospitals and residency programs rank the students that they would like to accept. It's like a national homecoming dance, with students from every medical school standing along one wall looking nervous and hospitals from every state standing along the other wall, arms folded and letting the students sweat a bit.

On a single day in the spring of each year, computers match the wish lists of students with the offers from medical school hospitals and marriages are born. One minute every medical student in the country is waiting with baited breathe, and the next moment some are on their way to becoming brain surgeons and others are, well, rectal surgeons save lives too.

One of my professors at Stanford was a graduate of the Harvard Medical School and he had trained under a world-renowned vascular surgeon at the Massachusetts General Hospital. Knowing that I was interested in surgery, and apparently seeing something in me that I was afraid might not be there, he offered to make a personal recommendation to his old teacher back in Boston. It was the chance of a lifetime for me. His endorsement would go a long way toward getting me a surgical residency at Harvard.

I was excited and petrified at the same time. What if I didn't get accepted into the Harvard residency program? What if I did? What if I didn't have what it took to be a surgeon? What if I did? A million questions were rattling around in my head, but one was bothering me more than the others: how was I going to tell Annie that I wanted to drag her all the way across the country to Boston for the next five years? That was the question that had brought us to Point Reyes, a place where we had come whenever we needed to get away from everything and everybody.

Annie spread a blanket on the ground and carefully placed rocks on each of the four corners to keep it from becoming a kite in the wind. She opened a thermos and poured coffee into two large porcelain mugs. I wrapped my hands around the mug and sat down next to Annie. We gazed out at the horizon, pretending to be looking for whales. Annie didn't say anything. Like always, she knew when something was on my mind, and she gave me room. She sipped her coffee, patiently waiting for me to say whatever it was that I had brought her all the way out here to say. My coffee was almost cold before I summoned the courage to start.

"I had lunch with Dr. Stanfield last week," I began. Dr. Stanfield was the professor of vascular surgery who offered to recommend me to Harvard.

"Wow. What was the occasion?"

Annie knew enough about medical school to know that faculty physicians didn't make a habit out of having lunch with medical students.

"He knows I'm interested in surgery," I continued. "He studied under Cashman at Harvard. The same Cashman who's picture was on the cover of Time magazine. Dr. Stanfield offered to call Dr. Cashman and recommend me for a residency if I was interested."

I watched Annie's face for a look of disappointment. I knew that she would never come right out and say that she didn't want to move across the country, but I was afraid that I would see a telltale flicker of disappointment at the prospect. Instead, I saw an instantaneous look of reassurance. Without hesitating, Annie dispelled any fears that I had about disappointing her.

"Mike, that's unbelievable," she said, putting her arm around me. "Harvard? That's the chance of a lifetime."

For a moment, I didn't know what to say. I'd been preparing for a reluctant acceptance mixed with sadness over leaving California. Her enthusiasm caught me by surprise.

"You do know that Harvard's in Boston?" I asked, trying to leave the door open for her to express just a little disappointment, even light-hearted disappointment.

"I'd heard that," she quipped.

"Boston, Massachusetts?" I continued.

"Didn't they have a Tea Party a while back?" she asked.

"Are you ok with Boston?" I asked, becoming serious.

"Absolutely," she answered without blinking.

"It's a long way from home," I offered.

"Home is wherever we are," she answered.

"It's cold there," I said.

"Nothing's cold after South Bend," she replied.

"Wouldn't you be happier if I did my residency out here?"

"Wouldn't you be happier doing it in Boston?" she answered my question with a question.

"You'll be two thousand miles from your family," I observed.

"I'll come out to see them often," Annie said softly. "You'll be busy; I'll have a lot of time for visits home. Besides, you've been a thousand miles away from your folks for the last four years.

"Are you sure you'll be alright?" I asked.

"We'll be fine," she said, and then she kissed me.

We held each other for a long time without saying anything. In the warmth of her embrace, I could feel her letting go of everything familiar and holding tightly to us.

About a year after Annie and I were married, my father was offered a promotion at work. He'd been offered promotions before, but they always came with strings attached, almost always involving relocation to plants in other parts of the country. While I was growing up, he had always turned down the promotions because he and my mother didn't want to pull me out of the neighborhood and away from my friends. Once I was out of the house and living in California, there was nothing to keep them there anymore.

When the offer came for a position in western Pennsylvania, he took it. The house had become haunted now that they were alone. Memories of Henry that my mother had been able to push into the background when we were all together took up residence in the old house now that she was there so much by herself. My dad saw the changes, and when the company asked him to move, he didn't think twice. They sold the house and moved during my second year of medical school. The timing was bad for me to get back, so I never did make it before they were gone.

Annie and I visited my parents in Pennsylvania every Christmas, and they took the train out to California twice to see us during my four years at Stanford. I missed them, but I was so busy with school that it was a lot easier on me than it was on them. Each time we saw them, the time went so quickly that it felt like we had just said hello when it was time to say goodbye. The partings never got any easier. In fact, as parents get older, each time you say goodbye it gets just a little harder, because you're seeing a few more gray hairs, a few more wrinkles around the eyes. I couldn't help staring at my father's hands. It's the hands that betray a person's age. The skin becomes thinner, freckles grow into splotches, and tiny creases begin to form between the thumb and forefinger.

Each time a visit came to a close, I made a mental note of my father's hands. Each time we said goodbye, another part of him stayed behind. I started to worry about how much was left. The pain of saying goodbye made it almost easier to allow more time to creep in between visits. It's funny…the more you miss someone, the harder it is to see them, because our hearts only have so many breakings in them.

When I was accepted for the surgical residency at Harvard, I thought that I would see more of my parents, since Boston is so much closer to western Pennsylvania. As it turned out, we didn't see them any more in Boston than we had in California. My schedule as a resident made medical school seem like a vacation, and once you're more than four hours apart, distance is a constant. So during the first two years of my residency, we got back to see my folks at Christmas, but now the visits were even shorter because we also had to travel to California to see Annie's family. I just grew accustomed to the long stretches of time between visits. I never grew accustomed to the partings.

My parents rarely called on the telephone. They were always afraid that they would be bothering us, so my mom wrote letters. Looking back, I wish that I had called them more often. I didn't have the excuse of not wanting to bother them, because I knew that they would be thrilled if I called. I just allowed myself to be busy, and I called when Annie told me to. That's another funny thing – a real difference between daughters and sons. Daughters talk to their parents every week, if not every day. Sons talk to their parents when their wives remind them that it has been too long since they called.

So I was surprised to hear Annie answer the telephone one evening and greet my mother. After pleasantries, Annie told my mom to call more often, and handed the telephone to me. I had just come home from a long shift at the hospital, and I was still wearing my surgical scrubs. I held the phone up to my ear with one hand and opened a can of soda with the other. I never took a drink of the soda.

My father had been having digestive problems, she said. Pain in his abdomen, nausea, lack of appetite. He had lost a lot of weight and my mother had finally convinced him to see a doctor. He had gone in for some tests to check out his gall bladder, but what they found was much worse. He had pancreatic cancer. My mom recited for me what the doctors had told her, but I already knew. While she was talking, my mind was three steps ahead, running all of the checklists and always coming to the same conclusion.

I tried to sound reassuring for my mother, but I'm not sure that it did any good. Her voice had a vaguely familiar hollowness that I had first overheard late at night when she and my father spoke outside of Henry's room, when they thought that I was asleep. It was the sound of sadness, tinged with resignation.

I told my mom to bring dad to Boston. I would arrange for him to be seen by Harvard's best specialists. I would look into available clinical trials, experimental drugs, anything and everything that could be done. The gesture was more for her and for me than it was for my father. Nothing that any doctors could do would change things for him, and in fact an argument could be made for doing less rather than more. For the time being, however, it was important that we convince ourselves that we had explored every option.

I offered to fly to Pennsylvania and bring them back to Boston, but my mother knew that my dad hated airplanes. They had always taken trains to and from California, and she said they would take the train out to Boston. If time had really mattered, I would have insisted that they fly, but unfortunately, one more day on the train wouldn't change anything. I spent the extra time talking with colleagues at the hospital, calling in favors to get him scheduled for examinations and diagnostic tests, and adjusting to the news.

Two days later, I was standing on the platform when the train from Pennsylvania rolled in. As the passengers disembarked, the platform became too crowded for me to see more than one or two cars of the train, so I stepped back and found a place that afforded me better sight lines. Four cars back from the engine, a conductor was lifting a battered suitcase down to the platform. I recognized the bag, and my eyes jumped back to the step of the train, where my mom was helping my dad down the stairs. For as long as I could remember, my dad had always helped my mom up and down stairs. Now here she was, helping him down the stairs of the train. I ran to help, getting there just as the conductor took one of my dad's elbows. I grabbed the other and we lifted him down to the platform. My heart sank when I felt how light he was.

When we had my dad safely on the platform, I gave him a hug. My hand came to rest between his shoulder blades, just as I remembered his having done to me so often when I was young. I kissed my mother on the cheek, and bent down to pick up their suitcase. My dad looked twenty years older than he had the last time I had seen him, less than a year ago. His eyes were tucked deeper in their sockets, his skin hung like a suit that was two sizes too big, and he was frighteningly pale. I knew the instant that I saw him step off the train that he would never get back on it.

Picking up the suitcase in my right hand, I took my father's elbow with my left. Moving slowly toward the front of the train and the terminal, I tried to sound confident.

"C'mon, Dad, let's go get you better."

He nodded and shuffled his feet, but no one was kidding themselves. We all knew what was coming.

The tests all came back just as expected. When they were talking to my parents, the doctors were guarded. They spoke in ambiguous terms, careful to neither give nor extinguish hope. With me, they were candid. He had only weeks at best, days at worst. They prescribed just enough morphine to dull the pain without dulling the senses. Chemotherapy was an option, but a poor one. The toxic side effects outweighed any possible benefit. This was one of the times in life when less was more.

Annie virtually lived in the hospital for the sixteen days that my father lasted. She sat with my mother when she needed company, and she disappeared when my parents needed to be alone. In a role that she would perfect later in life, when she adeptly stepped aside to make room in our daughters' lives for me, Annie seemed to know that I needed a little time with my father, and she would spirit my mom off for much needed respites away from the hospital.

I spent more time talking with my father during his last two weeks than I had since leaving home for Notre Dame. At first, characteristically, we talked about everything except his cancer or what we both knew was imminent. Toward the end, my father underwent a change of heart. He began making oblique references to what we should all be doing after he was gone. He reminisced about long ago times. He smiled. He laughed. We cried.

I was with my dad late one evening, and he was tired. Annie had taken my mother to a nearby beauty salon, and then out for dinner. It was a chance for my mother to have a break from the beeping machines, the harsh fluorescent lights, and the metallic smells of the hospital. I was on call but it was a slow night, and my friends were covering for me, so I had dropped by to visit with my dad in his room. As I passed by the foot of his bed, I glanced at his chart. There was a familiar small red sticker in the corner of the chart with the letters "DNR" reversed in white. Do

Not Resuscitate. It was a signal to the nurses and the attending physicians that my father wanted no heroic measures in the event that his heart or his breathing stopped. In medical jargon it meant do not resuscitate, but in plain English, it meant "I've had enough." I moved to the chair next to the bed and sat down as quietly as I could, trying not to wake him. His eyes fluttered open as soon as he sensed that I was there.

"Good to see you, Michael," he whispered.

"How ya doin' tonight, Dad?" I asked, trying to sound chipper.

"A little tired," he said with a weak smile.

I always started our conversations during those last days by talking of anything except his illness. If he wanted to change the subject, he could, but I always gave him the option of talking about anything else. I started to tell him about a major event in the news, but he interrupted me.

"Not sure how much longer now, Michael," he began.

How often I had wished that he would talk about me leaving for school, or about them moving away, but he never would. He always seemed to talk about anything but leaving. Now, when I wished more than ever that he would talk about anything else, he talked about leaving.

"You're still doing well, Dad," I lied.

He smiled again, and nodded. Then, he continued.

"Your mom has talked about going out to live with her sister in Colorado. Encourage her to do that. She shouldn't be alone."

"Okay, Dad," was all I could muster.

"She's always been proud of you, Michael. You weren't always there to hear her say it, but I was. You are the most important thing in her life."

I sat quietly and listened. I had the sense that my father was borrowing my mother to tell me things that he was thinking. Sometimes things are easier to say in the third person than in the first. We sat together for almost two hours, and my dad talked about my childhood and his. The memories came effortlessly for him, as if he was watching old black and white home movies. When he became too tired to continue, I reached out and took his hand in mine.

"Dad, do you remember what you told me the night I got married?"

He may or may not have remembered, but he knew that I was building up to something, so he stayed quiet and waited. I reminded us both of what he said in the twilight that night in Carmel.

"You said that every time we say goodbye, a part of us stays behind."

He nodded. "That's right."

"Well, for as many more days as we have, I'm going to say goodbye every night, because I want you to leave as much of yourself behind as you can."

My eyes were filled with tears, and my voice cracked. My dad squeezed my hand and looked at me with clear and fearless eyes.

"You've got everything you need, Michael."

He closed his eyes and drifted off to sleep. I sat beside him, watching his chest rise and fall, still holding his hand. The door opened quietly and my mom's silhouette was outlined in the bright lights of the hallway outside. She and Annie slipped into the room, speaking in whispers. They would stay with my dad for an hour or two, and then head back to our apartment for the night. I was on call, so I would be in the hospital all night. I stood up from the chair, bent down to my father's ear and whispered, "So long, Dad. I'll see you in the morning." My mom took my place at the bedside and I stepped out into the hall with Annie.

"How's she holding up?" I asked.

"As well as can be expected," Annie replied. "She has bouts of melancholy, but she's had time to get ready. She's very strong."

"She's been through this before," I said grimly.

"She'll be okay," Annie said, patting my arm. "Go ahead. We'll stay here a while longer, then I'll get your mom home to bed."

"Thanks, Annie."

"Thanks for what?"

"For treating them like they were your own parents."

"They are like my own parents, Mike. I love you."

"I love you, too."

I turned toward the nurses' station and reached to adjust my stethoscope, which was hooked around my shoulders as always. I took two steps and turned around, catching Annie just as she was going back into my dad's room.

"Annie?" I called. She turned, one hand still propping the door open.

"Yes?"

"Make sure they page me if anything happens." She nodded.

"I'll remind them before we leave," she said. Then she blew me a kiss.

My pager went off at 2:37 in the morning. Twice before that night, I had been paged by the emergency room to evaluate trauma patients. I instinctively reached for my pager and pressed the button that illuminated the message window. If it was the emergency room, the message would be flashing. I squeezed the pager and read the message: "Room 3215, STAT." Room 3215 was my father's room, and "STAT" means immediately in doctorspeak. I set off at a full sprint for the elevators. I could hear my heart pounding in my ears as I ran. I pressed the elevator button and bounced up and down on the balls of my feet while I waited for the doors to open.

When I reached the room, there was no commotion. The chief resident was waiting for me, but no one was rushing around; in fact, the only sign that anything was wrong was the bright overhead light. Ordinarily, overhead lights are turned off at night to allow patients to sleep. I looked at my dad, and it looked like he was asleep, but I knew better. I paused just long enough to detect no rhythmic rise or fall of his chest. I looked at the chief resident, who put his hand on my shoulder and said he was very sorry.

I slumped into the bedside chair and reached for my dad's hand. It was heavy. I laid his arm down gently and leaned forward against the rail of his bed. It took a conscious effort to breathe. I thought I had prepared myself for this moment, but you're never really ready. After a lifetime of leaving little bits of himself behind, my dad was gone.

Chapter 16

5:35 P.M.

THE TULLEY FUNERAL HOME WAS strategically located halfway between St. Basil's Church and the Immaculate Conception Cemetery. Winthrop Tulley's grandfather founded the business and handed it over to Winthrop's father, Percival Tulley. Percival Tulley was the coroner, a position that came in handy for someone in the funeral parlor business.

After taking over from his father, Percival Tulley expanded the business, making the most of his Irish connections among the constabulary and the city politicians. His plan was to open several additional parlors in other neighborhoods, and he would have built a mourning empire had he not been hit by lightning at the relatively early age of fifty-three. With his untimely passing, the business went to his son, Winthrop, who was only twenty-seven years old at the time. He had now been operating the business for fifty years.

I think what helped Mr. Tulley to be such a source of comfort to my parents when Henry died was the fact that he was only a few years older than they were. He had young children of his own at the time, so he was acutely aware of the pain they were feeling. He was just learning the funeral business, but he didn't need years of experience to understand the tragedy of burying a child. My mother always spoke well of Mr. Tulley and the kindness he had shown her at the time of Henry's passing.

Joe the Bum's dad went to school with Mr. Tulley. One summer while we were kids, Mr. Tulley decided to try a new service for his guests – valet parking. Joe the Bum's dad talked Mr. Tulley into hiring Joe and Pinhead to park cars. Neither Joe nor Pinhead had a driver's license at the time, but they both looked old for their ages. Always playing the angles, Joe's dad figured that they weren't actually driving the cars, they were just parking them.

Mr. Tulley gave Joe and Pinhead tuxedos to wear. Joe's tuxedo fit him okay, but Pinhead's pants were about three inches too short and his jacket sleeves stopped just below his elbows. Mr. Tulley apologized but said the tuxedos were left over from "clients" whose families had changed their minds at the last minute and asked to have their loved ones dressed casually instead. Afterward, they had never come back for the tuxedos.

Tulley's funeral home had four parlors, each decorated with flowered wallpaper, thick curtains, and comfortable couches and chairs. Mr. Tulley could handle four wakes at a time, and often did. Just inside the front door was a small sign with little white plastic letters that stuck to a black background. When more than one wake was going on at the same time, the names of each dearly departed would appear on the sign with the number of the parlor next to the name.

Joe the Bum and Pinhead were parking cars on the weekend after Salvatore "Digits" Pagnatelli passed away. Digits ran the numbers racket for years. He was a small-time crook who sent a percentage of his illegal gambling money to the big-time mobsters, who in turn left him alone. Digits was seventy-three when he passed away peacefully in his sleep. Joe the Bum and Pinhead didn't park many cars for the Pagnatelli wake; most of the visitors arrived in the back seats of limousines driven by guys in dark suits and dark sunglasses. After dropping their passengers off, the guys with the dark glasses drove up the block and parked in a long line along the curb. Mobsters don't like to leave their cars unattended or they tend to explode. Joe and Pinhead spent most of their time holding the doors open for the visitors, most of whom were even older than Digits.

It just so happened that on the same day that Digits Pagnatelli passed away, Teddy O'Shaughnessy died after a long illness. Teddy O'Shaughnessy had been a policeman for thirty-five years before retiring. He was what they called a "beat cop"; he had a section of the city that he was responsible for and he walked his "beat" every day. Everyone knew Teddy, and nearly everyone liked him. If an elderly neighbor was sick and unable to get out, Teddy O'Shaughnessy would pick up their medicine when he made his rounds, then drop it off at their house.

On the little sign at the top of the stairs in the foyer of the Tulley Funeral Home, the white plastic letters read "Pagnatelli, Parlor 4" and "O'Shaughnessy, Parlor 1". Since there were only two wakes that day, and both were expected to attract large turnouts, Mr. Tulley had placed them at opposite ends of the building, to provide as much privacy as possible. He was also sensitive to the fact that the two groups of mourners shared little in common.

Outside, Joe the Bum and Pinhead were standing near the curb when a line of police cars cruised up the block with their lights flashing but no sirens. The lead car stopped in front of the funeral home and four police officers stepped out wearing their dress blue uniforms with the gold buttons and their hats with gold shields. The officers stepped up onto the sidewalk and began forming a line, two by two. As each car rolled to a stop, four more policemen stepped out and lined up behind the others on the sidewalk. With twenty uniformed police officers in ten rows of two on the sidewalk, the last squad car stopped in front of Tulley's. Four Scottish pipers stepped out wearing kilts and carrying their bagpipes. The police department had sent an honor guard to pay its respects to Teddy O'Shaughnessy. As the police honor guard straightened its lines and prepared to enter the funeral home, Joe the Bum looked at Pinhead and smiled. "Stay here," said Joe, "I'll be right back."

Joe the Bum entered the funeral home and climbed the stairs. He stopped at the little black sign with the white letters. Looking around to make sure that no one was looking, Joe switched the "4" and the "1". He then went back down the stairs and opened the door just in time to hold it open for the police honor guard. The ten rows of policemen marched two by two into the funeral home while the bagpipers played "Danny Boy" at the rear of the formation. Row after row of uniformed officers climbed the stairs, checked the sign, and continued on to Parlor 4, where they expected to find Teddy O'Shaughnessy's wake. Inside Parlor 4 the friends and acquaintances of Digits Pagnatelli huddled in small clusters, talking in low tones.

Jimmy "Mailbag" Rossi was telling an off-color joke to "Joe Boots" Pasquale when he stopped in mid-sentence. Two uniformed police officers had just walked into the parlor. By the time Joe Boots turned to see what had caught the Mailbag's attention, there were four policemen standing in the doorway. A moment later, two more cops appeared behind the first four. Joe Boots and Mailbag Rossi looked at one another and said at the same time, "Raid!"

Hearing the word "raid" and seeing the police spilling into the room, the mourners scattered in every direction. There was a side entrance to the room that Mr. Tulley used to bring the casket into and out of the parlor. The septuagenarian mobsters began moving toward the side entrance as fast as their orthopedic shoes would take them. Meanwhile, not realizing that they were in the wrong room, the police honor guard continued marching into the parlor, forming a line around the perimeter of the room, with each officer standing at attention.

The bagpipers were making their way up the stairway as the first of the mobsters reached the top of the landing. Unable to move around the oversized bagpipes, the old crooks just stood at the top of the stairs until the cops in kilts moved past. As soon as the stairs were clear, Joe Boots, Jimmy the Mailbag, and thirty or forty crooked senior citizens rushed down the stairs and out the doors, which Joe the Bum and Pinhead were still holding open.

The first mobsters to make it outside began waving and gesturing to their drivers, who were parked up the block expecting not to be needed for another hour or more. Seeing the silver-haired retirees frantically waving and shuffling up the sidewalk toward them, the drivers scrambled to their cars and began a series of U-turns to pick up their bosses.

The last mobster to leave was standing on the curb leaning on his cane, nervously looking over his shoulder as if he expected the police to come pouring out of Tulley's Funeral Home at any moment. His car drew up alongside him and he grabbed the rear door handle, pulling up on it frantically. The door was either locked or jammed, because it wouldn't budge despite the old mobster yanking on the handle. The driver jumped out and began pulling on the door handle, but to no avail. The little old man began clubbing the huge driver with his cane. The driver ran around to the other side of the car and tried the other door, but the doors were clearly locked. While the driver was on the other side of the car, the ancient mobster jumped into the driver's seat, slammed the door, and drove off, leaving his driver standing in the middle of the street. Unable to nab Digits Pagnatelli in life, Teddy O'Shaughnessy had given him the raspberry in the hereafter.

Every once in a while, if the weather was lousy and we didn't have anything better to do, we would go down to Tulley's Funeral Home and hang out with Joe the Bum and Pinhead. There was a small room down the hall from the parlors where they parked caskets before or after a wake. The morticians called the room the "on deck circle", borrowing the term from baseball that refers to the area where the next batter waits before his turn at the plate.

We were killing time at Tulley's one afternoon when the Reverend Wiley Graft's wake was being held in Parlor 3. Wiley Graft had been a fire and brimstone Baptist minister who was famous for his high-pitched voice and top of his lungs oratory from the church pulpit. Reverend Graft was a no-nonsense, no-compromise, no-excuses preacher with no tolerance for sinners. For Wiley Graft, there was right and everything else was wrong.

Pinhead and Joe the Bum were on their lunch break when Cuckoo and I stopped by. We were in the "on deck circle" when Skinny Boggs came upstairs from the cellar. Skinny had a job cleaning the preparation rooms, which is where the morticians prepared the dearly departed for presentation in their caskets. Skinny came into the on deck circle whistling, with his lunch in one hand and a rolled up magazine under his arm. There was a light knock at the door and the door opened. A casket was rolled in from the hallway by one of the assistant funeral directors. Reverend Graft's wake was scheduled to begin at two o'clock and the directors were still arranging chairs in Parlor 3, so they temporarily parked Wiley in the on deck circle.

Skinny Boggs was used to being around dead bodies, so he laid his lunch on the foot of the casket and leaned against it, unrolling the magazine that he was carrying. Nothing had changed since second grade. Skinny Boggs still had the largest collection of adult magazines in the neighborhood. He stood leaning up against Reverend Graft's casket eating a sandwich and reading the latest issue of "Nature Calls". Pinhead was complaining about how badly his tuxedo fit when we heard Mr. Tulley's voice just outside the door. Mr. Tulley almost never came into the on deck circle. He was always up in front greeting families and offering his condolences. Now he was right outside the door, and we heard him call to one of his assistants, "I'll bring Reverend Graft in. You set up the flowers, and please tell Mrs. Graft that I'll be with her momentarily."

Skinny Boggs leapt into action at the sound of Mr. Tulley's voice. Apparently Mr. Tully had already warned Skinny about his choice of literature around the funeral home, because Skinny was frantically looking for someplace to stash "Nature Calls". Just as the door swung open, Skinny Boggs slipped the magazine into the casket and eased the lid closed. He picked up his sandwich and tried to look nonchalant as Mr. Tulley entered the room.

"Hello boys," Mr. Tulley greeted us. He looked over at Joe the Bum and Pinhead, whose sleeves were hiked up even higher than usual. "The guests will be arriving any time now, boys, you'd better get back out front." Skinny Boggs couldn't get back down to the cellar fast enough. He stuffed the rest of his sandwich into his mouth and bounded down the stairs. Cuckoo and I stood to leave as Mr. Tulley eased the casket through the doorway and out into the hall.

In the hallway, Mr. Tulley turned the casket over to one of his assistants and made his way toward his office, straightening his tie. Mrs. Graft sat in a leather wingback chair in Mr. Tulley's office. She wore a tasteful black dress with a rather elaborate black hat, complete with black feathers and what looked like a silk fishing net that dropped from the brim of her hat to the middle of her face. Mr. Tulley greeted Mrs. Graft with elegance and charm. He spoke in hushed tones, nodded deferentially, and grasped Mrs. Graft's gloved hand in his for a long moment before letting go. Mr. Tulley was masterful at putting grieving relatives at ease.

Mrs. Graft waited for Mr. Tulley to move around his desk and sit down before asking, "Did everything go as planned?"

"Indeed," replied Mr. Tulley. "You'll be quite pleased."

"I bought the suit especially for the visitation," sighed Mrs. Graft.

"It fits him beautifully," reassured Mr. Tulley.

"Does he look natural?" asked Mrs. Graft.

Why people always ask if a dead body looks natural is a mystery. There is certainly nothing natural about being dead, and nothing natural looking about a dead body. Nevertheless, knowing what Mrs. Graft was hoping to hear, Mr. Tulley answered in his most reassuring tone.

"I think you'll find him to look quite natural."

Mrs. Graft smiled and nodded without saying anything. She pulled a handkerchief from the sleeve of her dress and dabbed her eyes. Mr. Tulley stood and reached for Mrs. Graft's hand, assisting her to her feet.

"Would you like to come with me?" invited Mr. Tulley.

"Of course," replied Mrs. Graft, taking his arm.

The assistant funeral director wheeled Wiley Graft's casket down the hall and into Parlor 3. He situated it directly in front of a stained glass window that was framed by heavy drapery on either side. Stooping to gather up several floral arrangements, he laid a spray of white carnations on the base of the casket and set the other two on either side of the guestbook.

Mr. Tulley escorted Mrs. Graft into the parlor and over to the guestbook. Mrs. Graft signed the book on the family page, and then followed Mr. Tulley over to the casket. Cuckoo and I were just reaching the top of the stairs on our way out as Mr. Tulley opened the casket with a flourish. Mrs. Graft tilted her head to get a better view of Reverend Wiley. Her eyes quickly moved from his peaceful expression to the crisp white collar of his heavily starched dress shirt, and the blue silk necktie with tiny gold crosses, then on down to the open copy of "Nature Calls" draped across his chest. Out in the foyer on the stairs, Cuckoo and I heard a piercing shriek followed by a dull thud. In the next instant, Mr. Tulley's voice, normally hushed and gentle, boomed through the funeral home.

"Mr. Boggs, you're fired!"

Mr. Tulley taught at the Fillmore School of Mortuary Science, or "Undertaker U" as its students and alumni referred to it. Every semester, Mr. Tulley would allow students to come to his funeral home and practice their craft. I guess he figured that it wasn't any worse than doctors practicing on real patients, and a lot less dangerous. The worst student that Mr. Tulley ever had was Stanley Kanapeck. Stanley was an idiot. He once shaved the beard off of an Orthodox Jewish man, reasoning that he looked "neater" for his wake and funeral. On more than one occasion, he'd set the deceased's facial features in a big smile, explaining that it would make people feel better to see them happy. But by far, Stanley's biggest screw up was Mr. Wendell H. Billingham III.

Wendell H. Billingham III was a very rich man. He also had an eye for younger women. He was eighty-seven years old when he died. Asleep in the bed next to him when he passed away was his thirty-one year old wife Bunny. Her real name was Elizabeth, but Wendell always called her Bunny. They had been married for nearly three months when Wendell's heart gave out. The paramedics hadn't been gone for twenty minutes before the bickering over the Billingham estate heated up. Wendell had three children, all in their late fifties and early sixties, and all with children of their own who were older than Bunny. Wendell's children, grandchildren, and three great-grandchildren had twelve million reasons to wish that he had never met Bunny.

The day that he left on his honeymoon with Bunny, Wendell stopped at his attorney's office and signed his new will, which gave half of his estate to Bunny and divided the remaining half among his family heirs. With twenty-four million dollars in net worth, Wendell's decision to amend his will had cost his relatives twelve million dollars. It was no surprise when his two sons and daughter, their lawyers, and their accountants all showed up in the office of Wendell's lawyer on the afternoon of his passing.

As Stanley Kanapeck stood in the cellar of the Tulley Funeral Home, preparing to preserve Wendell H. Billingham III's remains, Bunny Billingham's attorneys were filing motions and counter-motions in district court downtown. It would be impossible for all of the wrangling to be resolved before the wake, which started in a few hours. Stanley finished his work and put away his chemicals and supplies. Hanging on a coat rack was a navy blue pinstripe suit that cost more than Stanley's car was worth. Admiring the suit, Stanley dressed Wendell Billingham, taking a long time to get the knot in his necktie just right. When he finished tying Mr. Billingham's Italian shoes, Stanley carefully straightened the creases in his trousers. That's when he noticed his mistake.

Wendell H. Billingham III was impeccably dressed, but his body was not laying quite flat on the stainless steel tabletop. In fact, he was bent in the shape of a "V", like a boomerang. Stanley hurried over to the casket and rolled it over to the table. Carefully situating Mr. Billingham in the satin-lined casket, Stanley eased the lower half of the casket down on its hinges. Unfortunately, Mr. Billingham was just boomeranged enough that his head and his feet would not lie flat at the same time. If you pushed down on his shoulders, his feet came up, and if you pressed down on his feet, he sat up.

Not knowing what to do, Stanley laid Mr. Billingham's head and shoulders on the satin pillow. Looking around the shelves, he found a small block of wood. Lowering the bottom half of the casket until it just cleared Mr. Billingham's feet, Stanley wedged the block of wood into the casket's hinge to prevent it from closing all the way. He figured that he'd explain to Mr. Tulley later and they would fix things between the wake and the funeral. Stanley looked at his watch. He had just enough time to wheel Mr. Billingham up to Parlor 1 before the guests would start arriving. Checking the block of wood to be sure it was wedged tightly in the hinge, Stanley took Wendell H. Billingham III upstairs in the service elevator.

The tension in Parlor 1 was so thick that you could cut it with a knife. Wendell's children, grandchildren, and business associates stood in small groups or sat on couches and chairs on one side of the room. Bunny Billingham sat on the other side of the room. She was dressed completely in black. Her black leather pants were so tight that they looked like they were painted on. She wore black leather shoes with five-inch heels. Her black satin blouse had a plunging neckline that even Wendell's sons could not ignore. Sitting next to Bunny was her new boyfriend. He was also dressed in black, but most of his clothing said Harley-Davidson somewhere on it. In all of his experience in the funeral business, Mr. Tulley could not remember a widow bringing her new boyfriend to her husband's wake.

When it was time for the eulogy, Mr. Billingham's oldest son Skip, a silver-haired banker, stepped to the front of the room. He started out slowly, remembering things from his childhood and those of his siblings, though most of those memories didn't include Wendell, who had been too busy getting rich to be much of a family man. Skip spoke fondly of his mother, who was living comfortably in a house on the ocean with the twenty-five million dollars that the judge had awarded her when Wendell announced that he was leaving her for Bunny.

As he worked his way from days long ago to days months ago, Skip Billingham's voice went up an octave and beads of perspiration broke out on his forehead. He was clearly becoming agitated at the prospect of seeing Bunny and her biker boyfriend ride off with twelve million dollars in their saddlebags.

"My only regret," Skip continued, "is that my father lost his senses late in life and made some decisions that clearly indicate that he was not of sound mind and body."

One look at Bunny and you could wonder about the soundness of the old man's mind but his body seemed to have been quite fit.

"I asked my father on more than one occasion why he was behaving like a kid," Skip lamented. "He rarely answered, but when he did, he said, 'kids have more fun than old men'."

Moving over to the casket, Skip leaned against the polished bronze and looked down at his father. Running his hand along the casket, Skip said, "It's too late for him to tell us himself, so I will pose the question to all of you...why would a man who had worked all of his life to amass a fortune just hand that fortune over to someone who he only knew for four months?"

Everyone on the family side of the room shook their heads solemnly. Bunny sat next to the guy from Hell's Angels, chewing her gum loudly, and tugging at her blouse to expose more cleavage. Then Skip asked what he thought was a rhetorical question.

"If there is anyone here who can explain that to me, I'm listening."

He inadvertently bumped the casket, dislodging the wooden block from the hinges. The weight of the casket lid dropped full force on Mr. Billingham's feet, causing the boomerang to pivot. As if on cue, Wendell H. Billingham III sat bolt upright in his casket, drawing startled gasps from his heirs.

Bunny sprang to her feet, smiling. "You tell 'em, Binky!" she exclaimed, then she turned on her spiked heel, and stalked out of the room. Her boyfriend stood up more slowly. He paused at the doorway, turned to face Skip Billingham, raised a clenched fist and gave Skip the finger. Then he followed Bunny through the front door and out.

The funeral procession slowed as we approached the entrance to the Immaculate Conception Cemetery. An eight-foot tall wrought iron fence encircled the property. The entrance was flanked by two sets of iron gates set into stone pillars. The entry drive sloped up a gentle hill, then curved around and down to the right. We followed the hearse along the winding road and up another hill. At the crest of the hill was a gravel parking area. An elderly man with weathered features from years of working outdoors stood at the top of the hill, directing cars into the parking area. The hearse continued past the old man and down the hill. Everyone else pulled into the gravel lot and parked.

As I stepped out of the car, the change in temperature was immediately noticeable. The stifling heat had given way to a cool breeze. The sun had dipped behind clouds and the breeze actually made the air feel comfortable. I reached into the back seat and grabbed my suit jacket. For the first time all day, I could wear it outside. I clicked my keychain and the car doors locked. The horn honked and the headlights flashed to confirm that the car was locked.

I paused next to the car to look around. The hill commanded a view of most of the cemetery, one of the only rolling green patches of earth for miles in any direction. Down the hill to the right was an awning. Blue and white striped canvas stretched across four steel poles. The canvas was approximately ten feet square. Centered beneath the awning was a dark rectangular hole. Around the hole but still beneath the awning were two rows of wooden folding chairs. Off to the side was a mound of freshly turned dirt.

Pinhead and the black suits were sliding the casket out of the hearse and resting it on the small wheeled cart that they would use to roll it over to the gravesite. It was a relief not to see old Ned with his hand dolly. The funeral director helped Sister Thomas Aquinas out of the black Cadillac and escorted her over the uneven turf to the first row of wooden folding chairs. St. Basil's new pastor was walking slowly from his own car to the gravesite. He was wearing his black suit and white clerical collar. Draped over his shoulders and hanging down either side of his lapels was a deep purple sash.

It occurred to me as I watched everyone making their way down the hill that I hadn't moved. I was still standing beside the Lexus, my right hand leaning against the roof. As much as I dreaded the thought of it, it was unavoidable. It was time to go. The funeral director had evidently noticed me sitting in the church with Sister Thomas Aquinas. At the gravesite, he had placed his briefcase on the chair next to her to save it for me. When I came down the hill behind everyone else, he caught my eye and motioned me over. Sitting down between Sister Thomas Aquinas and Pinhead, I whispered "thank you" to the funeral director.

The new pastor's name was Father Christopher Donahue. He introduced himself before beginning the service and said that he was very lucky to have spent most of the past year at St. Basil's with Father Tim. He didn't say it, but it was implied that when Father Tim had become terminally ill, the Church had sent Father Christopher to learn the ropes while allowing Father Tim to remain involved in the parish to the end.

Reaching for his leather missal with the gilded pages, Father Christopher began by touching his hand to his forehead and saying, "In the name of the Father, and of the Son…"

I didn't hear much after that. My eyes moved along the bronze casket, taking in the ornamental hinges and decorative moldings. They then moved down and focused beneath the casket.

I found myself staring into the hole.

Chapter 17

DURING THE SUMMER AFTER WE graduated from St. Basil's, we started excavation and construction of what would turn out to be our meeting place throughout high school. Located in a far corner of an abandoned parcel of land that had once been an industrial complex, hidden from view from the street, was "the hole". None of us could recall how long the property had been abandoned. It was several blocks long and two blocks wide. For as long as any of us could remember, it had been a collection of old run down, vacant buildings, criss-crossed by rusting railroad tracks, and littered with empty oil drums.

Pinhead's dad said the city had thought about making it into a garbage dump, but that the union had threatened to go on strike if that happened. It was way too close to the alleys in the neighborhood, which meant that the garbage trucks could make two or three runs to the dump each day. The existing dump was so far away that the waterlogged trucks could only make one round trip per day. The union was determined to keep it that way.

At the back of the property ran what was once the main railroad spur. When the factories were all running at full capacity, trains would come and go, delivering raw materials and carrying away finished products. The trains had stopped coming when the factories shut down, but the old tracks were still where they'd always been. Along the backside of the old track bed, a hole had been dug into the side of the slope. It may have been someone needing a truckload of dirt to fill a hole someplace else. Whatever the reason, there was a hole carved into the railbed six feet high by almost fifteen feet long. It extended inward by five or six feet.

Cuckoo found the hole one afternoon while he was walking the railroad tracks looking for stones to play rockball. The gravel used in the beds of railroad tracks was always a great place to find stones that were roughly the size and shape of baseballs. He called the rest of us over and we began poking around the hole. It was quickly decided that with a little additional digging, the hole could be turned into a fist rate casino. We could move our card games, penny pitching, and dice racket off the sidewalk and almost indoors. With a little elbow grease, we'd have it made. Joe the Bum, Cuckoo, and I volunteered to bring shovels the following Saturday. Everyone else was supposed to scrounge for wood and other materials to shore up the walls of the hole. We would start construction on the weekend.

When Saturday came, I grabbed a shovel from the garage and headed off to the hole. When I got there, Pinhead was helping Danny Noonan stack some planks near the opening of the hole. The planks were all splattered with different colors of paint.

"Where'd you get the planks?" I asked.

"Off of some scaffolding down where they're fixing up that old firehouse," answered Pinhead.

"They just gave it to you?" I inquired suspiciously.

Pinhead shrugged. "They weren't using it."

"You mean they just left it?"

"Yeah. They went off to lunch."

Joe the Bum walked up carrying two shovels over his shoulder.

"Where'd you get the extra shovel?" Pinhead asked.

"They're both from down where my dad works," answered Joe.

"Ah, from the sewage plant?" cried Danny Noonan. "I don't wanna use a shovel from the sewage plant."

"Relax," said Joe, hauling the shovels off of his shoulder. "These are my *dad's* shovels...they've never been used."

A few minutes later, Cuckoo arrived carrying a rake.

"What in the hell are you doing with a rake?" asked Joe the Bum.

"The handle on our shovel was broken," explained Cuckoo.

"You'll come in handy in the fall," snorted the Bum.

We spent all day digging and shoving the purloined planking into the hole. By evening, we had a space about the size of a small bedroom. Over the rest of the summer, we added to it whenever we found materials, but mostly we just hung out there, playing cards, and getting ready for high school.

When school started in the fall, we spent less and less time at the hole. There were a lot of things going on in school and with the days getting shorter, there wasn't much time after school before it got too dark to see the cards. The novelty of sitting in a damp cave carved into the side of a hill wore off, and we quit going altogether sometime around Thanksgiving.

In the spring, we decided to make some improvements to the hole. Fat Peter's parents got new carpeting for their living room, and he talked them into letting us have the old carpet. We dragged the roll of carpeting through the neighborhood and over the railroad tracks. When we unrolled it in the hole, it looked like it was made for the place. We discovered that the power was still hooked up to an old maintenance shed in the corner of the property, so we ran two hundred yards of extension cords from the shed to the hole. Joe the Bum said the extension cords had "fallen off a truck", along with a shop light and a transistor radio. With carpeting and electricity, we were officially in business.

One afternoon in July, Pinhead and Danny Noonan showed up dragging a Lazy Boy recliner chair. Before anyone could ask them where it came from, Pinhead had it in the hole and was sitting in it with his feet up. Cuckoo looked at him with raised eyebrows and his palms up. Pinhead explained that he had been riding with his dad on the garbage truck, and they found it out in the alley. Someone had left it out with the trash. It was a ratty old thing and had more than a few spots where the fabric was worn all the way through to the springs, but it still had a few good days left in it.

We may have made the hole a little too comfortable. One afternoon when we arrived, we found a hobo living in it. He had stumbled across the place and decided to move in. He was sitting in our Lazy Boy listening to our radio and drinking whiskey from a half-empty bottle. When he saw us standing in the entrance, he barely even looked up.

"How's it goin?" he belched.

"Who are you?" asked Fat Peter.

"What's it to ya?" asked the hobo, wiping his nose with the back of his forearm.

"This is our place," interjected Cuckoo, pushing his glasses up his nose.

"I don't mind company," replied the hobo. He made no move to get up. It was clear that he was planning on staying. The hobo said his name was Skeeter, but he didn't give a last name. He told us that he was from "out west", but didn't say exactly where. There was something about him that made us all uneasy. He wasn't your run of the mill harmless hobo.

"How do you get money for food?" asked Fat Peter.

"Odd jobs," replied Skeeter, taking another long pull on his whiskey bottle.

None of us believed that Skeeter actually did odd jobs to earn money. He seemed to be the kind of guy who just took what he needed. He swiveled in the Lazy Boy and turned toward the opening of the hole. When he did, we noticed a scar that ran from his forehead down to his jaw.

"So Skeeter, how long you planning on staying around here?" asked Joe the Bum. He'd been around rough characters before, so he wasn't afraid of Skeeter.

"Dunno…" said Skeeter, "gotta lay low for a while, and this is as good a place as any."

"Why do you have to lay low?" asked Cuckoo.

"Cuz I killed a guy," answered Skeeter, without blinking.

We stood around shifting our weight from one foot to the other, not wanting to get too close to Skeeter. It was more likely than not that he had made up the story about killing someone just to frighten us away from the hole. If that was his plan, it was working. We needed a plan of our own, and right now we didn't have one. We weren't prepared for an all out confrontation just yet, so we retreated to consider our options. We left him sitting in our Lazy Boy recliner and headed back to Earl's Chicken Shack to talk about what to do next.

"I say let's just stay away from the hole for a while," said Cuckoo. "He'll move on soon enough, then we can go back."

"I say we call the cops," said Fat Peter. "If he did kill a guy, the cops'll lock him up and then we can get our stuff back."

"We'd have to testify," observed Joe the Bum, with all the confidence of a lawyer.

The thought of sitting in a courtroom looking at that scar while a lawyer asked us a million questions wasn't something any of us wanted to do. Besides, the cops might ask us where all the paint splattered planks came from. We decided that it was safest for us to just lay low away from the hole while Skeeter was laying low in the hole. Soon enough, he'd get back on a freight train and be on his way. In the meantime, we'd just take our card games back to the neighborhood sidewalks.

For the next three weeks, we stayed away from the hole. Every day or two, one of us would sneak over and see if there was any sign of Skeeter. Unfortunately, he seemed to have taken up permanent residence. One night, Danny Noonan had snuck over to check on things and saw Skeeter with two other hobos in the hole, all of them drinking out of paper sacks. Skeeter had begun entertaining visitors. If we didn't do something fast, word would spread through the hobo grapevine and we'd never get our place back. Finally, Joe the Bum and Danny Noonan decided to confront Skeeter. They decided to confront him with a bottle of whiskey that Joe took from his old man's stash.

When Danny and Joe the Bum arrived at the hole, Skeeter was dressed much more presentably than he had been on the night we first found him there. He was wearing a pair of gray pants and a shirt with buttons. Joe noticed an old duffel bag in the corner of the hole that we hadn't seen on our first encounter with Skeeter. The second set of clothes must have been in the bag. Hoping that the change of attire meant that Skeeter was preparing to leave, Joe asked, "Going somewhere, Skeeter?"

"Nah, just came back."

"From where?"

"Dinner. There was a nice spread after the funeral."

"Whose funeral?" asked Danny.

"How should I know?" said Skeeter, with a nasty smirk on his face.

"If you didn't know the person, why did you go to their funeral?" asked Danny, still not making the connection.

"For the food. I get the newspaper, watch the obituaries, and look for funeral announcements that say there's a reception to follow. Then I go pay my respects and stick around for the eats."

"No one asks you who you are?"

"Funerals ain't like weddings. They don't send out no invitations. If you just act like you knew the stiff and sound sad that they're dead, nobody bothers you. You grab a plate of food, sign the guest book, and you're out of there."

Skeeter settled back into the Lazy Boy and turned on the radio. Joe and Danny were disappointed to see that he was no closer to clearing out than he was three weeks ago when we'd first seen him. Skeeter spied the brown paper sack in Joe's hand.

"What's in the bag?" he demanded, pointing at Joe.

Joe looked at the sack in his hand. He'd forgotten about the bottle.

"Uh, it's whiskey," replied Joe. Skeeter's eyes flashed.

"Well, let's have a taste," he said, reaching for an old chipped coffee mug that he'd undoubtedly dug out of someone's trash.

Joe handed Skeeter the bottle, still in the paper bag.

"Join me boys?" invited Skeeter.

"No thanks," Joe answered. "You can have it."

Skeeter opened the bottle and poured half a mug of whiskey. Closing the bottle, he looked at Joe and Danny through narrow eyes. He survived on guile, and he was sharp enough to smell a rat.

"Thanks...but why the generosity?"

"Thought you might be shipping out," lied Joe, "Wanted to bring you one for the road."

"I kinda like it here," said Skeeter. "I think I'll stay a while...but thanks for the hooch."

Joe the Bum and Danny Noonan left Skeeter drinking Joe's dad's whiskey with his feet up on our recliner chair, listening to our radio. When they got back to Earl's Chicken Shack, where we were all waiting for them, Joe shook his head disgustedly. If we wanted Skeeter gone, he told us, something had to be done.

"I don't care if he did kill a guy – he's gotta go," Joe lamented.

"Yeah, but what can we do – call the cops?" asked Fat Peter hopefully, still thinking that life was on the legit.

"No, I've got a better idea," said Joe. "We meet here tomorrow night. We need a shopping cart, a padlock, a roll of duct tape, and another bottle of whiskey, but not a full bottle. Now, I've gotta go see Lou the Screw."

We split up the scavenger hunt. Pinhead would grab a shopping cart from the grocery store parking lot. Danny would snatch a bottle of whatever liquor was available at his house. His dad was usually halfway through a bottle of something – it helped to take the edge off of living with Duke Noonan. I offered to bring the tape and the padlock, though I had no idea what it was for. The next night, as planned, we met on the corner at the end of Joe the Bum's street. We were all there waiting for Joe. We were about to go to his house to find him when he came walking up from the other direction. He was walking quickly, almost if he had a train to catch.

Looking at Danny, Joe asked, "Did'ja get it?"

Danny held out a bottle that was about one-third full of a dark brown liquid.

"Rum? You brought rum?" asked Joe, incredulously.

"Hey, it was all I could find," protested Danny.

"Oh well, it'll have to do," sighed Joe, "Open the top."

Joe reached into his pocket and pulled out a handful of pills, capsules of some sort. He had twelve or fifteen of them. He began pulling the capsules apart, emptying the powder that they contained into the bottle of rum.

"What's that?" asked Cuckoo.

"It's Lou the Screw's fit medicine," answered Joe, without interrupting the work at hand. "Lou takes these to calm him down when he's having one of his fits. I went over to Lou's house and while I was in the bathroom, I grabbed a handful."

"You think somebody's gonna have a fit?" asked Fat Peter.

"They're tranquilizers," explained Joe, now taking on the air of a pharmacist. "One of them calms you down. Three of them calm you down enough to fall asleep. A handful of them will knock a guy on his ass."

"I don't get it," said Cuckoo, frowning.

"We're gonna relax Skeeter," said Joe, screwing the cap back onto the bottle of rum and shaking it vigorously.

Joe explained his plan to us in detail. When he finished, we were all smiling. It was a stroke of genius. If it worked, we'd be playing cards in the hole again tomorrow. If it didn't, well, none of us gave much thought to what would happen if it didn't work. If we had, we never would have gone through with it.

"Let's go," said Joe, and we were off to the hole.

Skeeter was in his usual spot, slouching in our Lazy Boy chair, when we got there. He seemed startled when we all walked in – obviously he wasn't expecting visitors. Following the script that Joe the Bum had laid out, Cuckoo stopped in his tracks, pretending to be surprised, and said, "Oh, Skeeter, we didn't think you'd be here."

"Why not?" scowled Skeeter. "Where else would I be?" He was in a foul mood.

"We kinda thought we could have the place back," implored Cuckoo, sounding pathetic.

"Why don't you guys just find another place to hang out?" said Skeeter, not really asking a question.

"Why don't you?" interrupted Pinhead, with as much false bravado as he could muster.

"Well now, let's see. Have you ever killed a guy?" asked Skeeter. Without even waiting for a reply, Skeeter waved his arm in a dismissing gesture. "Clear out guys. You can have the place back when I'm through with it, and I ain't through with it."

On cue, Joe the Bum, who was holding the bottle of rum, said, "C'mon guys. We don't want any trouble. Let's find another place to drink. I'm getting sick of this place anyway."

Joe's reference to drinking had just the effect that he knew it would. Skeeter's alcoholic antennae when up, and he quickly spotted the bottle in Joe's hand. Thinking he had already intimidated us with his bragging about killing a guy, Skeeter figured he might as well pick our pockets on our way out.

"Not so fast, you little bastards. You can just leave the bottle," he said, staring at Joe.

"I dunno, it's all we've got," said Joe, shifting the bottle to his other hand and moving away from Skeeter.

"Then get more," Skeeter said flatly. "But leave that here."

Joe the Bum feigned being afraid of the threatening tone, and tossed the bottle to Skeeter.

"Let's get outta here, guys," he said to the rest of us.

We walked out of the hole and made a lot of noise climbing the slope up to the abandoned railroad tracks. Then we quietly ran down the tracks a hundred yards and noiselessly slid back down the slope to a spot where we could see into the hole. We were in the dark, so even if Skeeter had looked right at us, he wouldn't have seen us.

Skeeter had forgotten about us, however, as soon as we had left. He was now thinking only about the rum. We watched as he poured himself a coffee mug of the brown liquid, then put the bottle to his lips and took a long drink. He then took his mug, returned to the recliner chair, and turned up the volume on the radio. We just sat in the dark and waited.

It wasn't long before Skeeter had emptied his coffee mug and was back up pouring himself another. As he had the first time, he again took a long drink directly from the bottle, this time draining it. Skeeter tossed the empty bottle out of the hole and into the weeds, then shuffled his feet over toward the Lazy Boy. This time, however, when he went to sit down, he missed the chair entirely and crashed to the floor, flat on his back. We waited a few minutes to be sure that he wasn't getting up. When it was obvious that he wasn't, we ran to the hole. Skeeter was making a noise somewhere between snoring and gargling.

Working quickly, four of us taped Skeeter's hands and feet together while Joe the Bum grabbed Skeeter's duffle bag. We dragged Skeeter and his belongings up the slope and across the railroad tracks to the shopping cart that Pinhead had parked there. We dumped Skeeter into the shopping cart, laid his duffel bag on his chest, and started pushing the cart toward the street. It was almost four blocks to the freight yard, which meant that we would pass beneath three streetlights pushing a shopping cart with a body in it. As we approached each corner, we looked in every direction to be sure no one would see us when we crossed under the light. When we arrived at the freight yard, Joe the Bum surveyed the scene, looking for a train with more than two engines. More than two engines meant that the train was headed most of the way across the country. Spotting a train with four engines running, their red lights flashing, Joe pointed and said, "there".

We pushed the shopping cart as far as we could before reaching the tracks. When we could wheel him no further, we lifted Skeeter out of the cart and carried him the rest of the way. Joe the Bum ran ahead, looking for open boxcars. Finding one, he crawled up inside; a moment later, he jumped down and ran to another open car. Appearing in the open door, he jumped down again and tried a third car. This time he stood in the doorway, waving us over. When we reached the boxcar, Joe reached down and grabbed Skeeter under the arms as we shoved from below. Checking to make sure that Skeeter was still snoring loudly, Joe laid Skeeter's duffle bag next to him, unwrapped the tape from his hands, hopped down, and pulled the boxcar door shut. Turning to me, he said, "Got the padlock?"

I reached into my pocket and tossed Joe the padlock. The key was in it. He slid the lock through the latch of the boxcar door and clicked it closed. He left the key in the lock, taping it securely in place to make it easy for the railroad guys to open it when the train reached its destination. Then he hopped down and we took off. When we were back in the neighborhood, Cuckoo asked no one in particular, "You think he'll come back?"

"Nah," answered Joe, "he won't wake up until Pennsylvania…and when he does, he won't be thinking of coming back here."

"How can you be so sure?" asked Pinhead.

"Cuz of what's in that boxcar," said Joe.

"What's in there?" asked Cuckoo.

"Whiskey," grinned Joe, "A boxcar load of whiskey."

It had been a few weeks since we'd sent Skeeter packing and moved back into the hole when Whitey Shelton stopped by. Whitey was still a foot shorter than everyone else and was still pulling stunts to make up for his lack of size. He was hatching a plot and he wanted our help pulling it off. Whitey walked into the hole, tipped an empty bucket upside down and sat down on it. He didn't waste any time getting right to his proposition.

"Guys, I know where we can get enough beer for the whole summer… for free."

He couldn't have attracted more attention if he had shouted "FIRE" in a crowded theater. Everyone stopped what they were doing and stared at Whitey.

"Where?" asked Joe the Bum.

"C'mon, I'll show ya," said Whitey, already on his way out of the hole. We followed Whitey up the slope and onto the abandoned railroad tracks. He followed the tracks across the old industrial complex, past several empty factories and boarded up warehouses. At the far end of the complex was a chain link fence. Inside the fence was a cinderblock building with no windows. Whitey stopped less than a hundred yards from the fence and said, "Just watch."

We stood around for a few minutes before hearing a metal garage door rattling open. A moment later a truck drove out of the cinderblock building. Painted on the side of the truck, in large white letters on a blue background, was Pabst Blue Ribbon. In smaller letters: 'the beer that made Milwaukee famous'. We stared in disbelief, too shocked to say anything. Whitey was thinking about knocking off a beer distributorship. We would have been less surprised if he'd said he was planning to swipe some gold from Fort Knox.

"You're crazy, Whitey," was all Pinhead could say.

"What if we got caught?" reasoned Fat Peter.

"You're crazy, Whitey," Pinhead said again.

"I got it all figured out," explained Whitey. "I been watching, and after all the delivery trucks come back at night, everybody leaves. There's nobody around. Not even a night watchman."

"They don't need a night watchman," said Joe the Bum matter-of-factly.

"Why not?" asked Cuckoo.

"Cuz' nobody would be crazy enough to swipe anything from that building," continued Joe.

"You're crazy, Whitey," mumbled Pinhead.

"Why not?" asked Cuckoo again.

"Cuz' the place is owned by the mob," concluded Joe the Bum. He folded his arms and stared at us, like an attorney resting his case for the jury.

Joe the Bum was right. The beer distributorships were not businesses that just anyone could open. To deliver beer to taverns, liquor stores, restaurants, and every other place in town that sold it, you had to have a contract with the breweries. The breweries didn't take out ads in the newspaper looking for distributors. They gave the distributorships to guys who could make sure that the breweries didn't have any problems like union strikes or other interruptions in their business. Those guys more often than not wore pinstriped suits and a lot of gold jewelry. Whitey was seriously thinking about swiping beer from mobsters. For years we had seen Whitey stand up to guys twice his size – he wouldn't back down even when he should. But this was completely different. This was nuts.

"You're crazy, Whitey," Pinhead reminded him.

"Ok, you guys don't have to do anything except help me stash the beer. I'll go in and get it. Then we'll stash it in the hole."

The idea of hiding a few cases of mob beer in the hole sounded simple but it was anything but. We all looked at each other and no one had to say a word. None of us wanted to risk it. Whitey was persistent, however, and he kept saying that he'd do all the hard work, all we had to do was help him stash the cases. In part because we didn't have enough sense to say no, and in part because we were afraid that if we did say no, Whitey would go ahead and try it on his own, we agreed to ditch a few cases of beer in the hole. Whitey must have known that if he gave us a chance to think about it, we'd come to our senses and change our minds, so he said we'd pull the job that night. Muttering among ourselves, we agreed to meet at the hole that night at dusk.

The sun was just setting when we all met at the hole. Pinhead brought an old tarpaulin from his dad's garage. He said that we should throw it over the cases of beer so they weren't in plain view. We cleared an area big enough to stack six or seven cases of beer, then laid the tarpaulin out on the floor so that we'd be ready to cover the boxes quickly when we returned.

We turned off the radio and the overhead light and ducked out into the darkness. It was a cloudy night, so there was no moonlight. We made our way through the dark toward the far end of the industrial complex. As we approached the cinderblock warehouse, we stopped to make sure that no one was around. A single light bulb burned over the front door of the building. Other than that, it was completely dark. We were about to move closer when we detected movement around the back of the beer warehouse. Our eyes had adjusted to the dark, so we were able to make out a figure moving slowly around the rear of the building. When the shadowy figure stopped moving, it blended back into the blackness. A faint red pinpoint of light glowed, and then disappeared. Whoever was back there was smoking.

"Let's get out of here," whispered Fat Peter, more scared than I'd ever seen him.

"Stay still," instructed Pinhead, putting a hand on Peter's shoulder, "if we move now, they'll see us."

After a few minutes, the shadow started moving again. It looked for an instant like it was moving straight toward us. Our hearts pounded in our chests as we crouched in the dark, not having any idea what to do if we were spotted. The shadow stopped when it reached the edge of the building, however, and we heard the sound of a tin can being thrown into a garbage can, then the lid of the garbage can being replaced. The shadow then moved back behind the building. A door opened at the rear of the building, throwing a shaft of light from inside out into the darkness. In the light, the shadow was revealed to be a tall guy wearing a baseball cap. He stepped into the building and closed the door behind him. The rear of the building returned to darkness.

A minute or two later, a tall guy wearing a baseball cap walked out of the front of the building. He paused beneath the bare light bulb, giving us a clear view of his features. It was the shadowy figure who had just walked in the back door. He turned a key in the lock, then turned and walked toward a pickup truck parked in the gravel driveway. He tossed the keys in the air once and caught them, then went straight to the pickup truck. The engine of the pickup truck turned over and the exhaust rumbled through a muffler that needed work. One headlight came on, the other remained dark. The guy with the baseball hat backed up, shifted into gear, and drove away.

Whitey whispered, "Wait for me here, I'll be right back." Before we could protest, he was off and running, bent over at the waist. He followed the fence line to the gravel driveway at the street. There was no gate across the driveway; the mob didn't need a gate. Whitey ducked around the corner of the fence and followed it back the way he had come, this time on the inside, making his way toward the rear of the building.

"Should we follow him?" asked Cuckoo. "How's he gonna carry the beer?"

"He said to wait here," answered Fat Peter with a quake in his voice. "I think we should wait." Waiting was always better than not waiting if you asked Fat Peter.

"When he gets inside, he'll signal us", said Joe the Bum.

"We'll wait here until he comes back for us," declared Pinhead, putting an end to the conversation.

We squinted in the dark, barely able to make out Whitey's shadow as he ran to the back of the warehouse. He went to the spot where the guy with the ball cap had entered the building. A moment later, he disappeared. Either Whitey had found the back door open and was inside the warehouse, or he was laying flat on the ground, perhaps hiding. If he had seen someone, he would have flattened out to get out of sight. We held our breath, looking at the last place that we had seen Whitey, hoping to catch sight of him. Just then, we heard the sound of a truck motor from inside the warehouse. Someone was still inside, and if they saw Whitey, it would be a disaster. We didn't know what to do. If we tried to help Whitey, we could all get caught. All we could do was stay put and hope that Whitey was hiding.

The garage door at the front of the warehouse rattled open, throwing light out onto the driveway outside. While we frantically searched the darkness for a sign of Whitey, the truck inside started pulling out into the gravel drive. As the cab of the truck cleared the edge of the building, there was Whitey, sitting behind the steering wheel, grinning from ear to ear, waving at us. We just stood there in the dark, our mouths hanging open, watching Whitey drive off with an entire truckload of the mob's beer. He turned out onto the street, stepped on the gas, and was gone. For a long time, no one said a word. Then Pinhead spoke for all of us.

"You're crazy, Whitey."

We scattered, running toward the neighborhood. No one knew what to do about Whitey. We didn't know where he was going, but we knew that we didn't want to be standing around the warehouse when the mob found out that one of their trucks was missing. Pinhead and I headed for my house, while Danny and Cuckoo went to Joe the Bum's. Fat Peter kept saying that we were going to get caught by the cops, and made a beeline for home. When Pinhead and I reached our porch, we ran into my parents sitting outside. We tried to act as nonchalantly as possible, though we were out of breath from running.

"Where have you boys been?" asked my mom.

"Just hanging around," I replied.

Before my mom could interrogate us, her attention was drawn to a loud noise coming up the street from the corner. A Pabst Blue Ribbon beer truck rumbled past the house and continued up the street, turning right at the next block. Only the top of the driver's head was visible through the open window as it rolled past.

"That looked like Whitey Shelton," my mom suggested.

"Nah," I dismissed, "What would Whitey be doing driving a beer truck?"

Pinhead had been watching the truck as it turned right at the corner. He looked at me and raised his eyebrows questioningly. I nodded almost imperceptibly.

"Ma, we'll be back in a little while," I called, as Pinhead and I walked through the yard and up the sidewalk. As soon as we were out of the line of sight from our porch, we broke into a run and followed the route that Whitey had taken a few minutes before. One block over was Joe the Bum's house. Another half block further was the alley behind Joe's garage. In the alley was the Pabst Blue Ribbon beer truck, with its rear door standing open. When we arrived, Whitey and Joe the Bum were in the truck, handing cases of beer down to Cuckoo, who was stacking them behind Joe's garage. When they had unloaded a dozen cases, Joe hopped down and helped Cuckoo move the cases into the garage. Whitey ran around to the cab of the truck and drove off down the alley.

Pinhead and I helped with the last few boxes. When we had them safely out of the alley, Joe said, "Let's go. We've gotta pick up Whitey." We piled into Joe's car and headed down the alley in the direction that the beer truck had gone. We drove to the sewage treatment plant. Joe knew his way around the plant, because he had spent the last summer riding with his dad, punching in, then riding back home. In the afternoons, Joe would drive back to the plant by himself and punch out for himself and his dad. Joe's dad had pulled some strings to get Joe a no-show job so he no longer had to drive back himself every afternoon to punch out. When we reached the sewage treatment plant, the parking lot was almost empty. There was a single car parked next to the door that led into the plant. Joe the Bum recognized the car.

"That's the Hump's car," he said, "Hump works the night shift – has for about twenty years. He punches in and goes to sleep until it's time to punch out and go home. He's a mailman during the day."

Joe pulled up to the entrance to the sewage plant parking lot, but didn't go in. Instead, he parked along the curb. He left the car running but turned off his headlights. We sat there in the dark with the engine running, waiting for Whitey. We were expecting Whitey to drive up in the beer truck, so we were startled when he appeared out of the dark, standing next to the car, staring into the passenger window. Pinhead slid across the front seat toward Joe the Bum, making room for Whitey. As soon as Whitey was in the car, Joe the Bum pulled away from the curb, his headlights still off.

The sewage treatment plant was more sewage than plant. There were seven or eight filtration pools surrounding one brick building that housed a series of pumps and valve controls. By opening or closing valves and turning certain pumps on and off in the right order, the plant operator moved water through the series of filtration pools. The filtration pools were filled with sewage in various stages of clean up. The smell was awful when the wind was blowing in the wrong direction. Almost no one came near the plant during the day; at night, the place was deserted. Pinhead turned to Whitey and asked the question that we were all dying to ask.

"Where's the truck?"

"At the plant," answered Whitey.

"The parking lot was empty," observed Cuckoo.

"I didn't exactly park it," said Whitey.

"Where'd you leave it?" asked Pinhead.

"I hopped out while it was still rolling," said Whitey, "and it sort of rolled into the slop."

Whitey had driven the mob's beer truck into the sewage treatment plant and pulled it up to one of the filtration pools. Slowing down almost to a stop, Whitey had hopped out of the cab and the truck simply rolled the rest of the way into the sewage pit. In sank into the smelly muck and disappeared.

Joe the Bum turned his headlights on and drove back to the neighborhood. He pulled into the alley behind his garage and again turned off his headlights. Joe and Whitey disappeared into the garage and reappeared carrying two cases of Pabst Blue Ribbon beer. They put the beer into the trunk of the car and went back into the garage. We piled out of the car to make room for the rest of the cases. When the car was loaded, Joe and Whitey got in and said they were going to move the beer to the hole. The rest of us left Joe and Whitey to their work and started home. Two guys would be less likely to get spotted over by the hole than six of us lugging cases of beer over the railroad tracks. We agreed to meet at the hole the next night. As Whitey closed the car door and stuck his head out of the window grinning, Pinhead couldn't resist reminding him, "You're crazy, Whitey."

The next day, when the beer truck was discovered missing at the warehouse, rumors began to fly around the neighborhood. One story had some mobsters from out of town stealing the truck to settle an old score that they had with the local mobsters. Another rumor was that one of the local truck drivers had been kidnapped along with his truck and was being held for ransom. A third story circulating was that the local mobsters had taken one of their own guys on a "one way ride" and ditched the beer truck along with the body. One thing was curious. With all of the rumors floating around, it was obvious that the mobsters had discovered that one of their beer trucks was missing. The curious thing was that they never called the police. They never officially reported the missing truck to anyone. They just went about their business as if nothing had happened.

There was one more rumor making its way around the neighborhood, and no one doubted that it was true. That rumor was that the mob was looking for whoever had stolen their truck, and that when they found out who it was, they would make an example out of them. The reason the mob didn't need to worry about people stealing from them was because everyone knew what would happen if you got caught. Everyone knew that you had to be crazy to swipe something from the mob. Everyone.

The day after Whitey dumped the beer truck into the filtration pool at the sewage treatment plant, Joe the Bum's dad came home from work early with a puzzled look on his face. He called Joe over to the car even before he got out in the driveway.

"You hear anything about that beer truck caper?" he asked Joe.

"Nope," Joe lied, "What about it?"

"Funny thing. They dumped some of the beer at the plant," explained Joe's dad. "The Hump came out to his car this morning before the morning crew got there and he saw about a dozen cases of beer floating in the #3 filtration pool."

"What'd he do?" asked Joe, getting a little nervous.

"He fished the cases out, hosed them off, and put them into his car. He hadn't heard about the truck disappearing from the warehouse yet, so he thought some pranksters had tossed a few cases of beer into the pool as a joke. He figured it was just his lucky day. When he got home and heard that the mob was missing a truckload of Pabst Blue Ribbon, he put two and two together and figured the safest thing to do was to start drinking the evidence."

"How many people know about it?" asked Joe, worried that the truck would be discovered at the bottom of the sewage pit.

"Only me," answered Joe's dad. "I told Hump to keep his mouth shut when he wasn't drinking the beer – he's been around the block enough to know when it's unhealthy to be noticed. I just can't figure out why some idiot would rob a mob warehouse and then toss some of the merchandise into a sewage pit. You'd have to be crazy."

Joe relaxed when he found out that only the Hump and his dad knew about the floating beer. Neither of those two guys would be poking around looking for answers. They were old hands at keeping out of trouble, and this was nothing but trouble. Things quieted down a few days after the truck disappeared. People whispered about how the mob was still looking for whoever took the truck, but no one had the slightest idea what had actually happened. A few weeks passed, and still no one was any closer to figuring out what had happened to the mob's beer truck. The only ones still thinking about it were the mobsters.

Chapter 18

6:45 P.M.

I JUMPED A BIT WHEN the cold droplets of water hit my hands and face. Father Christopher was blessing the casket with holy water, using a gold mallet-shaped contraption that he dipped into a gold bucket of water. He moved around the casket, sprinkling holy water as he went. When he returned to his place at the head of the casket, he laid the bucket down in the grass behind him and folded his hands.

"Some of you may not know that Father Tim was a decorated war hero," Father Christopher said proudly. "He was awarded a Purple Heart and a commendation for bravery in the Vietnam War."

I caught a break during my senior year of high school. My birthday was drawn very late in the military draft lottery. Every year, the draft board loaded 365 small metal cylinders into a giant drum...366 cylinders in leap years. Inside each cylinder was a birth date, a month and day. They pulled out cylinders and listed the dates in the order drawn. Then for the rest of the year, they drafted young men into the military by birth date, beginning at the top of the lottery list and continuing until they reached that year's allotment. In most years, they made it a little more than halfway through the list of birthdays. When I was eighteen, my birth date was drawn late for the draft year during which I would turn nineteen and become eligible for service.

Everyone who turned nineteen or twenty years old during the Vietnam War remembers when their birthday was drawn in the military draft lottery. It was a lottery that you wanted to lose. It was not uncommon for guys to claim religious or moral opposition to killing anyone, even in a war. The government had a name for them: "conscientious objectors". They were still inducted into the service, but efforts were made to give them jobs that did not involve shooting anyone. Other guys, maybe because they weren't sure that the conscientious objector program would work, just took off for Canada. I was lucky that my birthday was drawn so late in the lottery, because I am afraid I might have been one of the guys sneaking into Canada...not because of any deep religious or moral conviction. I was scared, plain and simple. In any case, my lottery pick meant that I would be off to college in the fall and not off to the jungles of Vietnam.

Father Tim was in no danger of being drafted. No one expected priests to carry rifles or shoot howitzers. Shortly after I left for college, however, Father Tim volunteered for the Marines. He went through basic training on Parris Island and became a Marine chaplain. By the end of my first semester in college, Father Tim was in Vietnam. His first tour of duty lasted two years. When it was time to come home, he volunteered to stay for another two years.

Father Christopher told us that Father Tim almost never talked about his experience in Vietnam. What Father Christopher knew he had learned from letters that Marines had written to Father Tim after the war, and by reading official accounts of the activities of Father Tim's unit. During the year that he had lived with Father Tim, and especially when Father Tim's health began to fail, Father Christopher had researched his war record in some detail.

It turns out that Father Tim was indeed a war hero. His platoon had been pinned down in a rice paddy on the edge of a thin strand of jungle. The enemy was pouring artillery shells down on the Marines and had set up a firing line in the trees. For two days and nights, Father Tim's platoon just took a pounding. Throughout the night, enemy soldiers blew whistles in the darkness. The shrill piercing whistles made the hair on a Marine's neck stand on end. It was impossible to sleep. No one knew when an all-out assault was coming.

The Marines periodically fired phosphorous flares into the night air. The flares cast a bright white glare over the open rice paddy and threw shadows into the jungle. The Marines had to make sure that the enemy stayed in the jungle and did not mount a charge across the open field, because that would have been catastrophic. As each flare exploded in the air, the Marines opened fire and shot at anything that moved or seemed to move ahead of them. The enemy stayed put, content to wait for daylight to resume shelling.

On the third morning, reinforcements finally arrived behind the Marines. They began shelling the edge of the jungle to create an opportunity for the Marines to pull back and regroup. The Marines, who had been lying in the swampy rice paddy for two days, methodically pulled back, alternately covering one another with bursts of machine gun fire. As the last of the platoon started back toward the reinforcements, two men were running side by side. A mortar shell landed between them, exploding with a flash of fire. Both men disappeared in the explosion.

One of the two Marines was killed instantly. The other was badly wounded. The United States Marine Corps has an inviolable creed – leave no Marine behind. Without hesitating, Father Tim took off running for the fallen Marine. Father Tim carried no gun. His helmet had a small white cross on it, probably too small to be seen from the jungle. As he lifted the injured Marine and started back toward his platoon, Father Tim was shot in the left leg. He stumbled, but kept staggering forward, carrying the injured Marine with him. Two members of the platoon jumped up and ran toward Father Tim. The rest of the platoon laid down a withering round of covering fire.

The two Marines reached Father Tim just as he stumbled again. They lifted Father Tim and the other wounded Marine and carried them back to the cover of the platoon. Father Tim and the Marine he had saved were placed on stretchers and carried farther back behind the line of firing. A medic cut Father Tim's pant leg open and breathed a sigh of relief when he saw that the bullet had missed the femoral artery. He wrapped the wound tightly and nodded to the stretcher-bearers, who lifted Father Tim and loaded him onto a helicopter for the short flight to the field hospital.

Three weeks after his surgery, Father Tim got his second chance to return home. He was in his second tour of duty, which meant that his injury was his ticket home. He thanked the officer who was trying to hand him his discharge pass, but said that he wanted to return to his unit. He rejoined the platoon and was still with them when the American Embassy in Saigon was evacuated at the end of the war. Father Tim was carrying a young Vietnamese orphan when he climbed from the roof of the embassy into one of the last helicopters to leave Saigon.

Father Tim was in Vietnam for the entire time that I was in college. After the war, he spent several years helping veterans who were struggling with the transition back into normal lives after the insanity of war. He had been there. He could relate to them. Eventually, Father Tim returned to the role of parish priest, and when he did, he returned to St. Basil's. By then, however, my parents had moved to Pennsylvania. With my mom and dad gone, I had never come back.

Sitting beneath the striped awning, I felt numb. I've had an awful lot on my mind over the past few days. I've been thinking of cutting back on my practice for some time now. It's easier for a surgeon to cut back than it is for a family doctor. Patients grow attached to family doctors, and they get upset if they get handed off to someone else half of the time if the doctor tries to cut back. Surgeons just take fewer referrals. With the kids almost grown, I've been thinking that it might be time to spend less time at the hospital and more time at home before they're gone altogether. Maybe even lend a hand with the wedding plans.

When I left Annie and the girls at the airport, I decided that it was definitely time to make a change. It will be a big step, but I'm ready to take it. Hearing of Father Tim's passing only made the decision easier. Time is slipping away, and I'm determined to grab onto as much of it as I can when the girls return from London. I'll do it in August. August is a month for big steps. I thought back to a long ago August of big steps. The August when I went off to college…and when Father Tim went off to war. When everything that had been the same for as long as I could remember would never be the same again. I thought back to the last time I ever saw Father Tim.

Chapter 19

It was August, and I would be heading off to college at the end of the following week. My parents wanted the family to go to Mass together on Sunday, so I put on a white shirt and a paisley tie and headed off with them to St. Basil's. It was humid and the sky was overcast. It felt like it might storm later in the day. I walked to St. Basil's with my folks. We made small talk about things that didn't matter, because no one wanted to talk about me leaving home the next week.

It's funny how you can't wait to get old enough to get out on your own, to make your own decisions, to be independent. Then when the moment arrives, your stomach turns upside down and you start wishing you had more time to be a kid. I remember walking to St. Basil's that last time feeling like I couldn't swallow. My throat felt swollen even though I knew it wasn't, and I was a little bit queasy in the stomach.

I wanted to say so many things to my parents as we made idle chatter that morning. I wanted to tell them that I'd miss them. That I was scared. I wanted them to tell me that they'd miss me. That they were scared. I wanted them to tell me that I was going to be alright; I wanted to tell them that they'd be alright too. Instead, we talked about the weather.

"Looks like it could storm," said my father, not even looking at the sky.

"Yeah," I agreed. "Could be a real doozy."

"Grass could use the rain," my dad mumbled, not looking at the ground.

We arrived at St. Basil's along with the rest of the neighborhood walkers coming to nine o'clock Mass. My dad held the door for my mom and then waited for me to follow her inside. As I passed him, he reached around and grabbed the back of my neck with an affectionate pinch, then patted me between the shoulder blades without saying a word.

We followed my mom up the center aisle of the church, to a pew several rows from the pulpit. After genuflecting, I slid into the pew between my parents and sat down. That's when I saw him. Benito Filosa was a regular at nine o'clock Mass at St. Basil's. He was sitting in his customary spot in the front pew across the aisle from where we were sitting. Benito Filosa was in the import/export business. No one knew what that meant exactly, but it obviously paid well. He drove a big black limousine – more precisely, he was driven around in a big black limousine by a guy in a dark suit who always wore sunglasses, even on cloudy days.

There had been whispers all the time while I was growing up in the neighborhood that Benito Filosa was in the Mafia. He had never been anything but kind to any of us who ever crossed paths with him. He was a generous donor to St. Basil's. He had helped out countless neighbors over the years. It was widely known that if you were in trouble you could go to see Benito Filosa and chances were good that your trouble would go away. There was one thing that none of us in the "Hole in the Wall Gang" knew about Benito Filosa. It's likely that our parents knew. It's almost certain that Joe the Bum's dad knew. In addition to being in the import/export business, Benito Filosa was the silent partner in the Pabst Blue Ribbon beer distributorship.

The pipe organ began playing Ave Maria, one of my favorite hymns. In the doorway of the sacristy appeared Father Tim, flanked on either side by altar boys who had been only four years old when Pinhead set fire to the incense and ruined a wedding. They made their way out to the altar, bowed together in unison, and turned to face the congregation. The first part of the Mass passed without incident. There were a few readings from the letters of St. Paul to the Corinthians. No one ever explained how St. Paul knew the Corinthians, or why he was always writing them letters, but the gospel is full of them. Obviously, St. Paul must have said one day, "I'm going away for a while," and the Corinthians must have said, "Well, don't forget to write."

After reading the gospel, Father Tim made his way over to the pulpit to deliver his sermon. It was warm in the church. The humidity outside made it even warmer than usual. Throughout the congregation, women were fanning themselves with the weekly parish bulletins. Father Tim cleared his throat and began his sermon with a sentence that grabbed the attention of everyone in the church. Bulletins stopped fanning and it became very quiet.

"A person would have to be crazy to steal a beer truck from the mob."

No one in the church moved. Benito Filosa didn't flinch. Father Tim paused to allow the statement to sink in. Parishioners were stunned. Father Tim had opened his Sunday sermon talking about beer trucks and mobsters.

"No one in their right mind would walk into a warehouse, and drive off with a truckload of beer that belonged to the Mafia," he continued.

If anyone had missed his opening salvo, Father Tim made sure that they didn't miss it the second time.

"We must ask God to grant us the strength to help those among us whose minds have gone fallow like fields in the desert that once yielded plentiful crops."

Father Tim was on a roll.

"The human mind is a paradox. It is capable of complex analysis and imaginative innovation. It led men to invent the machines and to calculate the mathematical equations that put John Glenn into orbit around the Earth. It gave Michelangelo the vision to create one of the world's great masterpieces on the ceiling of the Sistine Chapel. And it made one poor soul think that it was a good idea to swipe a beer truck from a mob warehouse."

There it was again. For some reason, Father Tim seemed bound and determined to focus his homily on the theft of some beer from a bunch of gangsters.

"God takes pity on the infirm, whether the infirmity is of body or mind," Father Tim ranted. "Surely the lesson that Jesus taught – to turn the other cheek – applies when the offender is of feeble mind and diminished capacity."

Father Tim was not exactly staring at Benito Filosa, but he looked in his direction often enough to be sure that he was listening. Benito sat stone-faced, barely blinking.

"Let us pray that the poor stranger who came into our midst and left in the middle of the night for a far off place finds peace in the forgiveness of God. Let us not seek to find him in that far off place, but instead let us wish for him the wisdom to find and follow the righteous way of the Lord."

That was the moment that I realized that something was up. Father Tim never preached like an evangelist. He never waved his arms over his head beseeching us to "find and follow the righteous way of the Lord." He would simply tell us to do the right thing. Father Tim always talked to you, not at you. So when I heard him sounding like one of those fire and brimstone faith healers who preached from the back of a wagon out near the county fair, I knew that he was up to something. I started to listen even more carefully, trying to figure out just what it was.

"And so, as we go forth into the coming week, let us be mindful of the frailty of others – let us be compassionate toward those in need – and let us allow that far off stranger to remind us that we are all vulnerable to the fragile nature of reason. It can be taken from us at any time, and we are dependent upon one another for understanding and support. May Almighty God bless you, in the name of the Father, and of the Son, and of the Holy Spirit, Amen."

That was it. He'd said it earlier and now he'd repeated it again. "...that far off stranger..." Father Tim was telling Benito Filosa and any other mobsters who might be listening that the poor soul who took their beer truck was not from around here and was miles away by now. But Whitey Shelton was a block and a half away. Obviously, Father Tim had no idea who had swiped that beer truck, or how close by they still were. Or did he?

The rest of the Mass seemed to pass quickly, probably because so many thoughts were running through my mind. When the pipe organ filled the rafters with "How Great Thou Art," Father Tim and the altar boys made their way back to the sacristy while the parishioners began filing out of church and into the humid morning outside.

When we reached the front doors of St. Basil's, I turned to my parents and said, "Would you mind if I came along in a little while? I'd like to ask Father Tim about something. I won't be long." My dad said sure, told me that they'd meet me at home, then glanced at the sky and said, "Keep an eye on the weather...looks like a storm brewing."

I stood on the church steps and watched my folks walking off toward home, together but alone. In a few days, I would leave for school, and from then on my folks would be exactly that...together but alone. I swallowed the lump in my throat and turned to go back into the church. The pews were empty and the scent of extinguished candles wafted through the air. I walked up that long center aisle, my footsteps echoing off of the polished marble floor.

The two young altar boys were just leaving the sacristy as I reached the doorway. I leaned against the doorjamb and watched Father Tim hanging up his vestments. He was wearing his familiar black pants, black shirt, and clerical collar. He sensed that someone was there, and he turned in my direction. When he saw me, his face broke into a wide smile.

"Michael, it's great to see you."

"You too, Father."

"You must be excited about heading off to Notre Dame."

"I am, I guess. Maybe a little nervous too."

"That's natural, Michael, but you'll be great."

"Thanks, Father. I've been thinking about how my folks will be – I'm not sure they're ready for me to go."

"They'll never be ready for you to go, Michael, but they'll be fine. It's a funny thing about parents. Part of them wants you to be little forever, but a bigger part of them knows that they are here to see to it that you grow away."

I moved across the sacristy to the table where I had sat waiting for Father Tim on the day when Sister Pius had caught us sampling the sacramental wine. Sitting down, I felt secure here talking to Father Tim.

"That was some sermon today, Father."

Father Tim raised his eyebrows and smiled.

"Did you like it?"

"...the wisdom to find and follow the righteous way of the Lord?" I asked, my voice showing my amusement.

"A little too much, do you think?" asked Father Tim, still smiling.

"A little out of character," I answered, smiling back at him.

I decided to just come right out and ask Father Tim what he had been up to. In all the years that I had known him, there was never a time when I thought I couldn't talk to him about anything that was on my mind.

"D'you think that whoever took the beer truck is really someplace far away?" I asked.

"What do you think?" He'd always had a knack for answering a question with a question.

Being just as evasive as Father Tim, I replied, "After listening to your sermon, it sure sounds like it."

"I guess someone could come to that conclusion, if they were listening," Father Tim mused.

"They sure could," I agreed. "Do you think Mr. Filosa was listening?" I asked.

"Hard to say," answered Father Tim, "but it looked like he was."

I wanted to just ask Father Tim if he knew that Whitey had stolen the beer truck from the mob. I wondered if his repeated references to a "far off stranger" were as deliberate a red herring as they seemed. I didn't ask, however, because I didn't want Father Tim asking me if I knew who had taken it. I was not prepared to answer that question. So I didn't ask. I just stood up and reached out to shake Father Tim's hand.

"Thanks for everything you've done for us, Father."

Father Tim started to extend his hand, then stopped. He stepped closer and hugged me, patting me between the shoulder blades just as my dad had always done. He stepped back and I thought I saw his eyes shining a little more than usual.

"Be happy, Michael."

I swallowed another lump in my throat and turned toward the side door that led directly outside. As I reached for the doorknob, Father Tim called after me.

"Michael."

"Yes, Father?"

"Tell Whitey I wish I could have been there to see it."

I laughed out loud, then said, "I'll tell him, Father."

I opened the door and began to step outside when I realized that it was pouring rain. The clouds that had been threatening all morning had turned inside out and it was a soaking downpour. Father Tim looked past me and out the door, then walked over to the closet where he had hung his vestments. Reaching in, he pulled out an umbrella. He walked over to the doorway and handed me the umbrella with a smile.

"You'd better take this," he said.

Remembering the time when we had walked together under his umbrella years before, I asked with a grin, "You're not going to walk me home?"

Father Tim's face became serious but still friendly.

"You don't need me holding your umbrella anymore, Michael."

I turned and walked out into the rain, listening to the pelting sounds and watching water dripping from each of the spines of the umbrella. When I reached the sidewalk, I turned and looked back to where Father Tim was standing. He smiled and nodded, then gave me a quick wave of his hand. I thought about Father Tim all the way home. I had no way of knowing it at that moment, but it was the last time that I would ever see him.

Epilogue

7:35 P.M.

THEY DON'T ACTUALLY LOWER THE casket into the ground like you see in the movies. They leave that for the cemetery workers to do after everyone has gone home. When Father Christopher finished his invocation, the small group of us at the gravesite stood and prepared to leave. I helped Sister Thomas Aquinas up and the funeral director approached to escort her back to his car. Without even thinking about it, I leaned down and kissed her gently on her cheek. I turned to Pinhead and shook his hand firmly. He said that we should get together to talk about old times, and I promised to try to get to one of his basketball games in the fall. I patted Pinhead on the shoulder and turned to make my way back up the hill. In the distance, the bells of St. Basil's tolled.

As I walked up the gentle slope toward my car, I noticed the crunch of gravel beneath my feet. I hadn't noticed it on the way down to the grave. The air that had begun to cool when we arrived now had the hint of a chill. Looking up into the fading light, I noticed clouds rolling in. A cold front was coming. It had been a long day, and as I reached the car I felt very tired. More tired than I ever remembered feeling. A low, ominous roll of thunder rumbled overhead as I clicked my keychain twice – clickitt, clickitt – and smiled.

The doors unlocked, the headlights flashed, and the interior lights came on. Reaching into the backseat to hang up my jacket, my eyes fell upon a thick manila envelope lying on the seat. I hadn't given the packet much thought all day, but now I picked it up and settled into the driver's seat, closing the door behind me.

The interior lights slowly faded, leaving me in complete darkness. With the inside lights no longer reflecting off of the windshield, I could just make out the outline of the tent covering Father Tim's casket down the hill. Every now and again distant lightning on the horizon would light up the sky just enough for me to see the tent and the mound of newly turned dirt beside it. Everyone was gone, and I wondered if the cemetery workers were sitting someplace waiting for me to leave before they returned.

Reaching overhead, I snapped on one of the interior reading lights and returned my attention to the bulging envelope in my lap. It was comforting to think that I had returned to St. Basil's today solely out of affection and respect for Father Tim. The truth was, however, that the contents of this envelope had been the real reason that I had come home.

Removing the stack of paper that I had read so many times already, I saw the familiar colored tabs running along the edge of the folder. My name and social security number appeared on the cover, right between "Johns Hopkins University Hospital" and "Medical Record". There must have been ten thousand words in that medical record, and even more numbers, charts, and graphs. But one word made all of the others meaningless: cancer.

I heard about Father Tim's passing on the day that the doctors told me that the cancer was back, and that this time we were out of options. They said I might have six months left, nine if I wanted to try a new experimental drug that five years from now might show real promise. I told the doctors that I would let them know about the new drug in a few days. I don't think I'll go back. There is a time to hold on tightly, and a time to let go. If you're lucky, each parting leaves a part of you behind.

Turning off the reading light and returning my gaze to the windshield, I strained to see the little tent at the bottom of the hill. It may have been my imagination, but the bells of St. Basil's sounded farther away. A flash in the sky, closer now, cast a momentary light on the gravesite. I blinked several times, afraid that the blurred image that I saw meant that I was crying again. But it wasn't tears.

It had begun to rain.

Acknowledgements

THE IDEA OF WRITING THIS book came to me after spending more afternoons than I can count laughing about our childhoods with Mike Sheppard, an old friend and great storyteller in his own right, who spent even more time in Catholic schools than I did. In the five years since writing the first line of the story, I have benefitted from patient friends and family whose perspectives made this a much better book.

I owe a debt of gratitude – and probably an apology – to the nuns and priests who worked so hard to get us to do the right things while we worked so hard not to listen. It turns out they were right all along.

Any resemblance between the characters in the book and real people, whether still with us or not, is unintended but unavoidable…because after all, there is a little of all of us in the story of Father Tim.

About the Author

Tom Robertson was born in Joliet, Illinois and attended Catholic schools for eight years, where he first learned to negotiate, on more than a few occasions reducing his sentence to time served for various venial sins and classroom transgressions. He graduated from the University of Illinois, where he played varsity baseball, and holds a Master's Degree in Business Administration from the University of Chicago. Tom lives in Frankfort, Illinois with his wife Sandy and their daughters, Katie & Kelsey.

Made in the USA
San Bernardino, CA
09 December 2019

61155180R00144